A Garland Series

Foundations of the Novel

Representative Early

Eighteenth-Century Fiction

A collection of 100 rare titles
reprinted in photo-facsimile in 71 volumes

Foundations of the Novel

compiled and edited by

Michael F. Shugrue
Secretary for English for the M.L.A.

with New Introductions for each volume by

Michael Shugrue, *City College of C.U.N.Y.*
Malcolm J. Bosse, *City College of C.U.N.Y.*
William Graves, *N.Y. Institute of Technology*
Josephine Grieder, *Rutgers University, Newark*

The Secret History of
the Present Intrigues of
the Court of Caramania

by

Eliza Haywood

with a new introduction
for the Garland Edition by
Josephine Grieder

Garland Publishing, Inc., New York & London

1972

Bibliographical note:

*This facsimile has been made from a copy in the
Beinecke Library of Yale University
(IK H336 727S)*

Library of Congress Cataloging in Publication Data

Haywood, Eliza (Fowler) 1693?-1756.
  The secret history of the present intrigues of
the court of Caramania, by Eliza Haywood. With a
new introd. for the Garland ed. by Josephine Grieder
348p.(Foundations of the novel)
  Original t.p. has imprint: London, Printed and sold
by the Booksellers of London and Westminster, 1727.
    I. Title. II. (Series)
PZ3.H3372Se2 [PR3506.H94]   823'.5   71-170571
ISBN 0-8240-0562-7

Introduction

Delighted, no doubt, by the success of her scandal chronicle Memoirs of a Certain Island Adjacent to the Kingdom of Utopia *(1725), Mrs. Eliza Haywood turned once again to the genre for the work here reprinted:* The Secret History of the Present Intrigues of the Court of Caramania *(1727). The public's reaction was all she might have wished; the work became nearly as popular as its predecessor. But at the same time — as will be seen later — it drew upon her the wrath of the literary establishment; and the damage done to her reputation was regrettable, for by pillorying her exclusively for the scandal they considered offensive, her enemies ignored entirely the very real literary advances that Mrs. Haywood made in this work.*

Caramania *is a regular scandal chronicle. Prince Theodore is, of course, George II, and his spouse Hyanthe Queen Caroline. Ismonda, Theodore's mistress, is Mrs. Henrietta Howard, and Adrastus, Ismonda's husband, is perpetually trying to win his wife away from the court, as did Colonel Howard. Several of George's mistresses are even identifiable: note Lutetia (Mary Bellenden, though the lady never actually yielded, as she does in the novel); and Euridice (Lady Charlotte Finch). The go-between Marmillio is the Earl of Scarborough; Aridanor and his wife Barsina represent the Duke and*

5

INTRODUCTION

Duchess of Argyle. But *unlike the* Memoirs of a Certain Island, *which is nothing but a choppy series of anecdotes connected only by their participants' devotion to the Enchanted Well,* Caramania *has an integrated plot (albeit with no end), a degree of characterization, and a consistent moral point of view. It is in every way a more sustained and more sophisticated literary effort than the former work.*

Mrs. Haywood begins the novel with the premise that things are seldom what they seem. Theodore, Prince of Caramania, has just married Hyanthe, the aging Princess of Anatolia, an alliance which liberates his subjects from the tribute they were paying to that kingdom; on all sides he is hailed as a savior and the guardian of public liberty. "But not to detain on the rack the Curiosity of my Reader, who by what I have said, cannot but imagine there was some other and more powerful motive for this Prince's Behaviour, than that which I have related, or than was publickly known" (p. 3), the authoress proceeds to reveal in a flashback that Theodore's passion for Hyanthe's waiting-woman Ismonda has brought about this marriage so that Ismonda may have a legitimate pretext to come to Caramania to be with her lover. The further history of Ismonda and Theodore holds together the various interwoven stories of the Prince's and the other courtiers' amorous adventures.

The characterization of these three personages is, if not profound, certainly more developed than anything in the Memoirs. *When Theodore, hitherto insensible to*

INTRODUCTION

feminine beauty, sees Ismonda, he is enchanted: "Unskill'd in Love, and all unstudied in the God's approach, and by what means he steals himself into the unguarded Soul, he knew not to what Guest he had given room; and innocently, at first, indulg'd the growing Anguish, nor thought what future Pains might be the consequence of the Present Joy he found in gazing on so dangerous an Object" (pp. 4-5). After he possesses her, he is filled with delight; "yet, dear as she was to him, the Love of Variety intervened" (p. 31), as it is to do many times during the work, and he betrays Ismonda with Lutetia. His escapades, if not pardoned, are at least explained. "In spite of the fixed Affection with which he regarded this Mistress of his Soul, he must sometimes devote his Body at other Shrines. He could not live without his Gallanteries; and Curiosity frequently supplied the room of liking, and led him to the ruin of many a believing Fair" (p. 83). As a prince, he has, of course, little difficulty in winning over a reluctant woman. The one time when he is advised to use force, he is "shock'd" by such a proposal because "he had an inimitable share of Good-nature, and as much Honour as was consistent with the Inconstancy of his Temper" (p. 337); but he overcomes his scruples and rapes Violetta anyway. Thus he pursues his pleasures, returning after each to Ismonda.

Ismonda deserves Theodore's loyalty; she is a loving mistress and a clever woman. It is she who persuades him that marriage to Hyanthe will facilitate their affair, and Marmillio praises her as a woman of "masculine

7

INTRODUCTION

Temper ... [who,] free from the Vanity and Tenaciousness of her Sex, could consent to see the Man most dear to her in a Rival's Arms" (p. 24). Continually menaced by the exposure of her affair with the Prince, she fences adroitly with her opponents. Though her husband Adrastus demands she return to his side in Anatolia, she always finds a plausible pretext to remain in Caramania; she successfully evades an affair with Aridanor. She is, in fact, "a Woman, who priz'd her Reputation above all things, excepting her Passion" (p. 300). She even learns to tolerate Theodore's multiple inconstancies, for when, after each adventure, he returns to her, "never had rewarded Passion fill'd them with Extasies more divine, more insupportable to staggering Sense!" (p. 217).

The affair between Theodore and Ismonda is eventually discovered by Hyanthe, of course, but the Princess reveals herself to be both perceptive and prudent − "indeed it must be confess'd, that never Wife was an Example of greater Resignation, Fortitude, and Moderation." She says nothing to the guilty pair; she chooses "not to seem to know what, acknowledging to know, she must resent, but had not the power of redressing." And Mrs. Haywood expands her admiration of Hyanthe's conduct into a general admonition to the female sex: "Would all Wives take this method, there would not so many of them become hateful to their Husbands, and despicable in the eyes of their Acquaintance" (p. 304). Theodore's reaction proves how effective such generosity is, for "if this Conduct

8

INTRODUCTION

did not make him love, it caused in him the extremest
Veneration and Esteem for her" (p. 305).

A fourth well-drawn character deserves notice:
Marmillio, Theodore's adviser and go-between. It is he
who promotes the affair between Ismonda and
Theodore, rescues the Prince from his unfortunate
entanglement with Lutetia, and even arranges the
scheme by which Theodore disguises himself as an
Egyptian eunuch in order to rape Violetta. No doubt he
deserves to be called "a Man . . . who, in every Action of
his Life, had testify'd no Sense of Pity, Gratitude, or
Honour" (p. 336). Nevertheless, he understands far
more clearly than anyone else human motivation and
how to manipulate it. His explanation of Ismonda's
seemingly unfaithful request that Theodore marry
Hyanthe is penetrating and persuasive: " 'Tis with ease
we endure a conjugal Rivalship, because we are pretty
certain that those Endearments are more the Effect of
Duty and Formality, than of Love" (p. 25). And when
Ismonda, learning of Theodore's first infidelity to her,
launches into a long tirade against him, Marmillio takes
no notice, for "he was too well acquainted with human
Nature, not to know that nothing violent is of long
continuance, and of all the Passions that invade the
Mind, none so shortliv'd as Rage; because none is so
painful to be borne, and were it to continue, must
convert to Madness" (p. 92).

In addition to subtler characterization, Mrs. Haywood
displays in Caramania a more consistent moral
viewpoint regarding the natures of man and woman and

9

the dilemma of sexual love. Women are in general passive creatures.[1] *Constancy is their chief character-istic. Men may have many loves, "But 'tis not so in our too faithful Sex," says Euridice; "one dear Idea takes up all the Soul, we have no room to entertain another, and but with scorn look down on those who would intrude" (p. 112). Men are, unfortunately for the ladies, more active as well as inconstant. "That is indeed the nature of your ungrateful Sex," protests Ismonda; " 'tis Difficulty that endears Enjoyment, and keeps Desire awake: Suspence alone secures the Lover's heart, for when we own we love, we are sure to lose him" (p. 78).*

Therefore, physical union is little other than a temporary satisfaction. The woman is led into it by blandishment, innocence, or ignorance — for Elaria, for example, "So swift the pleasing Ruin came, she had not time to know, much less to avert the Danger; and when compleated, could not be recall'd" (p. 189). The man pursues it purely out of desire — there are, in fact, four seductions, not to say rapes; but his goal once attained, he is satiated, and only from politeness does he cajole the woman out of her guilt feelings and feign an affection he no longer feels. The result is unsatisfactory, certainly, from a feminine point of view: "Few Men, if ever any were, are twice enamour'd of the same Object; their whole Life indeed is one continued Series of Change, but then it is still to new Desires: the Heart that is once estrang'd, is never to be recall'd; and though the foresaken Nymph is sure to have her present Rival in the same Condition with herself, yet must she not hope to

INTRODUCTION

reap any other Advantage, than Revenge" (p. 277).

Mrs. Haywood's attempt to introduce some degree of
literary sophistication into the scandal chronicle should
certainly be given credit; her characters in Caramania are
no longer the paper dolls of the Memoirs, and her moral
observations are confined less to particular vices and
directed more to general human nature. But her
contemporaries were primarily concerned with the
scandal; and the literary establishment, including Swift,
Arbuthnot, and particularly Pope, were decidedly
affronted by the insults they saw offered to their friend
Mrs. Henrietta Howard.[2] And thus, Eliza Haywood
became the heroine of one of the more vulgar episodes
in The Dunciad.[3] Chetwood and Curll, the two
publishers, compete in a pissing contest for "yon Juno
of majestic size, / With cow-like udders, and with ox-like
eyes"; after a number of graphic couplets, the latter
wins Eliza, the former a chamberpot. And so that no
one would mistake the identity of Juno, the Variorum
edition (1729) identified her as the "authoress of those
most scandalous books, call'd The Court of Carimania
[sic], and The New Utopia" (pp. 107-108). The
incident ruined her reputation. Though she did not
cease to write, almost never again did she put her name
to a title page. One hopes that the continued royalties
from her anonymous works were some small consolation
for Pope's malice.

Josephine Grieder

11

INTRODUCTION

NOTES

[1] *Mrs. Haywood does include some satirical portraits of women. Olimpia pretends to be a "man-hater" because she is ashamed of the affair she continues with the groom who first raped her. Idomeus, pursuing Luthelina, must ingratiate himself with her all-too-willing aged aunt who "in a very small time . . . became enamour'd of him to the utmost pitch of Dotage; which is all the Term one can afford to a Woman, who, at her Age, confesses a Passion that even Youth is put to the Blush to acknowledge" (p. 323). And Mazares gives a friend a little lesson in female psychology à propos of the cold, haughty Arsinoe, with whom he has been having an affair: "Your reserv'd and coy Women in Publick, are ever the most warmly amorous in private. — The Constraint they put on their Inclinations, in denying themselves those innocent liberties which others take, makes them break out with great force and vehemence, when once they give a loose to them" (p. 226).*

[2] *A particularly unjust reaction, since the portrait of Mrs. Howard (Ismonda) is presented with discretion and even admiration.*

[3] *A complete account of this affair is given by George Frisbie Whicher in* The Life and Romances of Mrs. Eliza Haywood *(New York: Columbia University Press, 1915), pp. 117-131.*

12

THE
SECRET HISTORY
OF THE
Preſent Intrigues
OF THE
Court of CARAMANIA.

THE
SECRET HISTORY
OF THE
Preſent Intrigues
OF THE
Court of CARAMANIA.

LONDON,

Printed : And Sold by the Bookſellers of
London and *Weſtminſter.*
M.DCC.XXVII.

THE
SECRET HISTORY
OF THE
Present Intrigues
OF THE
Court of CARAMANIA.

THE large and fertile Province of *Caramania* is ſituated in that part of *Aſia* which is call'd the *Minor* ; and was formerly in ſubjection to the Kings of *Anatolia* : but THEODORE, the preſent Prince, having married HYANTHE, a Daughter of the late Monarch, had in Dowry with her a general Releaſe from all Tri-

B   bute,

bute, Fealty, and Obedience, by which himself and Succeſſors are now dignified with the Title of *Sovereign Princes of* Caramania.

Nothing could more endear a Ruler to his People than did this Action of THEODORE's; it seem'd ſo magnanimous a proof of Love to his Country, that a young Prince, in the full Vigour of thoſe Deſires which Lovelineſs creates, and every way accompliſh'd to pleaſe the Fair, ſhould, neglecting all the Beauties of the laſt, and the preſent Advantages he might have enjoy'd in the Choice of another Bride, ſacrifice himſelf to a Princeſs much older than himſelf; and who, when in her Bloom of Youth, was miſtreſs of very few perſonal Charms, meerly to free his Subjects from a Dependance which had long been uneaſy to them; that they thought they could never too much expreſs their Senſe of the Obligations they had to him: Statues were in all publick Places erected to his honour! they almoſt adored him as a guardian God! nor could he appear in publick without the Drums, Trumpets, and other martial Muſick which accompany'd him, being drown'd in the louder Acclamations of the admiring Croud, who hanging on his Chariot-Wheels, ſeem'd to rend the very Skies with Cries of Joy! *Liberty* and THEODORE, was the word! *Liberty* and THEODORE, was all that could be heard.

Nor

Nor was this Action of his look'd on with wondring Admiration by the Populace only; those of the deepest penetration, and who made it most their business to pry into the Intrigues of State, could with all their search be able to ascribe no other Reason for it, than that which it had the appearance of: so happy was this Prince in the few trusted by him, and so little is human Wisdom capable of fathoming the Heart.

But not to detain on the rack the Curiosity of my Reader, who by what I have said, cannot but imagine there was some other and more powerful motive for this Prince's Behaviour, than that which I have related, or than was publickly known; I shall, in as brief a manner as the Subject will admit, give an account how very different from their seeming, were the real Inducements of THEODORE to act in the manner he had done.

Being, as I have already said, possess'd of many valuable Accomplishments, of an illustrious Birth, descended by his Mother's side from the Kings of ancient *Dacia*, and by his Father's from the great ARSACES, and in several memorable Engagements against the Inhabitants of *Mesopotamia* and the Lesser *Armenia* having very much signaliz'd his Conduct and Courage, he was look'd on as a Prince who would hereafter make a very distinguishable figure in the world; and his

Alliance

Alliance fought for by the neighbouring
Nations, as the only Security from his fuperior Power. The feveral Princeffes offer'd
to him in marriage, and the equal Advantages
which attended thofe Propofals, rendred
him divided in his Sentiments, and being
by his People prefs'd to make choice, he
took a Journey to *Anatolia*, with a defign
to confult that Monarch, and be directed by
him in the Affair.

At his arrival, he receiv'd the Compliments of all the Grandees of that Court;
among the number of whom, was ADRA-
STUS, a Lord of eminent Birth and Merit,
and highly in favour with his Royal Mafter;
which Confiderations obliging the Prince to
return his Vifit in perfon, he was entertain'd
in a manner becoming the Dignity of fo
illuftrious a Gueft: But that which crown'd
the Feaft, and heighten'd every pleafure, was
the prefence of the lovely ISMONDA, Wife
to ADRASTUS. The Heart of THEODORE,
till now infenfible of the Power of Beauty,
felt a ftrange Alteration at the fight of her, a
mixture of Delight and Pain diffus'd itfelf
through every glowing Fibre, tumultuous
Thrillings fill'd the Veins, and each warm
Artery confefs'd the new Defire! Unskill'd
in Love, and all unftudied in the God's approach, and by what means he fteals himfelf into the unguarded Soul, he knew not
to what Gueft he had given room; and innocently,

nocently, at firſt, indulg'd the growing Anguiſh, nor thought what future Pains might
be the conſequence of the preſent Joy he
found in gazing on ſo dangerous an Ob-
jeĉt. So loſt was he in the admiration of
her Charms, that had not MARMILLIO, (a
Caramanian Nobleman who from his Childhood had been bred up with him, had ever
been his greateſt Favourite, and had accompany'd him to *Anatolia* and in this Viſit)
reminded him that it grew late, he might
poſſibly have forgotten that Decorum which
is always obſerv'd between Perſons of ſhort
acquaintance, as was that he had with ADRA-
STUS, and by his long ſtay have occaſion'd
ſome Suſpicions in him, which would have
been of little advantage to the Paſſion he
had entertain'd.

'Tis certain that the Diſcretion of MAR-
MILLIO, who preſently ſaw the Condition
of his Prince, kept it from being perceiva-
ble by the Husband; but the fair Occaſion
was too ſenſible of the Force of her Charms,
to be deceiv'd in that manner; ſhe both
knew and triumph'd in the Conqueſt ſhe
had made; and tho' ſhe had hitherto regarded her Husband with more Tenderneſs
than is ordinarily found among Wives of
Quality, yet the thoughts of being belov'd
by ſo great and ſo lovely a Prince as THEO-
DORE, rouzing all that was vain or ambitious in her Soul, made her in very great

danger

danger of fwerving from that Duty, fhe had, till now, preferved with all imaginable ftrictnefs. She faw herfelf admired by him, was pleas'd with the difcovery, endeavour'd all fhe could to enhance the Efteem fhe had infpired, and how near fuch a Difpofition is to betraying the Heart, too many fine Ladies by fatal Experience can teftify.

THEODORE, on the other fide, was no fooner departed from the prefence of his adored ISMONDA, than he was convinced by the pain he was in, what fort of Paffion it was which he had entertain'd : That purling Pleafure, which at her every little Word or Motion, ran trickling through his Veins, was now fucceeded by a heavy Languor; that fprightly Joy which fo lately enliven'd all his Soul, the dear Infpirer abfent, gave way to a fullen Gloom, and the once calm Compofure of his Mind wholly chang'd to the reverfe of what it had been. MARMILLIO, of all his numerous Train, was the only Perfon to whom he communicated his Sentiments; nor did that Favourite omit making ufe of the Opportunity which this Confidante gave him, of more ingratiating himfelf to him, by foothing his new Paffion with a Profpect of Succefs : and as he had, from the firft View the Prince had of her, prefently perceiv'd with what Emotions he regarded her, fo was he not lefs watchful over the Behaviour of ISMONDA; and being

per-

perfectly well versed in the humour of that Sex, and having experienc'd the various Foibles by which they become a preyto the insinuations of those who attempt their Honour, he imagin'd that he saw enough in this Lady to keep her Lover from despair: and embellishing the real Opinion he had of her propensity to Love with all the pleasing additions his witty Invention cou'd supply him with, indulg'd the enamour'd THEODORE with Ideas too satisfactory to be repell'd, and prevented him from making even an Effort to vanquish those new Desires which had taken possession of his Soul.

He had after this many opportunities of seeing her; for being as great a Favourite with HYANTHE, as her Husband was with the King, she was scarce ever from that Princess; and the transported THEODORE, under the pretence of paying his Compliments to the eldest Daughter of a Monarch, to whom he then own'd himself a Subject, indulg'd his Wishes with the more delightful Conversation of her lovely Attendant. The great number of Nobility which continually crowded the Drawing-room of this Princess, gave liberty to those of them, who were desirous of it, of withdrawing into Parties, and as this Court was full of Gallantry, almost every one had his particular Engagement: It is not to be doubted but

that

that THEODORE laid hold on every occasion which prefented itfelf to him, of entertaining the Object of his Affections; and one day having drawn her to a Window which jutted out a confiderable way, and was feparated from the reft of the Room by a kind of Half-Alcove; he told her after fome difcourfe on ordinary Affairs, looking on her at the fame time with an unfpeakable tendernefs in his Eyes, that he had a Queftion to ask, which he paffionately long'd to be refolv'd in, but that it was of fuch a nature, as he durft not mention without having firft her promife of a faithful Anfwer. The grave and earneft manner in which thefe Words were delivered, created at firft fome little furprize in ISMONDA; but, prefently recovering her felf from it, and impatient for his meaning, affur'd him that whatever his demand was, fhe would reply to it with all imaginable Sincerity. It is then, Madam! *faid he,* if amidft all that fhow of happinefs, you feem to enjoy in a married State, you have never in fecret wifh'd that you had made lefs hafte to enter into it, and in fome meafure regretted the lofs of that Liberty a fingle Life affords? Tho' of all the Interrogatories which Invention cou'd infpire, or Language form, *anfwered fhe,* this is of a kind the moft foreign from my expectation; yet fince you have my promife, I

will

will not scruple to inform you as much of the matter as my own Heart is senfible of. Yes I will confefs, *continued fhe*, that tho' I have no reafon to complain, either of the want of Honour or Tendernefs in ADRA-STUS; I am not without fome fhare of that too common Foible of Humanity, which makes us place lefs Value on the things we are in poffeffion of, than thofe above our reach :——Whatever we may pretend, *Hope* is the moft pleafing Paffion of the Soul, and happy as I am, having enter'd into a State which deprives me of the power of expecting to be more fo, I cannot entertain myfelf with thofe delightful Ideas, which were the Companions of my Virgin Thoughts. Then Madam! *cry'd the Prince*, (interrupting her with a vifible tranf-port in his Voice and Eyes) you do not think ADRASTUS deferving the boundlefs Bleffings he enjoys? I think him worthy of much more, *refum'd fhe*, than is in the power of ISMONDA to beftow ; —— but yet, *continu'd fhe briskly*, who knows but in fpite of the little merit I am miftrefs of, Fortune and that unaccountable Caprice which fometimes rules the Heart, might, had I been in a condition to receive them, have favoured me with the Addreffes of fome Man fuperiour to ADRASTUS in Birth, in Power, in perfonal Perfections, and in every love-infpiring Grace : —— at leaft,

added

added she, more seriously, I might have flatter'd Imagination with such a hope, and grasp'd in Theory a Joy, the very shadow of which would have been preferable to the real Substance of that mean Content which I have made my Lot. If these words were not dictated by a Passion she had for the Person to whom they were addrefs'd, he could take them for no other than the effects of her desire of engaging him: He plainly saw, that if he was not belov'd by her, she took an infinite pleasure in believing herself belov'd by him ; and whether it was to her Tendernefs or Coquetry he was indebted for the condescensions she had made him, thought he had now a good opportunity of declaring himself, without any danger of incurring the Censure of being too presuming. Ah Madam! *cry'd he,* were what you say practicable in all Cafes, where the reality of our Wishes is unattainable, how much oblig'd to you would every Lover, and in particular the despairing THEODORE be, for prescribing him so eafy a way to Blifs? But alas, 'tis only the unprepoffeffed, and insensible, which can receive any benefit from your Instructions ; the Heart which can content itself with an imaginary enjoyment of its Desires, must not have for the Object of them a Perfection like that the adorable ISMONDA boafts.———You, whose excelling Charms juftly

juftly command the World, may at your
pleafure difpofe the Slaves as Fancy fhall
direct, but what relief for me? —— Ah!
how fhall I beguile the Tortures of a real
Defpair by an imaginary Joy? —— When in
emboldened Thought I feem to travel o'er
all your world of Beauty, and aim to tafte
a Blifs which even in Idea is too mighty
to be born, will not curft Reafon inter-
vene between me and the infupportable
Delight, reverfe my fate, convert my promifed Heaven to a certain Hell, and prefent the extatick Vifion in another's Arms?
——Can I indulge the rapturous Image of
ISMONDA's Charms, and not at the fame
time behold ADRASTUS in poffeffion of
them?

Here ceas'd the Prince; but ISMONDA,
tho' fhe had wifh'd, and from her firft acquaintance with him, expected a Declaration of this nature, had hitherto been fo
little accuftom'd to receive Gallantries, that
fhe could not defend herfelf from the Confufion with which this overwhelm'd her:
but the pleafure fhe conceiv'd at it, foon
diffipating all the Remonftrances of fhame
or virtuous refentment, fhe affected to take
all he had faid to her only as raillery and
the Effects of an over-gay difpofition, and
anfwered him in this manner: It muft be
confefs'd indeed, *faid fhe*, that you counterfeit the defpairing Lover with fo good

a

a grace, that fhould a Woman be vain e-
nough to believe you were in any danger
of becoming fuch in good earneft, not
ADRASTUS alone, but the nobleft Husband
in *Anatolia* would foon ceafe to be in a
condition capable of creating Envy : Since
therefore, of all mankind, you have the
moft reafon to hope every thing, expect e-
very thing, thofe delightful Ideas we have
been fpeaking of, can be no ftrangers to
your Soul, unlefs you are one of thofe
unreafonable ones whom nothing but the
real Subftance can content. Tho' the former part of what you have faid, *reply'd the
Prince*, contains a Compliment to which
I have no pretence, yet I cannot avoid fub-
fcribing myfelf to that Character you mention in the latter. Yes Madam! (*purfued
he, tenderly preffing her Hand*) I acknowledge that I am one of thofe who cannot
be fatisfied with the fhadow of a Bleffing.
Spirits may delight themfelves in an intel-
lectual Correfpondence with each other,
becaufe it is all they are capable of en-
joying ; but while the Soul is lodg'd in Flefh
and Blood, Defires of a different nature will
arife ; the Body claims its fhare of Joy, nor
will permit the other to be bleft alone.
Blefs me, *cry'd* ISMONDA, *interrupting him*,
how fuddenly is the turn of your Converfation alter'd ! — I thought, indeed, that
Air of humble diftance and defpair was little

tle conformable to your difpofition; —— this of the bold encroaching Lover is infinitely more natural, and fhows you have been more ufed to beftow Compaffion than ftand in need of it yourfelf. Whatever I have been, *refum'd he*, I am now undone if I want power to convince you that I have no other aim on Earth, than to receive from the divine ISMONDA fome tokens of it; —— if therefore the profeffions I have made you, of a Paffion the moft violent that ever was, appear too great a Prefumption, impute it to the extremity of that Anguifh which a hopelefs Flame creates, and which failing to move pity from the ador'd Object, in time confumes the Breaft which harbours it. Well, well, *faid fhe, ftill with an ironical tone and gefture*, when I am certain you are in a Condition, fuch as requires confolation, you fhall find me not ill natur'd enough to refufe it. What proofs do you demand, *rejoined he*; will nothing lefs than a Dagger, a Bowl of Poifon, or a Leap from fome fteep Promontory fuffice? Yes I affure you, *anfwer'd fhe, laughing*, I am for no fuch romantick flights: Teftimonies of a more modern fafhion will content me. —— But, *continued fhe*, perceiving two or three Ladies coming toward them, fome other time we'll talk further on this matter. The Company by this time having joined them, the Converfation grew general, nor had he all
that

that day a second opportunity of speaking to
her alone. He was, however, as he had
good reason, perfectly satisfied with the pro-
gress he had made: He very well knew Is-
MONDA was a Woman of too much penetration not to see into his Designs, and her
receiving the Declaration he had made her
only as a Jest; he took it, as really it was,
as the method she made choice of, to encourage his Addresses, without seeming to do
so. MARMILLIO, to whom he related the
whole Conversation that had pass'd between
them, was of the same opinion; and his
known Experience in the Affairs of Love,
made the Prince very much depend on his
Judgment : and never had Lover, while in
a state of Expectation, greater reason to be
satisfied with his Condition.

The next time he saw her, was in the
Gardens of the Palace Royal. She was
lying on a green Bank by the side of a Fountain, extended at full length, her Head only
a little reclin'd and leaning on her Arm,
her Eyes seem'd to swim in tender Languish-
ments, and an unusual Softness play'd about
her Mouth, with gentle Sighs her snowy Bosom heav'd, triumphant Love wanton'd thro'
all her Air, and every Part proclaim'd the
new Desire. A-while, unseen by her, the
amorous Prince stood gazing on her Charms,
taking an infinite pleasure in contemplating
her in this melting and love-inspiring Posture;

sture; especially when he reflected on the
great probability there was, that it was occasion'd by the thoughts of him, and that one
of these delightful Ideas they had been talking of at their last Interview, might now
take up her Mind. At last, considering that
if she should chance to lift up her Eyes and
discover him, it would testify but little of
that ardent Lover he had profess'd himself
to be, contented with that distant Prospect,
he drew near, and was on his knees before
her, where he remain'd some moments without rouzing her from her Resvery, so deeply was she plung'd in Thought; till no longer able to contain himself, he catch'd fast
hold of one of her Hands, and putting it
to his Mouth, seem'd to devour it with his
eager Kisses. She started at the sudden Pres-
sure, and her Surprize making her send forth
a little Shriek, kept the Prince from using
any efforts to prevent her rising from the
posture she was in; Good Heaven! *cry'd
she,* how have I been lost in Thought!
Might I presume to ask, *rejoin'd* THEO-
DORE, what has been the Subject of that
Contemplation, which has been so favourable to my Desires, of gazing on your Charms
uninterrupted, and unaw'd? Yes, *answer'd
she,* I will make no scruple of reposing a
Secret in your breast, which is of so much
consequence to your self. Love has been
the Theme of my Meditations: and the
happy

happy Object of that Paffion is no other than THEODORE. How, Madam, *cry'd he*, (not able to contain the Extafy with which thefe words fill'd all his Soul) is THEODORE the Object of ISMONDA's Love? and do you confefs it too?——Is it poffible that I am fo divinely blefs'd!——O catch the joyful Sound, ye gentle Winds, and bear it up to Heaven; there let it be regiftred, and every Saint and miniftring Angel witnefs the glorious Promife, and put it paft the lovely Maker's power ever to call it back! The Beauties of ISMONDA were at this Acclamation cover'd with a fcarlet Blufh, which was prefently fucceeded by a deadly Pale; when the Prince approaching her with all the Tranf-ports of an embolden'd Lover, was about to take her in his Arms, and reap fome fruits of that obliging Declaration fhe had made him: Forbear, my Lord! *faid fhe, half turning from him,* thefe Raptures are indeed a juft Return for the Paffion with which you are honour'd; but alas! it is not ISMONDA who is worthy of receiving them. Your Merits have had the effect which it is ordinary for them to infpire, on a Heart which the Glory of fubduing is fufficient to make yours exult with joy and vanity. As for me, think of me no otherwife than as of a Wretch whom Fate has caft in a Sphere be-neath Regard, as one who but at humble diftance dares look up to you; yet full of

ardent

ardent Zeal for your Profperity, wifhes you
ftill greater, happier, and more blefs'd, if
poffible, than Heaven itfelf has power to
make you. The Surprize which the Prince
was in at the firft part of this difcourfe, kept
him from giving any interruption to it, till
he found fhe had concluded : and when fhe
had, was divided in his Sentiments, whether he fhould anfwer to what fhe had faid
with an entreaty that fhe would explain
what it was fhe meant, by telling him he
had influenc'd a Heart more worthy; or return the obliging Softnefs with which fhe
ended, in Endearments fuch as her Behaviour feem'd to demand from a Man lefs
enamour'd, lefs tranfported with it than
himfelf. After a Paufe of about two moments, It is of little confequence to my
Peace, *faid he*, in whatfoever light my Merits may appear to the reft of the world, I
wifh to be agreeable but to IsMONDA; and
to prove you really wifh to fee me blefs'd to
that fuperlative degree you mention, you
muft believe 'tis only in your power to make
me fo——Think not therefore, *continued
he*, (preffing a fecond time her unrefifting
Hand with greater Tendernefs, if poffible,
than before) think not to put me off with
the mean Joys which any other Beauty has
the power to yield ; my high-rais'd Wifhes
aim at the fupremeft Blifs, nor will be fatif-
fied with aught but you ! Your Love alone

C   can

can give me perfect Happiness, your Cruelty alone can make me wretched. It was with a visible Satisfaction in her Eyes, mix'd with a tender Melancholy, that ISMONDA receiv'd this Declaration; and when she perceiv'd he had given over speaking, I know not, *answer'd she*, how far the natural Vanity of my Sex might induce me to believe what you have said, had I not a Rival with whom 'tis Treason to dispute any thing: it is the Princess, Sir, HYANTHE, who claims all your Devoirs, nor would forgive me even a Wish to entertain you in this manner.——I see already, *pursued she*, (after a little pause, and observing some Confusion in his Countenance) the Weakness of my Influence appears: the very Name of this too powerful Opposer robs me of all the Interest I had in you——yet do you owe me some Acknowledgement for the Intelligence: you might, perhaps, but for me, have long been uninform'd of the Happiness design'd you, and I will not lose one jot of those Privileges which are allow'd in such cases to Confidantes. Unjust ISMONDA, too lovely, cruel Trifler! *resumed the Prince;* why do you take a barbarous pleasure in raillying the pains you give? Were what you say concerning that Princess real, too well are those dear Eyes of yours acquainted with their force, to fear a Rival, or suspect your Lover's Truth. This is an Invention

tion forg'd, but to delay thofe Joys which
this blefs'd Opportunity feems to invite:
——But thus, *cry'd he, (catching her in
his Arms, and bearing her per force into
a little Grotto near the Fountain*) thus
will I difappoint the meafures thou wouldft
take; thus put an end to all the little Artifices which fear or modefty might tempt
thee to make tryal of, and be indeed as
blefs'd as thou haft lately wifh'd me.

'Tis certain that this Prince's defires were
now grown too violent for reftraint by any
common means, and nothing lefs than thofe
Ismonda took, could have oblig'd him to
defer one moment the perpetration of his
Paffion. Perceiving herfelf on the very
brink of falling a Sacrifice to a Paffion,
which fhe was not yet certain, was enough
eftablifh'd in his Heart to affure her of his
Conftancy and Gratitude, and that nothing
fhe could fay was of any efficacy to move
him from his Purpofe; fhe fnatch'd a Dagger, which he always wore by his fide, and
putting the Point of it to her Breaft, pro-
tefted by all the Gods of *Caramania*, that
fhe would that inftant dye it with her Life's-
Blood, if he would not fit calmly down
and liften to what fhe had to utter. She
fpoke this with fo refolute and determin'd
an Air, that the aftonifh'd THEODORE
trembled left fhe fhould execute what fhe
had menac'd, before he could convince her

of

of his readiness to obey her; and retiring
three or four Paces from her, threw himself upon his Knees, entreating she would
throw away a Weapon so unbecoming her
Sex, and the Power she had over him. No,
said she, 'tis necessary that I keep myself
thus arm'd, to prevent that which I am a-
bout to confess, from having an effect upon you, contrary to what I am willing to
permit. Know then, *continued she*, (with a
deep Sigh) that from the first moment you
arriv'd at the *Anatolian* Court, my Heart
has been your Prize; my Husband, you
know, with some other Noblemen, met
you on the Frontiers, and I with many
other Ladies stood at a Window to behold the Entrance of a Prince, whose
fame had fill'd us all with admiration.
Not an Eye, but what seem'd fix'd and ri-
veted upon your Charms; but all my Soul
flew into mine, to take the bright, the
dangerous Image in :—— when next I saw
you, 'twas at my own Apartment, you did
ADRASTUS the honour of a Visit, and by
that second View I was intirely lost.——I
acknowledge that never Woman loved with
a greater transcendency of Passion than
that I feel for you, and it is perhaps more
owing to the Zeal of my Affection that I
refuse giving you the Proof you ask of it,
than to my Virtue, my Duty, or any o-
ther consideration whatever.——Too much,
O

O Prince! I love you, to dare give a loose
to tendernefs without a Certainty, that I
fhall always be permitted to do fo : ——
fhould I indulge your prefent Wifhes and
my own, how fhould I be able to fupport
the dreadful Separation, which muft foon
attend this fhort-liv'd Heaven of felicity?
——Are not all the Princeffes of *Afia*
impatient to call you Husband?—— Are
you not come to *Anatolia*, meerly to confult its King which of them fhall have the
preference in your Choice; the great de-
cifion made, happy *Caramania* will again
receive its Lord, and poor ISMONDA be a-
bandoned to all the miferies which Defpair creates. A Flood of Tears here ftop'd
the farther Progrefs of her Words, and gave
the impatient THEODORE the opportunity
of replying in this manner : After this rapturous difcovery, *faid he,* think me not fo
ftupidly infenfible of the Blefling it affords,
or fo ungrateful for the Bounty, that on
any terms I could be obliged to quit *Anatolia* for ever. —— No, moft inchanting,
moft adorable ISMONDA, I fhould look on
all the Hours which cruel neceffity enforces me to pafs in abfence from you, as
fo many vacancies in Life; and foon as the
important plagues of State were over, haft
to thy Breaft, there lull my Cares to reft,
riot in Love, and in the prefent Joy, lofe
all the memory of the paft difquiet.——

C 3   Or;

Or, *continued he*, if you suspect my Constancy, be the Partner of my Journey, leave
Anatolia and this too long happy Husband,
and consent to share with me my Bed and
Power. Alas! *interrupted she*, what wild Chi-
mæras does distracted Passion form! I know
too well of what dangerous consequence to
Love are Time and Absence, to trust my
Heart with him who must abide their trial:
—Much less can I so far consult Self-interest,
as to enter into any measures for my own
Security, which must be the destruction of
your Peace, your Glory, and perhaps your
Life. I have already told you, that Hyanthe loves you, she will soon be offer'd to
you in marriage by her Father: should you
refuse this Princess, and at the same time
take with you her Woman, would not all
Anatolia, commanded by their King, and
urg'd to Vengeance by the wrong'd Adrastus, be arm'd against you? Would not
their Forces like a Torrent pour upon your
Country, depopulate your Cities, lay your
Palaces in ashes, and drive you out a
wretched Exile to mourn in some sad solitude the Ruins you had caus'd? No,
Theodore, there is but one way left which
can secure our Love: you must marry with
Hyanthe, and under the pretence of friendship and fidelity to her, I unsuspected may
exchange the Court of *Anatolia* for that of
Caramania. The confidence and favour
with

with which that Princefs graces me, will make it not feem ftrange, that I can leave a Husband, at leaft for a time, to accompany fo Royal and Kind a Miftrefs; nor will ADRASTUS, howe'er uneafy, dare to murmur at the Choice I make.

Nothing that the Prince had faid, could appear lefs confonant to Reafon than did this Propofal feem to him: He thought it fo foreign from the Principles, not only of the Paffion fhe had profefs'd, but alfo from Nature itfelf, that a Woman could of her own accord defire to fhare the Poffeffion of the Man fhe lov'd with another, that for a great while he was able to bring out no more than, Are you in earneft, Madam? ——Can you pretend to love, yet advife me to marry HYANTHE? —— Muft I to prove my conftancy be falfe? ——what incoherency of Thoughts are thefe! In fuch kind of Interrogatories did he exprefs the Amazement he was under, till fhe again repeating almoft the fame Arguments fhe had before made ufe of, to demonftrate the neceffity there was for his acting in the manner fhe advis'd, and that no other means could fecure either the Love, the Reputation, or the Intereft of both; he was half perfuaded to be of her mind, and confefs'd that in forming this Defign, fhe had teftified a Paffion more heroick, and more delicate than ever before he had any notion of. In

fine,

fine, fhe at laft obtained a promife from him, to accept of the Propofals fhe knew would be made him by the Father of Hy- ANTHE, and oblig'd him to content him- felf with her's, that as foon as ever that Affair was concluded on, fhe would deny him nothing.

Thus they parted, and when MARMILLIO, to whom the Prince, the moment he came home related every thing that had pafs'd, had a little confidered on the Advantages which might be hoped for in an Alliance with this Monarch; he encourag'd him to it by all means, prais'd the mafculine Temper of ISMONDA, who, free from the Vanity and Tenacioufnefs of her Sex, could confent to fee the Man moft dear to her in a Rival's Arms, in terms fo warm and elegant, that he was almoft doubtful if his Favourite regarded her not with the fame Eyes he did; and judging by that ftart of Jealoufy, which juft then rofe in his Soul, how terrible it muft be to fuffer an inva- der in that tender point, he could not tell how to reconcile it to reafon, that ISMON- DA could have the real Paffion for him fhe profefs'd. This Reflection making him grow penfive on the fudden, MARMILLIO intreat- ed to be told the meaning of it; which the Prince freely declaring, he endeavour- ed to eafe him of the Apprehenfions he labour'd under, in thefe or the like Terms:

I

I hope, my Royal Lord! *said he*, that there is little need of my ufing any Arguments to convince you, that I better know the Duty of a Subject than to difpute any thing with my Prince, or that I look on the Heart of ISMONDA, having receiv'd your Image, as a facred Temple which is not but with Reverence to be approached: but as to the unjuft Sufpicions you conceive of her, permit me to fet your judgment right; fhould I or any other Man attempt to rival you in her Enjoyment, the motive which would induce her yielding, muft be Love; neceffity, or even convenience could not be the Plea: it would certainly, therefore, denote the utmoft indifference in you to endure it, much more to approve of it. But the Cafe is widely different in your becoming the Husband of HYANTHE; the Love which ISMONDA is poffefs'd of for you, cannot be gratified without it; fhe has no other pretence to accompany you, fhe muft fhortly lofe you, 'tis to avoid being feparated from you, that fhe chufes to have you marry'd, and would rather fee you in another's Arms fometimes, than be certain fhe no more could hold you in her own. 'Tis with eafe we endure a conjugal Rival-fhip, becaufe we are pretty certain that thofe Endearments are more the Effect of Duty and Formality, than of Love: nor confequently can ISMONDA fuffer greater

dif-

difquiet to behold you the Husband of
HYANTHE, than it is to you to know her
the Wife of ADRASTUS. By thefe kind of
Reafonings he at laft entirely overcame the
ill humour of the Prince, and fully convinc'd him that it was both for the advantage of his Love and Intereft to match
himfelf in the manner fhe had counfelled.

Several days pafs'd over in this manner,
without any thing happening, which either
advanc'd or diminifh'd the hopes of this enamour'd Prince ; for tho' he loft no Opportunity of entertaining the lovely Object
of his Affections, and omitted nothing
which he thought might prevail on her
to confent to what both of them feem'd
to wifh with equal ardency, yet was fhe
ftill refolute; and the more violently he
enforc'd his preffures, the more feverely
did fhe repulfe them : At length, the long-
expected Propofition was made, the King
of *Anatolia* acquainted his illuftrious Gueft,
that he defired nothing fo much, as that
he fhould become his Son; and that fince
he thought fit to ask his Advice in the
Choice of a Wife, the Perfon he fhould
recommend to him fhould be no other than
HYANTHE, who he knew was highly fatisfied with his good Qualities, and that he
would give in Dowry with her, a full difcharge for ever, of that Tribute which had
hitherto been paid by the Princes of *Cara-*
mania

mania to the Crown of *Anatolia*. The secret Reward which ISMONDA was to give for the compliance of this Prince, made him anfwer in fuch a manner, as was very agreeable to the King's Defires : not the leaft Objection being made on either fide, every thing was immediately concluded on, and a Day appointed for the Celebration of the Marriage. Never was impatience e-qual to that of THEODORE, to bear to IS-MONDA the News that her Commands were now fulfill'd, and to demand the glorious recompence of his obedient Love : and that Lady, who with the Princefs had been conceal'd in a little Drawing-room, join-ing to the King's Clofet, on purpofe to hear in what manner he receiv'd the Offer, made an excufe, as foon as fhe found the Prince was about to take his leave, to retire to her own Apartment; not doubting but the hafte he made, was wholly on her account, and there prepared herfelf to receive him with all the tendernefs fhe had promis'd, or that he could expect to find in her. Never had the God of tender Wifhes a Sacrifice more ardent, or attended with a greater Zeal, than that now offered him by this enamour'd Pair : each ftrove to outvie the other in the foft Devotion; both yielded, and both conquer'd in their turn.

The Gratification of his Paffion made the tranfported THEODORE in fo good a

humour,

humour, that he found it no difficulty to
diffemble as muchTendernefs for HYANTHE,
as was neceffary for the concealment of his
Paffion for ISMONDA; and with fo much
conduct did thefe happy Lovers behave
themfelves to each other, both in their
Converfations in publick, and in the management of thofe fecret meetings, which
gave them the full Satisfaction of their
mutual Defires, that the Intrigue between
them, was never fo much as fufpected, e-
ven by thofe who had moft reafon to
carry an obfervant Eye, H Y A N T H E and
ADRASTUS.

The Day being arriv'd for the Solemniza-
tion of the Wedding, it was perform'd
with the utmoft magnificence: all the Nobility of both Sexes endeavour'd to appear
in the moft grand manner that their Abi-
lities would permit; the Ladies efpecially,
forgot no Ornaments which might add a
Luftre to their natural Charms : but ISMON-
DA, like a Star of fuperiour Magnitude,
eclips'd the Shine of every other Beauty;
that fweet Contentment which now fat
fmiling in her Eyes, improving all her Air,
and heightning every Grace, rendered her
not only more lovely than all the con-
temporary Fair-ones, but alfo excelling
what even herfelf had been ufed to appear :
Enjoyment had been fo far from leffening
the Ardors of THEODORE, that never had

he

he languish'd with more strong or vehement
Desires than at this moment; and she who
was perfectly well vers'd in the Language
of the Eyes, found enough in his to assure
her, that the yet untasted Pleasure he was
to reap that Night with HYANTHE, would
but faintly compensate for the want of
those which were in her power to bestow.
And exulting in the Triumph that she a-
lone was mistress of his *Soul*, easily absolv'd
her Fate, for the necessity there was, for
their common Interest, that his *Body* must,
at some times, be elsewhere devoted.

Poor HYANTHE, who had also the most
tender affection for the happy THEODORE,
contented herself with the Complaisance
he paid her, imagining the little warmth of
his Caresses were only owing to the fault
of Nature, and that all he knew of Love,
he felt for her. All Parties, therefore,
had something to delight themselves with,
and every one being satisfied in their several Circumstances, made it not their business to search into the private Behaviour
of each other.

The Time being at hand, in which it
was thought proper the Prince should return to *Caramania*, the punctual ISMONDA,
counterfeiting the extremest Friendship to
the Princess, entreated she would permit
her to attend her to her new Sovereignty,
and telling her, she should be the most un-

happy

happy Woman on earth, to be left behind her; that in her Journey, and in a place to whose Cuftoms and Manners fhe was wholly a ftranger, fhe might probably wifh for a Companion, to whom fhe could impart her Mind with that freedom which fhe had been accuftom'd to do to her; and conjured her to grant the Requeft fhe made, of being permitted to go with her: that the Princefs was both furpriz'd and pleas'd at fo uncommon a proof of Fidelity and Love, as this had the appearance of. And is it poffible, *faid fhe*, that Friendfhip can carry one to greater lengths than Love?———Can you fo eafily be prevail'd on to quit the Arms of a Husband whom you love, and by whom you are fo well belov'd, only to follow a Princefs who has it not in her power to give you any Bleffings proportion'd to thofe you leave behind? Your Service, *replied fhe*, O moft Excellent and Royal HYANTHE, I always look'd on as the fupremeft Bleffing of my Life; and while poffefs'd of that, can know no want of any other Happinefs: As for ADRASTUS, if his great Employments will not permit him wholly to take leave of *Anatolia*, the diftance between the Lands is not fo great, but that he may fometimes pay us a Vifit at the *Caramanian* Court: or when you are fettled there, and the knowledge of your Goodnefs makes you as dear to your Subjects there, as juftly here you
&c,

are, ISMONDA may be the better spared, and I may then return to ADRASTUS a Wife who prefers him to every thing but her Love and Duty to her Princess.

These kind of Discourses were too obliging to the Princess, for her to refuse the Purport of them ; and in spite of all the opposition which ADRASTUS could make, it was resolved that ISMONDA should attend her to *Caramania*.

Thus did this Prince purchase the Good-will of his Subjects, and the Admiration of the whole World, by the same means which secured to himself the Enjoyment of his Wishes, and at his return receiv'd the Thanks of an adoring People for an imaginary Obligation; being look'd on as the Father of his Country, for an Action only influenced by Self-satisfaction, and in which he had no other View than such as were very distant from deserving the Trophies erected to it.

But having done so much merely for the sake of ISMONDA, who would not believe his Soul so wholly devoted to her, that it could have left room for any other Idea ; yet, dear as she was to him, the Love of Variety intervened, and made him wish to taste new Joys in a young Beauty's Arms, whose Name was LUTETIA, the Daughter of a *Caramanian* Lord, and brought by him to Court, to attend the Princess on her first

arri-

arrival. His Sollicitations had the effect it was ufual for them to infpire, nor could thofe Charms from which all the Tyes of Duty and premier Engagements to one of the beft of Husbands, were too weak to de-fend the Heart of ISMONDA, fail of gaining a Conqueft over one fo unexperienc'd, fo unprejudiced, as was that of this young Maid. Soon did the eternally-fuccefsful THEODORE triumph in her Virgin Favours, and as foon, alas! did he forget the Blifs; the Image of ISMONDA now return'd with former force into his Soul, and reproach'd him in Idea, for having aim'd at Joys with any other Object: he regretted his Incon-ftancy, could not forgive himfelf for having once been falfe to her, who of all her Sex alone had the power of infpiring him with a ferious Paffion, and for whofe Love he thought himfelf fo much obliged, that the Service of his whole Life was too little to requite the Bleffing; and of that burning, that impatient Longing which lately fill'd all his Faculties for the innocent LUTETIA, no-thing was now remaining but a cool Pity for the Ruin he had involv'd her in.

The unhappy Victim of Defire immediate-ly perceiv'd to what a wretched ftate her eafy yielding, and her fond belief had reduced her; yet ftill loving him with an unbated Paffion, fhe forbore either to reproach or to complain of his Unkindnefs, nor but to

Heaven

Heaven and the unpitying Stars reveal'd her
weight of Anguish; till finding in herself
that common Confequence which attends
Raptures fuch as fhe too lavifhly had indulg'd, the terror of approaching Shame,
and the juft rage of an offended and difhonour'd Father, made her refolve to intreat
the Prince to find fome Expedient which
might fhelter her from the impending
Storm : but he fo carefully avoided all difcourfe with her in private, that tho' fhe
watch'd with all imaginable diligence, fhe
could never find an opportunity of fpeaking to him.   It would be but impertinent to
trouble my Reader with any repetition of
the Lamentations fhe made, or the fecret
Miferies of her tormented Mind ; it is very
eafy to conceive what a young Creature,
thus ruin'd, thus abandon'd, yet ftill loving
the dear Undoer, muft fuftain : I fhall only
fay, fhe wanted nothing but Courage, to
fend herfelf at once from the Vale of Wret-
chednefs into which her Inadvertency had
plung'd her, and difappoint the Infamy
which the condition fhe was in was fhortly
to bring upon her. But whether it were,
that fhe could not refolve to leave the
World while THEODORE was in it, or that
Life ftill flatter'd her with fome faint Hopes
that he might again return to her Embraces,
and blefs her with renew'd Endearments, fhe
could not, or fhe would not fly to that Re-

D   medy

medy to which the Desperate have usually
recourse: But still revolving in her Mind
some means to communicate her Condition
to him, who alone had the power of rendring it supportable; and still finding all
the Efforts she made for that purpose ineffectual, she at last took up a Resolution to
write, and in these terms related the Dictates of her Love, her Grief, and her Despair.

To the most Charming of his Sex, the ac-
complish'd THEODORE, *Prince of* Caramania.

   ' **I**S it because you are my Sovereign,
   ' that you imagine yourself absolv'd
' for my undoing?———Is it a part of your
' Prerogative to ruin and betray?———
' Can Royalty convert those Acts to Vir-
' tue, which in another Man wou'd be
' look'd on as the extremest Degrees of
' Vice?———Oh! no; Power is not a
' Sanction for Oppression.——— The Duty
' of a Prince is to redress, not offer In-
' juries.———Where but to the Throne
' should we appeal for Justice, or for Mer-
' cy?———How wretched then is poor
' LUTETIA's Case, wrong'd by the only
' Man who should protect her Innocence,
' or revenge her Ruin?———Oh Prince!
' have you not a thousand times swore
        ' you

' you lov'd me, that you would always do
' so, and that my Peace, my Intereſt, my
' Reputation, ſhould ever be valued by you
' as your own; yet have you not aban-
' don'd me to all the Miſeries of Deſpair
' and Shame!——To the juſt Upbraidings
' of the cenſorious World, and the more
' terrible Remora's of a guilty Mind?——
' Wild with unſated Love, with Tender-
' neſs abus'd, with the Horrors of approach-
' ing, ſure, irremediable Woe, I ſuffer more
' than Words can ſpeak, or Thought un-
' feeling it, conceive; yet are you the
' cruel, lovely Author of it unmov'd, un-
' touch'd, and pityleſs of all this mighty
' Load of Anguiſh:——But leſt you ſhould
' plead Ignorance of the moſt poignant part
' of my Misfortune, know I am with child;
' and as if it were not a ſufficient Curſe
' to wear your faithleſs Image in my Mind,
' Fate has decreed me to bear another,
' which ſoon will become paſt conceal-
' ment, and grow an undeniable Witneſs
' of its Mother's Shame.——Wretch that
' I am, to what muſt I have recourſe, by
' what Replies ſilence the juſt Reproaches
' of an enrag'd, diſgrac'd, and troubled Fa-
' ther!——— How excuſe my Crime to
' Heaven and HYANTHE!——How anſwer
' even the unhappy Product of your diſ-
' ſembled Raptures, whoſe guiltleſs Cries
' will every moment upbraid me for giv-

' ing

' ing it a Life, whose Portion must be on-
' ly Infamy!——Oh! I am lost for ever—
' undone in every Circumstance; yet let
' those Powers who know my Soul be
' judge, if all that can attend a Crime like
' mine, here, or hereafter, is half so dread-
' ful as the shock of being by you for-
' saken.——Bless'd with your Love, I
' could have defy'd my Fate, and with a
' Smile met every other Woe.—— Charm
' me then, once more, with Love restor'd:
' if ever I was worthy those soft Endear-
' ments which made Guilt so pleasing, I
' still am so; nor Age, nor Sickness has
' deform'd my Bloom; my Eyes, tho now
' o'erflow'd with Tears, would, at your
' presence, regain their usual Lustre, and
' that Vivacity, you have so often praised,
' again return, and quicken all my Air.—
' If I am chang'd in aught from what I
' was, 'tis you, O Prince! have made me
' so, and when you please can restore me
' to myself, and to those blisful Moments,
' which assur'd me nothing could give a
' greater Satisfaction to the royal THEO-
' DORE, than to know I was his

Faithful, and most

Passionately Devoted

LUTETIA.

P. S.

P. S. ' If urg'd by Griefs too mighty to
' be long fuftain'd, I do a defperate Mur-
' der on myfelf and the unhappy Unborn,
' let not my Rafhnefs, but your own Cru-
' elty, bear the blame; fince it is much
' eafier to live by your relenting, than to
' feek a Shelter in the Grave from your
' Inhumanity.———Once more I beg you
' to compaffionate my Miferies, and that
' you will no longer fhun a Wretch who
' cannot be but yours.'

She had written this Epiftle fome days,
and kept it in her Pocket, without being
able to get an opportunity of delivering it
to him, having no Perfon in the world to
whofe Truft fhe dare commit a Paper of
fo much confequence: At laft Fortune afforded one as ample, as the miferable Circumftances fhe was in could hope. HYAN-
THE being a little indifpos'd, kept her Chamber; and the Prince coming to vifit her,
at a time when none but LUTETIA happen'd to be in the Room, that unfortunate
Lady made a pretence of opening the Door
for him as he was going out, and flipp'd
the Letter into his hands with thefe Words:
I conjure you, my Lord! *faid fhe*, to read
that, and afford fome Anfwer to her who
is dying with your Unkindnefs. This not
being a place in which fhe could expect

him

him to make her any reply, fhe waited not
for it; but immediately retir'd to her Seat
at the foot of the Bed, where the Princefs
was reclin'd, and by that means loft the
fight of that Confufion with which the
Prince was cover'd at receiving a Salutation, which he had long fear'd to meet.

'Tis certain, that tho' he had but fmall
remains of that Paffion, which can properly be call'd Love, he had Honour and
Good-nature enough to make him extremely commiferate her Diftrefs, and felt a Concern for her, which might very well bear
the Name of the moft tender Friendfhip:
fain he would have talk'd to her, and let
her have known, by word of mouth, how
great a fhare he bore in her Misfortune;
but the Fears he was in, that a private Interview might by fome accident be difcover'd, and occafion fome Sufpicion of
the Truth, efpecially when the Condition
fhe was in fhould be made known, prevented him. He equally dreaded the Jealoufy of HYANTHE, or ISMONDA; the
one, Intereft of State oblig'd him to diffemble with; and the other, his ftill fincere
Affection made him fearful to offend.
Thefe Apprehenfions, mix'd with his Regard for LUTETIA, and the Uncertainty in
what manner he fhould behave toward her,
kept his Thoughts in a perpetual rack, till
after many Refolutions form'd and reject-
ed,

ed, he at length pitch'd on one, which
promis'd him some ease from that Dilemma
he had long been involv'd in.

MARMILLIO, who on all occasions, particularly in those of his Amours, was always
his Confidant and Adviser, was the Person to whom he apply'd himself in this
juncture ; and having made him acquainted
with the whole Affair, and show'd him the
Letter which LUTETIA had written, he
order'd him to wait on that Lady, to bear
to her his most tender Respects, and excuse
his not coming to her in Person, because it
might occasion some Jealousy in HYANTHE ;
who, he bid him say, had already given
some hints of a propensity in her Nature
to that Passion. He desired him also to
make use of his utmost Efforts to persuade
her to retire from Court for some time,
and that nothing should be wanting to make
whatever Solitude she should chuse agreeable.

It was with the greatest reason that
the Prince always made choice of this Favourite for the management of such Affairs,
because he was not only extremely faithful
to the Trust repos'd in him, but had also a
ready Wit and Invention capable of carrying on almost any Enterprize he took delight in, and had a Genius naturally turn'd to
Love-Intrigues. He assur'd the Prince, he
would do in every thing as he had directed,

and

and that he did not doubt but to plead so
succcfsfully with LUTETIA, as to make her
accecd to every thing they defired of her;
and alfo more contented in her Mind, than
fhe had been of a long time.

There is a great deal owing to the good
Inclination of the Perfon employ'd. MAR-
MILLIO went about this Affair with fo
much Refolution to accomplifh it, that he
could not fail of doing fo; and by tender
and obliging Words, at firft combating with
the Tears and Impatiencies of the unfortunate LUTETIA, by degrees brought her to
liften to his Arguments with Moderation,
and at laft to think her Circumftances lefs
wretched than fhe had believ'd them. He
affur'd her that fhe was as much as ever the
Object of the Prince's Affection, that there
was nothing he fo ardently long'd for, as an
opportunity to convince her of it, but that
the prefent fituation of Affairs would not
permit it. Time, *faid this fubtle Infinua-*
tor, will convince the fweet LUTETIA, that
nothing is fo dear to Prince THEODORE as
the poffeffion of her Beauties, and that he
but denies himfelf the prefent Blifs, till he
can bring about fome Defigns, which may
fecure him hereafter the uninterrupted Felicity—Had you feen, *continued he*, with
how much Agony of Soul he exprefs'd himfelf on this occafion, you would not blame
but pity him. Tell her, *faid he to me*,
MAR-

MARMILLIO, that all that her own foft
Thoughts can form of Love, I feel for her;
that in my unextinguiſhable Paſſion, there
is all the Tenderneſs of *Woman*, blended
with the moſt vigorous and burning Energy
of eager Wiſhing, that e'er enflam'd the
Heart of *Man*.——But, *purſu'd* MARMILLIO,
to tell you what he ſaid, is but to make
you half ſenſible of what he would have
you know—to do juſtice to his Meaning, I
muſt be able to ſpeak in the manner he
did, muſt aſſume a Softneſs which my
Voice is incapable of wearing; muſt teach
my Eyes to languiſh, and every Feature to
declare the God with which he is ſo powerfully inſpir'd.——I am, alas! an unfit
Proxy to reveal what 'tis he ſuffers, and how
much he loves; and if your own Imagination makes not up for what I am deficient
in, my Prince can never appear what in reality he is.

By theſe kind of Diſcourſes, ſhe was won
to believe herſelf as happy, as ſhe, indeed,
was miſerable: and now employing her
whole time in Artifices to conceal her
growing Shame, and to contrive ſome
plauſible excuſe for leaving the Court, ſhe
prepar'd herſelf to go to a private Lodging,
which the Care of MARMILLIO provided
for her, wholly ſatisfy'd with the Aſſu-
rances he every day continu'd to give her of
the Prince's inviolable Affection, and ſending

ing by the mouth of that Favourite, every thing she would have him know.

Thus was LUTETIA satisfy'd, and the Prince reliev'd from those Apprehensions which had been so uneasy to him, that the Fondness or Despair of that unhappy Creature might drive her to some extravagances of Behaviour, which might betray the whole Affair between them, either to HY-ANTHE, or to her whose Displeasure more he dreaded, ISMONDA: but little did MAR-MILLIO think, that while he was serving his Prince, he was involving himself in Difficulties, from which not all his Wit and Address could disengage him for a long time.

Being, as I have before observ'd, of an amorous Disposition, he was scarce ever without an Intrigue, and sometimes had three or four upon his hands at once. Among the number of those for whom he had entertain'd a Desire, was IRENE, a young Lady, whose Brother had been first Minister of State to the Father of THEODORE, and tho' somewhat less in favour than he had been, was yet a very considerable Man both in the Court, and in the Army. It was not without the utmost Labour, long Assi-duities, repeated Vows and Protestations, and a solemn Contract of Marriage, that MARMILLIO had prevail'd on her to allow him the gratification of his Passion; but nothing

thing being farther from his Intentions, than
to make good his Promises, he always found
some pretence for deferring the Celebration
of their Nuptials, whenever press'd to it by
her. Finding herself, at length, in the
same condition with the unfortunate Lu-
TETIA, she renew'd her Desires of becoming
his Wife with greater force than ever; but
he had artifice enough to turn those very
Reasons she made use of, against what she
desired : he told her, that should the Marriage now be solemniz'd, it would be a
plain Demonstration that there had been too
great an Intimacy between them; and that
it would be infinitely more for her Reputation to keep the whole Affair a Secret; still
continuing to assure her, that as soon as she
was deliver'd of her Burden, he would perform what she required, and he had sworn.
—He enforc'd these Arguments with so
much Wit and Eloquence, and accompany'd them with so great a show of Tenderness, that had the Person to whom they
were apply'd, been infinitely more practis'd
in Deceit than was IRENE, she might have
imagin'd it sincere. The pains he took to
make her easy, were not, however, so
much the Effect of Love as Fear; he dreaded
the great Power of her Brother, and the Influence which the Complaint of a Woman
of IRENE's Quality and Character would
have on the Senate, in case she should make

a

a publick claim of the Contract he had
made ; and being in his Nature a marriage-
hater, and the Defires he had for IRENE fully
fatiated by repeated and unreftrain'd Enjoyments, nothing could appear to him a
greater misfortune than to be compell'd to
become her Husband.

To add to the Indifference he already had
for this Lady, there was lately arriv'd at
the Court of *Caramania* a young Beauty,
with whom he fell paffionately in love,
as much as that Paffion can be call'd fo,
which tends to the Ruin of the Object admired. ARILLA, for that is her Name,
has Charms which might almoft juftify Inconftancy, and render the Complaints of
the Forfaken of no effect, where Youth and
Nature are to decide the Conteft. Often
had MARMILLIO lov'd, but ne'er, till now,
experienc'd with how much force the God
can actuate ; and finding from the exceffive
Modefty of this new Charmer, not the leaft
Shadow of a Hope to countenance his Defigns, he grew almoft mad ; Sleep was a
ftranger to his Nights, and Peace forfook
his Days : Yet not being of a humour on
which Defpair could eafily feize, he refolv'd
not to defift till he had try'd every way
which Love and Wit had the power of infpiring in the moft determin'd Heart. He
had, indeed, this to encourage his Attempts,
that he perceiv'd he was not difagreeable to
her ,

her; that he had only Virtue to oppofe, and no premier Inclination to another, or Averfion to him, made war againft his Hopes: he imagin'd therefore, that what Modefty and Virgin Bafhfulnefs refus'd to grant, if feiz'd by amorous Violence would not appear a Crime too great to be forgiven; having often in mind that faying of a famous *Englifh* Poet, which Language he underftood perfectly well :

Force is the laft Relief which Lovers find ;
And is the beft Excufe for Womankind.

His Experience in the humour of that Sex inform'd him, that many of them are too prudent to refent what is paft retrieve, and that moft are more willing to pardon a Prefumption of that kind when done, than to give their Confent to the committing it. The gentlenefs of ARILLA's Behaviour made him half affur'd fhe was of this Temper, and that he had nothing worfe to fear from her after the perpetration of his Defires, than he now fuftain'd in the vain Profecution of them.

Having fix'd himfelf in this Refolution, all he wanted was an opportunity to put it in practice; but tho' he fcarce loft fight of her one moment, and ftill obferv'd her Motions whether at Court or at her own Apartment, he could not for fome days fee

her

her alone, some impertinent Interruption
still broke off the preparatory Discourses he
was entertaining her with, to bring about
his Purpose; but at length his zealous Attendance met the Reward for which 'twas
paid. The Prince and Princess being gone
to take the Air together, attended by a great
Retinue, none of the Maids of the Bed-
Chamber, who were in waiting, happen'd to
be left at home, but ARILLA; who, desirous
of indulging her own Meditations, had pretended an Indisposition, and desired to be
excus'd from her Attendance. She had
shut herself into the Princess's Closet, de-
signing to pass some hours in private; when
MARMILLIO, whose Eyes were never off
her, having observ'd what had pass'd, took
the boldness to knock at the door: Little
imagining who it was, and unsuspecting the
instant Danger with which she was threatned,
she readily open'd it, and gave entrance to
the Man who came prepar'd to ruin her.
The Resolution with which he had arm'd
himself for this Encounter, gave a greater
fierceness to his Air, than, till this moment,
he had ever presum'd to approach her with;
which, together with his making fast the
Door, as soon as he was admitted, gave the
timorous Maid some apprehensions of his
Designs: What is it you mean, MARMILLIO?
*said she, in a trembling and scarce intelligi-
ble accent.* To do Justice, *reply'd he,* to
the burning Passion of my Soul, which I
too

too much have trifled with, and which will now no longer be deny'd.——Yield then, *purſu'd he, looking on her with Eyes that ſeem'd to flame with raging and impatient Love,* nor rob the Joys I come determin'd to poſſeſs of half their Sweetneſs, by a vain Reſiſtance, and unavailing Coyneſs.——You will not ſure, *cry'd ſhe, more frighted,* have recourſe to brutal Force?—— Conſider where we are, and who I am, a Maid of Quality, and under the immediate Care of Royal Power?——Not all the Powers, *interrupted he, catching her in his Arms,* of Heaven and Earth ſhall now deter MARMILLIO from his purpoſe—I love, and cannot live without you—give then to the Winds thy Fears, thy Scruples, and all the Foes of Pleaſure——indulge the raviſhing Delights which ſoft Deſire affords—let Love and Nature looſe, and take thy ſhare of Joy, nor ſuffer me to be bleſs'd alone.——He accompany'd theſe Words with Actions, ſuch as left her no room to doubt if her continuing to refuſe wou'd be of much conſequence to her Preſervation; and tho' ſhe was far from yielding, ſhe wanted, in this ſurprizing exigence, Spirit and Reſolution ſufficient to oppoſe in any manner which could oblige him to give over his Attempt.——In the midſt of Tears, Tremblings, faint Entreaties, and Reproaches, he accompliſh'd his Deſign, and not till he

had

had fnatch'd the guilty Blifs, gave himfelf
leifure to reply to what fhe faid.

But when fecure of his Defires, and poffefs'd of all his wild Paffion aim'd at, he then
exerted all thofe Arts which had entitled him
to fo many Succeffes with the Fair, to defend the Violence he had been guilty of.——
He employ'd that Wit and Eloquence which
Men generally make ufe of, to melt the
unwary Maid to grant what they wifh; to
argue her into a Belief, that fhe not only
ought to pardon, but alfo to approve of
what he had done, as the extremeft Teftimo-
ny of his unbounded Paffion, which would
not fuffer any Confiderations, not even
thofe of offending her, than which, *he
faid*, nothing could be more formidable, to
be an obftruction to the attainment of his
Hopes. The hurry and confufion of her
Thoughts, left her as little the power of
making any Anfwer to him, as his Impatiencies had permitted him before; and he
went on uninterrupted, with his Perfuafions,
vowing not to leave her till fhe had affur'd
him of his Pardon; which, at laft, reflecting that what had happen'd was now irremediable, fhe granted, and without a fecond
Ravifhment, fuffer'd him to take a full Enjoyment of thofe Charms which before had
blefs'd him but by halves.

The Cravings of tumultuous Paffion being thus appeas'd, and Tranquillity, now
fettled

settled in that Breaft, which lately fwell'd with the moft difturb'd Emotions, cool Re-collection had liberty to refume its place; and bethinking himfelf, that if the Princefs fhould return and furprize him in this privacy with her Woman, it would give occafion for Difcourfes, fuch as were no way agreeable to his prefent Circumftances, and the appearance of that Fidelity it behov'd him to behave with to IRENE, who was not yet retir'd from Court, and he very well knew kept a jealous Eye on all his Actions: he therefore took his leave of the undone ARILLA, giving her the liberty of indulging Meditation on what had paft, while he, gay and triumphant on the eafy Conqueft, retired to tafte the Joys of BAC-CHUS, who, with the God of Love, are the only Deities he acknowledges.

It was in the time that he was carrying on this double Intrigue with IRENE and ARILLA, that he was employ'd by the Prince to negotiate his Affair with LUTETIA; and being known to be very often with that Lady both in publick and private, his Innocence in that matter rendring him lefs cautious in being feen with her, than with thofe whom he vifited on his own account, the whole Court gave her to him for a Miftrefs. Some imagin'd he follicited her on honourable Terms, but others who were better acquainted with his Difpofition, and had

E

alfo

alſo ſome ſuſpicion of her Condition,
made no doubt, but that ſhe had yielded
to his Suit, on Terms leſs advantageous to
herſelf than Marriage. Among the number of thoſe whom theſe Diſcourſes reach'd,
were IRENE and ARILLA : few Women are
poſſeſs'd of greater ſhare of Pride, Spirit,
and Paſſion, than the former of theſe Ladies, which, join'd to the Power which the
Contract between them gave her over him,
and the Circumſtances to which her yielding
to his Preſſures had reduc'd her, made her
look upon this imaginary Wrong as the
moſt inſupportable Indignity, the common
Chat being confirm'd to her by ſome buſy
People, who pretended to be in the Secret,
either to make themſelves paſs for Perſons
of an extraordinary Intelligence, or gueſ-
ſing how the Affair ſtood between her and
MARMILLIO, talk'd in this manner on purpoſe to ſee how ſhe would reſent it. She
grew perfectly outrageous, ſwore ſhe wou'd
have Juſtice or Revenge; and he hapning to
come in to viſit her juſt in the moment
when her tempeſtuous Paſſion was work'd
up to the greateſt height that mortal Fury
can arrive at, ſhe fell on him with Imprecations and Revilings, ſuch as both terrify'd
and aſtoniſh'd him; but the extremity of her
Rage, rendering what ſhe ſaid ſcarce intelligible, and mentioning only that ſhe was
ill treated and neglected for a Rival's ſake,
with-

without naming LUTETIA; confcious
Guilt made him not imagine it was any
other than ARILLA that fhe meant, and
entreating her to hear him, was beginning to
fwear he never had a Thought of Tendernefs for that Young Lady, and that the devoirs he paid her, were only on the account
of a dear Friend, who was paffionately in
Love with her, and had employ'd him to
follicit his Caufe.——Can the divine IRENE,
faid he to her, with the moft tender Air,
be fo infenfible of her Power of Charming,
as to imagine the Man, whom fhe vouch-
fafes to blefs, can throw away a Wifh on
the mean Beauties which ARILLA boafts?
ARILLA! *cry'd fhe, interrupting him,* What
mean you by ARILLA? Do you hope by a
poor Equivocation to evade my juft Refentment? and by protefting your Innocence of
a Crime of which you are not fufpected,
filence the Accufations of that wherein you
are guilty?——Inconftant, ingrateful, and
perfidious Man! too well you know 'tis
not ARILLA, but LUTETIA, is the Object
of my Jealoufy. Now was MARMILLIO,
indeed, confounded; tho' wholly free from
the Crime with which he was charg'd on her
account, he was now fenfible, on Reflection,
that he had behav'd in a manner fuch as
might very well make him appear otherwife, and having thrown away on ARILLA's
fcore the only Excufe his Invention could

fup-

supply him with, had nothing now to alledge in vindication of his frequent Visits to LUTETIA ; unless he had acquainted her with the Secret of his Prince; and that, not all the Fears he was in from the Rage of IRENE, could make him venture to do.——— She was not only a very great Favourite with the Princess; but had also a more than ordinary Intimacy with ISMONDA, and how far Jealousy or Curiosity might transport her to mention the Affair, he knew not: He therefore thought it better to run the risque of whatever her Indignation might attempt against him, than dare the Displeasure of THEODORE in a Business of so much consequence. The confusion which appear'd in all his Air, and incapacity of answering to her Reproaches on this score, confirm'd her that they were but too just; and giving a loose to her impatient Rage, she said all that a jealous and distracted Woman could invent : mingling with her Reproaches, the most bitter Menaces, and vowing by every thing that was sacred, that she would reveal the whole Story to her Brother, who would not fail to call him to a severe account for the Dishonour he had brought upon his Family. MARMILLIO told her, with his accustom'd softness, that he had nothing to fear but her Disquiet ; and began to persuade her to more Moderation, entreating her to trust to time for an explanation

tion of his Innocence; and endeavouring by a thousand new-invented Oaths to bring her to the belief, that she alone was the Mistress of his Affections. But all his Artifices were vain; it was now too late to dissipate an Opinion which his Disorders had at first establish'd in her, and she rather seem'd more incensed that he pretended to deny the Fact for which he was accus'd, yet gave no reasons for his having acted in a manner which had made him be thought guilty; and looking on the present Tenderness of his Behaviour only as an Imposition, would not suffer him to proceed, but flew out of the Room from him, and shut herself into her Closet; whence, tho' he sent several Messages to her by her Servant, she would not be prevail'd on to come out till he had left her Apartment.

To heighten the Chagrin he conceiv'd at this Adventure, when he came home he found a Letter, which his Servant inform'd him had been left for him in the Morning. He presently knew the Character to be that of ARILLA, and was not a little surpriz'd at her writing to him, being that Night to meet her by appointment, at a House he had contriv'd on purpose for their secret Rendezvous, and where, in the full Enjoyment of his yet unsated Wishes, he had hoped to make himself some amends for the Vexations of the Day: opening it,

there-

therefore, with a mixture of Delight and
Fear, he found it contain'd these Lines.

To the Perjured and Inconstant MARMILLIO.

‘ THE Heart that has plurality of En-
‘ gagements, cannot be said to be
‘ truly affected with any one of them, nor
‘ consequently feel any great Concern at
‘ breaking off. —— In the Charms of
‘ LUTETIA, you will easily forget the in-
‘ ferior ones ARILLA is mistress of; yet it
‘ is so natural, at least to me, to expect a
‘ return equal in value to what I give, that
‘ I cannot be so fondly complaisant, as to
‘ make a Present of my Affections, where
‘ all the Reward I can hope to receive, is Hy-
‘ pocrisy and Deceit: neither am I enough
‘ experienc'd in the Custom of a Court, to
‘ approve, or indeed to know how to carry
‘ on the Gallantries I see so much in fa-
‘ shion.—— If I love at all, it must be
‘ with sincerity; I have not yet learned to
‘ parcel out my Heart, and divide my Ten-
‘ derness as I would do my Time, one
‘ Hour with this, the next with a different
‘ Admirer, a third with another, and so
‘ on, pretending equally alike to all:——
‘ No, he that has me, must have my whole
‘ Soul, and every Faculty must be the dear
‘ Engrosser's.—— This is indeed to love;
‘ all

' all other Paſſions which bear that Name,
' are no more than ſo many Prophanations
' of the Deity; and ſince no other can be
' hoped for in a Correſpondence with the
' falſe MARMILLIO, I abjure it for ever —
' Loſe not therefore any of thoſe Moments,
' which, doubtleſs, you may employ with
' more pleaſure, in vainly waiting for me
' at that Houſe which was intended for
' our meeting.—— It is not fit that Truth
' and Tenderneſs, like mine, ſhould be the
' Recompence of Perjury and Ingratitude,
' ſuch as yours; and tho by Violence you
' have already triumph'd over my defence-
' leſs Body, my Mind you never ſhall ſub-
' due.——Ruin'd as I am by your brutal
' Paſſion, my nobler Part is uncorrupted
' yet; nor will I ever, by a ſhameful yield-
' ing, become Partner in your Guilt, and
' the Aſſiſtant in my own Deſtruction.——
' If I complain not of the Injury you have
' done me, to aught but Heaven, impute
' it not to any Tenderneſs for you, but
' to my own Modeſty ;—— and the know-
' ledge that there is no Revenge I could
' take, which would be equal to your Crime:
' from your own changing Temper, I doubt
' not but to ſee worſe Effects fall on you,
' than any I could wiſh, much more inflict;
' ——in the perfect Aſſurance, therefore,
' that my Wrongs will not go unreveng'd
' by a Hand more capable of puniſhing, I

E 4   ' take

' take my everlasting leave, only concern'd
' that I cannot, without severely adding to
' the Misfortune I labour under, impart
' your Villany to the World, and preserve
' my too believing Sex from giving credit
' to your Vows, and being by your perni-
' cious Artifices ruin'd and undone, like

The Unfortunate

ARILLA.

P. S. ' I accuse you not with any hope
' of hearing you justified :————Attempt
' not therefore to deceive me a second
' time; I am convinced of your Infidelity
' to me, and new Passion for LUTETIA,
' and all you can urge will be in vain.——
' The Contents of this Epistle, are the Dic-
' tates of a Resolution, which it is not
' in your power to shake; and I should
' merit the Infamy which must attend me,
' if, after the Detection of your Baseness,
' I should put it in your power to aban-
' don me.———— I desire no Answer to
' this, nor will read any thing that comes
' from you; and because the sight of a
' Man, who has so greatly injur'd me, is an
' Aggravation of my Griefs, the only Fa-
' vour I request of you, is, to shun me as
' much as possible, while there is a Neces-
' sity of my appearing in publick: a few
' days shall put it out of yours or my own
                                    ' power

' power ever to meet again.——Once more
' eternally adieu.'

Never was Vexation fuperior to that
which the difappointed MARMILLIO was
involved in at reading thefe Lines; he flew
directly to her Apartment, but her Woman
was order'd to deny admittance to him: he
afterwards writ a Letter to her, protefting
his Innocence in the moft moving terms that
Love and Eloquence could infpire; but it
was the next moment fent back to him un-
open'd. It was in vain that he attempted to
fee her at Court; fhe had pretended a fudden Illnefs, and kept her Chamber. He
now perceiv'd indeed, that fhe was miftrefs
of a Refolution equal to what fhe boafted,
and infinitely fuperior to what he ever found
before in any of her Sex, and was as much at
a lofs in what manner he fhould go about
to overcome it, as he was unable to endure
the thoughts of her perfifting in it. To
add to his difquiets, he heard that fhe had
fent to intreat leave of the Princefs to retire into the Country; which being granted,
all things were preparing for her Journey,
and to what place was unknown. Never
was man in more perplexity of foul than was
he, equally divided between his grief for
the lofs of ARILLA, and his fears from what
might happen by the difpleafure of IRENE;
whom he could no way appeafe, tho' he

at-

attempted it by all the artifices Invention could supply him with. That Brother with whom she threaten'd him, having been some time on a foreign Embassy, was now on his return, and was expected in *Caramania* in a few days : what Shame had prevented herself from revealing to the Princess, he doubted whether she would scruple to make known to him, who, in the vindication of the Honour of his House, would certainly make his appeal to the Prince, for obliging him to the performance of his Contract. He was very sensible, that THEODORE could not well incur the displeasure of a Man so dear to the *Caramanians*, and who had been so great a Favourite with his Father; and the thoughts of being compel'd to marry a Woman for whom he no longer had the least Remains either of Inclination or Tenderness, were insupportable. Reflecting therefore, that he was brought under the necessity of these apprehensions only by his Fidelity to his Prince, and taking upon him the reputation of being enamour'd of LUTETIA, he took the liberty of complaining to him of it, disclosing the whole Story both of IRENE and ARILLA. A visible Trouble spread itself all over the Face of THEODORE while he was speaking, and when he found he had concluded, You were to blame, *answered he somewhat angrily,* to engage yourself so far with a Woman of

IRENE'S

IRENE's Quality, and who had such powerful Friends to back the Intercessions she may
make against you.——I know not how you
will be able to avoid making good to her
what you have vow'd——but as for ARIL-
LA, I look on that Affair of little confequence: you have enjoy'd, and must forget
her Charms. This Reply stung MARMIL-
LIO to the quick; he expected a different
Treatment from a Prince, whose Service
alone had involv'd him in these Difficulties;
and for a moment losing all regard to the
Character of the Person who had spoke,
Were it so easy to throw off the Impression
which Beauty makes, *said he*, your Highness would have been in less apprehensions
from ISMONDA; nor had I been overwhelm'd in the Disquiets I am at present
under, by becoming your Proxy to LUTE-
TIA. These words being utter'd with an
unusual warmth, made the Prince look on
them as an upbraiding; and conceiving the
utmost disdain at so insolent a presuming in
a Person whom he consider'd as his Creature, I am sorry, MARMILLIO, *resumed he*,
that I employ'd you in a business which you
imagine disadvantageous——there are many
of my Court who would have thought themselves highly favour'd, had I given them the
same mark of my Confidence, and perhaps
too would have been as capable of serving
me in any thing I had entrusted to their
Care:

Care: at leaft, when next I ftand in need of
a Friend, I fhall make trial of fome other.
In the mean time, *purfued he, in a Tone
which exprefs'd the utmoft diffatisfaction,*
I would have you remember, that whatever
parity there is between our Amours, there
is none between a Sovereign and his Subject; and learn from thence, that I alone,
of all the *Caramanians,* am born to act
without controul. MARMILLIO, who from
the moment he had fpoke thefe rafh words
was fenfible of his Boldnefs, and the effect
it would have on the haughty and refentful
Humour of this Prince, was about to fay
fomething which might compenfate for
his former Behaviour ; when THEODORE,
too much incens'd for further Converfation with him at this time, flew out of
the Room, bidding him be dumb, for he
had already faid enough to let him into the
Difpofition of the Perfon he had trufted.

MARMILLIO now found on how un-
ftable a Foundation the Favourites of Princes
build their Hopes, and that he had little
to expect from the Friendfhip of THEO-
DORE, in cafe IRENE fhould offer her
Complaint, as he made not the leaft queftion but fhe would, at the arrival of her
Brother. Amidft all thefe tumultuous Agitations, the Memory of ARILLA, and the
Impoffibility there feem'd of ever obtaining a Reconciliation there, rack'd him with
all

all the Torments which attend Defpair: in which Condition let us leave him, till frefh Intelligence fhall arrive; which I ex-pect in a few days, to gratify the Impa-tience of both my Reader and myfelf.

The End of the Firft Part.

PART

PART II.

FOR some Days never mortal Man labour'd under greater Perplexities than did MARMILLIO, burning with vain and unextinguishable Desires for the re-enjoyment of ARILLA; trembling with Apprehensions of what might ensue from the Jealousy of the haughty IRENE, and full of the utmost Discontent for the Displeasure of a Prince, whom he had serv'd so faithfully, and with so much hazard to himself; the painful *present*, the Fears of the *future*, and those Racks of Thought which are inseparable from a State of uncertainty, made his Mind a perfect Chaos of confus'd Idea's, incapable of Invention, Ease, or Resolution. He attended the Levee of THEODORE every day, as usual, however; but found that what had pass'd between them, had made a strange Alteration in the Behaviour of that Prince towards him: He found himself no longer honour'd with his Confidence, he spoke

not

not to him, but in general Conversation, and in the presence of Persons, who would not fail to have endeavour'd to find out the cause of so sudden an Estrangement of that Intimacy which had formerly been obferv'd between them : And what confirm'd him more than all, that there was little hope of a Reconciliation, was, that thofe very People who had most appear'd his Enemies, were most now incouraged by the changed Difpofition of his offended Sovereign : His Difcernment and piercing Penetration were now of no other fervice to him, than to torment him more ; he could not forbear accufing THEODORE of Ingratitude and Mutability, but was obliged to keep his Difcontents conceal'd ; and tho' he privately murmur'd, durft not complain, nor openly wear the leaft appearance of Difguft.

But tho for a time he had loft the Favour of his Prince, *Fortune*, who had not yet deferted him, fent him, when he leaft expected it, an opportunity of relieving himfelf from the worft and moft dangerous part of his Inquietudes. He was but juft rifen one Morning, when a Page of ISMONDA's came to acquaint him, that his Lady defir'd he would come immediately to her Apartment, without letting any Perfon into the Secret of her fending for him. The privacy of this Meffage gave him no fmall

Sur-

Surprize, yet not enough to hinder him
from returning an Anfwer full of Complaifance and Obedience. But tho he made
all imaginable hafte in dreffing and preparing himfelf to wait on her, the fame
Page came from her a fecond time, and
deliver'd him a Billet, in which he found
thefe Lines.

To MARMILLIO.

' THE Secrecy which I defign'd to
' entertain you with this Morning, is
' prevented, by the unexpected coming in of
' a Lady; I would have you, therefore,
' wait an Hour or two in your own Lodg-
' ings for the return of my Page, who I
' will fend to conduct you when it is a
' proper time. I have Bufinefs of the ut-
' moft confequence to impart to you, and
' flatter myfelf that you will not think it
' too great a trouble to be made the Con-
' fidant of her, who, on all occafions,
' will be ready to retaliate the Obliga-
' tion.'

ISMONDA.

There was fomething in this Impatiency,
which not all the Cunning of MARMIL-
LIO could enable him to fathom; he
paus'd a while upon it, but was oblig'd to
attend the Gratification of his high-rais'd
Curi-

Curiofity, till he fhould receive it from her
Mouth : but bethinking himfelf that fhe had
given herfelf the pains of putting Pen to
Paper, it might be expected he fhould reply in the fame manner ; he fat down to
his Efcritore, and writ her the following
Anfwer.

To the moft Excellent IsMONDA.

Madam,
‘ THE Honour of your Commands is
‘ of fo high a nature, that ’tis im-
‘ poffible for the Perfon who receives it to
‘ teftify his juft Senfibility any otherwife,
‘ than by an humble Obedience, and moft
‘ ftrict Integrity. If there are Qualifica-
‘ tions which may render me in any de-
‘ gree worthy of your Confidence, depend
‘ on finding both in

Your Devoted Servant,

MARMILLIO.

Having difpatch’d the Page with this, he
waited not long before that Emiffary came
back, to let him know the Coaft was
clear, and that his Lady expected him. It
was with a Pleafure infinitely more than
the Vexation of his prefent Circumftances
feem’d to allow of, that he obey’d this Sum-
F   mons ;

mons; and indeed one would think he had that moment been inſpired with the Spirit of Prophecy, and had foreknown the Good which this Adventure brought him, he engaged in it with ſo much Rea- dineſs and Alacrity.

As ſoon as he came into the preſence of ISMONDA, You wonder, MARMILLIO, *ſaid ſhe, with the moſt obliging Smile*, at the Speed and Privacy with which I entreated this Viſit might be accompany'd; but the Buſineſs I have to communicate, will im- mediately eaſe you of it :—— it being of too much conſequence to my Glory, my Intereſt, and my Peace of Mind, either to be delay'd, or expos'd to the Knowledge of any one but him, whoſe Advice I de- pend on for Relief.

Bleſſings, Madam, ſuch as you vouchſafe to ſhower upon me, *anſwer'd he*, cannot be received without a mixture of Surprize and Joy: The *one* muſt naturally flow from the Diſcovery that a Being ſo ſuperlatively exalted in all that's excellent, as is ISMON- DA, above what is ordinarily to be found in Humanity, ſhould ſtand in need of any Aſſiſtance, but what ſhe might find in her own Genius; and the *other*, from the Glo- ry of being choſe out from the leſs *happy*, tho perhaps more *deſerving* millions of Mankind, for ſo great a Truſt. 'Tis true, indeed, *continued he*, that when the Mind

is

is over-burthened with any secret Discontent, a faithful Confidant affords some ease: if therefore it be possible you should be thus opprefs'd, behold the Man who would chuse Death rather than Infidelity, Ingratitude, or Disobedience.

The good Opinion I have of you, *resum'd she, interrupting him,* renders these Professions needless; I already believe you possess'd of every thing I would wish to find in the Man of whom I would make a Friend :——nor will I listen to any further Asseverations——the time is too precious to be thrown away in idle Talk, and may much better be employ'd in that Advice and Consolation I expect from you.—— Oh ! MARMILLIO, (*pursued she, with a Sigh as if her Heart were bursting, and which, in spite of her Efforts to restrain them, forc'd some Tears from her Eyes*) I fear I am undone.——The Heart which to preserve I have forfeited my Honour, and that Duty which by the Laws of Heaven and Earth I owe ADRASTUS, forsook my native Country, forgot my nearest Friends, and abandon'd every thing which ought to have been dear, I doubt is lost, estrang'd for ever from me.——Ruin'd at once both in my Love and Pride, the World contains not so forlorn a Wretch, as she who lately was the envy'd, fortunate ISMONDA.

Here

Here the long-fmother'd Paffions of her
Soul rofe with too much Violence to
be repell'd ; again fhe figh'd, again fhe
wept, but was deny'd the ufe of Speech.
The Aftonifhment of MARMILLIO at this
ftrange Difcourfe, had the fame Effect on
him, as Rage and Grief had work'd on her;
and as fhe was for the prefent incapable of
proceeding in the Relation fhe was about
to make, fo was he of replying to what
fhe had faid. This dumb Scene lafted for
fome moments, both of them endeavouring, but in vain, to break it. MARMIL-
LIO was the firft who had that power, and
he made ufe of it to entreat her to reveal
at once the caufe of her Difquiet, protefting to her that nothing in him fhould be
wanting for the difcovery of the Truth,
and reftoring her to her former Tranquillity.

Oh! *faid fhe*, 'tis too plain that I have
loft the Empire I once poffefs'd over the
Heart of THEODORE; nor are you, MAR-
MILLIO, without your fhare of the Dif-
grace. That artful Sycophant ARBANES,
has found the means to triumph over both
of us; he now engroffes the Friendfhip of
that ungrateful Prince, and his Niece EU-
RIDICE, his more fond Affections. MAR-
MILLIO is now no more than a difcarded
Favourite, ISMONDA a forfaken Miftrefs.——
Much do I wonder that the Change has
efcaped

efcaped your notice, when every day the
perjur'd THEODORE retires himfelf from
publick View, and paffes whole Hours together with his new Choice, and her de-
figning Uncle. Laft night my Woman LY-
SETTA, the only one of all my Train whom
I ever made the Confidante of my Affection
for this ungrateful Man, inform'd me of
my Misfortune, having learn'd the Secret
from one that waits upon EURIDICE, and
is by that triumphant Rival entrufted with
the Affair.

She fpoke no more, expecting his Reply ;
which, after a little paufe, he gave her in
thefe terms : That in a late Suit, *faid he*,
which I too rafhly mov'd, I gain'd the difpleafure of my Prince, I am but too fenfible ; but cannot think the Royal THEODORE
fo much a Foe to his own Happinefs, as to
forfeit his Title to ISMONDA's Heart : Is-
MONDA, of whom I have heard him fpeak
with Praifes, fuch as can be only due to
Heaven and her.——Moft fure I am, you
are in this deceiv'd ; I cannot think the
united Charms of your whole Sex could
make him blind to yours, much lefs the
faint and fickly Beauties of the vain EURI-
DICE have the power to move him.——
He would have added fomething more, had
he not been prevented by ISMONDA, who
haftily interrupted him with thefe Words :
You are too loyal, MARMILLIO, *cry'd fhe*,
and

and too zealous for the Vindication of a
Prince, who no longer is worthy of the refpect you bear him.——What I have told
you, is but too fad a Truth : it is not only
to teftify his ill Humour to you, that he
affects a Kindnefs for your known Enemy
ARBANES ; Love alfo has a fhare in the
Change of his Behaviour. ——Unwilling
to believe LYSETTA's Story without further Confirmation, I went immediately to
the Houfe of curs'd ARBANES ; where, as
I enter'd, I faw the Guards of THEODORE,
and found the inconftant Prince feated fo
near EURIDICE, that he with eafe might
whifper in her Ear thofe Vows of Paffion
he fo well knows to make, and by which
ISMONDA was at firft betray'd, to think,
that to reward fuch Love, was glorious
Ruin——He ftarted at the fight of me,
and endeavour'd to conceal the Confufion
he was in, under the pretence of a fudden
Head-ach, and foon after took his leave. I
ftay'd not long, overwhelm'd with Rage
and Jealoufy, refolving at my return to pour
forth all the Anguifh of my Soul in the
moft keen Reproaches, but was in that, as in
all elfe, difappointed ; fome Ambaffadors
being arriv'd from *Anatolia*, demanded private Audience of him, and Bufinefs of
the State took up all his Hours till mid-
night ; at which time I was engag'd about
the Princefs, and have not yet had opportunity

tunity to execute my Purpofe. I am glad
of it, *faid* MARMILLIO. How! *cry'd fhe,*
what mean you? That you could not, *reply'd he,* unlefs grown quite indifferent,
you no longer wifh the continuance of his
Affections, have done any thing more
effectual for the lofs of them, than fuch a
Behaviour would have been.

Jealoufy is a Paffion which ought not to
be entertain'd by Lovers, but while they are
in a ftate of Expectation; before Enjoyment, it denotes an ardent and violent Affection, and to whatever Extremes it may
tranfport the Perfon in whofe Breaft 'tis
harbour'd, they ought to be forgiven, nay,
taken kindly; but afterwards, tho' the Motives are the fame, yet it becomes tirefome,
uneafy, and difobliging, and difcovers an
ill Opinion of the belov'd Object. Confider, Madam, *continu'd he,* that if your
Sufpicions are juft, Reproaches will be of
no fervice to retrieve that Heart which Tendernefs could not retain; but, if otherwife,
may with reafon give Offence, and if perfifted in, become fatal to the very Purpofe
their aim is to accomplifh. I cannot deny,
anfwer'd fhe, the truth of thefe Suggeftions,
I was myfelf always of the fame opinion,
and have wonder'd at the Folly of thofe
Women who I have feen taking thefe extravagant meafures for reclaiming the darling
Rover, which never ended but in a total

Breach,

Breach, and sometimes gave a Pretence for ill Treatment——but, O MARMILLIO! I was not then a Lover, I knew not what it was to feel the Stings of Tenderness abus'd————I then had Reason, but now, alas! have none. Yes, Madam, *refum'd* MARMILLIO, you testify by those very Words, that you have yet enough, would you but exert it———— Besides, permit me, most excellent ISMONDA! to entreat you would a little examine your own Heart, which few, when instigated by Passion, have the power to do; and tell me then if *Pride* has not an equal share with *Love*, in your Resentment. Can it be otherwise? *reply'd she, hastily:* What Woman can endure Neglect even from the Man she hates; much less where rewarded ardent Vows of everlasting Passion have sooth'd her Vanity into an assurance of her Lover's Truth?———— To be forsaken————Heavens! is there a Curse beyond it!————Besides, my Reputation is here concern'd, the Secret of my Intrigue will be discover'd by its breaking off: that Respect, that tender Friendship which THEODORE has paid me, once chang'd to cold Civility, or Disregard, will put People on an enquiry into the Cause, which easily enough may be discern'd; a sudden Estrangement is an infallible demonstration of a past Amour, and even HYANTHE herself would guess the Truth. 'Tis certain,
said

said he ; and to prevent it, I would thus advise. When next you fee the Prince, conceal, if poffible, all tokens of your Difcontent——Let him not think you jealous ; for if that Paffion once break out, tho' in the fofteft Terms, he will be ever on his guard ; and Caution breeds Difguft, which may in time make him more guilty than you at prefent think him. By feeming not to fufpect, you will keep him ever yours in fhow, even tho' he ceafes to be fo in reality ; by this means your Character remains unfully'd, and your Power as great, to the World's eye, as when you firft poffefs'd his fondeft Wifhes——Nor are thefe all the Advantages which from fuch a Behaviour may accrue——fuppofe fome fudden ftart of Fancy fhould, for a time, deprive you of his Heart, and lead his wandering Defires to the Enjoyment of another Object, what Method fo probable to reclaim him as this I recommend ?—— In acting thus, you are certain not to err, you infallibly fecure your Intereft and Reputation by it, and perhaps, alfo your Lover.—— To enable you to purfue it, Madam, *continu'd he*, have ftill before your Eyes the examples of thofe Women who have had ftrength of Refolution to take thofe Steps, and even in old Age, in the midft of Deformity and Wrinkles, preferv'd their Empire in fpite of the oppofing Charms of their more young and

lovely

lovely Rivals.————Remember the fam'd
Miſtreſs of the late *Armenian* Monarch;
was he not the wiſeſt and the greateſt King,
that, ſince the firſt ARSACES, ever ruled in
Aſia ? Yet did not this Woman, by her
ſubtilty, maintain a Power over him, ſuperior to what his whole Council, tho' compos'd of the moſt learned Men the World
produc'd, could boaſt? Did he tranſact any
material Affair without her ? Were there
any Promotions or Degradings in which ſhe
had not a hand ? Did he make War or Peace,
unasking her Opinion ? Did ſhe not with
him receive the Embaſſies of foreign Princes,
and according to her Judgment, did he not
form his Anſwers? In fine, ſhe was the ſo-
vereign Dictatreſs of all his Words and
Actions.————And pray, by what mea-
ſures did ſhe preſerve this abſolute Domi-
nion, but by thoſe I would ſet down to all
who are the Miſtreſſes of Kings? When
young, beautiful, and poſſeſs'd of Charms
untaſted, there needed no other attractions
to captivate an amorous Heart; but long
before her Bloom decay'd, her Power would
have diminiſh'd, had ſhe not maintain'd it by
theſe Means. A Monarch, ſuch as he was,
great, witty, lovely, gay, poſſeſs'd of every
Qualification that can adorn the Hero or the
Courtier, could not fail of exciting the
moſt tender Wiſhes: ſcarce a Virgin of his
Court, but in her Eyes, whenever he approach'd

proach'd her, difclos'd the Languifhments of her diffolving Soul ; nor was he always in- fenfible or regardlefs of the Conquefts he made. At firft, 'twas hard for her, who had been the fole engroffer of his Heart, to en- dure to fhare it with another; but foon did her Prudence get the better of this Weaknefs : fhe not only forbore to up- braid the Inconftancy fhe found him guilty of, but alfo forwarded, as much as was in her power, without feeming to do fo, his Amours with as many as he appear'd defi- rous of engaging. Of all the numerous Charmers who aim'd at the Secret to pleafe him, fhe alone had the Skill to do it always, becaufe fhe alone had enough the Com- mand of her own Paffions to obferve this Rule.

Another Inftance of this nature (*continu'd he, perceiving his Difcourfe made fome Impreffion on her*) the prefent Age prefents us with : The King of *Illyria* has a Miftrefs, who, by the fame Arts, has render'd herfelf fo neceffary to his Happinefs, that fhe pre- ferves as abfolute an Authority over him, as when in the full pride of glorious Beauty he languifh'd for Enjoyment, and reigns more than Queen, triumphant over an injur'd Wife, and flighted Family ; who, aw'd by her fuperior Power, dare but in whifpers breathe out their Repinings.

On

On the contrary, *added he*, pleaſe but to
turn your Eyes on the Effects of Jealouſy
diſclos'd : You are too well acquainted with
the Affairs of foreign Courts to need Intelligence from me, how the late King of *Cap-
padocia*, by publickly avowing his Suſpicions of his new wedded Bride, created in
her ſuch an averſion to him as never could be
remov'd. The Animoſities between them
were fatal to his Peace ; and, as 'tis thought,
his Life ; for he expir'd ſoon after without
any viſible Diſeaſe. You muſt alſo know,
and, I believe, are enough a Friend to
Dalmatia, to lament the Misfortunes which
the Prince of it ſuſtains through this deſtructive Paſſion. Had the fair Partner of
his Bed and Throne, to her other excellent
Qualifications, added Patience, how flouriſh-
ing a Monarchy might that have been ? Had
ſhe deſpis'd or check'd the Perſons, who,
perhaps, envious of her Happineſs, brought
her the News of a criminal Converſation between her Husband, and the Wife of a certain Nobleman of his Court, 'tis probable the
Amour would ſoon have known a period,
and ſhe been more endear'd than ever, by this
Indulgence to the Prince's Affections : but
inſtead of that, ſhe flies out into Extrava-
gancies unbecoming of her Rank, the Duty
of a Wife, or the common Intereſt of them
both. ——They part Houſes, have different Parties, they omit nothing which may
ex-

expofe each other: the Friends on both
fides finding their Endeavours vain to reconcile them, will no longer take part with
either.———— The Subjects following the
Example of their Sovereigns, run into Fac-
tions——the Foes of Monarchy make their
own ufe of thefe Diforders——Confufion
reigns at home, and foreign Enemies take
this opportunity of compaffing Defigns,
which elfe they never would have form'd.

But what occafion for me to draw In-
ferences from diftant Examples, ISMONDA
is herfelf a fhining one, that there are Women who can refift this Foible of the Sex.
You, who to fecure the Heart of THEO-
DORE, could confent, nay, oblige him
to marry with another; can, whenever
you pleafe to exert your Refolution, look
down only with Contempt on the little
Amufements with which he may divert
himfelf elfewhere.—— Be fatisfied, that not
EURIDICE, were fhe endued with all the
Charms which Nature ever gave to Woman,
wanting thofe you are poffefs'd of, can ever
have the power to fix him in a ferious Engagement with her.——Often has he *liked*,
but I, who from our Childhood have till
now been acquainted with his moft fecret
Thoughts, ne'er knew he *loved*, till bright
ISMONDA, with unequal Merit, taught him
what that Paffion was: nor do I think, and
from my Soul I fpeak it, the Tendernefs

of

of his Affection ever can be leffen'd, whatever the Ardours of it, by an unreftrain'd Poffeffion, may.

Aye, there's the point, *cry'd* ISMONDA; that is indeed the nature of your ungrateful Sex; 'tis Difficulty that endears Enjoyment, and keeps Defire awake: Sufpence alone fecures the Lover's Heart, for when we own we love, we are fure to lofe him.

As fhe was proceeding, one of her Women came in to inform her, that the *Anatolian* Ambaffadors having had audience of the Prince and Princefs, defir'd her leave to wait on her, having brought Letters from ADRASTUS, and fome of her near Kindred. Tho' fhe had a great defire to continue the Converfation fhe was upon, yet there was fo abfolute a Neceffity, that fhe fhould receive this Vifit, that fhe was obliged to difmifs him, with an Entreaty that he would return the fame Evening, and finifh the Argument he had begun; which he having promis'd, left her to prepare herfelf for the Reception of her expected Guefts, and retir'd to his own Apartment to meditate on this Adventure, and confult with himfelf how to make the beft ufe of it. The Truft which ISMONDA repofed in him, affured him of her Favour; but if fhe herfelf was in her decline, as fhe began to imagine, he confider'd her Friendfhip would be of little fervice; he therefore thought the wifeft Method

thod he could chuse, would be to take the Opportunity her Confidence had given him of making his Court to THEODORE, and by revealing to him all she had difcover'd of her Jealoufy, and proceeding to advife her, for the future, as he should direct, lay him under the Neceffity of a Reconciliation with him. After having throughly debated all the Reafons, which prefented themfelves for or againft acting in this manner, he found none fo fubftantial, as thofe which encouraged him in it. Being therefore come to a Refolution, all the difficulty lay in fpeaking to the Prince in private; he, fince the late difpute between them, having carefully avoided him: but that he foon found means to get over; he wrote a little Billet, which it was eafy for him to deliver to him, tho' in the prefence of all the World, becaufe it was ufual for all Petitions and Addreffes to pafs through his hands. The Contents of what he wrote, were as follows.

To Prince THEODORE, *Sovereign of* Caramania.

Royal Sir,
' THO' to have offended you, has de-
' prived me of all for which I va-
' lued Life, yet durft I not prefume to ut-
' ter my Complaints, till fome happy op-
' portunity

' portunity fhould arrive, to give me the
' means of teftifying, that whatever Faults
' Rafhnefs or Inadvertency might commit,
' you have not in the world a Subjeƈt
' more devoted ro your Intereft.   The
' wifh'd for Moment is mine; I have that
' to impart to you which is of the utmoft
' confequence, both to your Pleafures
' and domeftick Peace, and humbly beg
' the favour of a private Audience fome
' time this day :———— The Affair is of a
' nature too delicate to brock delay ; and
' if negleƈted, may involve you in many
' Difficulties, and take from me the power
' of acquiring that Glory which is the fole
' Aim of my Ambition, that of proving
' myfelf

My Royal Mafter's

Moft Humble, moft Faithful,
and moft Obedient Subjeƈt,
and Servant ever,

MARMILLIO.

It was now about the time in which the
Prince receiv'd the Lords who attended his
Levée ; and having finifh'd his fhort Epiftle,
he went to the Drawing-room, where he
gave it publickly into his Hand, entreating
he would immediately perufe it, for it
contain'd fome Matters of Importance.
Thefe

These Words made the Prince look earnestly on the Superscription, and knowing it to be MARMILLIO's own writing, he retired from the Company to a Window, where, having examined the Contents, he made a sign for him to approach; and as soon as he was near enough to be heard by him, Attend me in the Orange-Grove behind the Palace Garden, *said he*, I will dispatch these, and instantly be with you. He turn'd from him in uttering these Words, and the other making a low Bow, left the Room, and hasted to the Place appointed; where he remain'd not long, before the Prince appear'd: and tho' there was not that open Freedom in his Countenance, with which he had been accustomed to accost this favourite Promoter of his Pleasures, yet there was so great an Abatement of the Severity which lately had sat on it towards him, that he had reason to hope what he had to communicate, would entirely re-establish him in his former good Opinion and Confidence. I hope, MARMILLIO, *said he*, it is not to renew the Subject of our last private Conference, that you desired this meeting; for assure yourself, if it be, I shall answer you in no other terms than before, nor indeed is it in my power to do it. I should be more unworthy than you think me, my Royal Lord, *answer'd the other*, if I could presume so far as to

G   mingle

mingle my little Interests with yours, pretend to call an Affair of mine, though it were of Life and Death, of consequence to your Peace, as I inform'd you this is which I would now impart.——— But not to detain your Highness in suspence, be pleased to read this Summons, which early this morning I received.——— In speaking these words, he presented him with the Billet brought him by Ismonda's Page, which, when the Prince had look'd over with all imaginable demonstrations of Surprize, he proceeded to inform him all that had pass'd between them in her Apartment, not forgetting the least particular of the Discontent he found her in, or the Arguments he had made use of to dissipate it. He acquainted him also how their Conversation was interrupted by the Ambassadors; and that he was engaged to return to her that Evening. And having concluded his Narration, putting one knee to the ground, intreated him he would once more honour him with his Commands in this Affair.

It was with all possible Artifice, and Self-extolment, couch'd under the disguise of Humility, that he related this Story; but half the pains he took, would have sufficed: It contain'd, indeed, a matter of importance much greater than he himself imagin'd; the Prince, tho' he could not be called any other than constant to Ismonda, because he ne-

ver

ver ceafed to love her, and prefer her to her
whole Sex befide, was yet the moft changing
Man in his Amours that ever was. In fpite
of the fixed Affection with which he regarded this Miftrefs of his *Soul*, he muft
fometimes devote his *Body* at other Shrines.
He could not live without his Gallantries ;
and Curiofity frequently fupplied the room
of liking, and led him to the ruin of many a
believing Fair. EURIDICE was of that number : the fame wild and unftable Fires, which
had feduced LUTETIA, had an equal effect
on her ; both had alike been tempted ; both
had alike confented to his Wifhes ; and both,
with over-fondnefs, and a too eafy yielding,
became immediately the Objects of his Satiety and Contempt. The fears he was in of
ISMONDA making a difcovery of his Crime,
infinitely exceeded the pleafure he found in
committing it ; and the fervice MARMILLIO
had done to him, in eafing him of the Ap·
prehenfions he had labour'd under on LU-
TETIA's account, made him wifh for fuch
another Friend on that of EURIDICE ; who,
prefuming on the tender things he faid to
her, while folliciting her Love, took a fort
of privilege of following him from place to
place, and perfecuting him with inceffant
declarations of a Paffion which he no longer
wifh'd to infpire. For this reafon he was
extremely glad of a Pretence, without
any injury to his Dignity, by fubmitting

G 2   to

to a Subject, of being reconciled to MAR-
MILLIO : for tho' he knew he could not rid
him of the impertinent Tenderness of EU-
RIDICE, and the continual Dangers which
her Fondness involv'd him in, of the Affair
between them being discover'd, by taking
on himself the Character of her Lover, as he
had done in the same Case with LUTETIA, by
reason of his enmity with ARBANES; yet he
doubted not but his subtile-working Wit,
and ready Invention, would find out some
Expedient also in this Exigence, as it had
done in others. When first he read the
Letter ISMONDA had writ to him, and by the
beginning of his discourse, discover'd her
but too just Suspicions of EURIDICE, his
still enamour'd Heart heaved with tumultuous Beatings; her Grief and her Resentment
gave him Pangs, which since the full enjoyment of her Charms had left Despair no
room, he had never felt. Nor was he without fear that MARMILLIO, to revenge the
Coldness with which he had of late been
treated by him, might have said something
to have increased that Lady's Jealousy ; but
when these Doubts were cleared, and he was
convinced by many Oaths and Imprecations
of the service he had done him, in argu-
ing with her on so nice a Theme, he re-
pented there had ever been a Breach between them, and omitted nothing which
might testify the sense he had of his Fidelity,

lity, and steady Adherence to his Interest.
After a thousand demonstrations of an eternal Friendship on the one side, and Loyalty on the other, the new-restored Favourite reminded him, that he knew not
how soon he might be sent for by ISMON-
DA, and that it was therefore time they
should resolve in what manner to proceed. If, *said he*, tir'd and grown weary
with a long and uninterrupted series of possession, you wish the absence of ISMON-
DA; I believe it easy for me, in the present
struggles of her Soul, to turn the Scale wholly
on the side of Resentment, and talk her into a
resolution of quitting *Caramania* for ever.
Oh, no, *replied the Prince*, rather do all that's
in your power to stay her : In spite of the
little Infidelities I have been guilty of to her,
I cannot think of parting with her. The
faint Joys which other Beauties yield, but
more indear the rapturous Image of her
power of charming. Still in my Heart she
reigns unrivall'd and supreme ; and sooner
would I renounce my Life, than that more
precious Treasure, my only lov'd ISMONDA.

He then proceeded to relate to him his
Affair with EURIDICE ; and how uneasy
he was to get rid of a Passion he had not
intended should arrive at any greater heights
than would just influence her to the gratification of a transient Desire, it being only
such he felt for her. But long he dwelt not

on

on this Theme; a nearer and more poignant Vexation took up the greatest part of his thoughts: He told him, that the Lords of *Anatolia*, sent from that King in Embassy to him, had been employ'd by ADRASTUS to sollicit the return of his Wife; that they last Night had obtained leave of the Princess for her departure; and that there remained nothing now but her own consent for her removal. ——Therefore, to prevent this Journey, exert, *said he*, my dear MARMILLIO, your utmost Wit and Eloquence; for, since suspected by her in a Case where I am, alas! too guilty, I dare not meet the just upbraidings of her angry Eyes, till you have sooth'd her Soul into a Calm of full Assurance of my Love and Truth. Depend upon my Zeal, *answer'd he*, nor doubt, my Lord, but that those Arts which hitherto have been crowned with success, when employ'd for your Service, will not be less effectual than before. But, Royal THEODORE, *pursued he, after a little pause*, as our late estrangement from that Familiarity with which you used to honour me, has been the sole occasion of her confiding in the truth of what I shall relate in this Affair; the news of a sudden Reconciliation may render all I say suspected, and with reason give her some Apprehensions that I have betray'd her to you.—— I think it then better for your purpose, that I conceal

ceal my happy Reſtoration to your Favour, and that you perſiſt to treat me for ſome enſuing Days in the ſame manner, as firſt induced her to imagine that any unkindneſs of my Prince could oblige me to reveal aught to his prejudice.

THEODORE extremely approved of this Advice, not only for the Reaſons MARMIL-LIO urged, but alſo that too ſudden a Turn might alarm the Jealouſy of ARBANES and EURIDICE, and put them on ſome mea-ſures, which would unravel the Myſtery it was ſo much the intereſt of that Prince to conceal, both from HYANTHE and ISMON-DA. Every thing being thus concluded on between them, MARMILLIO took his leave, and return'd to his Lodgings, expecting a ſecond Summons from ISMONDA.

It was near Evening before that Lady ſent to him, and at his return he found her in a diſorder which it is impoſſible to repreſent. As ſoon as he enter'd the Clo-ſet, where for the ſake of privacy ſhe re-ceiv'd him, Oh, MARMILLIO, *ſaid ſhe*, the perjured THEODORE may now bear his ficti-tious Vows to as many as his inconſtant Wiſhes aim to undo, unfearing the Re-proaches of ISMONDA.—ADRASTUS will no longer live without me.——The Princeſs has conſented I ſhall return to *Anatolia* with the Lords employed in Embaſſy from thence ; nor can the love which ſtill my

Soul

Soul avows for your ungrateful Prince, furnifh me with a Pretence to ftay. —— See
here, *purfued fhe, plucking a Letter out of
her Pocket, and giving it him to read,* fee
here, what the injured, yet ever faithful,
ever tender ADRASTUS writes. MARMIL-
LIO replied no otherwife than by doing as
he was defired ; and unfolding the Paper,
he found in it thefe Lines :

To my For-ever-lov'd, but moft Unkind
ISMONDA.

'FAIN would I, my cruel Dear! ac-
' cufe you of injuftice to the fond Paf-
' fion with which I ever have regarded you ;
' and of your little conformity to thofe
' Rules by which all who yield to become
' Wives, ought to think themfelves bound :
' But, alas ! in fpite of that Authority which
' Marriage gives me over you, my Heart is
' too much your Slave, to permit me to
' make ufe of any other Arguments than
' fuch as flow from humble Love. —— Yet
' have I, O ISMONDA ! have I deferved this
' Ufage from you ? —— Or, could I, till fad
' Experience convinced me, have believed
' you would thus long have left me to mourn
' your unkind abfence in a widow'd State ?
' Remember, my everlafting Charmer, call
' back in Idea the paft Endearments of our
' mutual Tranfports ; and then reflect, if
'from

'from the blifsful moment which gave thee
'firft to my defiring Arms, I have done
'aught fhould make thee cold, neglectful,
'or in the leaft deviate from thy former
'Tendernefs.——In one of your Letters you
'feem to tax me with what I have but too
'much reafon to reproach you, want of
'Uneafinefs in this Separation. *Were it not
'fo*, fay you, *I fhould before this time have
'found a Pretence for coming to* Carama-
'nia : How unjuft is this Affertion, let your
'own Heart be judge. Well do you know
'the arbitrary Difpofition of our Monarch;
'and that the Employments I have under
'him will not fuffer me to quit his Palace
'even for a Day, without permiffion from
'himfelf. Heaven, and all here are witneffes
'what Interceffions I made to be one of the
'Perfons fix'd on for this Embaffy, but had
'no other Anfwer to my repeated Importu-
'nities, than this; *That if my fond Affe-
'ction for a Wife who had deferted me,
'was more valuable than his Service, I
'might in Banifhment enjoy that Bleffing,
'for never more muft I expect to return
'to* Anatolia. What canft thou now ob-
'ject? What Reafons find which can with-
'hold thee from my longing Arms? The
'Princefs is too good to aim at parting
'thofe whom facred Vows have join'd; and
'did not the fublimeft Paffion actuate my
'felf in that behalf, I fhould believe fome
other

' other and more powerful Motive than her
' Friendſhip, induced thee to forſake a Huſ-
' band whoſe very Life is bound up in thee.
' Some buſy Whiſperers would make me
' more unhappy than I am by ſuch Sug-
' geſtions ; but be aſſured, I ſlight them,
' nor can entertain one thought in prejudice
' of my ISMONDA's Honour.   It is not, how-
' ever, in my power, to ſuppreſs the Talk
' of others.—Haſte then to confute them by
' thy immediate Preſence, and look the
' ſharp-ey'd Monſter, *Slander*, dead! ——
' Thy own *Reputation*, as well as my *Love*,
' demands thee ; both of them once were
' dear, and I have hope thou art not chan-
' ged in all, and that the return of the Am-
' baſſadors will bring thee alſo to the Em-
' braces of him, who with the name of Huſ-
' band joins that of thy Lover and thy Ado-
' rer,

ADRASTUS.

Now, MARMILLIO, *ſaid ſhe*, (as ſoon as he
had done reading) what Anſwer can I make?
Or how refuſe the tender Preſſures of this
too indulgent Husband?—— Were THE-
ODORE all that my fond Soul could wiſh,
adorn'd with every Perfection of the Mind,
as well as the Body, I muſt be compell'd to
leave him ; and he does well, by the Proofs
he gives me of his Inconſtancy, to wean my
Affections from their former Ardency, and
make

make the Separation lefs terrible to be borne.
Ah Madam ! *reply'd he,* before you refolve
on quitting *Caramania,* confider well if
you are able to fuftain the Pangs of an
eternal Abfence from the Man you love ;
and who, in fpite of the difregard with
which of late he caufelefly has treated me,
I muft confefs, I think deferving of it.
Deceive not yourfelf, I beg you, by an Imagination that he is lefs dear to you, becaufe
he appears, at prefent, more unworthy
than you once believ'd.————Were he
indeed as ingrateful as you now fufpect
him, which yet I cannot think, 'twou'd coft
you many bitter Agonies e'er you extinguifh'd a Paffion fo well eftablifh'd in your
Soul. Should I then ftay, *interrupted fhe,*
till bare-fac'd Contempt, and open Scorn
fhall drive me hence ?————till publick ill
ufage fhall compel me to be gone, and demonftrate, indeed, that not HYANTHE, but
her perfidious Husband, influenc'd my
coming hither, and now enforces my departure ?————No, if I neglect this opportunity all-bounteous Heaven affords of reftoring myfelf to Honour and to Fame, juftly
fhould I defire to be a Wretch, whofe only
hope is to excite Compaffion. There was
fo much reafon in what fhe faid, that had
it not been utter'd with a warmth which denoted a greater fhare of Refentment than
Refolution, MARMILLIO would have entertain'd

tain'd but little expectation of Succefs : but
he was too well acquainted with human
Nature, not to know that nothing violent
is of long continuance, and of all the Paffions that invade the Mind, none fo fhort-
liv'd as Rage ; becaufe none is fo painful to
be borne, and were it to continue, muft convert to Madnefs. He therefore aim'd not to
oppofe it, and by feeming not to take the
part of THEODORE, he more effectually did
fo, than if he had made the moft folemn
affeverations of his believ'd Integrity ; and
when, by this Artifice, he found the late
flames of Indignation in her pretty well
abated, Let not falfe Fortitude beguile you,
Madam, *faid he*, the Ills which! threaten
you in *Caramania* are but in Imagination,
and are fcarce poffible ever to happen in
reality ; but in returning to *Anatolia*, you
run to certain Mifery, the worft of Woes,
that of loath'd Embraces, and the eternal
Prefence of the Man you hate ; for there's
no medium in conjugal Affection. In *Caramania*, you but fear the Lofs of THEO-
DORE ; in *Anatolia*, you are fure to be depriv'd of him for ever : nay, what is more,
depriv'd of him by your own fault. Here,
fhould he prove ungrateful or unkind, your
injur'd Soul might vent her Anguifh in Reproaches ; but now to leave him, on a bare
Sufpicion, would throw the weight of it
wholly on yourfelf, and when paft remedy,

dy, you'd curſe the Raſhneſs by which you
are undone.

By theſe kind of Arguments, that Reſolution, in which ſhe had imagin'd herſelf ſo
well fix'd, began to waver, and before he
left her half diſpos'd as he could wiſh, he
doubted not but the next Viſit that the
Prince ſhould make, would entirely perfect
what he had made ſo good a progreſs in;
and to that end, acquainted him immediately with the ſum of all the Converſation
he had with her. This Day, which was in
every thing to be a fortunate one to him,
concluded with the News, that the Mother
of IRENE being taken dangerouſly ill, had
ſent an expreſs for her to come to her Country Seat, at which ſhe was when ſeiz'd with
that Indiſpoſition; and that Lady could not
refuſe Obedience in ſo preſſing an occaſion. By this removal of IRENE's, he had
time for Contrivance; the Journey ſhe had
to take, was long, and he was not without
hope, that before her return, the Prince
being now more than ever oblig'd to be-
friend his Intereſt, join'd with the Power
ISMONDA, of whoſe Favour he was alſo certain, had with HYANTHE, would render ineffectual all the Complaints the Brother of
that wrong'd Lady ſhould make of his Behaviour.

But in the midſt of theſe Conſolatory
Reflections, the Idea of ARILLA ſtill fill'd

him

him with Difquiets; the difficulty of re-
eftablifhing himfelf in her Affections, en-
hanced the Value of them, and he languifh'd in unfpeakable Defires for that,
which had it appear'd attainable, he would
perhaps have flighted and avoided; fo con-
tradictory is the Temper of Mankind, and
fo much is Ingratitude ingrafted in their
very Natures, that it feems inherent to the
Sex to fhun what comes with eafe, and to
court Dangers and Inquietudes. The fond,
the tender Maid, is fure to meet difdain,
while the neglectful or humourous Coquette,
receives their moft ardent Affiduities. Security is the certain *Recipe* for their Paffion;
and the only way for the ador'd Object to
maintain her Conqueft, is to keep her Lover
in fufpence. MARMILLIO, at leaft, was of
this difpofition; and had the moft charming
Woman Nature ever made, been offer'd to
him in exchange for ARILLA, while fhe continu'd cruel, 'tis probable no Attractions
could have withdrawn his Heart, or made
any abatement in that excefs of Paffion
with which he now regarded her.

The defire of regaining her Affections,
being, at prefent, the fupremeft wifh of his
impatient Soul, he fet his whole Wits at
work for the accomplifhment of it; and
tho' he had been before refus'd admittance,
went again to vifit her: but meeting with
the fame treatment, entreated, by her Woman,

man, that he might see her, tho' it was
but for a moment; saying, he had something of more than ordinary importance to
speak to her about, before she took her Journey. On which, the Person to whom he
apply'd, return'd for answer, that her Lady
had chang'd her Mind, and intended still to
stay at Court; that Relation to whose House
she had design'd to retire, being about coming to Town herself. To find she staid,
and yet had Resolution enough to refuse
seeing him but in Places where their mutual
attendance render'd it impossible for her to
avoid him, and that even there she carefully
shunn'd giving him any opportunity of
speaking to her, made him know that a
Reconciliation with her, would be infinitely more difficult than he could have believ'd
it could be, while she continu'd in the way
of his Importunities; at last, bethinking
himself that as her Cruelty sprung only
from her Jealousy of LUTETIA, it was chiefly in the power of LUTETIA herself to
undeceive her: he therefore ventur'd to
make her the Confidante of his Passion for
ARILLA, and the unjust Suspicions that
Lady had conceiv'd on her account; and
begg'd that she would write a Line or two
which might convince her that it was on
a different score from that of Love he visited her. LUTETIA look'd on herself as under too many Obligations to him, to deny
the

the grant of so reasonable a Request: but
having obtained this Promise from her, a
new Objection rose in his Mind; which was,
that, considering what had pass'd between
him and ARILLA, it might be too great a
shock to her Modesty, to find that her sup-
posed Rival had been made acquainted with
the Affair. To remedy this Inconvenience,
however, he soon bethought him of an Expedient; which was, that the Letter should
be directed to himself. He communicated
his Sentiments to LUTETIA, who agree-
ing with his Notions, between them they
dictated these Lines.

To MARMILLIO.

'THOUGH there is not a Possibility
'   of hearing from the dear Engros-
'ser of my Soul, by any other means than
'through your generous Care; yet I can-
'not forbear smiling, to think of how dan-
'gerous a consequence it may prove to
'me.———The whole Court gives you
'to me as a Lover; and as I cannot believe
'a Man of so much Gallantry can be with-
'out his Amours, I am in daily Expecta-
'tions of finding the Effects of Jealousy
'from some outrageous and disgusted He-
'roine.———If conscious of a Passion for
'any darling Fair, for Heaven's sake unde-
'ceive her; I give you leave to call me
                                    'ugly,

‘ ugly, ill-shaped, unbred, and every thing
‘ that is disagreeable ; nor will be offend-
‘ ed at whatever Rudeness you treat me
‘ with, even to my face, before her, rather
‘ than expose me to her Censures, or your-
‘ self to her Resentment, for the sake of
‘ her who is already but too much obliged
‘ to you.

LUTETIA.

There was something so natural in the
turn of this Billet, that MARMILLIO was
half persuaded it would work the Effect
he aim'd at ; and as soon as it was finished,
took his leave of LUTETIA, and retir'd to
his own Apartment, to enclose it to ARIL-
LA : In the Cover he wrote in this manner.

*To my Ever-Ador'd, but Causelesly
Offended* ARILLA.

‘ THE most guilty Criminal that ever
‘ incur'd the Censure of the Law,
‘ is allow'd to plead before his Doom is
‘ pass'd ; but ARILLA more severe, thinks
‘ it enough to let me know of what I am
‘ accus'd, not gives me liberty to make my
‘ Defence.——Oh! how unjust is this !——
‘ Were there any ground for your Suspi-
‘ cions, were it possible for me to think,
‘ after the Enjoyment of your Charms, an-
‘ other Woman worth my Regard, that

H

‘ which

' which caus'd my Ingratitude and Incon-
' ftancy, would influence my Indifference
' alfo; your Refentment would have fail'd
' to work the Effect it has done on my
' too tender Heart; my reftlefs Days, and
' fleeplefs Nights, the unnumber'd Agonies
' of my tormented Thoughts, would not
' have reproach'd the Cruelty of ARILLA,
' nor fhould I have bethought me of fend-
' ing this undeniable Evidence of my In-
' nocence. I need not tell you, that the
' Author of it is belov'd by my moft par-
' ticular and intimate Friend, the Contents
' will let you know as much; but when
' you allow a Vifit from me, as furely now
' you will, I fhall inform you how, being
' by the Severity of an avaritious Parent de-
' ny'd the publick Gratification of his Wifhes
' in marrying with LUTETIA, he is com-
' pell'd to content himfelf with a fecret
' Correfpondence with her. I am the only
' Perfon entrufted with the Affair, nor can
' they, but thro' my means, or fee each
' other, or receive a Letter. This, my un-
' kind ARILLA, has occafion'd thofe fre-
' quent Vifits and Whifperings which have
' been obferv'd between us, and which has
' given me the reputation of her Lover.
' ——It now remains that I, in my turn,
' upbraid your want of Tendernefs, and
' Faith in thofe fincere Profeffions of eter-
' nal and unchangeable Affection, which I
                                    ' have

' have made you; but that I will defer till
' the blefs'd Hour of meeting, which, that
' you may in fome meafure repair the In-
' jury you have done me, you muft appoint
' with fpeed.————Then, if it be poffible
' for me to retain in your dear Society the
' leaft Remains of aught but Love and Joy,
' will I chide the Injuftice you have been
' guilty of, to

Your Paffionately Tender

and ever faithfully Devoted

MARMILLIO.

The Superfcription of this little Packet
he caus'd to be written by his *Valet de
Chambre*, having the Experience that nothing on which his own Character appear'd,
would be received; and having carefully
feal'd it up, fent it by a Perfon who was
entirely a Stranger both to her and her Servants, to be left at her Apartment; not
doubting but when fhe fhould, by the
ftrangenefs of the hand, be betray'd to o-
pen it, the very fight of LUTETIA's Name
to the enclofed, would excite her Curiofity
to read it; and the Satisfaction of that
Curiofity, fo throughly convince her of the
Error fhe had been in, that fhe would not fear
to confefs it in an immediate Anfwer.

He had but juft difpatch'd his Emiffary,
when a Gentleman belonging to THEODORE

came

came to let him know the Prince was in
his Clofet alone, and commanded his attendance: His Mind being now much more
at eafe, concerning his Affair with ARILLA,
than it had been for many days, he was the
better capacitated to look after thofe of another; not in the leaft imagining, but that the
Bufinefs on which he was now fent for, was
either to profecute the Deception he had
already fo fuccefsfully carry'd on with Is-
MONDA and LUTETIA, or forward his Attempts on fome new Beauty.

But how agreeably was he furpriz'd, when
he found his Conjectures had deceived him;
and that the Prince, after having receiv'd
him with a moft obliging Smile, and made
him fit down by him, began in this manner! The Services you have done me, MAR-
MILLIO, *said he*, are too great not to deferve my utmoft Acknowledgments: Your
Prudence has entirely eas'd me of thofe Apprehenfions I was continually involv'd in,
left the extravagant Fondnefs of LUTETIA
fhould expofe me to the Jealoufy of both
HYANTHE and ISMONDA, and I can never
too gratefully confider of what advantage
your Advice to the latter of thefe Ladies
has been to me; what you faid to her, has
made fo deep an Impreffion in my favour,
that fhe is now only at a lofs for fome
Excufe, to avoid going with the Ambaffadors to *Anatolia*; and that I doubt not but
                                    your

your Wit and Invention may supply her
with, before the time arrives which is al-
lotted for their Departure.———But Thanks
is a poor return for Fidelity such as yours,
especially from a Sovereign, in whose power
you may believe it is, to confer a more sub-
stantial Recompence. ———I am not without a just Sensibility of Favours done me,
tho' I do not always make show of it ; and
Fortune now seems to join in my good
Wishes, and gives me an opportunity of
proving, that it was not through Ingratitude that I deny'd MARMILLIO the Request
he made me on IRENE's score.———Rise,
*pursued he, perceiving he was about to
prostrate himself at his feet* ; I will have
no Submissions, 'tis sufficient that I know
you faithful to your Trust, obedient to my
Commands, and zealous for my Interest
and Happiness. To the purpose therefore
for which I sent : DORASPE, the Brother of
that Lady, since his return to *Caramania,*
is grown enamour'd of EURIDICE, and sol-
licits her Affection on honourable Terms.
ARBANES this day acquainted me with the
Offers he had made to her ; and guessing
at the reason of my late frequent Visits at
his House, told me, that no Consideration
of the Interest this Match would be to his
Family, should oblige him to give his Consent to it, till I had yielded mine. A
Thought immediately struck into my head,

that

that the Doatage of my unoffending Rival,
might be of the higheſt ſervice to my
Friend; and after pauſing a little on the
matter, I told him, that I could by no
means be content that EURIDICE ſhould
thus diſpoſe herſelf; but upon one Condition, which was this, that DORASPE ſhould,
at the ſame time, give IRENE to his Son
the young ERNESTUS.

I had ſcarce pronounced the Words, when
he reply'd, Alas! my Prince, the rich, the
haughty DORASPE would diſdain the Pro-
poſition, my Son has neither an Eſtate nor
Birth proportionable to that of IRENE.
'Tis true, *reſumed I, gravely*, but his own
Merit, and my Favour, may make up that
Deficiency; nor will it be more ſtrange to
thoſe that hear it, that IRENE ſhould marry with the Son of ARBANES, than that
DORASPE ſhould become the Bridegroom
of EURIDICE, a Maid as far beneath him
in the Qualifications you mention, as ER-
NESTUS to IRENE. ——— Beſides, *added I,
ſeeing him ſtrangely ſurpriz'd at my ſtart-
ing ſo unexpected a Propoſal*, beſides the
Welfare of your Family, I have other Reaſons to deſire this may be brought about;
your mortal Enemy, and the Man I hate,
has long ſollicited IRENE, and, if I may
ſpeak my thoughts, not without Succeſs:
MARMILLIO, I mean, *ſaid I*, has often
boaſted, that at the return of DORASPE to

Cara-

Caramania, his Marriage with his Sister
would be solemniz'd. This had the Effect
I wish'd, the old Man presently grew outrageous at the thoughts of mingling his Family with yours ; and encourag'd by the
Displeasure I feign'd to have conceiv'd a-
gainst you, utter'd all that implacable Malice could invent. I listen'd to him with
Patience, well knowing, that in this the
more I appear'd your Foe, the more I
prov'd my self your Friend ; till tired with
railing, I sent him to discourse the Matter
with DORASPE.

How much, my Royal Lord, *said* MAR-
MILLIO, I am indebted to your generous
Care, so far beyond the utmost of my De-
servings, words would but faintly represent ; yet cannot I imagine that in this, even
your good Wishes ever avail me more than
the knowledge I am honour'd with them ;
DORASPE never will consent to give IRENE
to ERNESTUS's Bed, or if he wou'd, she
sooner would chuse death. You know not,
reply'd the Prince, how far a fond Affection
may transport the one, or Resentment the
other : I am told DORASPE doats with so
blind a Passion on EURIDICE, that to obtain her he would scruple nothing ; then as
for IRENE, you know her Fortune, by her
dead Father's Will, is absolutely in the dis-
posal of this Brother : 'tis not her Interest to
disoblige him, which, join'd to your Un-

kindness

kindnefs and Neglect, may prompt her in
Revenge to you, and Complaifance to
DORASPE, to marry with your Enemy.——
Add to this, ERNESTUS is young, gay,
agreeable in his Perfon, and every way qua-
lify'd to pleafe the Fair——but fhou'd all
thefe Motives fail, fhould IRENE be lefs a
Woman than I think her, or DORASPE lefs
enamour'd than I am inform'd he is, ftill my
pretended hatred to you gives me an excufe
for putting a ftop to your Alliance with a
Family fo illuftrious and wealthy as is that
of his——'Tis therefore for our mutual
Satisfaction to perfift in this counterfeited
Variance, till we fee how our Interefts are
link'd. MARMILLIO, *continued he, taking
him by the Hand*, I, by this fortunate Diffimulation, have the means of ridding you
of a Miftrefs you no longer have any Affection for ; you, of preferving for me the
only Woman I ever did, or can adore.

Some other Difcourfes, much to the fame
purpofe as thefe already related, having paft
between them, MARMILLIO withdrew,
neither of them judging it proper they
fhould be long together, left it fhould be
difcover'd to the ruin of that Scheme, both
of them promis'd themfelves to find fo
much to the advantage of their Defigns.
Every thing neceffary for each other to know
at prefent, having been talk'd over, they
agreed to wear the moft diftant Looks imaginable

ginable in publick, and to meet as feldom
as could be avoided, in the carrying on
their Stratagems, even in private; the Ca-
binets of Princes being generally full of
Eyes, which are alfo too often attended
with Tongues.

THEODORE, now zealous for the Intereft
of this Favourite, forgot nothing of the
Promife he had made him, and the firft time
he faw the Brother of IRENE, accofted him
in thefe Terms. DORASPE, *faid he*, your
long abfence from *Caramania* may, perhaps, make you ignorant of many things
which have paft here of late: at your departure, MARMILLIO was a Perfon I very
much efteem'd; but fince that, he has been
guilty of Imprudences which have alter'd
the Sentiments I had of him. I fcarce believe any will have fo little Complaifance to
the Will of their Sovereign, as to contribute to the Promotion of a Man I am refolv'd to deprefs———I hope, therefore,
that there is nothing in the Report, that you
intend to add to the too great Poffeffions he
is already Mafter of, by giving him your
Sifter IRENE, and a large Dowry in Marriage with her. It would be neither conformable to her Intereft, or the Duty of a
Subject, *reply'd he, with all humility*, to
efpoufe the Man made wretched by your
Difpleafure; but if fond Love, and the
weaknefs of her Sex fhould influence her

in

in behalf of the fallen MARMILLIO, be assur'd, my Royal Lord, DORASPE never will consent to such a Match; and if he has IRENE, he shall take her portionless and unfriended. That is not all, *resum'd the Prince*, that I expect from one, who, I would fain believe, would serve me in more than an outside show;——'twill be enough for his ambitious Aims, that he has married the Sister of DORASPE.——Whoever IRENE chuses for a Husband, cannot be without Support and Friends; and tho' you withhold your Hand or Countenance to his Proceedings, there may be others of your Family less Dutiful and Loyal——I insist upon it, therefore, that on no Consideration he obtain that Title, and as the only certain means of preventing it, you immediately dispose of her to some one more worthy of her Charms. He spoke these last Words with so much warmth and vehemence, that the other, who very well knew his Disposition was somewhat Arbitrary, easily saw he was in this resolv'd to be obey'd; and after a little pause, To prove, *said he*, how sacred to DORASPE are all the Commands of his Sovereign, there is nothing in my power I would omit.——In a late Conversation with ARBANES, he propos'd his Son ERNESTUS; his Birth indeed but meanly answers ours, nor is his Fortune equivalent with what my brotherly Affection has

design'd

defign'd to make IRENE miftrefs of: yet if
I could prevail upon her, there are Reafons, which, with the approbation of your
Highnefs, would induce me to confent.
This was all the Prince waited for; and as
foon as he had done fpeaking, ERNESTUS
anfwer'd, He has a ftock of Merit which
may well excufe his other Wants; nor do
I think that you can find a Man more rich
in inward Virtues, and intrinfick Worth.
They muft be little acquainted with a
Court who do not know that the Dependants on a Prince's Favour, think nothing
too great a Sacrifice to offer for it. Add to
this, of itfelf a fufficient Motive, DORASPE
had the certainty of the gratification of his Paffion with EURIDICE; fo that, without any
further hefitation, he told the Prince that his
Will fhould be performed, as foon as IRENE
was returned from vifiting her fick Mother.

Thus far every thing went to the fatisfaction of ARBANES and ERNESTUS, (who
promifed themfelves prodigious Advantages
by thefe Nuptials) and to the fecret contentment of MARMILLIO : But in the midft
of thofe agreeable Reflections, which the
ready Affent of DORASPE had given them,
there arofe an obftacle which none of them
had apprehended. Not all the State and
Grandeur, which attended this Alliance,
could charm EURIDICE from her firft Vows;
the gay and glorious Profpect had no Attractions;

tractions for her conſtant Wiſhes; her Vir-
gin-*Heart*, with her Virgin-*Favours*, were
in the Prince's keeping; and ſhe thought it
more felicitous to continue in an obſcure
Life, bleſs'd but by ſtealth with his Endearments, than to blaze out in all the Pomp of
Wealth and Titles, with any other Man;
and thought it nobler Pleaſure to indulge
herſelf in Guilt and ſecret Infamy with him,
than ſhare all Honours with a noble Huſ-
band. Inſtead of receiving the news with
ſatisfaction, when ARBANES told her, that
every thing was agreed on between Do-
RASPE and himſelf, ſhe expreſſed the moſt
bitter diſcontent; reproach'd him as much
as the Character he bore, and her Obligations to him would permit, of Cruelty, and
want of Tenderneſs, in going about to force
her Inclinations; proteſting, that ſhe would
never make a Sacrifice of herſelf in that manner; nor would be influenced by any Con-
ſiderations to beſtow her Perſon where it
was impoſſible for her to give her Heart.——
It was in vain that both he and ERNESTUS
urg'd the Advantages of ſuch a Match, and
ſet before her eyes the Charms of Power
and Greatneſs : She was not to be moved,
either by the Perſuaſions of the one, or
the Menaces which the other, on whom ſhe
from her Childhood had been a dependant,
made uſe of. But when he repeated to her
ſome part of the Converſation he had had
with

with the Prince, and she found that he also had approved of it ; he, in whose Love she had so much confidence, as to imagine he would never be prevail'd on to relinquish the Title she had given him over her ; she fell into Agonies which were very near depriving her of her Senses; she raved, tore her Hair, exclaim'd against the Perjury and Ingratitude of THEODORE, and curs'd her own too unbelieving Nature, in terms which confirmed ARBANES in what he before suspected, that she had been seduced by the Insinuations of the Prince. Less troubled, however, at her fall from Virtue, than that the fondness of her Passion made her blind to the Interest of her Family, in the alliance with DORASPE, he took no notice to her of the *former*, but exerted all the Power he had over her, both by Blood and Bounty, to oblige her to consider the *latter*, as a reasonable Woman would do : but finding that she persisted in obstinacy, and that all he said to her seem'd rather to strengthen the Resolution she had taken of continuing in a single Life, he reported her Behaviour to the Prince; adding withal, that it was only from his own mouth that she would believe he had given his consent for her Marriage. Conscious of what had pass'd between them, and the Vows by which he had seduced her, fain would he have saved himself the shock of appearing in this Affair ;

fair; but finding it was abfolutely neceffary, both for the eafing himfelf of the
trouble of any future Diffimulation with
her, and accomplifhing the Promife he had
made to MARMILLIO, who but by this double
Marriage could be fet free from his Contract
with IRENE, he at laft confented to go to
the Houfe of ARBANES. Being brought into the Room where the unhappy Victim
of his inconftant Wifhes fat, all drown'd in
tears, and in a pofture which denoted the
moft deep Defpair, ARBANES withdrew, as
it were out of refpect, but in reality to
give him an opportunity of faying thofe
things to her, which it might not be proper
he fhould be witnefs of. The fad and de-
jected Air with which fhe receiv'd him, a
little mov'd his Soul; and fitting down by
her, and taking one of her Hands with a
Tendernefs which was not wholly feigned,
he intreated her to let him know the Caufe
of that Melancholy in which he found her.
Can you ask that? *faid fhe.* Ah, too lovely
cruel Prince! let your own Heart inform you:
Reflect on your late Indifference, your vain
Excufes for Abfence; your Coldnefs when,
unable to live without your fight, I forc'd
myfelf into your prefence.——On too folid a foundation, alas! were my Sufpicions
built, which told me you were falfe, and I
undone.——Now you confirm even more
than my worft fears fuggefted;——without

a

a Blush avow Inconstancy, nor seek Pretences for your Change of Humour, but throw me from you as a thing unworthy your regard.—— For by what softer Term can you call that Consent, which I am told you have given for my Marriage with Doraspe? As these kind of Reproaches were the Salutation he expected from her, so he had prepared himself with Answers for them. Unjust Euridice, *said he*, to censure that as Neglect, which was only caus'd by the most tender Care.——The Princess began, my Dearest, to suspect that some more powerful Call than Business drew me so often hither; nor could I have continued my frequent Visits, without prejudice to thy Reputation: Our Amour, which I would not have told thee but to clear my self, is already but too much whisper'd among the Courtiers; and daily did I expect 'twould reach Hyanthe's ears.—— I therefore denied my longing Wishes, for a time, the Blessing of thy Love, that I hereafter might enjoy it fearless and secure. Yet you would give me to another! *interrupted she*. Ah! Prince, how ill do your Actions and your Words agree! Have patience, sweet Euridice, *resumed he*, till you have heard me out. I was about to tell you, that I thought Heaven, in the Passion of Doraspe, sent you the means to make yourself and me as happy as our mutual Circumstances

could

could hope : A Wife has many Liberties, which in the niceneſs of a Virgin-State are not allow'd; and if in new Embraces you find not Joys which may utterly obliterate thoſe you have taſted in my once happy Arms, the Ceremony of Marriage has in it no Spell to hinder the Effects of Inclination. —— I am a Husband, yet love EURIDICE; why then ſhould not ſhe, when made a Wife, continue to bleſs her THEODORE ? Heavens! *cry'd ſhe*, how little delicate are the Notions of Mankind! How many Chambers do your Hearts contain for different Impreſſions and Degrees of Paſſion!——But 'tis not ſo in our too faithful Sex ; one dear Idea takes up all the Soul, we have no room to entertain another, and but with ſcorn look down on thoſe who would intrude.—— No, Prince, *purſued ſhe*, 'tis you alone I love ; nor can I think DORASPE worthy my regard. I ask it not for him, *replied the Prince*, but would wiſh you to have ſo much for yourſelf, as not to forfeit the Benefits which this Alliance offers, for a romantick Whim ; a Chimæra, which has no Being but in a diſtemper'd Imagination. —— Caſt your Eyes round the Court ; nay, examine the generality of the married World, you will find infinitely more who for Convenience wed, than Love.——Complaiſance is all that now-a-days is expected from a Husband ; and

good

good Conduct, to preserve her Reputation, from a Wife.

He then began to repeat to her those Arguments which ARBANES and ERNESTUS had before made use of, to convince her of the Joys which Wealth and Grandeur bless'd the Possessors of them with; but all he could urge on that head being ineffectual, he had again recourse to Dissimulation. And finding that she was proof against all temptations but his *Love*, he endeavour'd to make it appear, that the only way to secure *that*, was to marry with DORASPE; which, *he said*, by taking away all suspicion of their former Amour, would secure the continuance of it. And perceiving she still seem'd to doubt the sincerity of his Passion, he omitted nothing which might serve to assure her, that it flamed with the same ardency as ever. And because *Words* are look'd upon but as poor Demonstrations of a vigorous Affection, he forbore no *Actions* which might make him seem possess'd of it. The Impatience he had of accomplishing his Design, which he found could be done no other way than by well-deceiving her, supplied the place of amorous Inclination; and thus agitated, she found no difference between the warmth of his present Caresses, and those which first triumph'd o'er her violated Chastity: But still accompanying the highest Raptures of

I   their

their mutual Endearments with Expreſſions ſuch as theſe——— My dear EURIDICE! *would he cry,* Heaven cannot give a Joy beyond thee. ——And then———Could I conſent DORASPE ſhould partake theſe Joys but to ſecure the poſſeſſion of them to my ſelf!——— Thus, in thoſe very Tranſports which one would think ſhould moſt diſcloſe, and lay open all the Soul, did he diſguiſe the Purpoſes of his; and what was the effect of deep Deſign, ſeem'd artleſs Tenderneſs, and unbiaſs'd Love.

How eaſy is it for the darling Object of our Affections to perſuade us to almoſt any thing, eſpecially when we are made to believe the Arguments uſed to ſeduce us, are dictated by that Paſſion by which ourſelves are ruled. Rather than be deprived of the poſſeſſion of THEODORE, ſhe conſented to be poſſeſs'd by DORASPE, and aſſured the Prince before his departure, that ſhe would receive that Nobleman, when next he viſited her, as a Perſon ſhe intended to make her Husband.

This Difficulty ſo well got over, a new one preſented itſelf; DORASPE having writ to his Siſter concerning the deſign he had of marrying her to ERNESTUS, he received an Anſwer from her, which as ſoon as he had read, he communicated to the Prince; the Contents of it were as follows:

To

To DORASPE.

' TIS impoſſible for any Heart to be
' ſenſible of a more perfect Pleaſure
' than mine felt, at hearing my deareſt Bro-
' ther was returned in ſafety to *Carama-*
' *nia* ; I received your welcome Letter with
' all the Tranſports which can attend the
' moſt ſincere Affection : but whatever ſa-
' tisfaction the beginning of it afforded me,
' I ſoon found a conſiderable Allay. I know
' not whether my Grief, or my Surprize,
' was moſt predominant, when I came to
' that part of it which acquainted me you
' had made choice of a Husband for me ;
' and that the Man you thought worthy of
' that Alliance, was ERNESTUS. Had I re-
' ceived the news from any other hand, I
' ſhould have teſtified my disbelief by my
' diſdain. —— Nothing but yourſelf could
' have convinced me, that you could ſo far
' forget our Birth, as to look on the Son
' of ARBANES as a fit Match for the Siſter
' of DORASPE. —— To what motive can I
' aſcribe ſo ſtrange an alteration in your
' Humour ? For fain would I ſuppoſe it any
' thing rather than Unkindneſs, or a deſire
' of throwing off that Care you have ſo
' often promis'd ſhould end not but with
' Life ; and with which I have been hi-
' therto ſo bleſs'd, that I ne'er knew a Fa-

' ther's

' ther's Loss. ———— It is with the utmost
' Gratitude, Sir! I acknowledge the past Be-
' nefits I have received from your brotherly
' Affection and Indulgence; nor should any
' thing on my part be wanting to testify
' the just Sense I have of all your Good-
' ness; not even in this, the most difficult,
' and also most exceptionable Command
' you could lay on me, would I refuse
' obedience, were the grant of it in my
' power : But, alas! my Heart has been suf-
' ceptible of a Passion, which is too uni-
' versal not to be forgiven in a Person of
' my Years.———— In fine, MARMILLIO
' has woo'd, and won me; I am his by so-
' lemn Contract; we are confirm'd to each
' other by Obligations too strong to be
' dispensed with; and to go about to part
' us, would be to act in opposition to all
' the Laws of Heaven and Earth.————But I
' have much to say to you on this ac-
' count; too much, indeed, and too ma-
' terial to be trusted to Paper. ———— I
' shall, therefore, defer it till I am happy
' enough to see you, which I hope will
' be in a few days. ———— My Mother's
' Indisposition has almost left her.————
' Soon as her recovery is compleated, I
' will hasten to intreat your pardon for
' having proceeded thus far without ac-
' quainting you. ————In the mean time, I
       ' hope

' hope you will fufpend your but too juft
' Difpleafure, and believe me ever,

Your moft Affectionate Sifter,
Obliged Friend, and
Obedient Servant,

I R E N E.

The Prince now found that what MAR-
MILLIO had told him concerning the Difpofition of this Lady, was no more than
truth ; but as this was an Impediment,
which he could not but expect, he was the
better prepared to oppofe it. He told Do-
RASPE, in giving him back the Letter, that
if the Refolutions he had lately taken, were
to be moved by the ill-grounded Paffion
of a Woman who knew not her own Intereft, he muft not take it unkindly ; that
tho' he made MARMILLIO his Brother, that
Confideration would be too weak to protect him from his Refentment. He has
offended me, *faid he*, in a manner which
I cannot pardon, without an Injuftice to my
felf.—— And if IRENE marries him, 'tis
probable that it muft be in Exile only fhe
will have the opportunity to enjoy her Huf-
band. Thefe words, pronounced with the
utmoft Earneftnefs, join'd to what had been
faid before, and the late Behaviour of the
Prince to that feemingly difgraced Favourite,

I 3   made

made DORASPE not doubt the sincerity of
them, and fearing to become a Partner in
the Royal Displeasure, forgot nothing which
might testify he merited not to incur it; he
express'd himself in the most bitter Terms,
both against MARMILLIO and IRENE also,
for having enter'd into an Engagement of
that nature, without having first consulted
him; and concluded with repeated Asseverations, that nothing in his power should
be wanting to make her alter her Resolution, which if she still persisted in, he would
never see her more, nor contribute in the
least to her support. After giving the Prince
all the Assurances he was able, he retired
to his own Apartment, to prepare a Letter
for her, which should acquaint her with the
present Position of MARMILLIO's Affairs,
and his own determination, if she continued refractory to his Designs.

While MARMILLIO was thus happy in
the sincere Endeavours of his Prince to free
him from IRENE, he was no less fortunate
in his Designs on ARILLA; and in a few
Hours after the receipt of his, she sent him
the following reply.

To MARMILLIO.

' I Have too much Sincerity in my own
' Nature to believe the contrary in an-
' other, without very great Appearances;
' that

' that there were such on your account, your-
' self confesses; and if you believe I lov'd,
' as I have given but too convincing Proofs
' I do, you should have undeceived me
' sooner; and if there be any thing now
' remaining to make me doubt your Truth,
' 'tis, that you should thus long sustain In-
' quietudes, which it was in your power
' so easily to be freed from, and of which
' you must be certain I endur'd at least an
' equal Portion.——— Can any thing be
' more terrible, than to suppose Ingrati-
' tude and Falshood in the Person one sin-
' cerely loves?———To wish to hate, yet
' find all the Efforts one can make inef-
' fectual to attain that Passion?——— All
' this my anxious Soul has labour'd un-
' der; ought I not then to repay it in some
' measure?———Should I not make this Re-
' conciliation more difficult to be accom-
' plish'd?———And let you know the Tor-
' tures of Suspence, as I have those of ill-
' requited Love and Tenderness abus'd?—
' Most sure I am, I ought to do so; but
' though I am of a Humour nicely just to
' others, I am too liable to forget what is
' owing to myself: nor have I enough the
' power of disguising the Passions of my
' Soul, not to let you know that I receive
' this Evidence of your Integrity with a
' Joy, which no Expressions of it can make
' you comprehend: but if you are at lei-

I 4   ' sure

' sure this Evening, to make a Visit at that
' House which was before designed our
' Scene of Happiness, my Behaviour shall
' demonstrate with how ardent a Passion I
' am

My Dear MARMILLIO's

Eternally Devoted

ARILLA.

Mean and enervate would be all Descrip-
tion of what this now transported Lover
felt, at but the Prospect of approaching
Blifs; much more, when at the appointed
time he was in the real Possession of it:
the experienced Reader's Imagination alone
can do Justice to Extasies, which he will
own beyond the reach of Words. Buried,
therefore, in the tumultuous Transport, let
us leave him for a while, and return to
the enamour'd Prince, who was in daily
apprehension of being eternally depriv'd
of those Felicities his Favourite enjoy'd, in
the supremest manner that Youth and mutual Desire could yield.

As much as possible had he delay'd his
Answer to the *Anatolian* Ambassadors on
the Business they were sent on from their
King; but no longer being able to find any
Excuses to detain them, he was at last
oblig'd to deliver his Dispatches. They
were now preparing for their departure,
and

and ISMONDA at her wits ends for a Pretence
to ſtay behind them. HYANTHE had already given her conſent, nor could the
Prince interpoſe, without giving too plain a
Proof how deeply he was intereſted in it.
The melancholy Hours theſe Lovers now
paſs'd together, was proportion'd to the
height of Happineſs they had enjoy'd, while
no intruding Fears of ſeparation embitter'd
the Extaſy of rewarded Tenderneſs. Is-
MONDA, to her other Vexations, had that
added of being depriv'd of MARMILLIO,
from whoſe apt Invention and Advice, ſhe
might have hoped ſome Relief from the preſent exigence; ſhe durſt not publickly
countenance him for fear of diſobliging
the Prince, with whom ſhe, as well as the
reſt of the Court, believ'd him in diſgrace:
and THEODORE was now perpetually with
her, that ſhe had not an opportunity of entertaining him in private. But it was not
ſo with her impatient Lover; he fail'd not
to communicate the Misfortunes which
threaten'd the proſecution of his Love to
him, and conjure him to uſe his utmoſt
Efforts for finding out ſome Stratagem by
which he might preſerve this Darling of his
Soul. It is not to be doubted but that MAR-
MILLIO exerted his utmoſt skill to requite
the Obligations he had lately receiv'd from
the Friendſhip of the Prince, and to render
himſelf worthy of his reſtored Confidence;
yet

yet could not all his Subtilty find any Expedient which had the profpect of Succefs.
Never were any Perfons involv'd in a
more perplex'd *Dilemma* than were thefe
three; but by what means they were extricated from it, and who had the Glory of
inventing it, I fhall, at another opportunity, faithfully relate.

The End of the Second Part.

PART

PART III.

 HE Day prefix'd for the departure of the *Anatolian* Ambaſ-
ſadors being very near at hand,
not only THEODORE, but MAR-
MILLIO alſo, having ſo great
an Intereſt in preſerving himſelf in the
Favour he had lately regain'd, were almoſt diſtracted to find, that on cool Conſideration, every Stratagem that either of
them could invent for the detaining of Is-
MONDA, appear'd impracticable : but tho'
neither of them wanted Cunning nor Artifice, yet in the Affairs of Love, that Lady
gave an Inſtance, that no Subtilty can vie
with that of Woman's, when reſolute to
obtain her Purpoſe.

ADRASTUS had a Brother, who, by being
born ſome Years before him, depriv'd him of
a very great Title, hereditary to the elder Sons
of that Family ; but tho' the Dignity was
inſeparable from his Birth, there appear'd
even from his Childhood an incapacity of
ma-

managing the Eftate which was to defcend
with it; and when arriv'd at maturity, difcover'd fuch ftrange Caprices in his Humour,
as might very well pafs for the effects of
Idiotifm or Frenzy: The Father, therefore,
in his laft Teftament, wifely bequeath'd his
Lands to him who feem'd moft worthy of
them, leaving the other a fmall Annuity,
fufficient indeed to keep him from want,
but far from a competency of fupporting
him in a manner proportionable to the Honours of his Rank. CLOTUS, for that was
the Name of this unhappy Nobleman, was
much lefs concern'd for this Misfortune than
his Friends were for him; he had no Notions of Grandeur or Reputation, and having it in his power to indulge his Appetite
in thofe things he delighted in, which were
chiefly eating and drinking, not voluptu-
oufly, but in larger quantities than is confiftent with Moderation; he little regarded what the World faid of him, or envy'd
the auguft Figure of his younger Brother.
Never had he attempted to difturb him in
the peaceable enjoyments of thofe Reve-
nues which were his by Birthright, had not
the frequent Importunities of almoft as
many as were acquainted with him, in a
manner compell'd him to do it; and more
to get rid of their Admonitions, than to
gratify any Defire of his own, he at laft
confented to have recourfe to Law, and put
ADRAS-

ADRASTUS to the proof of the Juſtice of
their Father's Will. Tedious, and prodigious expenſive on both ſides was this Con-
troverſy, the Deciſion lying wholly on the
Queſtion, If *Clotus* ought, or ought not to
be term'd an *Idiot*. Many ridiculous In-
ſtances of his Folly were made known in
Court, but whether ſufficient to bring him,
ſtrictly ſpeaking, under that denomination,
the Judges of the Cauſe confeſs'd themſelves at a loſs, and from time to time de-
ferr'd their Sentence, and demanded yet
longer Conſideration, and more ſubſtantial
Proofs. One very great Reaſon of their
acting in this manner, one may, without being guilty of an Injury to any body, impute
to the great Intereſt of ADRASTUS; the ap-
prehenſion of offending the King in the
Perſon of his Favourite, no doubt, had
an Influence over thoſe, who from him had
recciv'd the Power of inſpecting into this
Affair. To add to this, ADRASTUS was in
poſſeſſion, CLOTUS but ſued to be ſo, and
could not make thoſe preſent Gratifications
for Favours done him, which his Brother
cou'd.——From the generous and obliging
Diſpoſition of the one, there was every
thing to be hoped, nothing from the mean
and degenerate Nature of the other.——
ADRASTUS had the favour of his Superiors, and was belov'd by his Equals ; CLOTUS
kept no Company but with thoſe beneath
him,

him, delighting himself only in vulgar
Conversation, and such, as having a dependance on him, bore with his Caprices, and
humour'd his Folly. The most disinterested
part of Mankind confess'd the excellent
Qualifications of ADRASTUS merited more
than he enjoy'd, and the greatest Sticklers
for Hereditary Right, could not forbear
avowing that they thought it a great pity
that CLOTUS had that Plea.——All these
Considerations, together with the unusual
prolongation of the Process, oblig'd some
of the greatest Men in the Kingdom to in-
terpose between them, and endeavour to
bring both the Brothers to terms of Accom-
modation. ADRASTUS was prevail'd on to
double the Annuity left by his Father's Will;
and the other having, besides his natural
aversion to Business, experienc'd those
Wants as well as Fatigues which attend a
necessitous Prosecution, was glad, at any
rate, to drop it, and readily accepted the
Proposals made to him by the Mediators.
Those who had flatter'd themselves with the
hope of making Fortunes out of the Estate
when in the possession of CLOTUS, finding
their Designs defeated by this Agreement,
went another way to work, which was to
persuade him to marry: they knew that if
he had a Son born in Wedlock, all the Pretences which ADRASTUS cou'd make, would
not be look'd upon as sufficient to debar the
Child

Child from inheriting the Eſtate of his An-
ceſtors; and to that end, Women were introduced to his Acquaintance, adorn'd and
recommended to him in ſuch a manner,
as they thought moſt likely to win him to
their purpoſe : More than once was he very
near falling into the Snare prepar'd for him,
and it was as much as all the good Management of ADRASTUS could do, to ſave him
from becoming the Husband of one who
liv'd by Proſtitution, and was brought to
him by ſome of thoſe Creatures he made
choice of for Companions, as a Lady of
Quality.

In this poſture ſtood the Affair, when
ISMONDA left the Kingdom of *Anatolia*;
and having learned from the Lords ſent in
Embaſſy, that there had been little Alteration ſince her Departure : Love, ingenious
in Invention, help'd her, out of this, to
form a plauſible Excuſe for delaying her
return. The Head of the *Magi* (which are
a ſort of ſecular Prieſts, who, by their
Function, are deny'd to marry) being lately dead, ſhe told the Prince that he muſt
reſerve that Honour for a Friend of hers,
who ſhe would ſend for to receive it : And,
ſaid ſhe, becauſe I know ſuch high Places
are not conferred without ſome view of
Intereſt, even by the Sovereign himſelf, I
will offer a Bribe, which I hope my deareſt
THEODORE will not think an inconſiderable
one :

one : It is, *pursued she, looking on him with Eyes which seem'd streaming with Desire,* the Assurance of continuing those Joys, you say, are in my power to give. The amorous Prince could not hear that she had even a thought of tarrying with him, without expressing himself in terms the most rapturous and endearing : but giving truce to them much sooner than else he would have done, to ask how the grant of what she demanded could be of service to their Love ; she gratify'd his impatient Curiosity, by letting him into the Disposition of CLOTUS, and the continual Fears ADRASTUS was involv'd in on the account of that unhappy Brother, left he should be prevail'd on to marry to the Disgrace of their noble Family, and the Ruin of his Hopes. She then named CLOTUS as the Person she desir'd should be chief of the *Magi* in *Caramania :* I know not, *said she,* if he will accept it, but my appearing as an Intercessor gives me an Excuse for staying, which will be less suspected than any I can make.———'Twould be endless to repeat the Retributions made her by the transported Prince, for this Testimony of the zealous Inclinations she had to remain with him ; he prais'd her Love, her Wit, the Obligations he had to her, in terms which demonstrated the Sense he had of them. Never had he been more charm'd with her

than

than at this inftant, and never had fhe received more ardent Proofs of the Sincerity
of his Paffion, than thofe which he now
gave her. Their mutual Extafy indulged,
they began to confult in what method they
fhould proceed in this Affair, fo as the turn
might not appear too quick, and render
the Defign of it liable to Conjecture: and
it was concluded, that HYANTHE fhould
in this, as fhe had been in every thing
elfe, be made the Property. ISMONDA,
after preparing her by fome neceffary
Profeffions of Tendernefs and Friendfhip,
fhould entreat her to follicit her Husband
for this Place for CLOTUS; which he at laft
fhould grant, tho' with a kind of Reluctance, and, as it were, wholly to oblige
the Princefs. ISMONDA doubted not of fuc-
ceeding with that eafy-temper'd Lady, who
fhe knew would take her defires of ftaying
in *Caramania*, as the Effect of Love to her;
and as foon as that Excefs of Fondnefs, with
which at this time both feem'd animated,
would give them leave to feparate, fhe went
to the royal Apartment to put in execution
the Stratagem fhe had contriv'd; and he
retir'd to his Clofet, where he fent for MAR-
MILLIO, not only to communicate to him
the Kindnefs of ISMONDA, but alfo to difcourfe with him on other Affairs of almoft
equal moment to his Peace.

K   H;

He imparted to him the Conversation he had with DORASPE, and the Contents of the Letter IRENE had sent to him; on which it was agreed, that, to give the greater Air of Reality to the pretended Animosity between them, MARMILLIO should withdraw from Court for a small time, whispering among his Acquaintance, before his Departure, that he had received a private Order for that purpose. The time also being near arrived in which LUTETIA expected to be deliver'd of her Burthen, it was judged convenient that she should be removed to a greater distance, and that MARMILLIO should continue visiting her, and carry on the Deceit till after her Delivery, lest the knowledge of her Misfortune, join'd to the Melancholy of her present Condition, should throw her into a Despair which might make her forget every thing, except the Wrong she had sustain'd, and drive her to some Extravagance which might unravel all; but that as soon as she was recover'd, he should, in as gentle terms as the Business would allow of, acquaint her with the Truth, and endeavour to make her sensible, that whatever Faults a Prince was guilty of, he was accountable only to the Gods: and if she was no longer capable of contributing to the Pleasure of her Sovereign, it was only her own Illfortune she must accuse, and that it was

the

the Duty of a Subject to study Obedience
and a patient Resignation. You must expect, *said* THEODORE, when first you urge
these Arguments, only such Answers to
them as are dictated by the extremest Rage;
but when Passion has had time to cool,
she will consider, that to appear contented
will be of the most advantage to her Reputation, and that to make a show of being otherwise, will be of no service, either to retrieve the Heart she no longer has
Charms to retain, or Power to resent the
Disappointment, since given by a hand
whence there is no appeal.

There was nothing he commanded that
this obedient Favourite did not readily promise, and doubted not but he should be
able to take such effectual Measures with
LUTETIA, as should prevent her from ever
being troublesome to him; nor did he find
the least Reluctance in any thing he was
to do, but that of leaving ARILLA, of
whom he as yet continu'd passionately fond;
but the Necessity of his own Affairs with
I R E N E, requiring the imaginary Disgrace to be carry'd on with the utmost Caution, gave him no room to make an Objection to the Proposal of his Prince; who
assuring him, that as soon as he had brought
about the Marriage of DORASPE and EU-
RIDICE, ERNESTUS and IRENE, he would
in publick testify the Friendship he now

K 2   bore

bore him in secret; they embraced and parted.

But with what Agonies of Mind the fond ARILLA received the news of her Lover's Banifhment, is fcarce to be imagined; he endeavour'd to comfort her in vain, fhe gave way to the Violence of her Grief, fhe fear'd for him and for herfelf; ——fhe trembled, left the Rage of an offended Sovereign fhould proceed yet farther; fhe knew not but he might be going to an eternal Exile, or perhaps be permitted to return, but on terms more cruel.——She doubted alfo the Force of her own Charms, and could not flatter herfelf with an Affurance, that in abfence they would maintain their Power.———Nothing could be more tender and moving, than were her Adjurations of Fidelity, nor than the Imprecations he made, if ever he prov'd falfe.—— Loving her with fo real a Paffion as he at that time did, it was as much as he could do to reftrain himfelf from letting her into the whole Myftery of his pretended Banifhment; and had it not been that the Secret of his Prince was mingled with his own, 'tis probable he had given her that Demonftration, how much his Soul was hers.—— He told her, however, the Place of his defign'd Retreat, affuring her he would write frequently, and entreating fhe would be as punctual in her Anfwers.

Having

Having taken his farewell of ARILLA, he went to LUTETIA, who believing every thing he did, was caus'd by the Care the Prince had of her Reputation, made no Objections to her removal; which MARMILLIO contriv'd to be to a place, where there was no Company among whom it was suppos'd she could make a Confidante. Then, after having taken a solemn leave of all his Friends, he departed on his voluntary Banishment.

This seeming Displeasure of the Prince, against a Man who had been so publickly known his greatest Favourite, occasion'd much Speculation among the Courtiers; some imputed the Cause to one thing, some to another, but not one among them had any suspicion of the Truth. ISMONDA was extremely surpriz'd at it, and more than once intreated to be inform'd of what was so puzzling to every body; but THEODORE, (as by what has been said of his Behaviour to EURIDICE, may easily be believ'd) knew how, in the midst of Raptures, to preserve Discretion, and would not suffer himself to be prevail'd on to explain the Mystery, evading giving any direct answer to the Interrogatories she made him; and only told her, that he found him too presuming on the familiarity with which he had treated him, and forbad him the Court to let him

see

fee he ſtood in no need of that Service on
which he had too much valu'd himſelf. Is-
MONDA, whoſe Suſpicions of EURIDICE
were not yet extinct, ſet it down in her own
Mind for a certainty, that he was diſcarded
for no other reaſon than to make room for
ARBANES, becauſe that was the only Motive which ſhe imagin'd the Prince would
have conceal'd from her. The Advice, how-
eꝛer, that MARMILLIO had given her, together with the intended Marriage of her
Rival, enabled her to refrain giving any
marks of Jealouſy ; and perceiving all the
Diſcourſe of MARMILLIO was unwelcome,
ſhe forbore to ſpeak any more of him till a
fitter opportunity ſhould offer for an attempt to make his Peace, which ſhe very
much wiſh'd to bring about, believing him
wholly in her Intereſt, and that ſhe might in
him have a vigilant Obſerver of the Prince's
Actions.

Thus was Deceit either to attain or conceal their ſeveral Deſigns, on every ſide
made uſe of. The Princeſs and DORASPE
were the only Perſons made Properties of,
without returning the Impoſition ; the former of them truly loving ISMONDA, was
glad of an opportunity to detain her, without obliging her to infringe the Duty of her
matrimonial Vow, and with the utmoſt Good-
Nature, and Sincerity, aſſured her ſhe
would

would exert her Interest with the Prince for conferring on CLOTUS the Honour she requested for him. And the other, wholly taken up and devoted to the Charms of EURIDICE, had not leisure to inspect into the secret Reasons which mov'd the Prince to appear so zealous for the marriage of ERNESTUS with IRENE; and the Banishment of MARMILLIO, confirming what the Prince had told him, he thought it also as much to the prejudice of IRENE herself, to think of him for a Husband, as the making him so, would be to the accomplishment of his own Designs on EURIDICE. He therefore wrote to her a second time, acquainting her with the present posture of Affairs; and mingling some Menaces with his Persuasions, to oblige her to consent to that which he imagin'd was the only means to establish both his and her own Happiness.

ISMONDA was all this while busily employ'd in her Sollicitations for the Brother of ADRASTUS; there was no body who seem'd to have any Interest with the Prince or Princess, that she did not engage to back her Intercessions: but the former, as was agreed between them, still evaded any positive determination, and continued neither granting, nor refusing, till the Eve before that Day in which the Ambassadors were to depart from *Caramania.* They waited on

her

her at her Apartment, to know her Refolution concerning accompanying them ; to
which fhe reply'd, That being negotiating an
Affair of the greateft Importance to her
Husband, which not being yet accomplifh'd, fhe could not, without an irreparable detriment to their mutural Intereft, leave
it in Sufpence: but intreated they would
deliver a Letter to him, the Contents whereof were in this manner.

To my dear ADRASTUS.

'HOW griev'd am I, that I cannot
' give that Proof of my Love and
' Duty which you require of me, without
' being guilty of a Prejudice to your Intereft,
' which would be more unpardonable than
' the feeming Unkindnefs of this Abfence.
' My faithful Heart, ever anxious for your
' eafe, has found the means, I hope, to
' put an eternal period to thofe Apprehen-
' fions you have long labour'd under, of the
' Marriage of your degenerate Brother.
' Among the unnumber'd Obligations I have
' receiv'd from the goodnefs of our excellent
' Princefs, fhe has taken the Affair between
' you and CLOTUS into Confideration, and
' made it the Bufinefs of many days, to fol-
' licite her Royal Confort for providing
' for him in a manner which will not take
' away,

' away, but rather add to the Honour of his
' illustrious Birth, and at the same time
' rid you of those Fears you are continually
' involved in on his account.——The Head
' of the *Magi* is lately dead, and that our
' Brother may succeed him, she exerts her
' utmost Interest; the Grant is not yet ab-
' solutely given, but I am in daily expecta-
' tion of the Prince's acceding to what
' she so earnestly desires of him.——Should
' I leave *Caramania* till this is quite com-
' pleated, enough there are who would use
' their utmost endeavours to make an ad-
' vantage of my absence for procuring the
' Honours which attend this Post, either for
' themselves or Friends.——Judge now, my
' for-ever-lov'd ADRASTUS, if you have
' reason to accuse me of want of Tender-
' ness, when all my Thoughts are taken up
' with studying your Felicity: be you as
' careful on your part, and inspire such
' Notions into the Breast of CLOTUS, as
' shall make him willing to receive a Fa-
' vour so advantageous for himself, and
' which fixes you in so entire a Security
' from any future Troubles on his score.——
' I shall say nothing in return to what you
' seem to hint at, of the little Artifices made
' use of by some base Detractors, to blast
' my Reputation; my Conduct will suffi-
' ciently vindicate my Innocence to the dif-
' interested World, as the nobler Proofs I

' give

' give my Tenderness, will, I hope, satisfy
' you, that I am,

With the utmost Sincerity,

My dear ADRASTUS,

Your truly Affectionate Wife,

Faithful Friend,

and most Obedient Servant,

ISMONDA.

P. S. ' Soon as the Affair of CLOTUS
' can be accomplish'd, and he is arriv'd in
' *Caramania*, and settled in his Post, ex-
' pect to receive a Wife; who, by the
' Testimonies she gives you of her Concern
' for you in absence, ought more to endear
' herself to your Affections and Esteem,
' than by all the little Fondnesses of her
' Sex when present. Once more, dearest
' of Mankind, Adieu.

Scarce ever had ISMONDA known a greater
Contentment, than that she felt at seeing
these Ambassadors depart without her; nor
could any thing have afforded more felicitous Reflections to THEODORE: a while
did both enjoy an uninterrupted Scene of
Pleasure, but *Fortune*, to let them see her
Power was absolute, raised them up new
Troubles, at a time when they thought
themselves most secure.

ARI-

ARIDANOR was one of the chief of the *Caramanian* Lords, and on the account of his high Birth, vaſt Poſſeſſions, and perſonal Accompliſhments, was held in the greateſt eſteem of any of the Noblemen of that Principality. He had been married ſome Years to a Lady whom his Inclination only had raiſed to that Honour, ſhe being far inferior to him in Extraction, and the Goods of Fortune : they had liv'd together in a perfect Amity, nor was there any thing in his Behaviour which denoted the leaſt Deviation from that Eſteem, which led him firſt to make choice of her for a Wife : But how uncertain is the Heart of Man ? On how weak a Foundation is the Happineſs of that Woman built, which depends upon the Faith of that inconſtant and ever-varying Sex ? The once-admired Beauties of BARSINA, for that is the Name of his Wife, were forgot in the Reflection of thoſe ISMONDA ſeem'd poſſeſs'd of ; and tho', in reality, leſs lovely than the other, to the chang'd Humour of ARIDANOR appear'd beyond compare.——Long had he in ſecret languiſh'd ; her Character and Behaviour ſtruck him with an Awe, which would not ſuffer him to reveal his Paſſion ; and, difficult as it is to ſmother Deſire, he concealed his ſo well, that even the Fair Inſpirer was ignorant of the Conqueſt ſhe had gain'd : but with what inexpreſſible

In-

Inquietudes he obtain'd this Maftery over himfelf, thofe only who have felt the like, are capable of conceiving : tho' hopelefs of Succefs, the bufy Flame would not, however, fuffer him to reft; he was a diligent Obferver of all the Words and Actions of Ismonda ; he had Spies about her whereever fhe went, and to watch about her Apartment, and bring him Intelligence of whateverVifits fhe received. Yet fo cautious was fhe in her Amour, that for a great while his Affiduity ferv'd but more to confirm him in the Opinion the whole Court had of her Virtue ; and he was about giving over the vain Purfuit of finding any thing which might encourage him to hope fhe had the leaft Propenfity to intrigue, when Chance prefented him with a Difcovery, which not all his Induftry could fupply him with.

The Evening before the Departure of the *Anatolian* Ambaffadors, the Princefs gave a fplendid Entertainment and Ball at her own Apartment: Aridanor was one of the invited Guefts; and never had he thought Ismonda more lovely, than he did that night. Among the dazling Affembly of Beauties, which feem'd each to ftrive who fhould excel her fair Cotemporaries in Magnificence of Apparel, and Blaze of Jewels, fhe alone attracted his Eyes; and, like the Sun, with a fuperior Brightnefs, eclipfed

clipfed the Shine of any other Charms.
It being cuftomary in fuch places, for the
young Ladies and Noblemen to retire now
and then in little Parties into the adjacent
Rooms, in order to entertain one another
with greater freedom than was becoming
in the royal Prefence ; ARIDANOR, not
to feem particularly grave, did as he faw
others do, and as himfelf had been ufed
to behave, but always took the opportunity
of going when ISMONDA was abfent : but
having more Inclination to indulge his own
Reflections, than enter into any Converfation
which would deprive him of the pleafure
of contemplating the Beauties of ISMONDA,
he withdrew into a Room which he faw
entirely free from Company ; and throwing
himfelf into an eafy Chair, gave a loofe to
Thought, and to the labouring Difquiets
of his o'er-burthen'd Soul. But he had not
been there many moments, before he faw
ISMONDA pafs fwiftly by him : he follow'd
her with his Eyes, and 'tis probable had
done fo with his Steps, had he not feen the
Prince, who, on fome occafion, was juft
then coming out of the Drawing-room ;
and meeting ISMONDA, cry'd to her in a
low Voice, yet loud enough for the afto-
nifhed Liftner to hear, My Angel ! my everlafting Charmer ! how infinitely furpaffing
all thy Sex befide is thy Perfection ! A
tender Preffure of her Hand, and languifh-
ing

ing Glance accompany'd this Expreffion, and perhaps had been fucceeded by others of the fame nature, if the fame Inftant a Crowd of Gentlemen had not been coming that way. ARIDANOR follow'd ISMONDA, unfeen by her, into the Drawing-room, more perplexed and confounded in his Mind, than can be well imagined; he feated himfelf oppofite to her, and could not look on her, without the Confufion of his Thoughts fhowing itfelf as vifibly in his Face, as would have appear'd in hers, had fhe been fenfible of the Difcovery he had made; but *Security* fupplying the place of *Innocence*, fhe look'd not guilty, becaufe not confcious fhe was thought fo.————
Never did Paffions war with greater Vehemence, than in the Bofom of this amazed Lover——He found 'twas true that the adorable Object of his Affections was not infenfible of an amorous Inclination; but then he found alfo they were already devoted, devoted to a Prince, whofe Property it was a kind of Treafon to invade.——
Tho' there had not been time for her to reply in words to that tender Salutation with which THEODORE had accofted her, yet he eafily perceiv'd by her manner of receiving it, as well as by the Air with which he fpoke, that he was not a Lover in the ftate of Hope, but of Poffeffion. He now experienced the Pangs which jealous Rage inflicts;

flicts; and this Difcovery being far from making any abatement in his Paffion, what he endured, is fcarce to be conceiv'd.

The natural Courage of his Sex, however, got at laft the Victory over the meaner E-motions with which he had been agitated : ——and no longer being poffefs'd by that Awe which had hitherto reftrain'd him from declaring himfelf, he refolved to do it the firft opportunity which fhould offer; and tho' almoft hopelefs of Succefs, imagin'd he fhould find fome Eafe in giving vent to the fecret Anguifh of his Soul. Being fixed in this Determination, he kept continually a-bout the Court; and inftead of vifiting at the Prince's Apartment, as he was accuf-tomed to do, he now paid all his Devoirs at that of the Princefs.——There he every day faw ISMONDA, talk'd to her in general Converfation with other Ladies, but for a great while endeavour'd in vain the means of entertaining her alone. The Difappoint-ment was indeed in great meafure owing to himfelf; for ever fince he had been fen-fible of her Amour with the Prince, he had taken lefs pains to conceal the Inclina-tions he had for her; no more with diftant humble Reverence did he approach her, with fierce Defire his fparkling Eyes now blazed.———— All his Difcourfe was on the Force of Love, and in her prefence breathed nothing but the wanton God.——

Not

Not one who heard him but plainly faw
the Agitations with which he was poffefs'd,
and fome there were, who wifhed themfelves the occafion.——Ismonda prefently
perceived the change of his Behaviour, and
alfo that it was to her own Charms he
owed this Transformation; but tho fhe was
not without fome fhare of that Vanity
which is accounted inherent to the Sex,
and could not be greatly difobliged at the
Conqueft fhe had made, yet fhe defir'd no
other Confirmation of it, than what fhe received in publick: for which reafon, fhe
always carefully avoided being left alone
with him, not doubting, by the freedom of
his Carriage to her before all the Court,
but that he would have Temerity enough,
the firft opportunity which prefented itfelf,
to declare in words that Paffion which his
fpeaking Looks had already fufficiently
made her acquainted with. Whenever fhe
met him in the Drawing-room, fhe either
kept clofe to the Princefs, or feem'd bufy
in difcourfe with fome other Ladies; and
when he came to vifit her, was either deny'd, or receiv'd him in company, who fhe
oblig'd to out-ftay him: but nothing is impoffible to the bold and daring; in fpite of
all her Caution, fhe was oblig'd, at laft, to
hear his Pretenfions, and to hear him in a
manner more alarming than fhe could have
expected or imagin'd.——He went one

Evening to her Apartment; and thofe Attendants who were generally waiting in the
outward Rooms, and from whom he had
fometimes received Anfwers, no way obliging to his Defires, happening to be all
out of the way, he pafs'd directly to that
where fhe generally received thofe who
came to vifit her: but finding it entirely
free from Company, went boldly through
it into her Bed-chamber, where fhe was fit-
ting in a carelefs pofture with a Book in her
hand, which fhe feem'd to be perufing with
a great deal of attention. She faw him not
at his firft entrance, and it would have afforded him an infinite Satisfaction, to have
ftood obferving her thus unperceiv'd by her,
but the difficulty he had found to get an
opportunity fuch as this, made him confider there was no time to be loft; and
walking haftily up to her, May I prefume,
Madam, *faid he*, to ask the Subject of
your Entertainment? She blufh'd and ftarted
at his unexpected Prefence; but recovering
herfelf immediately from the Confufion
which the fight of him had involv'd her in,
You feem in little need, my Lord, *reply'd*
fhe, of an Apology for a Demand fuch as
this, when you make none for entring my
private Lodgings without permiffion, or
even letting me know you intended me
the honour of a Vifit. She fpoke thefe
Words with an Air of fo much refent-

L   ment,

ment, as left him no room to doubt she guess'd the purpose of his coming, and had been sufficient to have deterred a Lover less prepar'd with Resolution from proceeding further. Nor could all the Courage he had muster'd up for this Encounter, enable him to endure the Severity of her Looks, without being a little daunted; but re-assuring himself as much as possible, I have too often, *reply'd he,* been repulsed in my Desires of a private Interview, not to have experienced of how little service my Submissions are: I therefore now come arm'd with all the boldness of despairing Love, to tell you, that tho' your Cruelty should render me the most wretched of created Beings, it cannot have the power to lessen my Adoration of you, nor make me cease to demonstrate the Influence your Charms has o'er me, by all the ways which raging Passion can invent. 'Tis well, my Lord, *resumed she, with the most haughty Air she was able to put on,* and you think this fit Discourse for the Husband of BARSINA to the Wife of ADRASTUS? True, Madam, *answered he briskly,* we both are married, but I believe neither of us are ignorant enough to imagine that Ceremony a sufficient Bar to put a stop to the Effects of Inclination. When Heaven form'd an Angel like ISMONDA, *continued he, softning his Voice, and taking one of her*
Hands

Hands in spite of her Efforts to hinder him, it defign'd her not a private Bleffing, an unrival'd Poffeffion would be a Joy too mighty for mortal Man to bear ; nor would almighty Wifdom have given you thefe Charms to blaft a thoufand Eyes, while one alone revels and basks in envy'd Enjoyment.———— No, you were created for delight, born to receive and to confer it in the moft fublime degree, and cannot, if you would, be cruel, where *Love* and *Merit* jointly plead for favour.————To the *latter* of thefe Requifites, I have indeed no title ; but fure the abundance of the *former* may, in fome part, attone for that Deficiency, and the other let your Compaffion fupply.———— O Ismonda ! *cry'd he, throwing himself at once upon her Bosom,* I cannot live without you, the burning Paffion of my impatient Soul no longer will brook Reftraint.———— I muft have eafe or die.————That fhe fuffered him to proceed thus far uninterrupted, was owing only to that mixture of Surprize and Rage, which the unlook'd-for Prefumption he was guilty of enflam'd her with, and for fome moments ftopp'd the utterance of her Words : fhe recover'd herfelf from the former but juft timely enough to prevent him from taking any greater Liberties with her, than Modefty would admit ; and the Violence of her Indignation giving her a lar-

ger

ger share of Strength than ordinary, she
unloosed herself from his Embrace, and
starting from the place in which she had
been sitting——How can you, dare you
treat me in this manner? *said she*; O that
ADRASTUS were here, and witness of the Affront!—She was able to bring out no more,
but seem'd half suffocated with the rising
Passions. The Absence of a Husband is indeed, *answered he*, no small Encouragement for a Lover ; but perhaps his Presence
might not at all times be so welcome as
now. As he pronounced these Words, his
very Eyes spoke Satyr, as well as his Tongue,
and made ISMONDA know he had a secret
meaning in them, which she wish'd, yet
dreaded to discover: But concealing her
Disorder as much as she could, It is not
always so *necessary*, (*said she:*) Nor so *convenient*, (*rejoin'd he immediately.*) But to
take part with ADRASTUS, is not the Busi-
of ARIDANOR ; as to accuse the Object of
his Desires, would ill become a Lover. In
speaking this, he turn'd hastily from her,
as she thought with a design to leave the
Room; but vastly different were his Intentions : he found there was little to be hoped
for the gratification of his Passion by Entreaties; and thinking he had already done
too much to be forgiven, resolv'd to make
himself amends for the long Pains he had
endured in the concealment of his Wishes,

and

and alſo to revenge himſelf on a Coyneſs
which he knew was not univerſal :————
and giving a ſudden Jump to the Door,
made it faſt immediately, and return'd to
ISMONDA and caught her in his Arms, before ſhe had time either to prevent him,
or ring the Bell for any of her Attendants to come in. In vain were all her
Strugglings, in vain her Menaces, he regarded not her Reproaches nor Remon-
ſtrances; and though the higher roſe his
amorous Rage, the more tempeſtuous her
Indignation grew, he delay'd any Endeavours to abate it, till the Fury of his own
ſhould be allay'd. She raved, ſhe tore, did
all that Woman could : but alas ! it was
not in the power of her own Strength to
ſave her, and ſhe was juſt on the point of
falling a Victim to the Fierceneſs of his ungovernable Paſſion, when ſome Ladies coming to viſit her, LYSETTA her favourite Woman not knowing any body was in the
Room with her, and imagining ſhe was
fallen aſleep, knock'd pretty loudly at the
Door : For Heaven's ſake, *cry'd* ISMONDA,
when ſhe heard it, ſuffer me not to be ex-
poſed————retire into my Cloſet for a moment, that it may not be known you have
attempted me in this manner. ARIDA-
NOR could not refuſe giving her this Proof
of his Reſpect, and went into his concealment, tho' not without ſome Curſes on

L 3   the

the Interruption ; which, however, he was
refolv'd to repair, after the departure of
thofe who had given it him. The diforder
Ismonda was in, made her little capable of
receiving Company ; and tho' fhe rejoic'd it
was no other Perfon than Lysetta at the
Door, yet was fhe vex'd, that having not
given Orders to be deny'd, fhe was oblig'd
to fee thefe Ladies in this difcompofure of
her Temper. Setting herfelf in as much
order as the time would admit, fhe went
into her Drawing-room where her Guefts im-
patiently expected her approach ; in the
hurry of her Thoughts, forgetting to take
the Key out of the Clofet-door where Aridanor was hid.

Lysetta ftay'd not long in the Chamber after Ismonda had left it, and one of
the inferior Servants hapning to come in to
look for fomething fhe had mifplac'd, unluckily for her Lady's Reputation, went to
fearch for it in that Clofet ; fhe no fooner
open'd the Door, than Aridanor thinking it was Ismonda, bolted out upon her.
The fight of a Man in that place, made her
give a great Shriek, which alarming the
Family, fome of them ran up to know what
had occafion'd it ; but before they cou'd get
into the Chamber, Aridanor had Prefence
enough of mind to throw the Wench a
Purfe of Guineas, and bidding her be fecret, withdrew into his Cell, and held the

Door

Door faft on the infide. Several Interrogatories being put to the Maid, who could not
yet recover herfelf from the fright, fhe anfwer'd, that going to reach fomething from
the Top of the Cabinet, a great Rat had
jump'd down, and had occafion'd her crying out. No body fufpecting the Truth of
what fhe faid, they all went away and left
her; and as foon as ARIDANOR heard they
were gone, he came out, and charging her
that had difcover'd him never to mention
the leaft tittle of what fhe knew, either to
any of the Houfe, nor even to her Lady
herfelf, added fomething more to the Prefent he had already made her, and going
into his Concealment, defir'd fhe would
lock the Door upon him as fhe had found it,
and quit the Chamber before ISMONDA
fhould return to it. She was too well paid
not to be obedient to his Commands as far
as was in her power; but how far that extended, as to the gift of Secrecy, will hereafter appear.

ISMONDA, who knew nothing of all this
(having been in the Garden when the outcry
was made) being impatient to get rid of her
Company, complain'd of a violent Head-ach,
and by that means oblig'd them to take leave
much fooner than elfe 'tis probable they
would have done: but when left alone,
was very much at a lofs by what means fhe
fhould releafe her Prifoner, without letting

him

him be seen by the Servants; and confe-
quen tlygiving them to underftand that he
had been all this time conceal'd there. She
found there was no poffibility of doing it
without the help of LYSETTA; to her,
therefore, fhe communicated the whole
Affair, bidding her fend the Men on different Errands abroad, fome one way, fome
another; and contrive fome Bufinefs to employ the Women, that they might not come
into the upper Apartments till ARIDANOR
fhould be gone. LYSETTA, than whom no
body could be more fit for the Truft repos'd in her, having done as fhe was order'd, return'd to her Lady, and let her
know the Coaft was clear, on which, having bid her wait in the next Room, thinking it not fafe, as indeed fhe well might,
to truft herfelf a fecond time with a Man,
who had already prov'd, whatever his Profeffions of Adorations were, how little he
regarded her Anger, fhe went into the
Chamber and releas'd him; who had
pafs'd his Time pleafantly enough, flatter-
ing himfelf with the Thoughts, how dear
he fhould, at his coming out, make his
Fair Jaylor pay for his Confinement. But
how great was his Difappointment, when
the Door being open'd, at the fame time
that he faw ISMONDA, he faw her Woman alfo in an oppofite Room; who,
though not near enough to hear what
was

was said between them, was not enough remov'd to give him any opportunity of acting in the manner he defign'd. He was
now, in fpite of his refolves, oblig'd to
have recourfe to entreaties, and fet forth
the Violence of his Paffion in fuch humble
and perfuafive Terms, that had not the moft
potent Prepoffeffion that ever was, enabled
her to refift his Importunities, ADRASTUS
had been in no fmall danger of being injur'd the fame way by ARIDANOR, as he had
been by the Prince of *Caramania*. But that
ever-prefent Idea kept her firm and im-
moveable by any other Charms or Sollicitations, and the little Inclination fhe had to
hear him, join'd with the Apprehenfions
that he might poffibly be known to have
been there in private, made her exprefs an
Impatience for his leaving her Apartment,
which fufficiently affur'd him, all the tender
Arguments he cou'd urge, would be but
thrown away. He refum'd, as his laft hope,
that boldnefs he had lately caft afide, and told
her, that he was but too fenfible her Cruelty to him fprung from other Reafons than
thofe fhe was willing to confefs, and that to
his certain knowledge, there was a happy
Man who triumph'd over his unavailing
Preffures, and the Honour of ADRASTUS.
This Reproach, confirming her in the Fears
which fome Hints he had before given her,
that her Reputation was not altogether fo

clear

clear as fhe had imagin'd, fpread o'er her Face
a vifible Confufion : but willing to conceal it as much as poffible, fhe anfwer'd him
in Terms full of Refentment, telling him,
that if he perfifted to talk to her in that manner, fhe would complain to the Princefs of
the Affront. To the Prince you mean, Madam, *anfwer'd he*, it does indeed concern
him to filence fuch Difcourfes ; nay, blufh
not, beautiful ISMONDA ! *continued he, perceiving her grow extremely red*, I have indeed attain'd that Secret, but be affur'd it
never has efcap'd my Lips but to yourfelf,
nor never fhall, unlefs your continu'd Scorn
fhould drive me mad, and render me incapable of confidering what I owe to you,
and to my Sovereign. In what a condition ISMONDA was at finding herfelf detected in a guilt which fhe believ'd conceal'd
from all the World, and to find it known
to him, who aim'd at making an advantage
of the Difcovery, fo contrary to her Inclinations, to her Honour, to the Obligation
fhe had to her belov'd THEODORE, let any
one be judge, whofe Strength of Imagination can enable them to put themfelves in
her Circumftances. At firft, Surprize, and
inward Vexation made her dumb ; but when
fhe fpoke, it was with fuch Affeverations
of her Innocence, as had not his own Eyes
and Ears been Evidences againft the Truth
of what fhe faid, he would have given the

                                          lye

lye to any other Proofs; but too well convinc'd of the certainty of his Misfortune,
he let her know Denials were in vain, and
gave her Hints too plain, for her not to underſtand him, that to aſſure his Secrecy ſhe
muſt confer on him ſome part of thoſe Favours, ſhe had beſtow'd with ſo much pro-
fuſeneſs on his Royal Rival : which, tho'
ſhe was far from promiſing, he had the Satisfaction to obſerve what he ſaid, had a
very great influence over her, and was not
now without hope that her *Fear* might
work that Effect in his favour, which her *Inclination* refus'd to do.   Fain would he have
taken the advantage which the Confuſion of
her Thoughts ſeem'd to afford him to compleat his Wiſhes ; but all he could ſay, was ineffectual to perſuade her to diſpatch LYSETTA,
who ſtill continu'd in the next Room, which
being ſeparated from that in which they
were only by a Glaſs-Door, gave her a full
Proſpect of all that paſs'd ; and finding that
ſhe requir'd only time for Conſideration,
and inſiſted on his leaving her as a Teſtimony of that Obedience ſhe might expect
from a Lover, he thought it beſt to comply
with her Deſires, and departed with a kind
of an aſſur'd Expectation of being happy the
next Viſit he made ; which, before he would
be prevail'd on to quit the Room, he engaged her Promiſe ſhould be the enſuing
day.

Never

Never was a Mind involv'd in greater
or more violent Perturbations than that of
Ismonda; it is impoſſible for any Woman
to have a juſter Senſe of Reputation than
had ſhe, and the Apprehenſions of what ſhe
might ſuffer that way from the Rage of a
diſappointed Lover, was worſe than Death
to her: yet reſolute never to yield to what
he deſired, her hurrying Thoughts form'd
ſometimes one Scheme, and ſometimes a-
nother for the Prevention of that ſo much
dreaded Evil.——To acquaint his Wife with
his attempt upon her, ſhe conſider'd would
but incenſe him more, and provoke him to
divulge that, which elſe, perhaps, his own
Honour would oblige him to conceal; and
to let the Prince know what had paſs'd, ſhe
fear'd might occaſion that paſſionate Lover
to treat him in a manner which would make
him underſtand ſhe had betray'd him.— The
more ſhe reflected on the Conſequences of
revealing the Preſumption he had been guilty
of, the more dangerous it appear'd; and ſhe
found it beſt, on all accounts, to proceed
with him only by fair means, and palliate
the bitterneſs of her refuſal by giving it him
in the ſofteſt and moſt obliging Terms.

When, therefore, according to appointment, he came the next day, ſhe arm'd herſelf, as much as poſſible, with Patience, to
bear whatever Reflections Jealouſy and diſappointed Love might caſt on her; and,

per-

perceiving, at his firſt Entrance, that he took it ill, ſhe receiv'd him in a publick Room free to the acceſs of as many as came to viſit her, ſhe doubted not, but when ſhe had declar'd herſelf more fully, he would omit no Severities of Reproach which his Good-breeding would allow him to make: and hearing him beginning to complain of the litrle Inclination he found in her to oblige him, I will not deceive you my Lord, *ſaid ſhe*; I confeſs your Merits are ſuch as juſtly might expect to engage a more deſerving Heart, but mine is prepoſſeſs'd already, taken up with an Idea which will admit no room for any other——I therefore beg, for your own eaſe and mine, you will deſiſt the hopeleſs Proſecution, and think BARSINA only worthy your Deſires, as you are the ſole Object of hers. ARIDANOR, who was by Nature ſomewhat raſh and fiery in all his Paſſions, could not endure any thing that look'd like an Admonition without returning it. The Merits of BARSINA, Madam, *anſwer'd he*, are not unknown to me, nor is Fame dumb in thoſe ADRASTUS is poſſeſs'd of; but ſince both of us have teſtify'd an Inclination to experience the Pleaſures Variety affords, the Crime is not, I preſume, leſs pardonable in ARIDANOR, than it is in ISMONDA, unleſs it can be prov'd, that the Charms of *Royalty* are ſuperior to thoſe of *Beauty*: Be at once, therefore, lovely Creature!

ture! *continu'd he*, kind and prudent, fecure your Secret by binding to your Service
the only Man who has it in his power to
betray it, and blefs a Lover to whom you
are more dear than Words can fpeak. You
give but a very fmall Proof that I am fo, *reply'd fhe, no longer able to contain herfelf,*
when you would obtain that by *Menaces;*
which you ought rather to attempt by *Perfuafions* ; but know, that I defpife whatever Afperfions *Jealoufy* may fuggeft, or
Malice invent againft my Honour; and dare
believe, my Conduct has been fuch, as will
render ineffectual all can be urg'd to blaft
it :——but were I guilty in the manner you
feem to think, the imagin'd Partner of my
Crime, methinks, fhould awe you into Silence, were you *affur'd* of what, at moft,
you but *fufpect*. To practife that Prudence
you would prefcribe to me, you fhould confider that the Royal THEODORE is above the
Fears either of *Rivalfhip,* or *Accufation.*
The Vehemence and Spirit with which fhe
utter'd thefe Words, and that Fire which
fparkled in her Eyes all the time fhe was
fpeaking, fufficiently denoted the inward
Indignation of her Soul, and made him repent he had touch'd her in fo nice a part;
but all he could fay afterwards, was in vain
to pacify her, fhe look'd not on him but
with reluctance and difdain, and having feveral times forbad him ever to fpeak to her
on

on the unwelcome Theme of his Paſſion,
took her leave of him with a conſtrain'd
Civility, and went into another Room, leaving him alone to murmur at the ill ſucceſs
of his Deſigns.

'Tis certain that nothing could exceed
the Vexation he was in at this diſappoint-
ment of his high-rais'd Expectations; but
notwithſtanding the Treatment he had received from her, and that firm Reſolution
with which ſhe expreſſed herſelf, 'tis probable he had not yet given over the vain
purſuit, had not Fortune ſent her a deli-
verance from his Perſecutions by a way ſhe
little thought of.

Rage and Deſpair rendring him unfit for
Company, or Converſation, when he left
the Apartment of ISMONDA, he went to indulge his Diſcontents in the Gardens of the
Palace, it being a time of day in which the
Walks were generally empty; but finding
more Perſons there than he expected, the
preſent Melancholy of his Diſpoſition led
him into the Wilderneſs, where having wan-
der'd ſome time thro' the thickeſt part of it,
he thought he heard Womens Voices at a
little diſtance from him. The Perturbations
he was in, not having quite extinguiſh'd Curioſity, he drew nearer the Place whence
the Sound proceeded, and continued moving with a ſoft and ſlow Pace, till he came
ſo cloſe to the Grotto where they were ſitting,

ting, that he could diftinctly hear not only
the Words of her that fpoke, but alfo the
very Sighs with which the other liftned to
her Difcourfe. I cannot imagine, *faid
one of them*, wherefore you trufted me
with the fecret of your Paffion, unlefs it
were either with an Intent that I fhould af-
fift you in the gratification of it; or ftreng-
then your Refolution with fome Arguments
to enable you to overcome it : the one neither my Honour, nor my Character in the
World will permit me to do; and the other,
I am afraid, will be impoffible to accomplifh.————When Love once fettles itfelf
in a Heart fo young as yours for a deferving Object, how vain are the Efforts of
Reafon to expel it!————The firft Impreffion
is not without the greateft difficulty erafed;
and it feems like tearing part of the Soul
with it, when one but goes about to drive
it thence. Ah! my dear Coufin, *replied
the other*, how often have I experienced
the Pangs you fpeak of! Nor had I own'd
the Folly as well as Guilt of my unhappy
Flame, but that it grew too mighty for reftraint, and from your tender Friendfhip
hoped to find fome pity.————Too well, alas!
I am convinced that till I ceafe to live, I
cannot ceafe to love; and Heaven knows
wou'd fooner chufe to die, than purchafe
Blifs with lofs of Honour. Flatter not
yourfelf, *refumed fhe that had fpoken firft*,
my

my lov'd ELARIA! with fuch romantick
Notions; if Virtue is too weak to keep you
from Defire, fhe will not have the power
to defend you from gratifying that Defire,
when once the Means are offer'd. —— You
know not yet what 'tis to love, and have
the darling Object of your fond Affection
kneel at your Feet, breathing foft Vows of
everlaftingTruth, eternalArdors; ——then,
with fweet Violence, feize your refifting
Hand, and prefs it to his Breaft, which in
tumultuous .heavings confirms the language
of his Tongue; ——with wild Impatience,
and Longings untameable, at laft made bold,
rife to your Bofom, with burning Kiffes
melt your Refolves, and——— O hold!
cry'd the diffolving Languifher, interrupt-
ing her, I cannot bear the rapturous De-
fcription! Too many Charms the dangerous *Idea* yields, what then would the *Re-*
ality afford! —— Oh, fhould I ever fee the
godlike ARIDANOR thus, what would indeed become of me!

That this muft be a Surprize prodigioufly
agreeable to any Man, to find himfelf the
Author of fo fincere and ardent a Paffion
in the Heart of a young Maid, for whom
a thoufand noble Youths were dying, the
moft temperate of the Sex cannot but confefs. With what Emotions then did the
Breaft of ARIDANOR fwell at this difcovery? As much in love as he had been with

M   ISMONDA,

Ismonda, the improbability there now appear'd of gaining her, the Difdain with which he had been treated by her, and that changing Difpofition which is almoft inherent to the Nature of Mankind, all join'd together to make way for the new Impreffion of Elaria's Charms ; and he hefitated not a moment if he fhould not, the firft opportunity, act that part which her experienc'd Confidante had fo lively reprefented. The two Ladies had fome further Converfation ; but he fearing to be difcover'd to have been lift'ning, and by that means put the young Elaria more on her guard ; and alfo thinking he had heard enough to know how to proceed for the fatisfaction of thofe Defires fhe had acknowledged, and which he too now felt, he withdrew with the fame Caution with which he had advanced, and was got quite out of the Wildernefs before they had any defign of leaving it.

Never was there a more pleafing Cure for an unavailing and hopelefs Paffion, than that which Aridanor found in his for Ismonda, in the love of Elaria : She was extremely young and beautiful ; and by that Converfation which gave him the knowledge of her Wifhes, he found her Soul as tender and amorous as he could defire, in the Woman he made choice of for a Miftrefs ; and doubted not but in

her

her Enjoyment, he fhould find thofe Joys
which are never to be tafted but where
mutual Warmth excites the enamour'd Pair.
No difficulties appear'd to threaten him with
oppofition, or even delays in this Purfuit.
Inclination had already done his work ; her
Heart was his ; and Affiduities, diftant Homage, Vows, Sighs, Tears, Cries, Imprecations, and all the firft Artillery of Love,
were needlefs ; and he had no more to
combat with, than the faint ftrugglings of
Virgin Bafhfulnefs, to become mafter of
her *Body* as he was of her *Soul*. Nor
was it hard to find an opportunity for the
accomplifhment of this defign : She was
continually at Court, her Father, the Che-
valier ORSAMES, having a great Place under the Prince, had an ambition of preferring her, who was his only Daughter, to
the Service of the Princefs, in quality of
one of thofe young Ladies who make her
Train, whenever fhe appears in Publick,
are under her immediate Care, and receive
no other Salary for their Attendance, than
the Honour of being permitted to give it:
but there being only a certain number of
them allowed, fhe was obliged to wait till
a Vacancy arrived, either by the Marriage
or Death of one of thofe who were already
entertained. This Hope, together with her
fecret Paffion for ARIDANOR, made her feldom from a Place which gave her the op-

p or-portunity of indulging her Wifhes with the fight of him who was fo dear to her, and at the fame time of forwarding her Intereft.

Having drefs'd himfelf with the utmoft care and exactnefs, he went the next day to the Drawing-room of the Princefs ; and having paid the ufual Compliments to her, threw his Eyes o'er the Circle in fearch of ELARIA; who, till he appear'd, thinking nothing worthy her Attention, had retir'd to a Corner-window, which happening to be open, fhe was looking out, 'tis probable rather to avoid being engaged in Converfa-tion by thofe within, than that fhe found any Diverfion in the Objects which pre-fented themfelves from without.—— How natural is it (*faid he, ftepping to her, and leaning over her, as fhe was ftooping to the Window*) for us to know our own Per-fections! The fweet ELARIA, confcious of her power of pleafing, and fecure of the Admiration of as many as have the blef-fing of her Acquaintance, neglects the Hearts fhe holds in Chains, and fends her Charms abroad in fearch of more.————Elfe, why are thofe Eyes withdrawn, to whofe at-tractive Graces the Royal Prefence is in-debted for fome part, I am certain, of this Affembly, who come in *fhew* to pay their Homage there, but in *reality* devote it only here.—— The Confufion of ELARIA was fo great, to find the Object of her Af-

fections

fections so near her, (for she saw him not come into the Room) and at receiving this unexpected Compliment from him, that for some moments she could answer him no otherwise than by Blushes ; but endeavouring to overcome it as much as possible,—— I am too inconsiderable, my Lord, *said she*, to have enough of these fine things said to me, to be able to return them in the manner you may expect ; and must pardon me, if I express some Surprize, that, among so great a number of Beauties, who also are expert in those Turns of Wit and Raillery you Men of Gallantry so much delight in ; you should chuse to divert yourself with an unexperienced Maid, who has passed the most parts of those Years she owes to Nature in a Rural Life, remote from Courts, and ignorant of the politer World. To testify, Madam, *replied he*, how little I deserve that you should think my words had any other meaning, than the sincerest Dictates of an enamour'd Soul ; as also to prove the Opinion I have of your good Judgment, never will I address you by those Methods which ordinarily work their desired Effect on the vainer part of your Sex. I consider ELARIA as much beyond the rest of Womankind in Prudence, as she is in Beauty, and will endeavour to convince her of my Adoration only by such means as shall be consistent with the nicest Decorum, and of no prejudice to Reputation ; which I con-

fess,

fefs, indeed, our Ladies feem a little too
negligent in preferving. Happily for her to
whom in the prefent Emotions of her Soul
it had been impoffible to have continued
this Difcourfe, without confirming him in
what he was already but too well acquainted
with, fome Ladies with ERNESTUS came
to the place where they were; and the Converfation growing general, deliver'd her at
that time from giving any demonftrations
of a Paffion, fhe defired nothing more of
Heaven, than to enable her to conceal.

Having thus broke the ice, he omitted
no opportunities of talking to her, which he
could take, whithout rendring the Deference
he paid her liable to obfervation. The
Court is never without a great number of
Ladies, who, either thro' Malice or Curiofity, make it their bufinefs to pry into the
Motives which induce People to particular
Converfations; and tho' the love of Variety inclin'd him to feek in other Embraces thofe Joys which the unreftrain'd poffeffion of BARSINA no longer yielded, he
yet had Tendernefs enough for her to forbear giving her any Demonftrations of his
Change; and for that Reafon, as well as
the Promife he had made ELARIA, of never doing any thing which might prejudice
her Character, he entertain'd her not but
at fuch times as it might not appear he had
any defign in it.

But

But as if the purfuit of this Adventure was not fufficient to take up his Thoughts, and entirely erafe all the Remainders of his old Paffion for ISMONDA, another offer'd itfelf to him, which afforded him no lefs Surprize, and was not alfo without its fhare of Pleafure.

ZELINDA, a diftant Relation of ELARIA, and the fame whom fhe had made the Confidante of her fecret Paffion, when he overheard them in the Wildernefs, was a young Lady of an uncommon Gaiety of Humour: fhe had been lately married to a Nobleman of very great Poffeffions; but the Charaƈter of a Wife reftrain'd her not from indulging herfelf in all thofe Liberties fhe enjoy'd when in a ftate which render'd her Aƈtions accountable to none but her own Confcience. She had for a confiderable time made fuch Advances to ARIDANOR, as he could impute to nothing but a fecret liking of his Perfon. The Inclinations he then had for ISMONDA, kept him, however, from taking any great notice of her Behaviour; and the Converfation between her and ELARIA afterwards, made him imagine the defire fhe feem'd to have of engaging him, was only on the fcore of that fair Friend: till one day happening to be in a little Room joining to that in which the Princefs kept her State, laughing with fome Ladies, who had withdrawn for a little Re-

M 4   laxation

laxation of that grave Formality they were
oblig'd to wear in the Royal Presence, ZE-
LINDA came in; and giving him a little
Blow on the Shoulder with her Fan, Where
shall one expect to find ARIDANOR, *said
she*, but where there is the greatest Con-
course of Beauties?——— But I am resolv'd
to try how far your Complaisance will ex-
tend, when at war with your Inclination.
———You must pass some part of this
Evening at *Ombre* with me and another
Lady as far from handsome as myself, without any other Temptation in the World,
but the hope of winning our Money.———
What say you, my Lord! *continued she,
plucking him by the Arm after her free manner*, dare you accept the Challenge? or
cannot your Good-breeding furnish you
with Arms to resist the more potent Excite-
ments of your Desires to be in another
place? In some Cases, Madam! *reply'd he
gallantly*, what passes for *Cowardice*, is
really *Discretion;* and if that other Lady
should be like ZELINDA, a Heart susceptible
of Passion, and hopeless of succeeding,
might well seek Evasions to avoid so dangerous an Encounter.———But since it is
impossible for two Objects, tho' equally
charming, at the same *Time* to work the
same *Effect*, I am apprehensive of being
no further enslav'd than I already am, and
with Pride and Pleasure accept the honour
of

of your Summons. At five, *said she*, I
shall expect you, the Rendezvous is to be
at my Apartment; and because we are resolved to have you to ourselves, I will order my People to deny admittance to all
impertinent Interrupters. The greater Privacy, the more Contentment, Madam, *answered he*; you may depend on my Obedience and Impatience for the happy Hour.
There pass'd no more between them; having made this Appointment, she turn'd upon her heel, and went out of the Room,
with the same gay Air with which she had
enter'd it. ARIDANOR spent not much
time in guessing who the other Lady should
be she spoke of; he doubted not but it
was ELARIA, who, no longer able to contain the long-smother'd Passion of her Soul,
had prevail'd on the Good-nature of her
Cousin, to take this Method of bringing
them together, without plainly demonstra-
ting the Design of her own. He intended to
have told that Lady of the Invitation he
had receiv'd from ZELINDA, and that it
was his hope, as well as his desire, that
the third Person, who was to compleat the
Set, was no other than herself: but the
Drawing-room being extremely full of Company, and BARSINA one of the Number
who compos'd it, he forbore entering into
any Conversation with her that day.

The

The Hour being arriv'd in which he was
to go to ZELINDA's; he waited not till
the ſtriking of a ſecond Clock ſhould remind him his Preſence was expected: but
rather preventing than exceeding the time
prefixed, he went full of Contemplations
on what the Iſſue of this Viſit would be; but
little conjecturing the Truth, or in the
leaſt imagining the purpoſe for which he
was invited.

I told you, *ſaid ſhe to him, as ſoon as
the firſt Salutations were over,* that I had
an intent to puniſh you; but little did I
think the Mortification would have been ſo
ſevere as now it happens.——The Lady
who had promis'd to make one at *Ombre*,
has juſt now ſent word ſhe cannot come,
and you will be conſtrain'd either to paſs your
time with one who has it not in her power
to do any thing to make herſelf agreeable
to you, or acknowledge, by ſome faint
Excuſe for leaving me, that you had not
come, but for the hope of being more
pleaſingly entertain'd. If any body ſuffers
by this Accident, *anſwered he*, it can be
only yourſelf.——I am too ſenſible of the
Bleſſing of being admitted to a private Converſation with a Lady of your Beauty and
Accompliſhments, to be able to part with it
without the utmoſt Regret.——I am afraid
my Inclination will, in ſpite of me, get
the better of Good-manners, and you will

be compell'd more than once to look upon
your Watch, and remind me it grows late,
before you get rid of your Gueſt. I expected no leſs than this, *reſumed ſhe*, from
the well-known Gallantry of ARIDANOR ;
but to which-ever of theſe Motives, your
Inclination, or Good-manners, I am indebted for your ſtay, I ought to make it as
agreeable as I can : and ſince the deſign of
your coming was play, what think you of
a Game at *Piquet?* To which he having
agreed, Cards were immediately brought
in by her Woman, who no ſooner had ſet
the Table, than ſhe immediately withdrew,
ſhutting the Door after her.

They continued playing a conſiderable
time, but ZELINDA play'd the Game ſo ill,
that it might eaſily be perceiv'd her Thoughts
were employ'd a different way. ARIDA-
NOR alſo had his Cogitations, nor well
knew how to form a Judgment of her Behaviour ; but he remain'd not long in this
Dilemma : ſhe threw the Cards out of her
Hand on a ſudden, and affecting to ſtart at
ſomething which juſt then came into her
Head——— Bleſs me ! *cry'd ſhe*, what will
my Servants think that I have order'd myſelf to be deny'd to all the World, while
I am lock'd up in private with the moſt a-
greeable of his Sex !——— Theſe Words
opening his Eyes, he wonder'd at himſelf
that he had ſo long been dull ; and by her

Example,

Example, laying afide the Cards, Did the
divine ZELINDA think me fo, *faid he*, we
might have employ'd our time much better
than in this infipid Diverfion.——— But it
is not yet too late, *continued he, drawing
his Chair near to hers*, to repair what we
have loft——the future Moments may attone for the omiffion we have been guilty
of in the paft.——— How ftrangely you
talk, *refumed fhe*, is it impoffible for ARI-
DANOR to be alone with a Woman, who
is young, and accounted tolerably agreeable, without having fuch odd Fancies in
his Head? Whatever may be poffible to
me, *reply'd he*, I am fure it is not for the
enchanting ZELINDA to be feen by any
Man, without creating in him a Defire of
being alone with her. Well, *faid fhe*, it
muft be confefs'd, that you have the beft
turn of Raillery of any Man about Court.
——But prithee let's be ferious, or elfe to
Cards again. As much in earneft as you
pleafe, Madam! *rejoin'd he, taking her in
his Arms, and beginning to treat her with
fome Familiarities, which gave her indeed
no room to doubt fhe had been difappointed
in her Expectations.* Heavens! *cry'd fhe,
with an Air of Aftonifhment, and making
fome few faint Efforts to difirgage herfelf,* what is it you mean to do?——But I
fee what encourages you——you know well
enough my Husband is out of town——
that

that all my Servants are out of hearing——
that my Bed-Chamber is in the very next
Room——that I am but a weak Woman,
and that you are the moft engaging Creature that ever was born——but if ever I
give you fuch an Opportunity again——
It fhall be my fault if I make not the beft
ufe of this, *faid he, redoubling the Freedoms he had already began with her:* and
by this time fired with that Paffion, which
is often miftaken for Love, and is ordinarily more fuccefsful, he bore her to the
Chamber, to which, by forbidding, fhe invited him, and for fome Moments loft all
remembrance of both ISMONDA and ELA-
RIA.

Tho' this Amour was too fudden to afford much Delicacy, yet as ZELINDA was
a very lovely Woman, and of a humour
prodigioufly entertaining, it was not only to
oblige her, that ARIDANOR refolved to continue a Correfpondence with her of the
fame kind he had begun, nor were his
Tranfports feigned, or the Proteftations he
made her of an eternal Gratitude wholly
compofed of Deceit. In the midft of their
Endearments, fhe alfo threw off her Affectation, confefs'd fhe had long languifhed
for him with an unfpeakable Defire; that
fhe had appointed him to come with no
other view, than to try how far he liked
her; naturally concluding, that if he thought
her

her worthy his Addresses, he would not neglect so favourable an opportunity of making them. They parted not till it was very late, nor without mutual Assurances of frequently renewing those Delights, with which neither of them as yet were satiated.

This Darling of the Fair, the happy ARIDANOR, past the remainder of the Night in Contemplations perfectly pleasing : to be beloved by two such Women as ELARIA and ZELINDA, was sufficient to gratify the Vanity of any Man, and tho the Method the latter of them had taken to engage him, had something in it very extraordinary, yet imputing it to the Violence of her Passion, it did not in the least abate his Esteem of her.

Yet could not this Intrigue justly bear any other Name than that of an Amusement; it engross'd not the Soul, it chas'd no other Ideas thence; it was enough, that when they were together, that each was the sole Object of the other's Affections; apart they had different Sentiments, and the free Mind disdaining all restraint, refus'd admittance to no pleasing Image. One thing, however, ARIDANOR took care of, which was never to engage ELARIA in a particular Conversation when ZELINDA was present; fearing with reason, that the Jealousy of that Lady once alarm'd, might make her take some Steps which might put a stop to the Gratification of his Desires on this young Beauty.

Nor

Nor was he without apprehensions, that
all his caution in this Affair might be in
vain; he knew how far the innocent Lan-
guisher had already betray'd herself to her,
and it was highly probable that the next
time they were alone together, she would
also make her acquainted with the Declarations he had made to her; for which reason
he kept them, as much as possible, asunder,
by engaging either the one or the other in
Appointments with himself. As yet no
opportunity had offer'd, in which he could
take those advantages the Passion of ELA-
RIA had given him over her; and this Affair,
which from the knowledge of her Sentiments threatned so little difficulty in accomplishing, he found infinitely more hard
than he could have imagin'd. He was often
alone with her indeed, but then it was only
in such places as gave him no assurance he
should not meet with an Interruption. She
had no Apartment, as yet, assign'd her in
the Palace, and to visit her at her Father's
House, would have been far from advancing his Designs; to entreat her to accompany him to any place of privacy, he thought
would too plainly let her into his Reasons for
such a Request, and give a Shock to her Modesty, which would enable her to *refuse*,
tho' her Wishes should with the utmost ardency prompt her to *grant*.————Long
was he debating within himself what course

to take, and had till now, perhaps, been undetermin'd, had Chance not interpos'd, and put a period to the Conteſt.

As he was one day in the Apartment of HYANTHE, he heard that Princeſs call for EURIDICE, who was then walking in the Gardens of the Palace with ELARIA; he happen'd to ſee them as he was looking out of the Window, and immediately made an Errand down to tell her, that her attendance was required; on which, ſhe haſtily taking leave of ELARIA, that intended Victim of his amorous Flames was left alone with him. It preſently came into his Head, to make that place in which he firſt receiv'd the knowledge of her Love, the Scene of his accompliſhing it, and entertaining her with diſcourſes too pleaſing to her Wiſhes for her to break them off, ſhe was inſenſibly led to the Gate which open'd into the Wilderneſs; which he puſhing back with his Hand in order to go in, her good Angel, that moment, warning her of the Danger to which ſhe was about to be expos'd, Let us turn back, my Lord, *ſaid ſhe*, the wild Solitude of this place has nothing agreeable in it.—— Yet it was here, Madam! *anſwer'd he*, that I receiv'd that Inſpiration which makes all my Merit ——'twas here the God of Love firſt ſhow'd me what his Power could do—— Permit me to conduct you, and I will ſhow you that very ſpot of Earth whence came the

bliſs-

blifsful Arrow which fix'd me ever yours.
It was not in the power of ELARIA to comprehend the Myftery of thefe Words, and
while fhe was paufing on the meaning of
them, he took her by the Hand and drew her
into that Retirement, which feem'd, indeed,
defign'd by Nature for an Amorous Rendezvous.———On the ftill rifing Camomile
no Tracks appear'd to guide obfervance on
the wanderer's Steps, and the clofe meeting
Trees deny'd accefs even to the Eye of
PHOEBUS; a thoufand little Grots on every
fide, arch'd o'er with mingling Boughs, invited to repofe within their fweet recefs.
Can any thing, faid ARIDANOR, be more
indulging to the Mind than this delightful
Shade?———How could I here lie down,
forgetful of the World, its Cares, its noify
Pleafures, and quite diffolv'd and ravifh'd in
the Contemplation of ELARIA's Charms,
enjoy, in Theory, fuch Raptures as only fhe
herfelf could add to. Let any Woman
who has experienc'd the force of Love, confider and pity the Confufion of this unhappy Maid, divided between Fear and foft
Defire, ftruggling with all her might to
fmother both, yet both apparent to the
watchful Lover.———He took no advantage however of what he faw, nor prefs'd
her in any manner which could alarm her
Modefty, till they came to that Thicket where
he had overheard her Converfation with

N   ZE-

ZELINDA——but then catching her at once
in his Arms, and ravishing ten thousand
Kisses from her trembling Lips in the few
Steps he had to carry her, he bore her
to the inmost and most dark part of the
Grot, before, in the surprize this sudden
alteration of his Behaviour involv'd her in,
she had the power of making use of any
Arguments or Persuasions to oblige him to
desist.——'Twas here, *said he*, that Passion first took birth from Hope, and here
shall Hope expire in sure Possession, and
Passion receive its due Reward.——These
Words were accompany'd by Actions suited
to the meaning of them.——At first she had
not the power of entreating, and soon it
was too late ; the resolute ARIDANOR let
her know what 'twas he aim'd at, and accomplish'd it almost at the same time.——So
immediate was her Ruin, that before she
cou'd think by what means she might avert
it, there was no more to fear——it was not
now in Prayers, in Menaces, in Artifices, nor
even Heaven itself to save her ; the fatal Deed
was done, the cruel Transport over, irrevo-
cable Time not Destiny can recall, or make
what has been, to have never been :——
In floods of Tears her struggling Griefs
sought ease, and virtuous Resentment fain
would have found vent in keen Reproaches,
but more mighty Love here interpos'd, new
form'd her Words, and what was design'd
for

for Fury, expreſs'd only Tenderneſs; and all that her utmoſt Efforts could bring forth of upbraidings, was only, Oh ARIDANOR! too lovely cruel ARIDANOR, why have you undone me? And then immediately after, teſtifying that the fears of his future Unkindneſs were more terrible than the preſent ruin of her Honour; You will not love me always, *would ſhe cry.*————It is not to be ſuppos'd that ſuch a Man as ARIDANOR was wanting in his endeavours to make her ſatisfy'd with what had paſs'd between them, nor that loving to that infinite degree ſhe did, thoſe endeavours were altogether unſucceſsful. A Perſon truly inſpir'd with a great Paſſion, never wonders at, nor can condemn the Exceſs of it in another; and tho' thoſe Deſires with which the Soul of ARIDANOR was poſſeſs'd for the Enjoyment of ELARIA, were not of that kind which may juſtly bear the denomination of a perfect Tenderneſs, yet as he had always diſguis'd them in ſo artful a manner, as could make her believe them to be no otherwiſe, it was the ſame thing to her, and work'd the ſame effect as if in reality. At length, won over by his Arguments to think Obedience to the Laws of Nature no Crime but in Imagination, ſhe yielded to renew'd Endearments, and met the guilty Joy with equal Warmth and Tranſports inconceivable. Being ask'd by her, if her Couſin had be-

tray'd

tray'd the Secret of her Paffion to him, and
by that breach of Truft encourag'd him to
make an attempt of the kind he had done;
he affur'd her that fhe had not, and very
frankly confefs'd in what manner the knowledge of her Sentiments had reach'd his
Ears. But tho, in juftice to ZELINDA, he
clear'd her of this imagin'd Infidelity, he
gave ELARIA fome hints, that it would not
be prudent to make her any further a Confidante in the Affair.

With how much eafe do Men, when
once they go about it, banifh an Idea they
have been the moft violently charm'd with!
It is moft certain, that ARIDANOR had felt
for ISMONDA more than ever was in the power
of either ZELINDA or ELARIA to infpire;
yet that being a hopelefs Paffion, in giving
way to thefe Amufements, he found that
eafe which a Woman, in the like Circumftances, can feldom, if ever, arrive at, till
Death at once puts a period to her Love and
her Defires. He divided all thofe hours
which he could borrow from the Bufinefs of
the State, or his own domeftick Affairs, between thefe two Ladies, and for fome time
manag'd the Intrigue with both fo well, that
neither of them had the leaft Sufpicion that
fhe had a Rival in the other.

But while he was thus endeavouring to
forget ISMONDA, he obtain'd the Character
of being as happy with her, as his utmoft
Hopes

Hopes had once flatter'd him he should be :
That Servant-Maid who had discover'd him
in the Closet, found the Secret too mighty
for her Capacity to contain ; she cou'd not
forbear whispering it to some of her Companions, who happening to be of the same
Disposition, reveal'd it to as many more;
those imparted it to others, and so on, till
it became the common talk of all the inferior
Courtiers, and from them rose gradually to
the Ears of the Great ones. The Favour
she was in with the Princess, her Beauty, and
the Grandeur in which she liv'd, exposing
her to the Envy of the less Fortunate, she
wanted not a great number of those who
were glad of this occasion to blast her
Fame. BARSINA, scap'd not the News, and
having of late perceiv'd a more than ordinary coldness in her Husband, too readily,
for her Peace of Mind, gave credit to it.
The Princess was the only Person who dis-
believ'd it; she knew that ISMONDA had
ever behaved herself with an exemplary
Discretion and Modesty in the *Anatolian*
Court, and could not think she had de-
serv'd any other Character in *Caramania*;
however, she intended to speak to her of it
the first time she had an opportunity.

But what became of the enamour'd THE-
ODORE at this Report! Never before had
he experienc'd the Pangs of jealous Rage,
and unable to endure the first Emotions of

it,

it, he was going to her Apartment to reproach her in such terms as he thought her
Inconstancy merited from him ; but as he
was crossing a Gallery, which parted his
side from that of the Princess's Women, he
met DORASPE, who throwing himself at
his feet, conjured him to vouchsafe a private hearing of something which he had to
communicate. The Melancholy which appear'd in his Looks, and the Earnestness with
which he spoke, making it evident that
something very extraordinary had happen'd,
obliged the Prince to turn back ; and as
soon as they were together in his private
Closet, Oh, my royal Lord, *said that perplexed Nobleman*, never was a Mind tor-
tured with an Anguish superior to mine.
Cross'd in my Love, and wounded in my
Honour——IRENE, forgetful to what she
owes her Birth, has, in a mean Disguise,
forsook our Mother's House, and is retir'd
where search has yet been vain. ——A
Letter which she left behind her Toylet,
would persuade us the occasion of her flight
was only lest I should compel her to a Marriage with ERNESTUS, but the whole Country ascribes a different and more shameful
Cause. Some late Disorders have been ob-
served in her, which the Skilful will have
to be the Effects of Pregnancy; and much
I fear she has too much depended on her
Contract with MARMILLIO. ——Contented
should

should I be, if only she, who caused this Disgrace, were to endure the Infamy; but a Misfortune of this kind, reflects on all the Family of the Wretch so abandon'd, but most on me, as nearest in Blood, and once too in Affection.——Nor am I, *added he*, in loss of Honour only curs'd, ARBANES but this moment told me, that without I could prevail on IRENE to become the Bride of ERNESTUS, I must quit all hope of EURIDICE.—— There is something so very probable, *replied the Prince*, in the justice of the former part of your Fears, that I have nothing to offer for your Consolation; but that whatever Faults she may have been guilty of, she cannot so far demean herself, as not to add to the Honour of ERNESTUS, by becoming his Wife: you need not doubt, but that should even the knowledge of it reach his ears, he will still continue his Assiduities. And one thing, methinks, seems to forward your hopes, which is, that humbled by this Misfortune, she will no longer be refractory to your Desires. I would advise you, therefore, to be as secret as possible in the Affair; and while you press for the confirmation of your Happiness with EURIDICE, still keep their Expectations warm with the hope of IRENE: Feign some plausible Excuse for her remaining so long in the Country; and let them think she but delays, not denies what

N 4   you

you require. DORASPE, whoſe Mind was
full of inward Vexation, would fain have
engaged him in a longer Converſation, but
the Prince was not at this time in a fit ſtate
of humour to enter into long Diſcourſes ;
and pretending buſineſs, diſmiſſed him from
his preſence, with telling him, he would
talk further with him at ſome other opportunity.

But his impatience of ſpeaking to Is-
MONDA, being diſappointed by her being
not at her Apartment, when he went, Re-
collection repreſented to him, that it was
beſt not to accuſe her, till he could do
it in milder terms than as yet his Rage
would give him leave to do. He conſider'd that there was a poſſibility ſhe might
be wronged ; and if ſo, he knew very well
the greatneſs of her Spirit would not eaſily forgive an unjuſt Suſpicion, eſpecially
when declared with Ill-manners. He therefore reſolved not to ſee her in private, till
he had enough become maſter of himſelf to
talk to her with moderation ; and that what
he ſaid might appear rather as the effects of
thoſe tender Doubts which are almoſt inſeparable from Love, than as the dictates of
a jealous Reſentment, and a Paſſion which
look'd on itſelf as ill treated and deceiv'd.

The End of the Third Part.

PART

PART IV.

WHILE the Prince of CARAMANIA was labouring under the worſt Torments of the Mind, his unjuſtly ſuſpected Miſtreſs was rejoicing to find herſelf eas'd of the Perſecutions of his Rival. She had obſerv'd the Freedoms which of late had paſs'd between him and ZELINDA; and being perfectly acquainted with that Lady's Diſpoſition to Intrigue, did not doubt but that ARIDANOR had found the ſecret to pleaſe her. She was, however, prodigiouſly ſurprized to hear the Prince had been to viſit her; it not being his Cuſtom to come to her Apartment without ſending before, to inform her of it.——— LYSETTA had told her, that ſhe perceived an unuſual Gloom upon his Brow, and that he expreſs'd the utmoſt diſcontent at not meeting her at home. She alſo ſaw him the ſame Evening at the Princeſs's Apartment; and as Lovers eaſily underſtand
the

the Humour of each other, by their Eyes,
she thought she discover'd something in
his, that she was unacquainted with ; and a
certain Coldness and forced Civility in all
his Behaviour, the meaning of which she
could not comprehend : and being far from
guessing the truth, imputed the change of
his Countenance to the change of his Affections. Perceiving him the same the next
day when she saw him again, she made no
doubt but that the Charms of some new
Beauty had triumph'd over the Gratitude he
ow'd her, and began in secret to curse the
mutability of the Heart of Man.   Heartily
did she wish for MARMILLIO, whose coun-
sel, and perfect knowledge of the Humour
of his Prince, she imagin'd might have led
her through this Labyrinth, which at present seem'd so perplexing to her ; and having no body to whom she could impart
her Sentiments on this occasion, suffer'd
little less than the jealous and impatient
THEODORE.

In the mean time, the occasion of their
mutual Disquiets was not perfectly at ease ;
whilst Love was show'ring on him his choi-
cest Blessings in favour of the Fair, the wanton God prepared for him Perplexities at
home, which almost countervail'd the Pleasures he enjoy'd abroad. He had a Brother
whose Disposition was no less amorous than
his own ; he was also every way as well
qua-

qualified for Succefs ; feldom had he figh'd
in vain ; and wherefoever he carried his
Addreffes, the only certain way of depriving
them of their wonted Force, was not to hear
them. BARSINA, who had experienced the
Advantages a lovely Woman has by being
feen at Court ; where Beauty appears more
fplendid and illuftrious than it can do in a-
ny other Place, fent for a young Sifter, who
had more than a moderate fhare of Charms,
hoping that they might have the fame effect on fome Great Man, as thofe fhe was
miftrefs of, had work'd on ARIDANOR. AL-
MIRA, for that was her Name, was indeed
fo perfectly compleat, that fhe no fooner
appear'd, adorn'd and fet forth with all the
Advantages of Drefs and Grandeur, than fhe
attracted the Eyes of the whole Affembly : A
thoufand aching Hearts avow'd her Triumph,
a thoufand Stratagems were immediately
forming ; and fome too fuggefted by Honour, for the ingaging this new, and dazling
Beauty. But none was there on whom her
Charms had greater influence, than on the
Heart of IDOMEUS, the Brother of ARIDA-
NOR : He no fooner faw her, than he became enamour'd with her ; and no fooner
felt the Emotions of that Paffion, than he
fet his whole Wits at work for the gratification of it. He had a thoufand Opportunities, which the reft of her Admirers
wanted ; fhe was lodg'd in his Brother's Palace,

lace, was the Sifter of BARSINA; and by that
kind of relative Obligation, might take many Liberties with her, which from another would create fufpicion, and be look'd
on as too prefuming. Without feeming
therefore to make Love, he made it in the
moft effectual manner; and all that he did,
paffing for no more than the Complaifance
which was owing from him to the Sifter
of his Elder Brother's Wife, he was omitted in the Cautions given her how to behave to the others who declared themfelves
her Lovers; and he found the means to
fteal himfelf into her Affections, as though
without defign.——— She was young, unexperienced in the Artifices of Love, and
unknowing of the Snare laid for her, fell
into it with as much eafe as the watchful
Ruiner could wifh.———Being, in a manner,
one of the Family, he never wanted free
accefs to her Chamber; was frequently a-
lone with her; would fometimes pafs many
hours with her in reading; playing on the
Mufick, in which he was an admirable Pro-
ficient; or in telling her the Court-news.
The mutual liking which both teftified of
the other's Company, was afcribed by BAR-
SINA only to a conformity in their Hu-
mours; and ARIDANOR, who better knew
his Brother's Conftitution, was at this time
too much engaged in his own Amours, to
obferve that which was carrying on between
them.

them. Repeated Opportunities, and a certain Languishment in the Eyes of the fair ALMIRA, which she had not the artifice to conceal, at length embolden'd the impatient Lover to endeavour the accomplishment of his desires. And one day, when BARSINA was abroad, he took the advantage of being alone with her, and at once attempted and attain'd all that he wish'd, or hoped to enjoy. So swift the pleasing Ruin came, she had not time to *know*, much less to *avert* the Danger; and when compleated, could not be recall'd.

The difficulty of a Lover is to *obtain*; his Point once gain'd, 'tis easy to maintain his Power; and rarely, if ever, does that Woman, who has yielded through Inclination, repent so far of what she has done, as not to suffer the dear Youth to repeat those Joys by which she was at first abandon'd to the soft Perdition. IDOMEUS and ALMIRA, unfearing Satiety, and thinking themselves secure from all Discovery and Blame, indulg'd their mutual Flames to all the wild excess of guilty Rapture.——IDOMEUS, notwithstanding the natural Inconstancy of his Disposition, confess'd Delights in this young Beauty's Arms, which for a time engaged him wholly hers; and to the ravish'd Soul of fond ALMIRA, he seem'd more than mortal.——Each seem'd to vye with the other which should exceed in Passion,

fion, and moſt diſſolve in criminal Deſire.
——— But this was but for a time : Soon
the ſweetneſs of their too extravagant Bliſs,
was to be imbitter'd. ALMIRA found herſelf with child ; and by communicating the
knowledge of this Misfortune to her Lover,
perceived ſhe had not only the Melancholy,
and, if divulg'd, *Shame* of her Condition
to ſuſtain, but alſo, that the Author of it
ſeem'd rather more uneaſy for himſelf than
her. He talk'd of nothing but the Diſpleaſure of ARIDANOR, and the Reproaches of
BARSINA, and ſeem'd more to upbraid than
pity the Effect of their once fervent Love.
It is needleſs to ſay how terrible a ſhock
this muſt be to a Woman, who, in ſuch a
Circumſtance expects Conſolation only ;
and certainly deſerves it from the Man to
whoſe fatal and undoing Artifices ſhe is indebted for her approaching Miſery. 'Tis
eaſy to imagine ſhe felt all that Ingratitude,
and Tenderneſs abuſed could inflict ; yet
would not the Mildneſs of her Nature ſuffer her to ſay any thing which could be
called ſevere : but, when he deſired, that
both for his and her own ſake ſhe would
keep it ſecret, Alas ! *cry'd ſhe*, are Impoſ-
ſibilities to be expected from me ? ——— Am
I not in the Houſe with my Siſter, from
whoſe penetrating Judgment I might as
well hope to blind the Eye of Heaven, as
hide it long.——— And when, or how can I
re-

remove? What pretence have I for leaving her? Or, if I could invent one, to
whom should I apply? I have no Acquaintance here, no Bosom-Friend, to whom I
might impart the Mystery, and expect relief. Something must be done, *replied he
coldly;* and tho' the management of such
Affairs is more properly the business of
your Sex, than ours, I will endeavour to
find some Person with whom you may remain; but should the Secret be made known,
I think it will be infinitely less vexatious
to us both, to have the Suspicion light on
any other Man than me.———— It may occasion a Breach between ARIDANOR and
BARSINA, which never, perhaps, will be made
up.————I would have you, therefore, dear
ALMIRA! entirely to conceal your Tenderness for me, or that I feel for you. ——
But this, *pursued he, perceiving she was
bursting into tears at his words,* is all but
supposition.——I hope we may order it so,
that all those from whom we would conceal it, should have no conjecture of
the reason which induces you to remove,
which yet you need not think of for a long
time.

Reflecting within himself, that he had
not at the first discovery of this Event, behaved with that softness which he ought to
have done, he endeavour'd to repair that
Fault, by saying a great many kind and
ten-

tender things to her. But, alas! the little
Compaſſion he had teſtified for the Ruin he
had brought on her, had already pierced her
Heart too far, for all the Fondneſs that he
could afterwards expreſs, to remove. She
rightly judged, that thoſe Emotions of the
Mind, which in a ſurprize the unguarded
Soul ſends forth, are more to be believ'd
than all the Tongue can ſpeak, when Re-
collection has given room for Artifice; and
contemplating her Condition with Eyes
unprejudiced, ſhe ſaw the miſery of it, nor
could be blind to that proſpect of mingled
Infamy and Horror, which open'd itſelf to
her affrighted View.

Her Griefs, join'd to thoſe Diſorders natural to Women in the like Circumſtances,
threw her into ſuch a deep Melancholy and
Indiſpoſition, that ſhe was unfit for Company; ſhe kept her Chamber, and even
there avoided being ſeen as much as poſſible, even by any of the Family; ſhe fan-
cied that whoever look'd on her would
gueſs the occaſion of her alter'd Countenance, and gave way to ſo terrible a Deſpair, that had it been of long continuance,
muſt certainly have ended in Madneſs. Her
refuſing ſometimes, even to admit her Siſter, made IDOMEUS not attempt going into her Chamber; not that he doubted her
readineſs to accept his Viſit, but he thought
that to be received when all the World be-
ſide

fide were denied, would look too particular not to cause inspection into the reason
of so strange a Behaviour. Being vex'd at
the heart at her proceeding in this manner, he writ a Letter of Advice to her,
which one day, when with BARSINA he was
sitting with her, he slipt into her hand unperceiv'd by that unsuspecting Lady. The
Contents of it were as follows.

To the Lovely ALMIRA.

'WHY do you express a Terror left
' your Secret should be divulg'd,
' and at the same time take the most effectual
' means to make it so? — Can any thing be
' more contrary to Prudence than your Be-
' haviour? —— Will not your alter'd Looks
' put People on an enquiry into the oc-
' cafion? —And that unusual Sadness which
' fits upon your Brow, convince them that
' there is something more than Indisposition
' in the case? ——Why, my Dearest! have
' you so little regard either of yourself, or
' me?—— You fancy your Condition infi-
' nitely worse than it is: How many Ladies
' have been, and doubtless are now in the
' same, yet retain their accustomed Gaiety,
' and pass unsuspected by the most diligent
' observers? —— For Heaven's fake call your
' Reason to your aid, and consider what it
' is you do, and what it is you would a-
O   ' void.

' void.——It is yet a long time before the
' Myſtery is in any danger, but from your-
' ſelf, of being made known ; and you may
' depend on my Care to take ſuch mea-
' ſures as ſhall ſecure your Reputation, and
' afford you all the Conſolation you can
' wiſh.—— Reſume, therefore, your former
' Sprightlineſs, and let thoſe Eyes which firſt
' lit up my Love, ſtill ſhine, and bleſs me
' with their chearing Glances.—Nor let any
' Jealouſy of Love diſturb thy gentle Soul.
' Believe me, my Adorable, thou art now as
' dear, as charming to my raviſh'd Thoughts,
' as in the extatic moment of our firſt En-
' joyment.——How cruel are you then, to
' anticipate the worſt that Time or Age could
' do!—— How many blisful Hours have we
' loſt by this unkind Retirement !——Scarce
' could I ſuffer more, wer't thou inconſtant !
' Throw off then a Sadneſs ſo much an
' Enemy to Love, to thy Reputation, and
' to our mutual Contentment ; and let us
' once more haſten to thoſe Joys which
' only thou canſt give, and none can be
' capable of receiving in a manner more
' ſublime, than,

> ' My For-ever-lov'd ALMIRA's
>> ' Moſt paſſionately Devoted,
>>> ' And Faithful
>>>> ' IDOMEUS.
>>>>> ' P. S.

P. S. ‘ As a Proof of that Tenderneſs
‘ you have ſo often ſworn, I again entreat
‘ you will let me ſee you in publick to-
‘ morrow, which is the only means that
‘ can ſecure us that Happineſs in private,
‘ which I ſtill flatter myſelf you languiſh
‘ for, with the ſame Ardour you once con-
‘ feſs’d, and I ſtill feel. Adieu ! my Char-
‘ mer.’

As the chief reaſon of that Diſcontent
which had ſeiz’d upon her Spirits, was the
belief that ſhe was now grown indifferent
to the dear Ruiner, the hope that ſhe had
wrong’d him by an unjuſt Suſpicion, diſſi-
pated the greateſt part of it : and as her
Deſpair decreaſed, the force of Reaſon
ſtrengthen’d itſelf in her. She ſaw, indeed,
that ſhe had taken wrong ſteps for the concealment of what ſhe ſo much fear’d ſhould
be diſcover’d, and wonder’d how ſhe could
have been ſo loſt to Thought, as to be guilty of it. A thouſand and a thouſand times
ſhe kiſs’d the dear Teſtimony of her Lover’s
Truth, and reſolv’d not to delay Obedience
to the purport. She therefore order’d her
Woman, that ſame Evening, to let her Siſter know that ſhe was better, and deſired
her Company ; which that affectionate Lady rejoicing to hear, went to her immediately, and found her even beyond Ex-

pectation

pectation in fo fhort a time recovered. The
next day fhe dined at table with the Family, and fome Strangers, who happen'd to
be there that day.

The Gardens belonging to the Palace of
ARIDANOR being extremely pleafant, they
all adjourn'd to pafs fome part of the Mid-
day's Heat in thofe refrefhing Groves : As
they were walking up an Alley, which led
to that delightful Recefs to which they
were going, ARIDANOR, who happen'd to
be behind ALMIRA, faw that in plucking
a Handkerchief out of her Pocket, fhe
dropped a Paper; which he ftooping haftily
to take up, with a defign to reftore to her,
he faw it was his Brother's Hand. The
Surprize he was in, to fee it in a Direction
to a Lady, who, till fhe came to live at his
Houfe, he never had the leaft acquaintance
with, and fince had Opportunities too frequently for fpeech to have any occafion
that he could think on to employ his Pen,
made him alter his defign of returning it
to her : and as none in the company faw
him take it up, he put it into his Pocket,
refolving to inform himfelf of this Secret;
and imagining there muft be fomething more
than ordinary in it, he foon made an Excufe for leaving his Guefts, and retired to
his Clofet for the fatisfaction of his Curiofity.

I doubt not but my Reader eafily be-
lieves this Letter was that which IDOMEUS
had

had writ to the diſconſolate ALMIRA, to
perſuade her to take other meaſures than
thoſe her late Sorrows had obliged her to
give into, and indeed was the only one he
had at that time ever written to her. It
is impoſſible to know whether Aſtoniſh-
ment or Vexation was the moſt predominant in the Mind of ARIDANOR, at this
Explanation of his Siſter's, till now, myſterious Griefs, or if he more condemned his
Brother for his Attempt on a Woman ſo
nearly related to his Wife, or her for taking
ſo little care to conceal what had paſs'd
between them.——IDOMEUS has reaſon to
accuſe her, *ſaid he to himſelf, as ſoon as he
had done reading;* would any Woman, poſſeſs'd of the ſmalleſt ſhare of Senſe, have
acted as ſhe has done? Her Melancholy, her
Diſorders, which ſhe ſcarce aim'd at diſ-
guiſing, might, without the help of
this Letter, had we not all been blinded
by our good Opinion, have let us into the
whole Secret?——'Twas wrong in him,
however, to engage in an Intrigue with the
Siſter of BARSINA, nor can I eaſily forgive
him for the Diſquiets it may poſſibly
create.

He was for ſome time divided in his Sentiments, whether he ſhould take any notice
of the Diſcovery he had made, or not; but
fearing it might be further blazed, through
Negligence, or Imprudence, at laſt reſolv'd

not

not to conceal it. As he was in thefe Cogitations, his Brother, who wondred at his
leaving the Company in fo abrupt a manner, came to feek him: he found him with
the Letter in his hand, which, as foon as he
faw him enter the Room, he threw to him,
telling him he ought to be more careful to
whom he writ; and fince he had been
guilty of fo great a Fault, in a Family where
nothing but the utmoft Refpect was owing
from him, he fhould at leaft have warned
the Perfon with whom he committed it,
to be more cautious of his and her own
Secret. Thefe Words, and the fight of the
Paper, fo much confounded him, that for
fome moments he was wholly bereft of
Speech; and when he had the ufe of it,
was little able to employ it in any Arguments, which might excufe what he had
done. ARIDANOR, however, continued
not long the Severities with which he had
accofted him; he could not heartily condemn that in his Brother to which himfelf
had but too great a Propenfity, and more
frequently indulg'd than check'd.——And
as his greateft Perplexity was, left what had
happen'd fhould come to the knowledge of
BARSINA, he charg'd him to behave to
ALMIRA in fuch a manner, as fhould prevent her from giving any caufe of Sufpicion, either through Inadvertency, or Defign. They had a long Converfation together

gether on this Subject, which, at their return to the Company, ARIDANOR excufed,
by faying, he had juft received fome Letters
from the Country, which required an immediate difpatch in anfwering. But the
firft time IDOMEUS found himfelf alone
with ALMIRA, he gently reproved her for
the omiffion fhe had been guilty of, in
not burning his Letter, which he told
her he had found, his Brother having defired fhe might not know he was in the
Secret. Suppofe, *faid he*, that BARSINA,
or ARIDANOR, had taken it up, it was but
our Good-fortune which prevented our Secret from being difcover'd by thofe from
whom 'tis moft our Intereft to conceal it;
they were both in company when the fatal Scroll dropp'd from your Pocket, and
might have feen it as well as I. Poor AL-
MIRA trembled all the time he was fpeaking, and could not for a good while get
over the Horror it involv'd her in, but even
to think how near fhe had been to what
fhe moft dreaded : This danger made her
readily agree with him to be more cautious
and circumfpect than they had been, to be
lefs frequently alone together than formerly, and on no occafion whatever to behave in a manner which could awaken Obfervation to a Scrutiny into their Difpofi-
tions. IDOMEUS did not fail to acquaint
his Brother with the Difcourfe which had

pafs'd

pafs'd between them, and the Refolutions
which both of them had taken to regulate
their future Conduct; yet was he not perfectly at cafe: he knew very well, that to
keep the Condition in which ALMIRA was,
eternally a Secret, there were a million of
Chances againft one; and could not defend himfelf from the Apprehenfions he
was daily perfecuted with. This Accident
ferv'd to let him know, that BARSINA was
more dear to him, than he himfelf was
fenfible of before; fince it was the fole
fear of giving her difquiet, which occa-
fioned fo much in his own Breaft.

To make the Proverb good, which fays,
*That one Vexation feldom arrives without
being attended by others*; while he was
ftruggling with that which the knowledge
of IDOMEUS's Intrigue had given him, he
received no inconfiderable Addition to it,
through the Jealoufy of ZELINDA. That
Lady, as well as others, had heard the Story,
at which the whole Court diverted themfelves, of ARIDANOR having been lock'd up
in the Clofet of ISMONDA; and remembring
that fhe had formerly obferv'd he had treated her with a Complaifance, which might
very well be taken for Love, and that of
late they had feem'd to fhun each other's
Prefence, and if they met, behav'd with
a Coldnefs and Difrefpect unbecoming
of either of their Characters; in reality,
fhe

she made no doubt but there was an Amour, and that perceiving it grew talk'd of, they had agreed to affect this Indifference in publick, that the Fondnefs which in private they indulged, might be lefs liable to Sufpicion.—— She had an extraordinary opinion of herfelf, and thought that when she condefcended to favour a Man in the manner she had done ARIDANOR, he ought to banish all former Impreffions from his Soul, and devote it wholly to her. But refolving to be fully affur'd, that he was falfe, before she gave him any Proofs that she was jealous, she carefully obferv'd all his Words and Actions, when in the prefence of ISMONDA; but that indrawn notice of his Eyes, which was occafion'd by Refentment, and the Fears of relapfing into his former Paffion, she took for the Effects of Caution, and imagin'd he look'd not on her, becaufe fenfible he could not look on her without difcovering too great a Tendernefs: In fine, every thing she heard, every thing she faw, more confirming her that the report of the Amour between them was not without reafon; she was beginning to confider in what terms she should reproach him, and more expofe her Rival to the Ridicule of the Court. She happen'd to be alone in the Palace-Gardens one Evening, indulging her Ill-humour, when she faw ARIDANOR pafs fwiftly by, unfeeing her, and go directly

rectly to the Gate which led into the Wilderness. The Solitude of the Place which
she saw him enter, and the haste he made
to arrive at it, had very much the Air of
an amorous Rendezvous, and she bless'd
her good Stars for giving her this opportunity of detecting him. She consider'd
not long therefore, what it was she had to
do; but following the Path he took, was
in the Wilderness a very few Minutes behind him: She left not a Grotto unsearch'd
all the way she went; but Fortune not yet
directing her to the right, so much time
was spent, that she disappointed not the
Persons she fought, of accomplishing the Intent they had in meeting. 'Tis impossible
to express how much Vexation this Reflection gave her; but resolving to make
herself amends, by the Revenge she would
hereafter take on the Reputation of her Rival, she prosecuted her search: and being
at last come to that place, which was in
reality the Scene of their stolen Joys, she
saw ARIDANOR come out of the most dark
and shady Recess the whole Wilderness afforded, and to her unspeakable Surprize,
not ISMONDA, but ELARIA in his hand.

Never were any Persons more cover'd
with Confusion than were these three; 'tis
difficult to say which of them had the greatest share of it; ELARIA at perceiving her
Amour

Amour was difcover'd ; ARIDANOR that it
was fo, by the very Woman, from whom,
next his Wife, he would moft carefully have
conceal'd it ; or ZELINDA, at finding herfelf miftaken in the Object of her Jealoufy.
This Lady, however, had the advantage of
firft being able to recollect herfelf, and with
the moft fcornful and malicious Smile fhe
could put on, accofted ARIDANOR in thefe
terms : I thought to have found you in other
Company, my Lord, *faid fhe*; nor could I have
believ'd, without having been convinc'd of it
by my own Eyes, that a Girl fo unexperienc'd in Converfation as ELARIA is, could
attract a Man of your Lordfhip's nice Gouft
half a minute ; much lefs could I have
thought (*continued fhe, turning her Eyes
on* ELARIA, *whofe Face through fhame
and anger was dy'd all over with a fcarlet
blufh*) that the Modefty of my feemingly innocent Coufin would have fuffer'd her to
make amorous Appointments.———— Heavens ! *cry'd fhe,* How could you be fo inde-
cent, fo horridly wicked, as to commit fuch
an Action in the face of the Sun ? If Love
be a Crime, *reply'd* ARIDANOR, *vex'd to
the very Soul,* I know not why it fhould be
abfolv'd at one time more than another——
Circumftances indeed may very much ex-
tenuate or alleviate the Guilt, and you know
very well, Madam! that there are fome
Ladies who think that Paffion is in itfelf

an

an excuse for breaking through the strictest Tyes.————Let us talk no more, therefore, I beseech you of this matter, ELARIA is perfectly innocent of what you seem to accuse her————I met her here by chance, and thinking it unbecoming in a Lady of her Age to give way to those Reflections the Melancholy of this solitary Place inspires, offer'd my Service to conduct her back to the Palace. Extremely well, *resum'd* ZELINDA *peevishly*; and your Lordship too came here to indulge Chagrin?————But now I think on't, that may possibly be true; you like being alone sometimes, or you would not have had patience to have been lock'd up for two long hours in the Closet of Ismonda.————You see, my Lord, *added she, seeing him look prodigiously amaz'd at these Words*, that I have a perfect Intelligence of your Amours, and it must be confess'd indeed, that you are a Man of admirable Address to carry on so many different ones at the same time, all too with Women of the Court, and yet preserve yourself from the Effects of Jealousy. Jealousy, Madam! *answer'd he*; if I gave cause for it, it would be of little service to the Woman who testify'd it to a Man of my Disposition; and I would, above all things, have her who thinks my Esteem worthy of her regard, to abstain from that pernicious Passion, 'tis the very poison of Love; nor
would

would I search for Pleasure in a Bed of
Snakes, tho' cover'd with a VENUS. Most
Heroically indeed, *said* ZELINDA, you assert
the Prerogative of your Sex; and since you
are of this humour, I congratulate your
Choice; from the tame humble Spirit of E-
LARIA you fear no Reproaches: perhaps she
thinks your Love, at least the show of it, so
great a Favour, that she ought not to repine
at the share you bestow of it on others—But,
continu'd she, with the utmost spite, for
fear she should not enough know how to
express her Gratitude, ORSAMES shall in-
struct her what to do, nor will I delay one
moment acquainting him with the Honour
his Family receives in the deference you pay
his Daughter. I hope then, Madam! *answer'd*
he, provok'd beyond measure at this Menace,
that you will not forget to inform him also,
that however ELARIA may have prov'd,
there are other Ladies of his Family who do
not love Ingratitude, and chuse rather to
confer Favours unask'd, than refuse them
when they are the Merit of a long Service.
ZELINDA could not avoid hearing this Reproach, tho she seem'd not to do so; and
having turn'd upon her heel just as she had
concluded the Words already repeated, was
tripping away as fast she could when he began to speak, and turn'd not back to continue a Conversation in which she had little reason to expect she should have the better.   Poor

Poor ELARIA, who all the time she had
been there, had not utter'd a Syllable, nor
dared, through Fear and Shame, scarce to lift
up her Eyes, now turn'd them on her dear
Undoer; and pouring forth at the same
time a torrent of Tears, What will become
of me, my Lord?' *said she* ; this cruel Woman will certainly betray me, and I no
more can see my Father's face. This La-
mentation was more cutting to ARIDANOR,
than all the Raillery of the other had been,
not only that he was really concern'd for
what might happen, through the Pride and
Jealousy of her offended Rival, but also
that this Demand included something of a
Dependance on him, which was no ways
pleasing to him. Disguising therefore all
the fears he had of ZELINDA'S making good
her Threats, Why are you terrify'd, my dear
ELARIA? *said he:* Your Cousin will not
certainly be so base as to expose you, nor
can I think she would be the bearer of a
Theme so unwelcome to a Father's ear.——
Besides, she can at most but have a suspicion
of our Amour, and will not venture to
make what is in her but bare Imagination,
pass on others for current Truth.————Depend on it, *continued he, finding her still
unsatisfy'd,* there is nothing in what you apprehend, nor do I foresee any Consequence
from this Meeting, half so bad as the present
Discomposure of your Mind.——Clear up
then,

then, my Angel, thy drooping Spirits, and believe I suffer more in the sight of thy Disorders, than any thing which can ensue will make thee feel.

He pursued his Endeavours to re-assure her all the way they walk'd together, and being come within the Garden, he took leave and separated, because the Walks were at that time very full of Company. BARSINA and ALMIRA, with some other Ladies, appear'd at a little distance ; to whom he immediately join'd himself, as did ELARIA with two or three who she saw together of her acquaintance.

But too true a Presage had this unhappy Beauty of her approaching Misfortune : At her coming home, she found ZELINDA there before her, and by her Countenance, as well as by the mingled Grief and Indignation which she beheld in that of both her Parents, immediately knew the Evil she so much dreaded, had in reality befallen her. The Servants, who at her entrance into the Room, were waiting, being dismiss'd, she continu'd not a moment in suspence. ORSAMES, with all the marks of the most violent Fury in his Voice and Eyes, took her by the trembling Arm, and accosted her in these Terms : Is it possible, *said he*, that thou can'st so much degenerate from thy Mother's Virtue, and thy Father's Spirit, as to submit thy self the Slave of base Desires?
and

and forgetful of thy own and House's Honour, yield to become the loose Diversion
of an idle Hour, and fit Society for none but
such as live by Prostitution?——Speak, *pur-
su'd he, (growing more fierce, as by her Tears
and Tremblings he found more reason to believe the Truth of what he had heard)* art
thou this Wretch?————Hast thou at once
cast off all Sense of Honour, Virtue, and
Reputation? With infinite difficulty, she
at last faintly answer'd, No; but was unable to bring forth more: and the griev'd Father still persisting in his Reproaches, which
were seconded by the more peircing, if possible, Sorrows of a most tender Mother,
struck so deeply to the fair Offender's Heart,
that she fell fainting at their feet, happy,
in a short Cessation, from the Pangs of
Thought, and the just Sense of her forlorn
Condition, and the sad State to which she
had reduced Parents to whom she had been
so dear.

Never was a Scene more moving, the
mournful Mother weeping o'er her ruin'd
Offspring; the unhappy Father divided between Grief, and Rage, and Pity; Revilings
fill'd his mouth, but the fast Sighs which
every now and then broke in upon his
Words, and stopp'd the struggling Accents,
declar'd there was a stock of Tenderness
within, which would not suffer him to forget it was his darling Daughter he was about

to

to curfe : with fudden ftarts like thofe
which Frenzy caufes, he ftood and gaz'd on
the ftill dear, tho' ruin'd Beauty, while the
no lefs afflicted, tho more patient Mother,
was with ZELINDA, employing their utmoft care to recover her from the Swoon
which confcious Guilt and Shame had
thrown her in. As foon as fhe came to herfelf, Alas! my dear Coufin, *faid* ZELINDA
to her, how griev'd am I to fee you thus !——
yet I could not refolve to fee you perfevere
in a Conduct fo difhonourable to yourfelf
and Family, without informing thofe of it,
who only can oblige you to regulate it for
the future.——You know, that when firft
you made me the Confidante of your unhappy Paffion for this deftructive ARIDA-
NOR, I did not fail to fet before your Eyes
the danger of giving way to it ; I reminded
you of his being married, and of the Gaity
of his Humour, which would not fuffer him
to lofe any opportunity you fhould give him
of taking an advantage over you——You
promis'd then to take my Counfel, and
while I hoped you did, forbore to utter the
leaft fyllable of what I knew : but you
have now undone yourfelf in every Circumftance ; and would to Heaven, *added
fhe, with a feign'd Sigh,* I were the only
Perfon about Court to whom your Secret
were divulg'd ; but you have been too pub-

P   lick

lick in your Amour, not to have made even
BARSINA herself fufpect it.

In this manner, under the pretence of
Friendfhip and Concern for her, did fhe go
on perfecuting her unfortunate Coufin,
and while fhe feem'd to pity the Condition
of fo near a Relation, fecretly triumph'd in
expofing a Rival; who, too artlefs and unexperienced in Deceit, had nothing to anfwer
which cou'd make her be thought lefs guilty
than fhe had been reprefented : and the perplex'd ORSAMES, and her troubled Mother,
had from her own Behaviour but too many
Confirmations of the Truth of what they
had been told by ZELINDA. Refolving
therefore to put a period to an Affair fo
offenfive to Virtue and to their Honour,
they fent her down to a Relation they had
in a far diftant Country, ordering her to
be ftrictly watch'd and kept there, and even
deny'd the privilege of Pen or Paper, to
the end that fhe might have no means of informing ARIDANOR of the place of her
abode, or encourage him to attempt any
thing for the recovering her.

But, alas! this laft part of the Charge
they gave, might have been fpared; the
Paffion of ARIDANOR had already had its
fill, and had no longer thofe impatient
Longings, which put Men on combating
with the greateft Difficulties for the Gratification.———He was, indeed, infinitely
vex'd,

vex'd, that ZELINDA had fo much reafon to
fufpect her Coufin had given him the fame
Proofs of an ungovernable Tendernefs which
herfelf had done, becaufe he doubted not
but that her Jealoufy, join'd with that natural Propenfity moft Women have to expofe the Faults of each other, would make
her difclofe this to as many as fhe was acquainted with.

ELARIA was no fooner fent away, than
he was inform'd of it by fhe who had occafion'd it : If I have not the power over your
Affections, *faid fhe haughtily*, you fee I can
over thofe you have preferred to me; ELA-
RIA is gone to a place, whence all your
Love will not afford you the means to
bring her back.———This News was far
from being fo great a trouble to him, as
ZELINDA imagin'd it would be; and taking
this opportunity, which her Jealoufy gave
him, of being rid of both at once, he told
her, that he loved Tranquillity too well, to
part with it on any confideration; that he
would not be made uneafy by the Caprice
of any Woman; and that, in fine, he found
fo much trouble in Intrigue, that he would,
for the future, confine his whole Defires in
the compafs of BARSINA's Arms. Thefe
Words were like a Thunder-clap to the
Ears of her to whom they were addrefs'd;
who, expecting no fuch matter, and ftill
finding too many Charms in him to con-

fent

fent to part with him, endeavour'd to excufe the Rafhnefs of her Jealoufy, and pro-
tefted fhe would no more pry into his
Amours, or attempt to difturb him in the
purfuit of any thing in which he propos'd
a Pleafure. ARIDANOR wanted not Good-
nature ; and feeing fhe had fubmitted to
his Humour fo much beyond what he could
have imagin'd from one of hers, he thought
it too much to humble her Spirit, and
make miferable her Love at the fame time :
and taking her in his Arms, affur'd her he
would not only forgive what fhe had done
on the fcore of ELARIA, but alfo continue his Affections to her, with the fame
Tendernefs and Ardour as before. Now
was fhe as happy in her own Imagination,
as fhe had made her Rival wretched ; but
how long Fate permitted her this Bleffing, we
fhall hereafter difcover. The chief Subjects
of our Hiftory, THEODORE and ISMONDA,
at prefent claim our Attention, and require
we fhould look into the means by which
they were extricated from that Labyrinth
of Perplexities, in which we lately left them
bewilder'd and involv'd.

The good Princefs, extremely troubled
at the Report which was fpread abroad of
her Favourite, delay'd not to acquaint her
with what fhe had heard : And the Vexation ISMONDA conceiv'd at fo unlook'd-for
an Injury to her Reputation, had been in-
fup-

supportable, had it not been sweeten'd by the belief, that this it was which occasion'd the late change in the behaviour of the Prince toward her; and that it was not to the want of Constancy in him, but the Jealousy he had of hers, she ow'd the Estrangement which for some days had been between them. She attested her Innocence with all the Asseverations which her desire of being clear'd could suggest; and fearing that every thing which came from herself might be liable to Suspicion, entreated her royal Mistress to put the same Questions to ARIDANOR as she had done to her : No, no, *said she*, I am enough convinc'd by what yourself assures me; but if I were not so, should little depend on what a Lover should alledge in the Vindication of a Mistress.——I doubt not but ARIDANOR has honour enough rather to endure the reproach of not having been able to please a Lady, than boast the Favours he receives from her, to the prejudice of her Reputation. After some little time being past m these kind of Discourses, ISMONDA retir'd to her own Apartment, to ruminate on what she had heard, and consider what means were best for her to make use of, in order to undeceive the Prince from the unjust Opinion she now not doubted but he had entertain'd of her. And not having any opportunity of holding a long Conver-

sation,

fation, he having refrain'd vifiting her of
late, fhe refolv'd to write to him in fuch a
manner, as fhould engage him to come, if,
with his good opinion of her Conduct, he
had not alfo thrown off all the Tendernefs
he once had for her. Nothing being fo
terrible to a Woman of Spirit as Sufpence,
fhe delay'd not to enforce the Certainty of
her Fate, by employing her Pen to him in
this manner.

ISMONDA *to* THEODORE, *the dear Sovereign
of her Soul, and only Ruler of all her
Thoughts, her Words, and Actions.*

'WHAT Terrors, O thou Life of all
'   my Joys! what a wild Maze of
' Fears, and Doubts, and Jealoufies, and
' difmal Apprehenfions, have you fuffer'd
' me to be involv'd in!——What from
' your alter'd Looks and Abfence could I
' conjecture, but that I was undone, my
' Love grown taftelefs, and my Form un-
' pleafing to your Eyes?——— 'Tis but
' this moment that I had room to hope it
' was not fo, and blefs the happy Scandal
' which gives me leave to think 'tis not In-
' difference, or Hate, that keeps you from
' me.——Be angry, be jealous, but ftill re-
' tain your Love; my Innocence and un-
' fhaken Faith will, fome time or other,
' find the way to chafe the two former
'   Paffions

' Paffions from your Breaft, but the latter,
' if once loft, is never to be retriev'd. ——
' The Princefs, more kind than THEODORE,
' has inform'd me of the Afperfions thrown
' on me on ARIDANOR's fcore.——Oh,
' Prince! could you believe me guilty?—
' But I will not accufe you, but myfelf,
' for not revealing to you fooner the whole
' Hiftory of that Affair, which has occa-
' fioned me this Taint in my Reputation,
' and you thefe needlefs Jealoufies. ——
' Think, I conjure you, my dear Prince;
' but fure I need not remind you of it;
' would I have forfaken the faithful Arms
' of fond ADRASTUS, my native Country,
' and unnumbred Friends, forfeited that
' Virtue which from my Youth I ftrictly had
' preferv'd, and run fo imminent a Hazard
' of lofing my Character, equally precious
' with my Life; would I have done all this
' to purchafe THEODORE's Affection, if I
' had thought it fo mean a Bleffing, as to
' confent to part with it in exchange for
' ARIDANOR?—— O, 'tis an Injury to my
' Underftanding, as well as to my Truth,
' to imagine, that, after thee, there is any
' thing in the whole Sex befide, capable of
' attracting my Regard.——Hafte then, and
' do me juftice.——I live not but for thee,
' and if fo wretched to be depriv'd of that
' only Aim, only Ambition of my defiring

' Soul,

‘ Soul, thy Love, ſhall return to *Anatolia*,
‘ and die, as I have liv'd,

My Ador'd THEODORE's,

ever Paſſionately Faithful,

ISMONDA.

She ſent this by a Page, whoſe Fidelity
ſhe had experienc'd, ordering him to obſerve when the Prince was retiring to his
Cloſet, as it was his Cuſtom to do every
Evening, and deliver the Paper into his
own hands. He fail'd not to obey punctu-
ally the Directions ſhe gave him, and inſtead of loſing any time in writing, he ſent
her back for anſwer, by word of mouth,
that in half an hour he would ſee her at
her own Apartment. There needed no
more to convince this perfect Lover of her
Truth, than telling him ſo; · he had this
juſt opinion of all great Spirits, that whatever Faults they may be guilty of, they never are of Inſincerity, and that her's was
of that kind, he had had a thouſand In-
ſtances.———He now gave to the Winds
his late Diſtruſt, and if he had any Uneaſineſs, it was in the reflection how much
he had been to blame, to give any entrance
to a Paſſion ſo mean as Jealouſy,———
Her rightly applying the cauſe of his eſtrange-
ing himſelf in the manner he had done for
ſome days, was a new Charm to his tranſported

ported Soul.——— How much beyond her
Sex, in every thing, is that Woman! *said
he to himself;* how far from their little
Doubts, and impertinent Apprehenfions!
She fees into the moft hidden Meanings,
and never judges but with almighty Reafon.——— And then again would he cry
out, How unworthy am I to poffefs fuch
Excellence, who could fufpect her for any
thing lefs than fhe appears?——She is a-
bove Hypocrify, or the meaner views
of vulgar Spirits, and in every Action denotes a generous and difinterefted Flame,
and that not the *Royalty,* but the *Perfon*
of the happy THEODORE, was the Object
of her Affections.

With thefe rapturous Reflections did he
entertain himfelf while alone; but when
they met, where is the Pen which can defcribe the mighty Joy! The Pleafures of Reconciliation between Lovers is unfpeakable,
unconceivable but by thofe who have felt
what 'tis to have the fwelling Heart long
torn with anxious Doubts, and fired with
Jealoufy, at once reftor'd to Peace, to Happinefs, and all that Heaven of Felicity which
mutual Love affords. Such was the ftate
this blifsful Pair now fhar'd, and never had
rewarded Paffion fill'd them with Extafies
more divine, more infupportable to ftagger-
ing Senfe! They were fo great, they fcarce
were to be borne, and to have been more,
                                        muft

muft have been fatal.——So little is Humanity capable of fuftaining the Emotions of
the Spirit, were there not Bars by Nature
planted to reftrain its force.

In the firft Truce from fpeechlefs Tranfports, and tumultuous Bliffes, Ismonda re-
counted to him the whole Hiftory of the
Perfecutions fhe had received from Aridanor, and the reafon of her concealing him
in the Clofet; but by what means this
came to be known, neither of them could
imagine. No body could think that Aridanor had fo little Honour, as to mention
fuch an Adventure, had it terminated to his
advantage, much lefs when it happen'd fo
much the contrary. And the Fidelity of
Lysetta, who was the only Perfon whom
Ismonda had trufted with that Affair, had
been too much experienced, to permit a
doubt on her fide. It gave alfo fome little
Difcontent to Theodore, to be told that
their Amour was fufpected, efpecially by a
Perfon, who, being an unhappy Rival, might
fuffer the Dictates of his *Malice*, to overcome thofe of his *Generofity* : but Ismonda
foon eas'd him of thofe Apprehenfions, by
telling him, that fhe had obferv'd a more
than ordinary Familiarity between him and
Zelinda; that fhe was more than half affured, there was an Intimacy between
them; and that he had now forgotten the
Paffion he formerly profefs'd for her, and
the

the Treatment he had receiv'd from her.
It was eafy indeed at this time, to drive
all Confiderations, which were uneafy, from
a Mind which refolv'd to devote itfelf wholly to Love and Pleafure.——He fpoke of it
no more, and the remaining moments they
pafs'd together, were only taken up with
mutual Endearments.

To add to the Contentment of this once
more happy Prince, he receiv'd news from
MARMILLIO, that LUTETIA was not only
brought to bed, but alfo, that the Child fhe
went with expired almoft as foon as born,
and that that Favourite had made a confiderable progrefs in the Task enjoin'd him,
of reconciling her to the thoughts of being
no longer of fervice to the pleafure of her
Prince. All dangers of any difcovery from
that quarter being pretty well over, he refolv'd, for the future, never to be guilty of
any thing, which, if ISMONDA were witnefs
of, would caufe any Interruption in their
Love. He had nothing now to apprehend,
but on the fcore of EURIDICE; and Do-
RASPE continually folliciting him to influence ARBANES to confent to their Nuptials before thofe of IRENE with ERNESTUS
could be celebrated; he thought it beft to
yield to his Entreaties, and at the fame
time oblige himfelf, by feeing that Lady
difpofed of, in a manner which would take
from her the power of expreffing a Tendernefs

derneſs which laid him under a Neceſſity
of diſſembling with her; yet ſtill retaining
a deſire of delivering MARMILLIO from the
ſame Troubles himſelf had been involv'd
in, he oblig'd DORASPE to ſign the Articles
of Marriage for IRENE with ERNESTUS, before he mention'd the Affair to ARBANES.
But that being done, the other was well
pleaſed to conſent to the promotion of
his Neice, not doubting but that of his
Son would immediately enſue. DORASPE
was tranſported at the Conceſſion, ARBA-
NES well ſatisfied, EURIDICE was the only
Perſon who expreſſed any Reluctance; and
it was not without ten thouſand Vows, and
well-diſſembled Ardours of continued Tenderneſs, that THEODORE at laſt perſuaded
that Lady to yield to be another's, that ſhe
might with the more ſecurity be alſo his.
Every thing, however, being at laſt agreed
on, the Day for the Wedding was appointed, and all neceſſary Preparations were order'd to make it magnificent, and becoming the Quality of DORASPE, and the paſſionate Affection he had for EURIDICE.

But as if the love of Intrigue was to be
inſpir'd in all who came to the Court of
Caramania, CLEOMENES, the Brother of
MARMILLIO, who ſince the ſuppoſed Diſgrace of that Favourite, was obliged to be
continually there, becauſe the Prince could
with leſs ſuſpicion both give and receive
Letter_s

Letters through his means, than any other, became extremely enamour'd with ATTA-LINDA, the Wife of a certain Nobleman, diſtinguiſh'd by the Title of *The Good-natured Lord.* What firſt gave it him, was, that happening to find a moſt paſſionate Love-letter directed to his Wife, and alſo Thanks for having received ſome Favours beyond what could be taken for the effects of an ordinary Complaiſance, he put it into his Pocket very carefully; and the firſt time he was alone with her, return'd it to her without the leaſt Marks of Jealouſy or Ill-humour; ſaying only, *My Dear, I wiſh you would be more careful of Papers of this nature. 'Twas well it fell into no other hands than mine.* ——*If it had, I know not what might have become of your Reputation.* ——— His Valet, who happen'd to be in the next Room, and overheard what paſs'd between them on this ſcore, thought the manner of his Behaviour ſo very extraordinary, that he could not forbear relating it to ſome of his Intimates, they to others, and ſo on, till it became a Jeſt, not only through the Court, but the whole Town.

This Story, of which CLEOMENES was inform'd, gave him encouragement to hope he ſhould not be unſucceſsful in his Amour. What more could a Lover wiſh, than ſuch a Proof of the eaſy Temper of the Husband he would impoſe upon,

and

and the amorous Difpofition of the Wife
he would feduce! ———— The Beauties of
ATTALINDA no longer gave him Pain, but
Pleafure; becaufe he look'd upon her as
already won, even before he had an opportunity of attempting it, which he imagin'd
was all that was neceffary to make him
mafter of his utmoft Defires. But, in fpite
of the hopes with which he flatter'd himfelf, he found it not fo eafy a matter as he
had imagin'd, to get the liberty of fpeaking to her alone; fhe was fcarce ever to be
feen without ARSINOE with her; and the
prefence of that Lady, who declar'd herfelf a profefs'd Enemy to Intrigue, and all
the Diverfions of the gay World, gave him
many difappointments, when he came fully
prepared with Arguments, and Affurance
to back them, for the declaration of his
Paffion. The little conformity which there
appear'd to be in the Notions of thefe Ladies, the one always alert and chearful, the
other grave, formal and precife, made every
body wonder at the Intimacy between them;
but CLEOMENES, who made it his bufinefs
more than any other, to dive into the Reafon, could not help believing, that the demure Countenance might be capable of
concealing an Inclination which might render her no unfit Companion for the o-
ther, who more openly betray'd the Im-
pulfe of Defire. As he was one day rumi-
nating

nating within himſelf in what manner he
ſhould proceed, either to make a Confidante
of this Shadow of his Miſtreſs, or contrive
ſome Stratagem which might render them
leſs inſeparable, a young Nobleman, called
MAZARES, with whom he was extremely
intimate, came to viſit him; and after ſome
little diſcourſe on ordinary Affairs, Dear
CLEOMENES, *ſaid he*, I have a Secret to diſcloſe to you, but you muſt firſt ſwear to
me never to reveal it; and alſo, that you
will aſſiſt me to get rid of a very trouble-
ſome buſineſs, which I have unwarily engaged in. I never knew People, *replied
he*, make a Confidant of any one, without
having ſome deſign in it. ——They make it
a favour that they truſt us, but always require ſomething of us which more than
counterbalances the Pleaſure of being privy
to the Affair.——But ſetting Raillery apart,
purſued he, you need not doubt either my
fidelity or readineſs to oblige you in any
thing in my power. I do not, *reſumed the
other*; nor is the Task difficult, nor to a
Man of your Conſtitution diſpleaſing, that
I would enjoin you.—— But not to keep
you in ſuſpence, you muſt know I have, for
a conſiderable time, had an Intrigue with
one of the fineſt Women about the Court,
but the Affair is now grown old to me—I
have had her ſo long, that ſhe is become as
inſipid as a Wife;—— yet does ſhe not perceive

ceive it, but continues so surfeitingly fond,
that I am quite sick of the very Name of
Love ; and were it not that I have a sort of
an Inclination to a very fine Woman that
is continually with her, I should find some
pretence or other to quarrel with her : but
such is my unhappy State, that I cannot
see ATTALINDA without her ; and am therefore compell'd to dissemble a Passion for the
one, in hope the other will discover by my
Eyes that I have a real one for her.

ATTALINDA ! *cried* CLEOMENES, *more
surprized than can be well express'd*; then
it is ARSINOE whom you have possess'd,
and are grown weary of. Your guess is
right, *answer'd* MAZARES; I have had her
these two Months, and yet the unreasona-
ble Creature expects I should meet her with
the same warmth of Inclination, as when
the Novelty of her Beauties fir'd.——— See,
continued he, what a Billet I receiv'd from
her this morning ! In speaking these words,
he plucked a Letter out of his Pocket, and
delivering it to CLEOMENES, he found it
contain'd these words :

*To the dear Charmer of my Soul, the Ac-
complish'd* MAZARES.

' I Have not closed my Eyes this Night.
' ——— All my hours since last I saw you,
' have been taken up with the cruel Reflections

'flections you caused in me. —— For Hea-
'ven's sake, what did you mean by saying
'you were obliged to go out of Town for
'a whole Month? Do you think it pos-
'sible for me to live so long without you?
'Or that I can, with any tolerable degree
'of patience, think I have forfeited my
'Honour, for a Man who is capable of sup-
'porting such an Absence? —— But I hope
'you spoke it with no other design than
'to make trial of my Love; for I cannot
'see that any Motives, unless it is Inclina-
'tion, should necessitate your going. ——
'However it be, I beg to be assured, and
'that you will not delay one moment the
'satisfaction I require. —— I am now a-
'lone in my Chamber, whence I will not
'stir till I have your Answer. —— I wish
'you would come yourself, and by your
'dear presence this Morning, make some
'reparation for the disquiets of the Night.
'—— If you are free from Company, let
'the Bearer conduct you to the impatient
'Arms of

'   The Languishing

'   ' A R S I N O E.

Good Heaven! *cry'd* CLEOMENES, *as soon
as he had read it,* who will hereafter trust
a Woman when she professes Virtue! ——
The seemingly cold ARSINOE, write a Bil-

Q   let

let of this nature!—scarce can I believe my
Eyes! —Oh, *replied the other*, your reserv'd
and coy Women in publick, are ever the moſt
warmly amorous in private. ——The Con-
ſtraint they put on their Inclinations, in
denying themſelves thoſe innocent Liberties which others take, makes them break
out with greater force and vehemence, when
once they give a looſe to them. —— If
you would chuſe a Miſtreſs, who, like *Se-
mele*, wiſhes to be clasp'd in Flames, ſeek
her among the demure and the preciſe.——
The gay and chearful Girl, evaporates her
Spirits in ſuperficial Gallantries ; but the ſly
ſilent Maid longs for more ſubſtantial Joys,
receives the welcome Bliſs with double ea-
gerneſs, and never knows Satiety. But ſhe
can give it, *interrupted* CLEOMENES, *laughing*, or you would not complain of this Diſpoſition in ARSINOE. 'Tis true, my Friend,
replied the other, the Delights of Love, when
purſued with too much violence at firſt,
degenerate by ſwift degrees into Diſguſt.
——The Bleſſings which ARSINOE afforded,
were too extravagant to laſt ;—— and what
was once the higheſt Joy tranſported Nature
was capable of receiving, is now become a
Toil, a kind of Penance for paſs'd Pleaſures. I underſtand you, *ſaid* CLEOME-
NES, you have entertain'd a new Deſire,
and for that reaſon would be glad to get
rid of your Obligations to the old one.
You

You have hit it, *refumed* MAZARES, and you are the Perfon I have pitch'd on to do me this Service.————. I have many reafons to believe it is not *me*, but my *Sex*, that AR-SINOE is in love with; tho' did fhe really find any thing in me more agreeable than the generality of Mankind, I doubt not but the fuperior Perfections of CLEOMENES might, with a very little pains, oblige her to change her Sentiments in his favour. I will not return your Lordfhip's Compli-ment, *faid he*, becaufe 'tis natural to flatter the Vanity of thofe from whom we expect Favours.——— But, pray, of what ufe can I be to you in this Affair ? ——— You know ARSINOE and ATTALINDA are fo perpe-tually together, that there is not a poffi-bility of fpeaking to either of them, with-out making a Confidante of the other. As for that, I have laid a Scheme, *replied* MA-ZARES; we will go together this Afternoon, to vifit ATTALINDA, where I know we fhall find ARSINOE. You fhall intreat the favour of the latter to give you leave to talk to her one moment in private; on which fhe will certainly take you into the Garden, or fome other Room.———You may then make what Pretenfions you pleafe to her; and to fecond your Arguments, I will give you this Letter, which you may tell her I dropp'd by accident. ——— Accufe me of want of that Care I ought to have taken

of

of her Reputation ; fay any thing which Invention can fupply you with, to render me
unworthy of the happinefs of her Love ;
but be fure to make no mention of that I
have for ATTALINDA.—— I am certain
you may prevail on her as far as you pleafe,
if you follow thefe meafures. ——— At
leaft, if you fhould fail in that, you will
not in convincing me of your Friendfhip,
and engaging my utmoft Gratitude and Services. CLEOMENES, who, all the time he
had been fpeaking, had been cafting about
in his mind, how to make the beft Advantage of this Adventure for his own Defigns, readily promifed to do all that was
defired of him ; and as foon as they thought
it a proper hour, both went to the Houfe of
ATTALINDA, where, as MAZARES faid, they
found ARSINOE ; but fome other Ladies alfo
being prefent, gave CLEOMENES an inexpref-
fible fatisfaction, that while he was entertaining ARSINOE, as he had agreed to do, the o-
ther would be deprived of the opportunity of
making his Addreffes to ATTALINDA. Nothing could be more furprized than was AR-
SINOE, at his defiring to fpeak to her in private ; fhe having no farther acquaintance with
him, than by feeing him fometimes in the
Drawing-Room, or at Church. She withdrew
with him, however, to a Window, which
was a confiderable diftance from the Company ; but he not thinking it remote enough
for

for what he had to fay, Madam, *cry'd he*, I beg you would permit me to attend you to fome other Place; what I have to communicate, will, I fear, occafion fome Diforders in you, which you will not think proper fhould be obferv'd by fo many Witneffes. Tho', *faid fhe*, I cannot comprehend what bufinefs a Perfon fo much a ftranger to me, as CLEOMENES, can have with me, yet I fhall make no fcruple of lift'ning to it; believing my Character and Reputation are too well known to you, to encourage you to entertain me in any manner which may be offenfive to that ftrict Referve and Modefty by which I regulate my Conduct. It was as much as he could do to reftrain a Smile from breaking out at thefe words; but compofing his Countenance to as much Gravity as was poffible, Would to Heaven, Madam, *anfwered he*, that all who have the bleffing of converfing with you, were as zealous for your Honour as CLEOMENES will foon have an opportunity of proving himfelf. There needed no more to make her as impatient for going with him, as he exprefs'd that fhe fhould do fo. She found there was fomething myfterious couch'd in what he faid, and was eager for an Explanation.—— She therefore led him into ATTALINDA's Clofet, which happen'd to be open, and was at the end of a long Gallery, between which and the Room where they

Q 3 left

left the Company, were many others, which
secured whatever pass'd from the hearing
of any but themselves. But for the greater
Surety, as soon as they enter'd, he made fast
the Door; which observing, she look'd a little confounded at, I beseech you, Madam!
said he, be not in any apprehensions of
danger from my proceeding; what I do, is
to preserve your Honour, not attempt a
violation of it. In speaking these Words,
he oblig'd her to sit down, and placing himself by her, immediately took out the Letter which she had written to MAZARES, and
which that treacherous Lover had given him
on purpose to show her.——Do you know
the Contents of this, beautiful ARSINOE?
said he. Let any one judge what a Woman
who pretended to the severest Virtue, must
feel at finding herself thus expos'd; at first
she rav'd, deny'd that she had ever written
it, and cry'd it was a Plot contriv'd to blast
her Reputation: but CLEOMENES soon
brought her to talk in another manner, by
convincing her that he was but too well
assur'd of the Condescensions she had made
MAZARES, relating to her many other par-
ticulars of her Behaviour to him, which
made her know he must have had the
whole History from that unfaithful Man.

What, *cry'd she, bursting into Tears, so
soon as he had done speaking*, is it possible
that he should be so monstrous a Villain to

be-

betray the Faults his Perjury has made me guilty of!——Oh wretched Woman, *conti-nu'd she*, what will become of me? my Reputation, which is dearer to me than my Life, is loft for ever. No, Madam, *re-join'd she*, I believe the Secret is only lodg'd in my Breaft, which, be aſſur'd, I would ſuffer my Heart to be pluck'd thence, e'er I'll part with it. But wherefore, *ſaid she*, for what Reaſon did he make you his Confidant?—— To reveal that, *anſwer'd he*, I muſt be as guilty to him as he has been to you; but yet, *continu'd he, after a little Pauſe, as tho' he was divided in his Sentiments whether to proceed or not*, I cannot ſuffer a Lady, ſuch as the incomparable ARSINOE, to be injur'd in a manner ſo cruel and ſo baſe, without giving her warning of the Villany deſign'd againſt her, much leſs can I conſent to be a ſharer in the Guilt.—— Know then, Madam, that all I hitherto have ſaid, has been by his Commiſſion—— He is grown weary of your Charms, and would transfer the right you have given him over you to me, while he with greater liberty purſues the yet untaſted Sweets of ATTALINDA's Beauty.—— He bid me addreſs you in the manner of a Lover, and to prepare your Heart for an Impreſſion in my favour, permitted me to ſay whatever I thought fit, excepting only that of his Love to ATTALINDA, or that I came by the

know-

knowledge of your Amour with him from his own Mouth: on all fides therefore you were to have been made the Property; but I have a Soul too honeft to join in the Deceit———have confefs'd to you all the Truth of the Affair, and ask no other Recompence, than that you will not betray me to him——Make your own ufe of what I have reveal'd, or to forget or reclaim the ungrateful Rover; but let him not know that I entertain'd you with any other Difcourfe than that of my own Paffion. You are as generous as he is the contrary, *faid fhe*, nor fhall you have reafon to repent fo difinterefted a Proof of your Good-nature: ——But, *purfu'd fhe, looking kindly on him*, is there no way by which I may return the Obligation? Yes, Madam! *anfwer'd he, who having his head full of the Thoughts of* ATTALINDA, *did not prefently fathom the meaning of what fhe faid*, 'tis greatly in your power to contribute to my Felicity; I am not lefs fenfible of the Charms of ATTALINDA than is MAZARES; you have an influence over her, and by inclining her to favour me, you may doubly reward the Service I have done you, and, at the fame time, punifh my ungrateful Rival. 'Twas eafy to perceive a vifible Alteration in that Lady's Countenance at this Requeft. MAZARES, *anfwer'd fhe peevifhly*, has render'd himfelf equally unworthy of my Refentment,

ment, as of my Love; I defpife the Wretch,
nor from this moment will ever think of him
but with the utmoft contempt; ——but as for
ATTALINDA, fhe is wholly taken up with
young PHILARCHUS: I wou'd not have you
give way to Defires, which I am certain will
be unavailing——leave it to the vile MAZARES
to love and to defpair; I would have you
as happy as your good Qualities and Ac-
complifhments deferve, which is infinitely
more than ATTALINDA, were fhe kind,
could make you——for be affur'd, a diftant view of her is beft; fhe has a thoufand
Imperfections, which difguft thofe who are
permitted a nearer Converfation with her,
nor would PHILARCHUS fo long have devoted himfelf to her, were it not for the
rich Prefents fhe is continually making him;
which, to a Man of his narrow Fortune,
are too acceptable not to engage the return
fhe expects from them.———But tell me,
*added fhe, taking him by the Hand, and
gently preffing it,* is there nothing elfe in
which I can oblige you? Nothing, Madam!
*anfwer'd he, by this time being perfectly
inform'd what it was fhe aim'd at,* in which
I dare hope you will. You wrong me
then, *return'd fhe haftily,* by Heaven there
is nothing in my power I will refufe you——
think, therefore, if there is no other Lady
with whom I have an Intereft, whofe Love
might make you happy——I dare anfwer

for

for her, whoever fhe be, fhe cannot long
hold out againft fo many Charms as you are
mafter of, efpecially when I fhall repeat all
your Perfections over to her in fuch Terms
as cannot fail to raife Defire.——Inftruct me
then which of the Train of Beauties that
grace the *Caramanian* Court, you wou'd
moft gladly have in your Arms this moment;
——I have fworn to do my utmoft to bring
her to you, and you need not doubt but I
will keep my Promife.

ARSINOE was a very lovely Woman, and
the new Paffion with which fhe now was
animated, added a frefh luftre to her Eyes,
and a more lively red upon her glowing
Cheeks; CLEOMENES was naturally amorous, and when urg'd in this manner, muft,
indeed, not have been a modern Man, to
have been without thofe Emotions fhe fo
plainly aim'd to infpire in him——They
were alone—the Door fhut——fo many
Temptations joining with that which Curiofity afforded, made him but little hefitate
what Anfwer he fhould make; he took her
in his Arms, and crying, Who that had the
privilege of chufing, not only in the Court
of *Caramania*, but in the whole World befide, would think any but ARSINOE worthy his Regard, proceeded to Freedoms
with her of that kind, which I muft leave
to the Reader's Imagination to reprefent ;— I
fhall only fay, that they were not difpleafing

to

to her, and, telling him further, that since
he had her Vow, she could not refuse the
Performance of it, if requir'd, yielded
without even a shew of Reluctance to all
he attempted, exacting from him only a
Promise that her Reputation should be safe;
which he protesting to preserve inviolably,
some moments were past in those Extasies,
which, MAZARES had before acquainted
him, were in the power of this Lady to bestow and to receive.

At their return to the Company, whoever had been sensible in what manner they
had pass'd the time of their absence, would
have been surpriz'd to see much less appearance of Confusion in the face of AR-
SINOE, than in that of CLEOMENES; relying
on her Character, and the good Opinion
her pretences to Virtue had establish'd in
the World of her, made her enter with all
the assurance that the most perfect Innocence could have worn: but CLEOMENES
could not restrain his Blushes at the sight
of MAZARES and ATTALINDA, conscious
of the Crime he had been guilty of to
both, injuring the one by carrying to another some part of the Ardours he had
vow'd to himself he would reserve entirely
for her, and betraying that which he had
so faithfully promis'd the other to keep secret. MAZARES, however, who little suspected him either for his Rival, or Deceiver,

was

was impatient to know the Event of his Converſation with Arsinoe, and therefore took leave of the Ladies in a ſhort time. Cleomenes having been introduced to their acquaintance but by his means, had no Excuſe to ſtay behind him, and was neceſſitated to anſwer to all the Interrogatories made him by his Friend, before he had any time to reflect in what manner it was beſt for him to reply. He would not, however, let him know the ſudden Conqueſt he had obtain'd over the Lady, who had that very moment ſent ſo paſſionate a Declaration of Love to himſelf, leſt the Pique it might give his Pride, might occaſion him to reproach her with her Inconſtancy, and by that means ſhe alſo be provok'd to unravel the whole Diſcourſe between them concerning Attalinda. He told him, therefore, that he had found her not conſenting to the Profeſſions he had made her, nor yet not altogether ſo averſe, as to give him any great occaſion to fear he ſhould not be able to do him the ſervice he required, of eaſing him of the trouble of her Affections. Mazares was perfectly contented with this Account, nor imagin'd there was any thing more had paſs'd between them, than what he was acquainted with : Arsinoe, as ſhe had promiſed Cleomenes, not breaking out into any Demonſtrations of Rage, which might give him occaſion to believe himself betray'd by the Person whom he had trusted.

But in a very few days after, that Lady had an opportunity of venting the secret spite she had conceived against him. The long-wish'd moment at last arriv'd, in which he told ATTALINDA that she was the dearest thing on Earth: but nothing could be more unwelcome to her, than such a Declaration; she was herself too deeply engaged with PHILARCHUS, to think of any other Man, and also knowing him to have been the Darling of her dear Friend ARSINOE's Soul, he of his whole Sex was the last by whom she would suffer herself to be address'd. She express'd her Sentiments on this occasion with all the plainness imaginable, protesting she would acquaint his Mistress with his Ingratitude and Falshood: nor did she fail to do as she had said; and ARSINOE, glad to be told it by her, immediately writ him a Letter as full of Upbraidings as the other had been of Fondness, forbidding him ever to see her more, and loading him with every opprobrious Name which witty Malice could invent. But her Indignation was now depriv'd of all its power of giving pain, and he could have been very merry with her Resentment, had he not discover'd by it that ATTALINDA was, in good earnest, resolv'd to put a period to his Hopes. He communicated this Letter, and

the

the Converſation he had with ATTALINDA,
which occaſion'd it, to CLEOMENES, who
had alſo his ſhare of Pain and Pleaſure in
the hearing it : It delighted him above mea-
ſure, that ſhe had repulſ'd him with ſo much
Vigour; but then the Apprehenſions, that
for the ſake of her dear PHILARCHUS, ſhe
would alſo treat himſelf ſo on the like occaſion, embitter'd all the Sweets of her Behaviour to his Rival ; and this Conſideration, together with that of the Probability
there was that ARSINOE would endeavour
to prejudice him in the opinion of that
Lady, made him defer for a time declaring
the Paſſion he had for her; but endur'd
Agonies in this Reſtraint, which not all the
Favours he receiv'd from ARSINOE could
atone for.

But while he was thus languiſhing for
ATTALINDA, and but vainly endeavouring
to forget her in the Arms of ARSINOE, an
Adventure happen'd to him; which, if it
did not wholly engroſs his Thoughts, took
up ſo much of 'em, at leaſt, as to make
him induſtrious for an Explanation of it.
One day, when he was abroad, a Letter was
left for him by an unknown Perſon, in which
he found theſe Lines.

To the Agreeable CLEOMENES.

‘ IF your Eyes do not very much belye
‘   your Heart, there is a ſtock of amo-
‘ rous Inclinations there, which it is im-
‘ poſſible

‘ poffible for the faint Charms of ARSINOE
‘ to take wholly up.————I affure you there
‘ is a Lady, who looks on the regards you
‘ pay the Leavings of MAZARES, with a fe-
‘ cret Contempt of the Choice you have
‘ made.———If therefore you do not think
‘ yourfelf bound to an eternal Conftancy
‘ to one, who never had the leaft fhare of
‘ it in her own Soul, either to you or any
‘ other, caft your Eyes round the Circle,
‘ and give a proof of that Penetration you
‘ are fo much fam'd for, by difcovering in
‘ the Countenance the Heart which lan-
‘ guifhes for you.———— To direct your
‘ fearch, I muft inform you that fhe is
‘ young, gay, a Woman of Quality, and,
‘ if the Opinion of the World may be
‘ taken, not unlovely.———— She is every
‘ day at Court, it was there fhe firft be-
‘ held you, and was charm'd; and to take
‘ from you all fears that her Paffion aims
‘ at Marriage, to which I know you have
‘ an Averfion, fhe is already wedded, and
‘ can have no other view, than to prove
‘ herfelf

The moft Lovely CLEOMENES's

      moft Paffionately Devoted.

There was nothing in this Billet more
furprizing to him, than to find, that not
only his Intrigue with ARSINOE was difcover'd,

cover'd, but alſo, that ſhe had been the Miſtreſs of MAZARES. She was by the generality of the World, taken for a Woman
of the moſt ſevere Virtue that could be,
and how this kind Unknown came to have
ſo perfect a knowledge of her Humour and
Affairs, ſeem'd to him the moſt aſtoniſhing
thing in nature. He ſometimes imagin'd it
had been written by herſelf to try his Con-
ſtancy, but then the Hand being vaſtly different, and the little probability there was
ſhe would uſe any other in ſuch a Buſineſs, made him reject that Suppoſition. The
Earneſtneſs with which he look'd in the
Face of every Lady in the Drawing-room,
who had the leaſt Conformity with the Perſon deſcrib'd in the Letter, gave ſo much
Diverſion to her who wrote it, as half countervail'd the Vexation ſhe was in, that he
could not yet diſcover who ſhe was.

In this Dilemma we muſt leave them for
a ſhort time, the more material Affairs of
their Superiors having now found a turn as
perplexing as unlook'd for.

The End of the Fourth Part.

PART

PART V.

SMONDA had but juſt begun to taſte the Sweets which Reconciliation yields, when a new and unexpect- ed Interruption inform'd her no ſettled Tranquillity could be hoped for, in an Amour ſo doubly criminal as was hers. She was ſitting in her Cloſet indulging the delightful Contemplation of rewarded Love, and the Perfections of her admired THEO- DORE, when LYSETTA told her a Perſon deſired to be admitted, who ſaid he came from *Anatolia*, and was commiſſion'd by ADRASTUS to attend her. Tho' at every Meſſage from that injur'd Husband, ſhe felt Emotions which only the Guilty are capable of knowing; yet ſhe was now ſeiz'd with an unuſual Diſorder, a Fluttering and Con- fuſion of Spirit, which at that time ſhe was unable to account for: She order'd, however, that the Perſon who occaſion'd it ſhould be introduced, which as ſoon as

R   he

he was, he deliver'd her a Letter, in which
he found thefe Words.

To my Regardlefs, but ftill Lov'd
Ismonda.

'   HOW great my Difappointment was
'   to fee the *Anatolian* Lords return
'   without you, I need not go about to de-
'   fcribe; you know too well the tender
'   Paffion of my Soul, to be ignorant that
'   nothing could be more afflicting, more
'   fevere.—You gave me, however, a reafon
'   for your ftay, which, if real, I ought to
'   be pleas'd with, tho' I cannot approve;
'   little lefs of Policy, and more of Love,
'   would have made me blefs'd; but that
'   time is paft, and I will therefore add no
'   more on what cannot be recall'd; what is
'   to come, is fufficient to take up all my
'   Thoughts.——You have now no longer an
'   excufe for abfence, my Brother refufes to
'   accept the Title of one of the *Magi*, and
'   thofe Interceffions which have deprived
'   me of you, are now as infignificant to
'   my Intereft, as they have been prejudi-
'   cial to my Peace of Mind.———I beg,
'   therefore, that you will fet forward for
'   *Anatolia* with all poffible Expedition; I
'   have fent a Perfon to conduct you, un-
'   der whofe care you might truft yourfelf
'   a much greater Journey.——— I can no
                                    longer

' longer live without you, and fhould you by
' any vain Pretence endeavour to delude my
' impatient Wifhes, I fhould, regardlefs of
' my Ruin, and forgetful of what I owe my
' Royal Mafter, come in Perfon to bring
' you back—O therefore let me owe that to
' yourfelf, which elfe I am refolv'd to be in
' Poffeffion of by my own Power, and that
' right the Law has given me over you.——
' I now *entreat* you as a *Lover*, but would
' have you remember, that when I pleafe,
' I may exert the *Husband*, and *command*
' you.———Drive me not to Extremities,
' I conjure you, for the fake of both of us,
' but haften to redeem that Character your
' late Behaviour has but too much forfeit-
' ed, and reftore long abfent Peace and Hap-
' pinefs to

> Your paffionately Tender and
>
> ever Faithful Husband,
>
> ADRASTUS.

' *P. S.* One thing I had forgot, ufe me
' well in the Perfon of my Friend, pro-
' vide an Apartment near you, if you have
' not room for him in your own : he is
' entirely a Stranger in *Caramania*, and has
' no other Bufinefs there, than to oblige me
' in conducting you. Once more, my
' deareft ISMONDA, for a fhort time, *Adieu.*

Had

Had a sudden peal of Thunder cleft the
Palace-Roof, and threaten'd all beneath
with inftant Death, fcarce could it have
ftruck more terror into the guilty Soul of
this Fair Criminal, than did the reading this
Letter inflict on her.——She faw the Patience
of her injur'd Lord was now entirely worn
out, fhe was left without Excufe, or almoft
a poffibility of continuing any longer in
Caramania, and the thoughts of quitting
her dear Prince, was fomething fo terrible,
that nothing is more ftrange, than that fhe
had prefence enough of Mind to reftrain the
burfting Grief from fhowing itfelf in her
Countenance in the prefence of this Perfon,
who fhe eafily perceiv'd was fent as a Spy
on her Actions. She forc'd herfelf however to treat him with all imaginable Complaifance, and told him, that in every thing
in her power fhe would teftify the Love fhe
bore ADRASTUS; and as he had defir'd in
his Letter that he might be lodg'd near her,
fhe would order an Apartment for him ad-
joining to her own : But, *faid fhe,* I know
not yet how far I may be able to comply
with his Defires of returning to ANATOLIA;
the Princefs will, I know, exert her Authority to keep me with her, and ADRASTUS
is not ignorant what we both owe to the
Birth and Virtues of that excellent Lady,
nor the Obligations I in particular have to
her, both by Duty and the tendereft Affection.

Nor

Nor is the juſt Ismonda to be told, *anſwer'd
he*, how far all other Duties and Affections
are to yield to thoſe which Marriage makes :
Nor can my Lord believe that Princeſs, who
is herſelf ſo bright an Example of Conjugal Love, would, on any conſideration, occaſion a breach of it in others————But, I
hope, *continu'd he*, there will be no need of
Arguments to convince you how highly re-
quiſite it is you ſhould return to a Husband
to whom you are ſo dear, and who is reſolv'd to be no longer ſeparated from you.
All things muſt give way to Neceſſity, *ré-
ſum'd ſhe coldly*, but, if you pleaſe, we
will talk further of this Affair ſome other
time. The fatigue of ſo long a Journey
requires repoſe, my Servants ſhall conduct
you to a Chamber, and in the mean time I
will acquaint Hyanthe with the Buſineſs of
your coming. In ſpeaking theſe Words, ſhe
rang for her Attendants ; two of the Grooms
of her Chamber immediately entering, ſhe
commanded them to ſhow the Stranger to
the beſt of thoſe Apartments ſhe could
call her own ; and, as ſhe had ſaid, went
directly to the Princeſs, and communicated
to her the whole Affair, telling her that nothing could be ſo afflicting to her, as the
Thoughts of quitting her Service, and entreating, ſhe would permit her ſtay ; and
that ſhe might not be forc'd from her, to in-
tercede with the Prince for ſome Poſt of

Ho-

Honour which might engage ADRASTUS to
come alſo, and live with her in *Caramania*.
The Princeſs paus'd ſome time before ſhe
made any Anſwer to this Requeſt; and after
ſhe had, as ſhe thought, juſtly weigh'd the
Reaſons of the other, I can never, *ſaid ſhe,*
too gratefully acknowledge the Obligations
I have to your Friendſhip, in preferring my
Service to the Society of ſo tender a Husband as is ADRASTUS; I have many times
reflected on ſo unexampled a Proof of your
Regard for me, with all the Admirations it
merits : but notwithſtanding all this, my
dear ISMONDA! the cenſorious World is of
another Opinion; in ſpite of all the Arguments I can bring in your Vindication, they
will aſcribe your ſtay in *Caramania*, to
other Motives than your Friendſhip for me.
In fine, I need not repeat the unwelcome
Name, ARIDANOR has the glory of inſpi-
ring you with Inclinations to the prejudice of
ADRASTUS, nor do I ſee how it will be at
all conſiſtent with that Fame all Women of
Virtue ought to endeavour to preſerve, if
you tarry longer from the Arms of that indulgent, yet impatient Husband.——Cou'd
he, indeed, be prevail'd on to live among
us, your Reputation, as well as his Deſires,
would be ſecur'd, and Friendſhip no longer
be at variance with Duty. Oh it remains in
you, my Gracious Princeſs! *reply'd* ISMON-
DA, to reconcile theſe ſeeming Oppoſites—

were

were half the Honours he enjoys in *Anatolia*, offer'd him in *Caramania*, I know he
gladly would accept the Change——Influence therefore, I once more conjure you,
the Royal THEODORE to make this Tryal of
him; which if he should refuse, I shall have
good cause to doubt his Love, not he to
question mine. Well, *said* HYANTHE, to
prove how unwilling I am to lose you but
for your own Honour's sake, I will do as
you desire, nor do I doubt to gain the Prince
to equal all the Dignities your Husband is
possess'd of through my Father's Favour——
but I foresee the Proffer will be ineffectual,
he will make the same Objection against
leaving the Service of his Royal Master, as
you have show'd Reluctance to quit a Mistress——however, nothing on my part
shall be left undone. ISMONDA had no time
to answer this Condescension, any otherwise than by a low Reverence; some Ladies
coming in, broke off the Conversation,
and ISMONDA disengaging herself as soon as
possible, went to seek the Prince, to relate
what had pass'd, and prepare him for the
Request HYANTHE had promis'd her to make
him.

Nothing cou'd be more transporting to
THEODORE than this new Proof of her Affection: He prais'd her Love and Wit in
terms proportionable to the Idea he had of
them, and told her, that as her Tenderness

R 4   had

had never yet fail'd to supply her with some
pretence or other for an opportunity of suf-
fering him to indulge his Passion; he doubted not but Fate would at last be kind, and
by some unexpected Event, consent to bless
their mutual Ardor, and save her the pains
of farther Invention. Neither of them i-
magin'd ADRASTUS would quit his Interest
in ANATOLIA, even tho the Prince of *Caramania* should offer him the half of his
Dominions. The time therefore that ISMON-
DA could hope to gain by this Stratagem,
was no longer than it would take up to send
a Messenger to him, and receive an Answer
from him; she then doubted not but she
should a second time be remanded back, and
'twas probable, with greater absoluteness
than before; and even in the mean time,
must be oblig'd to preserve a much greater
caution in her Behaviour than before the coming of this Spy she had occasion to do.
The Prince therefore visited her not at home,
and they were forc'd to enjoy the Society of
each other in a more stolen and less frequent
manner than ever, which gave Pains to both
of them, which only a Lover equally restrain'd, equally impatient, can be capable
of conceiving.

CLEARCHUS, for that was the Name of
the Person commission'd by ADRASTUS, was
for some time kept in play by the Subtilty of ISMONDA, being every day told by
that

that Lady, that all she did was for the advantage of her Husband, as well as her own Satisfaction, which she confess'd she could more perfectly enjoy in *Caramania*, than in *Anatolia*, tho' it were the place of her Nativity; because the Friendship she had for the Princess would not suffer her to part from her, if there were a possibility of avoiding it, without incurring the Displeasure of ADRASTUS.——Of how much force these kind of Discourses were on the Person to whom they were made, the Reader will, in a little time, be sensible; he made a show, however, of acquiescing to all she said; and she had no reason but to believe he was as much deceived by them as she could wish.

Thus did some Weeks pass over, till the amorous THEODORE, no longer able to live without a nearer Conversation with his beloved ISMONDA, than what a publick view afforded him, made an Appointment with her to pass some part of the Night in the Palace-Garden; which she, no less impatient and passionate than himself, consented to, well pleas'd. He feign'd himself a little indispos'd, and said he would lie on his own side, ordering the Captain of his Guard to suffer none to enter into his Apartment, till he received permission from himself. ISMONDA, who, since the arrival of CLEARCHUS, had never supp'd from

him,

him, made an excuse for doing it now,
by telling him, that on the account of the
Prince's abfence, fhe was obliged to ftay
with the Princefs till fhe fell afleep, and
perhaps fhould not return to her Apartment till it was very late.——— Both of
them having thus managed the Affair, came
by back ways, unperceiv'd, as they imagin'd,
by any Perfon, to the Rendezvous: But
fcarce had one fond Embrace proclaim'd the
Joy which this meeting infufed into the
Souls of both, before a Voice, well-known
to ISMONDA, cry'd out, At length art thou
detected, thou vile Adulterefs! thy Perjuries,
thy Deceits at laft laid open!—— A ruftling
thro' the Leaves accompany'd thefe Words,
which prov'd the Perfon who fpoke them
was making his way as faft as he could to
take other Revenge on thofe he had furpriz'd, than this Interruption could inflict:
but being in a Walk on the back-fide of
that Arbor which the Lovers had made
choice of, he found it impoffible to reach
them that way, and was coming round to
meet them the other, when ISMONDA, who,
even in this the greateft Exigence fhe had
ever experienced, or that any Woman could
be in, ftill retain'd her ufual prefence of
Mind, prevented the Prince from drawing
his Sword, as he was about to do, by faying in a low Voice, Think not of Revenge
or Vindication, the only way for both of

us

us to fecure our Loves and Reputations, is
to fly.——It is my Husband whom I hear.——
ADRASTUS! *cry'd the Prince:* The fame,
refumed fhe; make to the Palace with all
fpeed. Never was Confufion equal to that
of THEODORE; fcarce could he move, much
lefs have the power of Thought what was
beft for him to do, till animated by her
Words and Example, he follow'd her in
the Path fhe took, which being a fhort Cut
to the back Gate, by which fhe had enter'd,
they foon approach'd it; when he turning to
her, to ask how fhe would proceed, Take
no care for me, my deareft Prince, *faid
fhe,* but go to your Apartment; I will haften to that of the Princefs, and perhaps
order it fo, that this may be of advantage
to our Love, rather than the contrary. She
ftay'd not for any Anfwer, but ran directly to HYANTHE's, and THEODORE pafs'd
forward to his own, in a Diforder and Per-
turbation of Spirit, which cannot be exprefs'd. The Princefs was in bed when
ISMONDA came into the Anti-chamber; but
fome of her Ladies being there, fhe made
an excufe, that fhe had defign'd to fit by
the Princefs; but fince fhe had no need of
her attendance, fhe would ftay a while with
them.——One of them was employ'd in
reading to the others a diverting Book, juft
then publifh'd by fome modern Wit; but
what attention ISMONDA gave to it, may
easily

eafily be guefs'd. This was, however, a good Opportunity for her to indulge Reflection, and give a little loofe to the Amazement fhe was in: She thought herfelf perfectly certain, that it was the Voice of ADRASTUS fhe had heard, but how he had been concealed in *Caramania*, fhe could not imagine; if it were really him, and that he had follow'd her to the Garden, as fhe could not well doubt of both, fhe confider'd that there was no Relief, but an abfolute Denial. She had carefully look'd round about, when fhe enter'd the Arbor, and was fure there was none near at that time; therefore it muft be only Conjecture in him, that fhe was the Perfon whom he had furprized. She endeavour'd therefore all fhe could to overcome every thing that might denote Fear, which fhe believ'd was all that would make her appear guilty. In thefe Cogitations, we muft quit her, to fee what became of the Perfon who had occafion'd them.

ADRASTUS, for it was, indeed, no other, having, with much difficulty, at laft prevailed on the King of *Anatolia* to permit him to go in fearch of his Wife, too juftly fearing there were Motives far different from thofe fhe pretended for her ftay, accompany'd CLEARCHUS to *Caramania*, and being difguis'd in the Habit of a Servant, was entertain'd as one belonging to
the

the Family of ISMONDA, where he had the opportunity of obferving and knowing much more than ever would have reach'd his Ears had he appear'd as himfelf.————— Among that fort of Converfation in which he was now engaged, there is infinitely more to be learn'd than in any other: they talk without referve of the Foibles of their Superiors, and being frequently oblig'd to be trufted, make no fcruple of exchanging one Secret for another.————ADRASTUS foon perceiv'd the Genius of his new Acquaintance, and by relating to them fome fictitious Adventures of his pretended Mafter, got from ARANTE and the reft of them all that they knew of the real ones of their Miftrefs; from that Wench he heard the Story which had fo much occafion'd the Laughter of the Court, concerning the Captivity of ARIDANOR in the Clofet of ISMONDA, and every body being poffefs'd with an Opinion of an Intrigue between them, a thoufand little Circumftances, all Invention, were added to the Truth, and left him no room to hope but that fhe was really as guilty with him as was reported. Refolving, however, to be more affur'd before he difcover'd himfelf, he watch'd her every motion, but till that night, had never feen any thing which could be call'd a proof of what he fear'd: but being told by CLEARCHUS that fhe had excufed Supping at home

on

on account of the Princefs, he was determin'd to know if in that fhe was fincere or
not. As he was on the fcout in one of the
darkeft and moft retired Avenues of the Palace, he faw a Perfon muffled up in his
Cloak pafs haftily by him, and go into the
Garden, and foon after ISMONDA hurry
along the fame way: Never was a Heart
more rack'd than that of this unhappy Gentleman; the fears he had, that he fhould be
afcertain'd of what he had yet but fufpected,
were more terrible to him than the fufpence
had been, and much ado had he to prevent
himfelf from calling to her as fhe went, and
faying to her, Come back ISMONDA, let not
Detection prove me the Wretch I dread to
be——Come back, and fuffer me to retain
the thought, that there is a poffibility thou
art not falfe. 'Tis probable, indeed, that
had fhe not pafs'd too quick to fuffer her to
take notice of any thing, fome Word or
Motion, in fpite of him, had difcover'd the
Emotions of his Soul, and awaken'd Obfervation to infpect into the Caufe. Seeing her
enter the Garden, where but the moment
before he had feen the Perfon, whom he
miftook for ARIDANOR, but was indeed
the Prince, had gone, he made no doubt
but that it was an Affignation. The different Paffions with which he was agitated at
but the fuppofition of the Injury he was
about to fuffer, render'd him unable immediately

diately to affure himfelf; but rouzing, as
much as poffible, from that Lethargy of
Thought he had been in, he alfo pufh'd back
the Wicket, and went into the Garden:
but there being two Walks which met at
that Entrance, he was uncertain which it
was, they, whom he fought, had took; and
happening to make choice of the wrong,
could neither fee nor hear any thing of them
till he came to that Arbor, where being no
Paffage on the fide he was, he but vainly endeavour'd to get through, when he cry'd
out to them in the manner already mention'd, and occafion'd their flight. The way
being twice as long from where he was to
the Arbor, as it was from it to the Palace, they had time to fettle themfelves, as I
have reprefented, before he could arrive at
the place where he firft perceiv'd they were.
He fpent fome hours, after he found they
were gone, in giving vent to the Diftraction
he was in, at this plain Demonftration of his
Misfortune. Vex'd he was that he had difcover'd himfelf, fince he had been prevented from appearing in the manner he had defign'd to do, and it was now too late for
him to refume his difguife, not doubting
but that ISMONDA had known his Voice.——
He wifh'd he had remain'd yet a little longer
time conceal'd, but then reflecting that he
already had feen enough, and needed no
more to be convinc'd of the Infidelity of
that

that fair Hypocrite, he ceas'd to be uneasy at the Interruption he had given, and bent his whole Thoughts on Revenge, and the manner in which he would accomplish it. At his return to the Palace, he went to the Chamber of CLEARCHUS, where being inform'd she was not yet come home, he dress'd himself in one of those Habits he had been accustom'd to wear when he was call'd ADRASTUS, and as soon as he was ready, sent a Page to search for her, who having heard her say she was going to HY-ANTHE, went no farther than the Apartment of that Princess, and having acquainted her with his Message, and from whom he re-ceiv'd it, she summon'd all the Courage she was Mistress of to arm her for this Encoun-ter; and having prepar'd herself beyond Ima-gination, she flew to the Room where she was told he was, and preventing his ap-proach to her, threw her Arms about his Neck, crying, My dear ADRASTUS, by what Miracle is it that I behold you here? Has my good Angel whisper'd in your Ear the good I am about to do for you, and you thus kindly come and spare me the pains of sending? Yes, Madam, *answer'd he, dif-engaging himself as soon as possible from her Caresses, and turning from her with a Countenance which denoted the mingled Rage and Grief of his tormented Soul,* I am too well satisfy'd what it is you do for me;

me; and after the knowledge that you have been falſe, nothing could ſo much aſtoniſh me, as that there is a poſſibility for Vice, like yours, to wear the ſhape of Virtue———Good Heaven, *purſu'd he wildly,* why do you ſuffer that Face ſtill to retain its ſhow of Innocence? Why is not her Form grown black and horrid, like her polluted Soul? ſome publick mark of Infamy ſhould appear to warn unwary Gazers from her deſtructive Charms.———Oh all ye Gods of *Caramania, interrupted ſhe, and offering to take his Hand,* what ſudden Frenzy has poſſeſs'd my Lord? Off thou Adultereſs, *reſum'd he, throwing her from him,* well may'ſt thou call on foreign Deities, thy own have long ſince forſaken thee———when for the Embraces of a Stranger, the curs'd ARIDANOR, thou did'ſt refuſe thoſe of a once fond doating Husband.———Shame, and the worſt of Crimes has been thy Choice, and Hell and Horrour ſhall reward thee for it. Not all the Terror which conſcious Guilt had before involv'd her in, was equal to the Joy ſhe now conceiv'd at his miſtake. Innocent of this Accuſation, ſhe threw off the ſupplicating Air ſhe had put on, and aſſuming one all haughtineſs, Unjuſt ADRASTUS, *ſaid ſhe,* is it thus that you return the Obligations you have to me? Am I, for having preſerv'd my Honour inviolable from all the Artifices, nay, combated

even

even with the Force of that feducing Lord,
to be reproached ?——Injurious Man, never
will I forgive the wrong thou haft done me,
nor, fhould'ft thou repent of what thou haft
faid in Rivers of inceffant Tears, any more
will know thee by the Name of Husband, or
fhare the Bed of one who has fo much pro-
faned my Virtue. Scarce could he contain
himfelf in hearing her fpeak in this manner,
from expreffing his Rage in fomething more
violent than Words.——More than once
he laid his Hand upon his Sword, but CLE-
ARCHUS reftrain'd him from going farther—
O more than Impudence, *cry'd he, ftamp-
ing and walking about the Room in a diforder'd motion*——Language has no Name to
diftinguifh this Behaviour, which would not
wrong the monftrous Meaning——had not
my own Eyes and Ears betray'd the horrid
Secret, I know not but in fpite of all I
have been told, my foolifh Heart would
yet have doubted if fhe had been bafe——
But to give the lye to all my Senfes, nay,
when her own have inform'd her that they
have been Witnefs of her Crime, is fomething which fure fhe could not have learn'd
in any School but that of Hell.——Were
not your perfidious Arms, *continu'd he,
turning to her,* clofe lock'd about the Adul-
terer's Neck ?——Did not fhort Sighs and
mingling Kiffes proclaim a mutual eagernefs
for the guilty Joy, when my abus'd Patience,
no

no longer able to endure the fhocking Scene,
made me break out, and vainly ftruggle for
a Paffage to reach the hated Heart of your
Undoer? All a Madman's Dream, *reply'd
fhe fcornfully*; When or where was I fo
kind? Can you deny it? *faid he :* Was it
not now, this very Night, in the Palace-
Garden?——Oh! had you not both been
too well acquainted with the Place, my Rage
had overtaken your flight, and put you paft
the power of urging me yet more by fo ob-
ftinate a Contradiction——but it is not
yet too late, *added he,* and fuc'. Examples
will I make——Compofe yourfelf to fleep,
refum'd fhe, and to-morrow I will talk with
you before thofe who are better Judges of
my Conduct. In fpeaking this, fhe flung out
of the Room, CLEARCHUS preventing him
from detaining her, and half perfuaded of
her Innocence, with fo much Serenity and
unfhaken Temper had fhe behav'd : Are
you certain, my Lord! *faid he to him,* that
you have not been deceiv'd? to me, Appearances on her fide ftand fair ; fhe told me
fhe was going to the Apartment of the Princefs, and it was there, when fent for, fhe
was found : With what probability then could
it be fhe whom you faw in the Palace-Garden? you might probably be deceiv'd by the
faint glimmerings of the uncertain Moon,
and having the Image of ISMONDA ever prefent to your Eyes, might, with eafe, miftake

fome

some other for her. This Suggestion of
CLEARCHUS made him perfectly outrageous; what, *said he*, do my very Friends
conspire against me, and take the Wanton's
part?——How could I be deceiv'd, when free
from Passion, and scarce believing my Misfortune, she pass'd so close to the place in
which I stood, a little nearer and she had difcover'd me? it was not by the Moon's faint
light I saw her then, but by the unerring
Lamps which fill the Palace-Gallery. He
added many more Circumstances, which but
too plainly prov'd he could not have been
mistaken, and after passing the remainder
of the night in Discourses suitable to the Occasion, he wrote a little Note to ARIDANOR,
which he oblig'd CLEARCHUS to carry to
him, the Contents whereof were as follows.

To ARIDANOR.

' A S you are conscious of having in-
' jur'd me, so are you also sensible
' what kind of Reparation is expected from
' a Man of Honour: As I am too much a
' Stranger in *Caramania* to know what
' place is most proper for such an Interview,
' I leave it to your appointment, as also
' whether with or without Seconds; tho
' since the quarrel concerns none but our-
' selves, I think it needless to interest any
' other in it: however, if you are of a dif-
' ferent Opinion, I am not unprovided of a
' Friend,

' Friend, pleafe to let me know your Re-
' folution by the Bearer, and alfo where
' about an hour hence I may hope to find
' you.——Tho a Stranger to my Perfon, I
' believe you have heard too much of my
' Character to think me unworthy of your
' Sword, when I fhall inform you I am
' call'd

ADRASTUS.

Loth was CLEARCHUS to be the Bearer
of this Mandate, yet as the Affair feem'd to
be, could offer nothing in oppofition to it;
he therefore went about the execution of his
Commiffion, but found fome difficulty in
being introduced to the prefence of ARI-
DANOR, who was not yet rifen : however,
on telling the Servant that his Bufinefs was
of a nature which would not brook delay,
he was admitted. He deliver'd the Billet to
him while he was in Bed, and having read
it, heard him call for Pen and Paper immediately, and in a fmall time receiv'd an Anfwer from his own Hand; which returning
with to ADRASTUS, he communicated to
him : it contain'd thefe Words.

To ADRASTUS.

' THO I am as much a Stranger to the
' Guilt of which you feem to accufe
' me, as I am to your Perfon, and cannot
' imagine by what means I fhould poffibly

S 3   ' have

' have injur'd one fo much a Stranger, yet
' am I ready to give you what Satisfaction
' you fhall think proper ; which, that you
' may the better judge, I will meet you in
' the Wildernefs, behind the Palace-Gar-
' den, within this Hour at furtheft.——I
' am of your mind, that there is no occafion
' for Witneffes of what we have to fay, and
' fhall therefore come alone.

ARIDANOR.

He has anfwer'd like a Man of Honour,
nor could any other, *faid* ADRASTUS, *with
a Sigh,* have deprived me of the Affections
of ISMONDA : he pafs'd fome little time in
Difcourfes of the fame nature, after which
he embrac'd CLEARCHUS, and went to the
place appointed, where he had not walk'd
above the Space of a minute, before he faw
ARIDANOR approach ; he had the advantage as having feen him while he remain'd
with CLEARCHUS in difguife, but ARIDA-
NOR who knew him not, was at a lofs whether he was his Antagonift or not, till plucking off his Hat and approaching him, You
are punctual, my Lord ! *faid he,* nor did I
expect other from your Character ; the Man
who dares commit an Injury, fhould alfo
dare as boldly to defend it. Yes, ADRAS-
TUS, *reply'd* ARIDANOR, nor is it that I fear
your Sword that I defire fome Speech before
we engage, but becaufe thofe Actions cannot

not, with juſtice, be call'd brave, to which
we are only inſtigated by our Paſſions; I
ſhould be glad to know the Reaſon why we
are Enemies. Oh ye Gods! *cry'd the other,*
tranſported with Rage, is that a Queſtion
for ARIDANOR to ask the Husband of Is-
MONDA?——Can he believe me ignorant
of the wrong he has done me?——Or
does he inſult the Shame he has brought
on me, and would make me the Reporter of
my own Infamy? ADRASTUS, *reſum'd he,*
I have not wrong'd you—but ſince you have
nam'd ISMONDA, I am no longer at a loſs to
gueſs the Cauſe of your too juſtifiable, tho
miſtaken Rage —— O! *continu'd he,*
after a pauſe, that you knew me better,
that you might not think 'twas Cowardice
prompted my Tongue, I would reveal a Secret.——Speak it, *interrupted* ADRASTUS,
your Fame in Battle has been too well eſtabliſh'd to ſuffer ſuch a Thought—if there
be aught concerning my Diſhonour more
than yet I know, be generous and tell me.
You yet know nothing, *reply'd* ARIDANOR,
but are abus'd by falſe Intelligence; but
longer ſhall you not——I have conſider'd,
and find 'twould be meer Madneſs, and not
Bravery, to ſuffer you to continue in a
Miſtake which might not only be fatal to
one or both of us, but alſo add new Tri-
umphs, and full Security to the fair falſe
ISMONDA, and her great Seducer————for

ſhould

fhould you fall by me, or I by you, the
Death of either would be welcome Ti-
dings; by mine, they would be rid of,
perhaps, the only Perfon who has it in
his power to betray their Secret; and
by yours, the fears of Separation would no
more difturb the guilty Pair.

I will not therefore fight with thee, A-
DRASTUS, on this Theme, at leaft not till
you have heard the Truth.——— O fpeak
it, *cry'd the diftracted Husband!* my Soul
is all Aftonifhment; if I have been deceiv'd, and wrong'd your Virtue, I will entreat your Pardon in the humbleft manner.
Calm the tempeftuous Paffions of your
Grief, if poffible, *refum'd* ARIDANOR; you
have not wrong'd me, neither am I guilty;
I am, and am not innocent——well may
you feem amazed, but foon will I explain
the Myftery.——— Know then, ISMONDA
fcorns to fin beneath a Prince; and had
there not been a THEODORE, ADRASTUS
would have had no room for fufpicion of
ARIDANOR. Here the impatient Soul of
this afflicted Man was able to contain no
longer; but cafting a furious Look, and lift-
ing up his Hands, as tho' he would accufe
Heaven of his Misfortune, Gods! Gods!
cry'd he, can it be poffible?——— The
Prince!——the Husband of HYANTHE attempt the Honour of her Friend, her Bofom Favourite!——But tell me, *continued*
he,

he, turning his Eyes on ARIDANOR, inform me, generous Lord, the whole of this
vile Secret; let me not linger in a Life of
Torment, but kill me at once with aſſuring
me 'tis ſo. I wiſh that I could ſay there
was a hope it were not, *reſumed the
other*; but becauſe it would be mean-
ſoul'd in me to reveal the Crimes of o-
thers, while I conceal my own, I will
confeſs, that when the knowledge of the
Prince's Happineſs made bold my hopes, I
too preſumed to talk to her of Love; but
with ſuch force did ſhe repel my Suit,
that ſoon I dropp'd the fruitleſs Proſecution. Yet one thing more I have to ask,
ſaid ADRASTUS, and I conjure you, by your
Honour, hide not the Truth: Were you
not late laſt Night in the Gardens of the
Palace? No, by Heaven, *anſwered* ARI-
DANOR; but as I croſs'd the Gallery, I ſaw
your royal Rival cloſe muffled in his Cloak,
and unattended, paſs that way.——'Twas
him then I miſtook for you, *cry'd the tormented* ADRASTUS; Oh that my Sword unknowing him had reach'd his Heart!——
Oh that I were ſtill in ignorance by whom
I am abus'd! ſome lucky Moment might
then have thrown me on him, and I might
have taken that juſt Revenge on the De-
ſtroyer of my Honour, which now the
Name of THEODORE debars me from ——
were it any other than the Husband of

HYANTHE, tho' guarded by the brighteſt of the celeſtial Beings, he ſhould not 'ſcape my Rage.——Damnation! *purſued he,* all other Curſes of the offended Gods, are mean to bearing Injuries as I muſt do.

A conſiderable time was paſs'd between the one, relating all he knew of this Adventure; and the other, in exclaiming on the Severity of his Fate, and the Falſhood of ISMONDA: After which they parted, and ADRASTUS return'd to the Apartment of his Wife, who he found abroad; ſhe was gone to the Princeſs, to acquaint her with the arrival of ADRASTUS, and his unjuſt Suſpicions of her. He had ſcarce finiſhed the account he was giving to CLEARCHUS, of what had paſs'd between him and ARIDANOR, when one of the Princeſs's Pages came to let him know ſhe expected to ſee him; having been inform'd his Wife was already with her, he doubted not but ſhe had made her Complaint to that deceiv'd Lady, and was in a Perplexity which cannot be deſcrib'd, in what manner he ſhould defend his Accuſations againſt her, without, at the ſame time, proclaiming the Guilt of the Prince; which not only the Admonitions of CLEARCHUS, but his own Reaſon alſo perſuaded him it was wholly improper to do. The Affair was nice, and in the preſent Confuſion of his Thoughts, he found himſelf incapable of managing it;

yet

yet was there an abfolute Neceffity of o-
beying the Summons of a Princefs, who
was the Daughter of his Mafter. He therefore compos'd himfelf as much as poffible
to attend her. He found her in her
Clofet entirely alone, ISMONDA having entreated not to be prefent during this Converfation. How comes it, ADRASTUS, *faid
fhe, as foon as he approached,* that you
have conceal'd yourfelf in *Caramania?* I
thought the Love and Duty you pay my
royal Father, had extended to all belonging to him, and that the firft Vifit you had
made, had been to me. Pardon, bright
Princefs! *anfwer'd he,* this feeming neglect
of that Regard due to your high Birth, and
more illuftrious Virtues; but there were
Reafons for the Concealment of my Arrival, which could not be difpenfed with,
and which have made me guilty of Omif-
fions both to Heaven and you. I fear thofe
Reafons, *faid* HYANTHE, are fuch as cannot be approv'd by the Well-wifhers of
your Fame, or Peace of Mind: I hear, and
grieve to hear, ftrange Stories of your alter'd Humour.———Believe me, ADRASTUS,
Jealoufy is the worft Paffion of the Soul,
and when 'tis caufelefs, is an Offence to
Virtue fcarcely pardonable. I am of the
fame opinion, Madam, *anfwer'd he*; and
becaufe I would not give it entrance, endeavour'd to arrive at certainty.———And how

far

far have you fucceeded? *interrupted the Princefs.*

Now was this unhappy Husband in the ut-moft Dilemma, in what manner to reply: but a fudden Thought coming that moment into his head, after a moment's Paufe; So far, Madam, *anfwer'd he*, as has ferv'd to convince me that I have been deceiv'd by falfe Reports, and have injur'd by an un-juft Sufpicion——ARIDANOR. He was go-ing to fay his Wife, but could not force his Tongue fo much to belye his Heart. And not ISMONDA too? *demanded the Princefs.* When fhe returns to *Anatolia, refumed he*, what my opinion is of her, will fhow itfelf.———I therefore befeech your Highnefs, *continued he, putting one Knee to the Ground,* that you will no longer countenance her ftay, nor fuffer her to fkreen under your facred Umbrage the little Regard fhe has teftify'd to my Defires. Far be it from me, *reply'd fhe*, who am myfelf a Wife, to go about to hinder one who is a Wife from that Obe-dience the Name of Husband claims; but as I would not have her wanting in her Duty, fo I hope you will remember there is alfo fome required from you, and not by harfh Treatment, or too great an Exer-tion of your Authority oblige her to re-pent fhe ever put it in your power. Here the Memory of the former Tendernefs he

had

had expreſſed to her, and her Ingratitude
ſince, made him ſhake with inward Agony.
How I have behav'd, Madam, *ſaid he,*
yourſelf has been a Witneſs.——— In what
manner I ſhall behave, will be owing to
her Actions. I comprehend not the meaning of theſe myſterious Words, *reply'd the*
Princeſs, who was entirely prepoſſeſs'd by
what that ſubtle Woman had ſaid to her;
you ſeem to have ſtill a reſerve of Indignation in your Soul, which may make her
fear the Uſage I have mention'd: And as
her Friendſhip for me has been her only
Crime, it lies on me to engage her Pardon; which you muſt give, ADRASTUS,
purſued ſhe ſmiling, or I ſhall think you
look on me as a Rival. I neither can, nor
ought, *anſwered he,* to refuſe any thing
to the Daughter of my Sovereign, and a
Princeſs illuſtrious for a thouſand Virtues,
but moſt for her heavenly Sweetneſs of
Diſpoſition; and while ISMONDA has had
ſo bright a Pattern, methinks it is impoſſible ſhe ſhould have err'd.——— I inſiſt
therefore on no more than that ſhe prepare
with all expedition to depart with me for
Anatolia.

The Princeſs, well pleaſed with thinking ſhe had brought about this Reconciliation, endeavour'd to perſuade him to continue with them in *Caramania,* aſſuring
him that the Prince her Husband would

put

put him into Pofts of Honour equivalent
to thofe he enjoy'd in *Anatolia*. But before his Tongue could bring forth a refufal
of this Offer, his Looks demonftrated how
unwelcome it was to him. At the Name
of THEODORE, fcarce could he refrain from
uttering all he knew, and the Reafons that
Prince had for engaging his ftay ; but the
regard he had for the Quiet of the happily
deceived HYANTHE, prevented him : and
he only excufed himfelf from accepting
any Favours offer'd him by her Husband, on
the account of thofe he had received from
her Father, whofe Service, while he could
be of any ufe to him, Gratitude he faid
would not permit him to leave. Though
the Princefs, truly loving ISMONDA, urg'd
him as ftrenuoufly as the Cafe would permit, yet could fhe alledge but little, befides
her own Defires, againft the Juftice of thofe
Arguments he made ufe of to back his Denial, and fhe was oblig'd at laft to own that
he was in the right, and confent to difcharge
ISMONDA from her Service.

ADRASTUS had no fooner difengaged
himfelf from the Princefs, than he return'd
to the Apartment of his Wife, where he
communicated to CLEARCHUS every particular of the Converfation which had pafs'd
between him and HYANTHE ; but when he
came to that which related the promife of
his Pardon to ISMONDA, and his defign of
taking

taking her with him to *Anatolia*, nothing
could be more amaz'd, than was his Friend:
And can you then, *said he, interrupting him*,
so readily forgive what but some hours
since you swore, that to the last Moments
of your Life, you would endeavour to revenge?——Does the Name of Prince so far
alleviate the Guilt, that you can consent to
live again with the false fair Ismonda? A
gloomy Smile at this Interrogation diffused
itself around the Mouth of this offended
Husband; No, Clearchus! *resumed he*,
think not so meanly of Adrastus, 'tis to
accomplish that Revenge, at which I can arrive no other way, that I affect this Patience,
this tame forgiving Nature.—— Should I
leave her in *Caramania*, what more could
the adulterous Pair desire? But I will divide them——divide them for ever——
give them to know some part of the Hells
they have on me inflicted——and to prevent a second Injury of this kind from any
other Man, soon as she arrives in *Anatolia*,
shall she be immur'd among the Vestals. The
Surprize which Clearchus had at first
conceiv'd, was now succeeded by an adequate Admiration; he applauded his Conduct, and encouraged him in this Resolution, with all the Eloquence he was master of.

　While they were talking, Ismonda, who
by the Princess had been inform'd of what
　　　　　　　　　　　　　　　　he

he faid, came in; and with an Air of Haughtinefs, with which fhe, but in vain, endeavour'd to mingle a little Sweetnefs: Now, my Lord, *faid fhe*, I hope you are convinced of the Injury your miftaken Rage has done me, and are prepar'd to ask my pardon. We will talk no more, Madam, *reply'd he*, either of Injuries or Pardon, it will be time enough when we come to *Anatolia*; and the greater fpeed you make in getting ready for this Journey, the more I fhall be inclinable to think you wifh a more perfect Reconciliation between us, than can be made in *Caramania*. I know not, *faid fhe*, whether I fhall accept it on thofe terms, or not. And with thefe Words left the Room, refufing to hold any further Converfation with him, tho' he call'd after her to affure her he would afford it on no other, nor would confent to bed with her, or call her by the name of Wife, while fhe continued in *Caramania*.

Nor did he ftagger in this Refolution, but went with CLEARCHUS immediately out of the Palace, and took private Lodgings at fome diftance from it. Nothing certainly ever equal'd the Perplexity of ISMONDA at this fudden turn of her Fate, unlefs it were that in which her belov'd THEODORE was involv'd. Neither of them could now invent the leaft plaufible Pretext, ADRASTUS had refus'd all Offices which might detain
him

him in *Caramania*; the Princess had given
her Consent that Ismonda should depart,
and there appear'd no way of preventing
this Misfortune to their Love, but such as
must have open'd the Eyes not only of the
Princess, but the whole Nation also, to see
into the long hid Secret. Marmillio was
now a Person whose Presence and Advice
was thought exceeding necessary, and the
Prince was beginning to think by what means
he should recall him, without the Eclat of
his restoration into Favour being prejudicial
to himself; when Cleomenes acquainted
him, that his Brother having receiv'd News
that Irene had died in Childbirth, desired
nothing more than his Highness's Permission to return.

This was welcome News to Theodore,
he sent an immediate dispatch that he should
come with all possible expedition, giving
out among his Courtiers, that as that Favourite had incurr'd his displeasure only for
a rash Word, he thought he had sufficiently
punish'd him for so trivial a Fault. Nor
did this Alteration impede his Desires of
seeing Euridice the Bride of Doraspe,
but on the contrary, it very much forwarded that Marriage; for Arbanes, by the return of Marmillio, being frustrated of
the Expectations with which he had flatter'd
himself of being the chief Favourite of his
Sovereign, and receiving the consequential

T   Be-

Benefits of such a Trust, thought it best not to neglect that only means which now remain'd of advancing his Family, by an Alliance with one so powerful as that of Doraspe ; and since Death had disappointed his Son Ernestus of his hope of Irene, he was resolv'd for the future never to leave any thing to Time or Chance, and hurry'd the slow Euridice to Nuptials, which in her Soul were little less detestable to her than the Grave.

Marmillio had many Friends who truly lov'd him, and sincerely rejoic'd at his Re-establishment ; but theirs was a Joy faint and languid, when compar'd with that which fill'd the Soul of the transported Arilla. The News of it no sooner reach'd her Ears, than she again indulg'd the pleasing Idea of rewarded Passion——again prepar'd to meet the Joys of Love——and her heav'd Bosom swell'd with renew'd Desires; but alas ! little did the false Man merit so true a Passion: Far different from her Expectations, were the Caresses with which he now receiv'd her Ardors !——Absence had quite estrang'd his fickle Heart, and a new Object obliterated almost the Memory of the former.

While depriv'd of the Pleasures of the Court, he cou'd not live without his Amusements ; being invited after a Hunting Match, to the House of a wealthy Commoner in that part of the Country which he had chose

for

for his Retirement, he became fo much enamour'd of the fair CARICLEA, the Wife of that Gentleman to whom he was a Gueft, that the Idea of ARILLA, to whom he had been fo much devoted, foon loft all the Empire over his Soul.——Perfectly skill'd in the undoing Art, he exerted all for the obtaining this new Conqueft, and the unwary Liftner, too weakly guarded, became a Prey to his deftructive Infinuations. The unfufpecting Husband, far from gueffing at the Motive which occafion'd the frequent Vifits he now receiv'd from him, took them as fo many Proofs of his Friendfhip, and was tranfported at the deference paid him by a Man of MARMILLIO's Quality, from all the other Gentlemen of the County. He had a young Sifter equally lovely with CA-RICLEA, tho' of another fort of Beauty ; this blooming Creature, when MARMIL-LIO found himfelf recall'd to Court, he perfuaded to go with him, telling her, he would introduce her to the Service of the Princefs, which would not only improve her in Converfation, but alfo throw her in the way of Fortune : there was no doubt, he faid, but Charms fuch as hers would appear, when fet forth to advantage, might make up for the deficiencies of Birth, and entitle her to a Husband among the firft Rank of the Nobility. CARICLEA feem'd of the fame Opinion, and infufing fome

Prin-

Principles of Ambition into the Mind of the young Girl, made her continually teaze her Brother for his Confent; which he at laft gave, on Condition his Wife would accompany her, and fee her fettled with the Princefs before fhe left her. This was all that the guilty Pair defir'd; MARMILLIO not yet grown weary of the Charms of CARICLEA, and divided between his Love Intereft, had form'd this Stratagem for the Gratification of both; and the Fair Tranfgreffor was infinitely pleas'd, to think how freely fhe might indulge her Paffion when abfent from her Husband, who, by reafon of a publick Office he bore in the Country, cou'd not leave it.

Depending therefore on the Virtue of his Wife, he gave his Sifter wholly to her Care as to her Behaviour, and recommending her Preferment to MARMILLIO, who had promis'd fuch great Things, fuffer'd them to take leave without the leaft fufpicion of what they defign'd, or that the innocent Maid was the Property which they made ufe of for no other purpofe than his Difhonour.

For fome time after they came to Court, CARICLEA maintain'd her Empire over the Heart of him who had brought her to it; and when it decreas'd, ARILLA profited not by the Change : nothing being more true than that Saying of an *Englifh* Poet;

To

*To Love once paſt we cannot backward
      move;
Call Teſterday again, and I may love.*

Few Men, if ever any were, are twice
enamour'd of the ſame Object; their
whole Life indeed is one continued Series
of Change, but then it is ſtill to new Deſires: the Heart that is once eſtrang'd, is never to be recall'd; and though the forſaken
Nymph is ſure to have her preſent Rival
in the ſame Condition with herſelf, yet
muſt ſhe not hope to reap any other Advantage, than Revenge. ARILLA ſoon perceiv'd ſhe owed her Misfortune to the Beauties of CARICLEA, and had Wit enough to
know that Complaints would be of little
ſervice to eſtabliſh her in the Affections of
this ungrateful Man. Unable therefore to
endure the ſight of what was ſo diſtracting
to her, ſhe quitted the Service of the Princeſs, and retired to the Houſe of a Relation in the Country, with a Reſolution never to return, unleſs her Reaſon could ſo
far get the better of her Paſſion, as to give
her Courage to look on all he did with the
Eyes of Indifference and Contempt.

Her removal made room for VIOLETTA,
ſo was the Siſter of the Husband of CARI-
CLEA called: And MARMILLIO, as much
to leave that Lady (whoſe abſence he now

began

began to wish, as much as he had done her presence) no pretence of staying, as to comply with the Promise he had made her Husband, neglected not this opportunity of introducing this young Beauty. There were no Obstacles to her reception, she was well accomplish'd, and of a Family inferiour to none, who were not of the Nobility. HYANTHE accepted her with her usual Affability and Sweetness, and assured CARICLEA, who accompany'd her to the Presence-Chamber, that there were none among her Train of noble Maids, whom she would treat with greater Kindness.

VIOLETTA thus fix'd at Court, CARICLEA was oblig'd to return home, and sav'd herself the Grief of being forsaken : The necessity of her Departure engaging MARMILLIO to entertain her with the appearance of the same Ardours, as those with which he first seduced her easy Heart ; and she parted with this Satisfaction in her mind, that she left him involv'd in equal Sorrow, and that his Inclinations would bring him in a short time to visit her.

Next to the fear'd IRENE, nothing had ever given him more Pleasure, than to be freed from ARILLA, and this last Conquest of his victorious Wiles: he was now at liberty to prosecute a new Design, which his ever-waving Passion had form'd against the the Virtue of OLIMPIA, a young Lady of

ex-

exquifite Beauty and Accomplishments, but
efteem'd a Man-hater, and 'tis probable the
difficulty that appear'd in gaining her, was
no lefs an inducement to him than any other
Charm.————He long'd to triumph over
fo rigid a Virtue——He thought it would
be an infinite Satisfaction to know himfelf
poffefs'd of what fo many had languish'd for
inj vain, and refolv'd to leave no means un-
try'd to bring her into the number of thofe
who were unable to withftand his Sollicitations. Many propofals greatly to the advantage of her Fortune had been made her,
yet was fhe fo far from accepting them, that
tho' fhe had, at the firft acquaintance with
them, declar'd a liking of their Converfation, they no fooner appear'd as Lovers,
than fhe immediately defpis'd and us'd them
ill; and to prevent all further Importunities of the like nature, at laft treated the
whole Sex with a Contempt which was
fcarce reconcileable to Good Breeding.
MARMILLIO had frequently been in her
Company, and had found the Effects of this
Humour in common with the reft of Mankind, yet did it not deter him; and fetting
himfelf to dive into the fecret of a Difpofition fo foreign to all that is natural, he
thought it muft proceed either from a fecret
Paffion fhe had entertain'd for fome one
Man, that had created in her an averfion
to all others; or elfe, that it was no more

than

than Affectation, and that she imagin'd by
seeming to *Hate*, she might give the greater loose to *Love*, unperceiv'd and unsuspected. His Business therefore, was to find
out which of these two Motives was the
right; but by what means he should make
this Discovery, he was for some time at a
loss; and was indeed at last indebted for it
only to an Accident as whimsical in effect,
as it was ruinous to the Honour and future
Reputation of this seemingly reserv'd Lady.

Happening to pass by her House one Night
when it was very late, he saw the Door
wide open, and no Servant near it, nor any
Light appearing at the Windows, he presently imagin'd it might have been broken
open by Thieves; and having two Men with
him, he made them go into the Hall, and
call to the Footmen, but none answering
for a long time, he grew convinc'd that his
Conjectures had been true, and made yet
a louder Noise. At length a Fellow came
running down stairs half naked, and with
all the marks of fright and astonishment on
his Face, Are any of the Family beside your
self, *said* MARMILLIO, awake? No, my
Lord, *answer'd he*. Your Lady then, *resum'd he*, is doubtless robb'd: And then told
him in what manner he had seen the Door,
and the occasion of his coming in at that
unseasonable hour. On which, the Fellow

ran

ran up ftairs to call his Companions, who
being all foundly fleeping, were not very
eafy to be rouz'd from it.——All the Men,
and Maid-Servants, being at laft alarm'd,
they went up and down the Houfe with
Lights, endeavouring to difcover at what
place the Rogues had enter'd, or what they
had taken away. OLIMPIA's Woman ran
into her Chamber, to apprize her Lady of
what had happen'd; but not finding her
there, fhriek'd out, that the Thieves had
ftole away her Lady: on which, every body going into that Room, they found it
ftripp'd of all the rich Things in it, which
could conveniently be carry'd away; her
dreffing Plate, a fine Watch and Equipage,
which, at her going to Bed, were always
hung in a Cafe made on purpofe for them;
her Cabinet broken open, and her Jewels and Money taken out. There was indeed fufficient in this Room to glut the
Avarice of thefe nocturnal Pilferers; and
either being fatisfy'd with their Booty, or
fearful of Difcovery, they went into no
other, as might be fuppos'd; for every thing
ftood as it did in all the other Apartments.
As MARMILLIO, with the Servants of this
Lady, were fearching the Houfe, one of
them cry'd out, that the Door which open'd
into the Garden was unbarr'd; on which the
reft going toward it, found it was fo indeed,
and were then no longer at a lofs by what
means

means the Rogues had gotten entrance : e-
very one, however, MARMILLIO efpecially, being in great Concern what was
become of OLIMPIA, fome of the Footmen ran with lighted Torches into the Garden, where in a clofe Arbor they found her
bound and gagg'd, and, to their great amazement, the uglieft and moft dirty of her
Grooms in the fame pofture. Scarce would
the wonder which they all were involv'd in,
permit them to deliver her from that uneafy
State ; but MARMILLIO, who had more
Prefence of Mind, was the firft who gave
her any Affiftance, and taking the Gag out
of her Mouth, reftor'd her to the ufe of
Speech, while the others were bufily employ'd in unfaftning the Cords which had
rudely been twifted round her Legs and
Arms. It was expected that fhe would have
related to them, fo foon as fhe had power,
how fhe came to be thus expos'd, but fhe appear'd in too great a Confufion to do it ;
and when MARMILLIO, having his own fecret Reafons for the Queftion, ask'd her how
it came to pafs that fhe chofe fo odd and fo
dangerous an hour for walking, fhe anfwer'd nothing. And when he more ma-
licioufly demanded, if it were with her
knowledge that the Groom was in the
Garden at the fame time her Ladyfhip had
chofe to make it the place of her Retirement, fhe feem'd ready to die with Shame
and

and Vexation; and inſtead of thanking
MARMILLIO for the timely aſſiſtance he
had given her, ſhe flung abruptly from him,
crying, I cannot imagine what Accident or
Deſign ſhould bring you here at this time.
He endeavour'd not to ſtay her, nor had
any further buſineſs to remain there any
longer himſelf, but went thro' the Houſe,
and into his Chair, impatient till he was at
home, to examine the Contents of a ſmall
piece of Paper which he had taken up in
the Arbor of OLIMPIA's Garden, and lay
near the Groom; and which, 'twas probable,
the Thieves in rifling his Pockets had let
fall. He had no ſooner enter'd his Cloſet,
than opening it, he found it contain'd theſe
Lines.

'Tho' I have turn'd away the Wench,
'whoſe inquiſitive Diſpoſition gave me
'juſt cauſe of Fear, yet am I ſtill appre-
'henſive of diſcovery, by ſome unlucky
'Accident or other.—— We cannot, my
'dear SILO, be perfectly ſecure, while we
'continue our Endearments in my Cham-
'ber; I will therefore quit my Bed when
'all the Family are drown'd in ſleep, and
'ſteal down to the cloſe Arbor at the far-
'ther end of the Garden, where I ſhall ex-
'pect you with all the Impatience of the
'moſt doating Affection.'

Doating, indeed, cry'd MARMILLIO to
himſelf, as ſoon as he had done reading;
was

was ever fuch monftruous Hypocrify! 'Tis
certain, that tho' he had not that opinion
of her Virtue, which the generality of the
World had, yet he could never imagine
fhe would have ftoop'd fo low as her own
Groom, if he had not feen the Confirmation of it under her own hand, which he
knew perfectly well, having often feen it
on feveral Occafions. He could not forbear laughing, however, when he confider'd on the whimficalnefs of this Adventure : It was plain, that the Thieves coming
over the Wall with a defign to rob the
Houfe, had found the Miftrefs of it with
her humble Enamorato in that Arbor ; and
having bound and gagg'd them, found an
eafy opportunity to compafs their Defign.

Having a little given way to the Diverfion of his Humour on this comical Affair,
his more ferious Inclinations refumed fome
part of their former force : I fay, fome
part ; for after the knowledge how much
OLIMPIA had demean'd herfelf, he had not
thofe paffionate Defires for her Enjoyment
as before. It was Curiofity, and perhaps
fome mixture of a more bafe Paffion, which
made him now refolve not to relinquifh
his Pretenfions ; and encourag'd by the difcovery he had made, prefs'd on her in fo
clofe a manner, that it oblig'd her to make
ufe of all the Invectives fhe could mufter
up againft the Sex, to make him defift :

and

and perceiving that thofe Artifices, which
had been fatal to fo many of the believing
Fair, had no influence on her, he grew at
laft fo piqued, that, without any regard to
her Quality, or thofe Vows of an eternal
Adoration he had made her, he upbraided
her with Hypocrify and Deceit; and to
prove that he knew her pretended Virtue
all a Cheat, reveal'd to her by what means
he had been acquainted with the Conde-
fcenfions with which fhe had favour'd SILO,
and theaten'd to make the Affair publick
to the whole Town, if fhe confented not
to bribe him in the manner' he defir'd.
Nothing can be imagin'd of Fear, Vexation, and Surprize, fuperiour to what OLIM-
PIA endur'd in this fhock; at firft fhe raged,
forfwore all he alledged, and branded him
with Injuftice and Barbarity, in terms the
moft opprobrious that Paffion could fuggeft:
but all fhe faid having no other effect, than to
make him more refolute to expofe her, fhe
fell into as mean Submiffions, entreating
him to pity the Weaknefs fhe had been
guilty of, and not ruin her for ever, by
revealing what he had difcover'd. She told
him that SILO, by concealing himfelf in
her Chamber, had at firft ravifh'd her Virgin Favours, Shame preventing her from
alarming the Family; becaufe that, while a-
fleep, he had prefumed too far for her to fuffer to be made publick; and that fince, more

out

out of fear of being betray'd by his Malice,
she had yielded to repeat the guilty Joy,
than out of any Pleasure she took in the
Caresses of a Wretch so much beneath her;
and that the Reflection how cruelly her Virtue had been triumph'd over by him, had
been the occasion of that Hatred she express'd to all Mankind in general. And
can you not, *said* MARMILLIO, assume
Courage enough to throw off such a bold
Invader?———What matters it, in what
manner he shall speak; who will believe
the Words of a discarded Servant?———
A Villain so audacious should rather have
met the Punishment of his Crime from
your offended Hand, than reap'd Reward.—
But you have since forgiven, and no doubt
love the Wretch.———No, by my hopes of
Happiness, *resumed she*; and had I any
Friend would rid me of him, should think
myself oblig'd past Recompence.——— But
to whom could I apply for such a Favour,
without relating the cause of my Disgust;
you are the first Discoverer of this horrid
Secret, and if indeed you lov'd me, would
not endure a Rival such as he to be possess'd of the Advantages he is. What can I
do, *reply'd* MARMILLIO, to a Creature unworthy of my Sword? O! there are a
thousand, *said she*, who, for a trifling Reward, would send him from the World.
As dissolute as MARMILLIO was, the
thoughts

thoughts of Murder fhock'd him, efpecially
when propos'd by a Woman, and one who
had willingly continued in the neareft Intimacy with the Perfon fhe would deftroy.
There are Countries, Madam, *anfwer'd he,
after a little Paufe,* where thofe *Bravoes*
you talk of are eafy to be found; but if
there are any of that Calling in *Caramania,* I proteft to you I know them not.
———— However, *continued he, when he
had again taken a little time for Confideration,* I will endeavour to give you the Eafe
you feem to wifh, though by means lefs
cruel than you mention'd. I care not by
what way, *faid fhe,* you fecure my Reputation from his Tongue, and deliver me
from the Conftraint I am under, in fuffering his odious Careffes; and my Heart, my
Soul, my All fhall be at your devotion.
MARMILLIO would fain have receiv'd his
Hire before his Work was done, but OLIM-
PIA would not confent: No, my Lord,
faid fhe, when he importun'd her, fet me
free from the detefted Obligations I am under, and I can then receive your Embraces
with fatisfaction. He was able to obtain
no more of her, and took his leave to go
about the Execution of what he had promifed, which he accomplifhed by thefe
means.

He had an acquaintance with a Captain,
who traded to the farther part of the Wef-
tern

tern Ocean, the Ship was at that time ready
to set sail: and OLIMPIA sending SILO
on board, under pretence of carrying a Letter to the Captain, which he was to deliver
to some Friend she had in that Country for
which he was bound; the poor Fellow
was immediately clapp'd under Hatches,
and, like other Felons, was made a Transport
for the Theft he had committed on his Lady's Honour. After which, MARMILLIO
received from OLIMPIA as full a Gratification of his Desires, as he had hoped, or she
had promised.

While the elder Brother was thus engaged, the younger was not left without his
Amusements. ARSINOE had Fondness e-
nough for him to oblige her to an endeavour to attract all his Moments; but in
spite of all she could do, his Heart could
not disentangle itself from that Snare, which
the Charms of ATTALINDA had spread a-
bout it. The unknown Lady also, who had
writ so obliging a Letter to him, sometimes
came in for a part in his divided Sentiments; Love of the one, and Curiosity to
discover the other, took up so much of
his Thoughts, that it was as much as all
the Endearments of ARSINOE could boast,
to claim a small share in his Inclinations.
He would have given almost any thing he
was master of, to have known who the
Lady was, whom he had made such an Impression

preſſion on ; but not all his Penetration
could ſerve him ſo far, and he was as much
to ſeek as ever, when he received a ſecond Billet from her, which contained theſe Lines.

To the Accompliſh'd CLEOMENES.

'HOW long will you ſuffer yourſelf
' to be accus'd of Unkindneſs, or
' Stupidity ? For to one of theſe two muſt
' be aſcrib'd your refuſing that Return my
' Paſſion hoped.——But perhaps you are
' not yet inſenſible on whom your Charms
' have wrought this Effect, and find nothing
' in me which can induce you to more
' than Compaſſion for the Languiſhments
' you have caus'd.——I wiſh to Heaven
' I knew the happy Beauty for whom you
' are ungrateful to all others : if worthy of
' yourLove, I might endure my Fate with leſs
' regret ; but if to the faint and proſtituted
' Graces of ARSINOE I owe the Miſery of
' hopeleſs Tenderneſs, I muſt confeſs that
' I am not able to ſupport the Shock.——
' I beg, therefore, that you will gratify me
' in one Requeſt ; which is, that if that
' Creature be not the Miſtreſs of your Af-
' fections, you will come into the Draw-
' ing-room to-morrow with a white Fea-
' ther in your Hat, inſtead of a crimſon
' one, which you have been accuſtom'd to
' wear ; but if ſhe be, which, alas ! I too

U   ' much

‘ much fear, make no alteration in your
‘ Drefs.————This, if you oblige me in,
‘ I will not fail to requite by fome Favour
‘ or other, which fhall be adequate to the
‘ Obligation.—— Farewel! I wifh you were
‘ lefs lovely, or I more worthy of attract-
‘ ing your kind Wifhes.’

Yours, Tenderly Devoted.

At fight of the Hand, which he perfectly knew again, he hoped this was an Eclair-
ciffement of what he fo much defired to
know ; but perceiving that this CYNTHIA
ftill concealed herfelf behind a Cloud, he
was more uneafy and difcontented than before. He did not fail, however, to oblige
her in the Requeft fhe had made him, and
appear’d the next day drefs’d after the richeft
and moft becoming manner he could invent, and a milk-white Feather in his Hat.
—— There was a great Court that day ;
but among all the Ladies who were there,
tho’ he look’d in the Faces of them all,
with Eyes the moft enquiring that could
be, he faw nothing in any of them which
could give him any light into the Truth.
As he was in a deep Cogitation on this
Affair, ATTALINDA came to the place
where he was ftanding ; and giving him a little rap on the Arm, You feem, *faid fhe*, another Man, methinks, to-day, CLEOMENES!
Pray

Pray to what fair Lady's Eyes do we owe the Alteration of your Colours, and your Humour? Thefe Words proceeding from a Mouth which had fo much charm'd him, made him immediately refume his former Vivacity: and looking on her with the moft tender Air, The Change of my Colours, Madam, *anfwer'd he*, is not a Symptom of the Alteration of my Heart, which never was fenfible of a true Paffion, but for one Object, nor never can defcend beneath the glorious Flame with which at firft it was infpired. Few Men, *faid fhe*, fpeak with this warmth of an abfent Miftrefs; and by your declaring yourfelf in this manner, I cannot but imagine I am of the acquaintance of this happy Lady.——If fo, make no fcruple to reveal who fhe is, I affure you I can be a faithful Confidante. She is indeed of your acquaintance, *reply'd he*, and I am confident will act in every thing according to your Defires:—— But before I prefume to name her to you, I muft engage your Promife to plead my Caufe with the utmoft Eloquence, and all the Arguments of prevailing Love.——Tell her I love her more than Words can fpeak——that all my Nights and Days are taken up in Contemplation on her Charms ——that I have no Wifh but what is her's. ——She forms my Dreams, and renders all my waking Moments happy, or curs'd, according

U 2

cording

cording as she smiles or frowns.——Tell
her, that for a long Age of Days I thus
have languish'd; and tho' I never yet have
dar'd to reveal my Passion, it has taken too
deep a root ever to be remov'd, or banish'd
from my Soul. The Face of ATTALINDA
was sometimes cover'd with a scarlet Blush,
at others, with a livid Paleness while he was
speaking : which he observing, interpreted
not to his disadvantage, and in spite of all
he had been told of her Passion for PHI-
LARCHUS, from that moment conceiv'd a
hope of being able to supplant him. Well,
said she, with a Countenance in which Joy
and Fear were visibly painted, when I
know to whom I should address these Discourses, I will not omit any thing which
may promise you Success: and, indeed, I
think a Passion such as you describe, join'd
with your other Merits, may almost assure
you of it. These Expressions, and the Air
with which they were pronounced, was a
sufficient Encouragement for him to declare
what he had till now, but with the utmost
Pain, conceal'd. He presently told her it
was no other than herself, and demanded
the performance of her Promise; on which
she look'd a little grave : But tho' she drew
her Features into an Air of the most re-
servedness she could assume, yet he easily
saw she was not in the least offended at
what he had said. This is strange Discourse,
resumed

refumed fhe, from one who I know profeffes himfelf the Lover of ARSINOE. The moft modeft Virgin, when attack'd with the profaneft Impudence, could not appear with greater Confufion, than did CLEOMENES at the Name of ARSINOE; he could not have imagin'd that a Lady who was fo fevere on the Failings of others, would herfelf expofe her own, nor was there any probability ATTALINDA could have this Information from any other hand: But recovering himfelf as well as he could, he thought it better to relate the Truth of every thing, which he did exactly, tho' in a fafhion as favourable as he could for AR-SINOE. There is not one tittle of this Adventure, *faid fhe, laughing, as foon as he had done fpeaking,* but what I have heard; with this addition to it, that you had with a great deal of Wit and Ill-nature ridicul'd my want of Beauty, and fpoke things fo greatly to my difadvantage, that I muft confefs I had not fo ill an opinion of myfelf, as to believe————I pretend not to Beauty, yet know I am not ugly :————— My Humour is not the moft entertaining in the world, neither is it difagreeable; nor am I quite a Fool, or have a ftinking Breath, or a thoufand other Imperfections, which I am told you branded me with.

CLEOMENES had fcarce Patience to hear her talk in this manner, without interrupting; but finding fhe feem'd not to give credit to fo cruel an Afperfion, he was the more eafily fatisfy'd: but when he perceiv'd fhe had done, he entreated her to let him know by whom he had been fo barbaroufly wrong'd. A very little perfuafion ferv'd to prevail on her, to tell him it was from ARSINOE fhe had heard the Character he had given of her; which enraged him to that violent degree, that he made no fcruple of letting her know that Lady had turn'd her own Words upon him.

All this Difcourfe happening in the Prefence-Chamber, they had no opportunity to give each other thofe Teftimonies of their mutual Approbation, which both with equal Adour long'd for; but ATTALINDA giving him permiffion to vifit her in the Evening, fhe order'd things fo againft his coming, that he found no Obftacles to impede his Wifhes.

In fine, he obtain'd of her the Joy he fo long had languifh'd for; and in the Tranfports of their mutual Endearments, fhe confefs'd that it was from her he had received thofe two Letters, which had given him fo much difquiet, while ignorant of the Author. I always liked, *faid fhe*, and had an Affection for your Perfon; but when you came to vifit me with MAZARES, was more charmed with your Wit and Behaviour. When you were gone, ARSINOE made me
the

the Confidante of what had pass'd between
you, and the Baseness of MAZARES in having betray'd her to you.———— I was not
without some Envy, when I heard her speak
with how much Rapture you return'd the
Condescensions made you, but could not
believe she had Charms capable of secu-
ring your Heart for ever: And when she
told me that you had pass'd some Censures
on me, which I was conscious I did not
merit, I was so far from giving credit to
what she said, that I imagin'd you had mention'd me but with too much regard for
her Repose; and to prevent me from having the same Sentiments, had invented that
heap of Absurdities.————In order, therefore, to be upon the square with her, I
writ to you. The Success has answer'd my
utmost Wishes, and if you can resolve to
be constant, think myself the most fortunate
of my Sex, in having engaged you.

'Tis not to be suppos'd that there was
any Deficiency of Oaths or Vows, to make
her secure of his eternal Faith; and she was
Woman, easily deluded Woman, and gave
credit to all the Asseverations he made.
Being now possess'd of all the Intimacies
he wish'd, he took the liberty of complaining that he had still a fear, that her Heart
was not so wholly his, as the Ardency of
his Affection made him desire; and then
related, tho' not in terms which she could

U 4   be

be offended at, what he had been told concerning PHILARCHUS. ATTALINDA was perfectly free from all Hypocrify, and frankly confefs'd that fhe once had been poffefs'd of the moft tender Sentiments, in favour of that young Gentleman ; but that his Ingratitude had entirely erafed them, fhe having difcovered, that, in fpite of a thoufand Obligations he had to her, he made the moft folemn Proteftations of Affection to a mean Creature, inferiour to her in every Circumftance.

CLEOMENES lov'd her not the lefs for the Freedom with which fhe acknowledg'd the Folly of her former Fondnefs; and thinking himfelf perfectly happy in that fhe now teftified for him, nothing could be more felicitous, than the Moments they pafs'd together. The Good-nature and Indolence of the Husband gave them frequent opportunities of feeing each other, in as private a manner as either of them could wifh : ATTALINDA defir'd no other Proof of his Affection, than that he would entirely quit the Society of ARSINOE, which he accordingly did : Nor found he much Reluctance in his compliance with that Requeft. All naturally defpife what comes with too much eafe ; and that very Confideration fhould have made ATTALINDA, had fhe not been of a Difpofition too gay to be capable of any folid Reflection, tremble

ble at her own Fate, and remember that
nothing can be more true, than thoſe Words
of the Poet, which thus reminds that eaſy
Sex to be cautious in what manner they
beſtow their Favours :

All naturally fly what does purſue ;
'Tis fit Men ſhould be coy, when Women
woo.

The End of the Fifth Part.

PART

PART VI. and Laſt.

IT was not the Charms of OLIM-
PIA, or any other Woman, could
make MARMILLIO neglectful of
what he owed his Prince; he ſaw
him torn with the ſevereſt Anguiſh, for the
expected departure of his dear Miſtreſs; he
found alſo in that Lady a Deſpair which
nothing could ſurmount, and kept his Brain
on a continual rack, for ſome Stratagem to
prevent the Misfortune which both equally
dreaded.————But all his Invention now
was at a loſs; the Princeſs, whoſe Commands alone had the power to awe ADRAS-
TUS into ſilence, had given him her Promiſe, that ISMONDA ſhould go with him:
and tho' that ſubtile Woman omitted nothing which ſhe thought might prevail on
her, to retract what ſhe had ſaid, yet HY-
ANTHE continued firm in her Reſolution;
and the exceſſive Uneaſineſs which the other
expreſs'd at the thoughts of returning to
her

her native Country, to her Kindred, and
with a Husband, who had ever been moſt
tender of her, at length made every body
imagine there was ſomething more in this
Reluctance, than ſhe made ſhow of, and
occaſion'd a ſtricter Scrutiny into her Behaviour than uſual. The Prince for that
reaſon was now oblig'd to refrain from
ſeeing her, unleſs in publick; and whenever they had any thing to communicate
to each other, MARMILLIO was the Perſon
who convey'd the Letters and Meſſages.
Nothing, however, being concluded on to
ſtop the impending Evil, and the time prefix'd for the departure of ADRASTUS arriv'd, there remain'd no other Expedient,
than that ISMONDA ſhould openly refuſe
accompanying him, under the pretence, that
having jealous Notions in his Head, ſhe apprehended ſome ill-uſage from him. This
was an excuſe which paſs'd current but
with a very few, becauſe *Anatolia* being
the place of her Nativity, and where ſhe
had many great and powerful Relations,
to whom ſhe might apply in caſe of his
Unkindneſs, her Cauſes of Fear appear'd to
have no real Foundation. And nothing
was now more publickly talk'd of, than
that it was more her Averſion for ADRAS-
TUS, than Love for HYANTHE, which would
not ſuffer her to leave the Court of *Cara-*
mania. The Eyes of that Princeſs alſo being
now

now partly open, as to the Artifices of that fair Hypocrite, she talk'd to her in a manner, which convinced her she no longer thought herself obliged by her stay. How great a Vexation this was to a Woman, who priz'd her Reputation above all things, excepting her Passion, any one may judge. She gave herself up to the most terrible Reflections, she wept incessantly when in private, and could not so far restrain herself in publick, but that it was easy for any one who saw her, to perceive the trouble she was in. Nor did THEODORE think himself less unhappy, or had more the power of concealing his Chagrin; and their mutual Discontent was so apparent, that scarce any Person about Court, but *thought* as much as ARIDANOR *knew* of the Misfortune of ADRASTUS.

MARMILLIO, who was perfectly acquainted with what was said, endeavour'd to stifle such Conjectures, but in vain; every one whisper'd it about, and the Blindness of the Princess, and the Ingratitude of her Woman, became at once the Theme of both Pity and Detestation. ISMONDA, however, having long since abandon'd Virtue, was now preparing herself to oppose Shame; and since Love and Glory in her Circumstances were grown things incompatible, to preserve the one, chose to renounce the other; and at last brought her assurance to

so

fo high a pitch, as to tell the Princefs, that
if fhe difcharg'd her from her Service,
it was a Misfortune, which to bear fhe
muft ftudy Patience, but nothing but being banifh'd from *Caramania* fhould oblige
her to quit it :——Nor even then, would
it be to *Anatolia* fhe would repair. Your
Highnefs, *faid fhe refolutely*, has power to
drive me from a place where you are Sovereign, but not to confine me to the Houfe
of a Husband, whofe ill Treatment has render'd odious to me all places where he is,
and from whofe miftaken Jealoufy I have
reafon to apprehend the moft terrible Con-
fequences. The Prince, in whofe prefence
fhe utter'd this, imagin'd he might now add
fomething in her favour, without feeming
to do fo out of any other Motive, than
pity for her Misfortunes, and that Complaifance which might be expected from
him to a Woman of her Quality. The Secrets of Marriage, Madam, *faid he to the
Princefs*, are only known to Perfons united
in thofe Bonds, nor are any others a fit
Judge of the Caufes of domeftick Diffe-
rences. Pardon me, therefore, if I think
'twould be an Act of Cruelty to abandon
a Lady in her Extremity, who depends a-
lone on you for Protection, and what I am
certain your Goodnefs will hereafter regret,
when you fhall hear, as probably you may,
that this ADRASTUS, whom you think fo
juft,

juſt, ſhall make no other uſe of your diſ-
charging from your Service his Wife, than
to revenge himſelf on her for an imagin'd
Wrong.———— Jealouſy is a Paſſion the
moſt terrible, and leaſt capable of forgiving
of any, for which the Soul finds room ;
and I entreat, in favour of this afflicted Beauty, that you will not ſend her from you,
at a time when her only Aſylum is here.
Conſider, Madam ! *continued he, more ſtre-
nuouſly,* ſhe had not quitted *Anatolia,* but
for the dutiful Regard and Love ſhe bore
HYANTHE ; nor had ADRASTUS Notions to
her prejudice, but for the long abſence
which thoſe Motives occaſion'd : Shall you
then, you, for whoſe ſake ſhe has incurred
his Diſpleaſure, abandon her to the Effects
of it ?———— O ! let it never be ſaid a Sovereign has ſo ill requited the Faith and Zeal
of a Subject.

'Tis certain, that at the beginning of this
Diſcourſe he deſign'd not to purſue it ſo
far ; but having once open'd his Mouth, to
plead a Cauſe in which he was ſo deeply
intereſted, he could not ſo far be maſter of
himſelf, as to conclude juſt when it was
conſiſtent with Prudence. The Princeſs
look'd on him with a fix'd regard all the
time he was ſpeaking ; and as ſhe wanted
not Penetration, tho' for a long time deceived by her own Virtue into a Belief of
others, now ſaw what ſhe, of all the world,
was

was laſt convinc'd of. But as ſhe was Miſtreſs of great Wiſdom, Conduct, and Preſence of Mind, ſhe in a moment recollect-
ed what would beſt become her to do ; and
after taking a very little time for conſideration, anſwer'd him in this manner : Never ſhall it be ſaid, that a Wife, who boaſts
to know the Duty of that State, preſumed
to contradict her Husband's Will. Ismonda, Sir, ſhall ſtill continue in *Caramania* ;
but remember, that the only Incitement to
my Grant, is my Obedience.

Her Heart was now too full to utter
more, and retired that moment with pre-
cipitation into her Cloſet ; where ſhe ſhut
herſelf up, and gave a looſe to the over-
boiling Paſſions of her troubled Soul. She
now found that the hopes ſhe had long
flatter'd herſelf with, of being Miſtreſs of
the Affections of Theodore, were but in
vain ; and that while ſhe imagin'd ſhe had
the moſt faithful Friend in Ismonda, ſhe
had been cheriſhing a Viper to ſting her in
the moſt tender Part. It was with an in-
finity of Tenderneſs ſhe regarded her Huſ-
band, and was as ſenſible as Woman could
be, of the wrong he had done her Love
and Virtue ; yet did ſhe entertain no thoughts
of revenging it in the manner ſome Wives
would do, nor vented her Diſcontent in
Revilings, and Exclamations, as it is ordinary for Women to do on thoſe occaſions.

To

To Heaven alone did she complain, and from the divine Powers entreated either a Mitigation of her Misfortunes, or Patience to endure them.——— And indeed it must be confess'd, that never Wife was an Example of greater Resignation, Fortitude, and Moderation. She consider'd, that to fly into Passion, would but render her Condition worse, by exposing to the World her Husband's Weakness, and her want of that Power she ought to have over him; that Pity was but a poor Relief for a Misfortune such as her's, yet that was all she could expect by revealing it; and that to accuse the Prince with any terms of Wrath, would but provoke him to avow his Crime to her face, and by that means lay her under the necessity either of coming to an open Rupture with him, or, by brooking such a Contempt tamely, testify a meanness of Spirit, which was not in her nature. She chose therefore not to seem to know what, acknowledging to know, she must resent, but had not the power of redressing.

Would all Wives take this method, there would not so many of them become hateful to their Husbands, and despicable in the eyes of their Acquaintance, who, for the most part, more *scorn* than *pity* their want of Charms. Never was any Heart less capable of Hypocrisy, than that of HYAN-THE; and tho' her Prudence made her resolve,

folve, neither by her Words or Actions, to
give the Prince room to imagine fhe had
the leaft jealous Thought, yet could fhe
not at all times fo well difguife the Truth,
but that he difcover'd it : and if this Conduct did not make him love, it caufed in
him the extremeft Veneration and Efteem
for her. And fhe finding him increafe in
the Refpect he paid her, more eafily endured his want of Love, hoping that alfo
would enfue ; and that when fatiated with
the Poffeffion of unlicens'd Charms, he
might at laft return to thofe which had a
juft Claim to his Regard, and by his future
Tendernefs repay the too long neglected
Merits of a fuffering Wife. But in what
terms is it poffible to defcribe in any manner, which can give the Reader a juft Notion of it, the Diftraction of ADRASTUS,
when he found himfelf by this means difappointed of revenging the Injury he too
well knew was done him by this ungrateful Wife. He made his Complaint to all
to whom he fpoke, of the Injuftice done
him, in detaining from him the Woman,
whom by all the Laws of Heaven and
Earth was his, engaged the whole Body of
the reverend *Magi* to urge the Princefs in
his behalf; but all being unfuccefsful, fcarce
could he refrain from uttering all he knew,
and expofing the Guilt of THEODORE, which
he imagin'd was yet a Secret to HYANTHE :

X   yet

yet in fpite of the tempeftuous Paffion
which invaded him, and like an Earth
quake fhook his tormented Soul, fo
true was his Affection for his Sovereign,
that he forbore, painful as the Reftraint
was to him, uttering the leaft Syllable,
which might occafion a fufpicious Thought
to the prejudice of his Daughter's Repofe.
ARIDANOR and CLEARCHUS were the only
Perfons to whom he difcours'd with freedom of his Misfortune : and the former of
thefe was now involv'd in Vexations, which
left him little the power of liftening to
thofe of other People.

The Intrigue between him and ZELINDA
had now lafted a confiderable time for Perfons of their gay Temper ; the Condefcen-
fions fhe had made him, and the Submif-
fion fhe had teftify'd on the fcore of ELA-
RIA, however, making him imagine fhe
felt really for him what might be call'd a
true Affection, made him endeavour to be
as grateful as poffible : and tho' nothing
could be a Task more fevere than that he
impos'd on himfelf in this behaviour, he
exerted all the *Man* about him to diffemble a Tendernefs for her, equal to that fhe
had feem'd to have for him : but how eafy
is it for thofe who are at all acquainted with
the Paffion, to diftinguifh the true Ardours
from the counterfeit ? She plainly faw that
he would find nothing lefs difficult, than

to

to part from her, if he could find a hand-
fome pretence for it; which Indifference,
join'd to the inceffant Importunities of a
new Adorer, made her become as negligent in her Endearments, as of late fhe
had perceiv'd he was. And one Evening,
perceiving he came not at the appointed
Hour, fhe gave admittance to her new Enamorato; and to prevent any Interruption
in the Entertainment fhe was now refolv'd
to permit him to give her, writ to ARIDA-
NOR a Billet, containing thefe Lines.

To the Inconftant ARIDANOR.

'WHEN I fo readily forgave your
'   Intrigue with ELARIA, it was not
' that I lov'd too little, but too much; ill
' therefore does your Indifference repay fo
' true a Paffion, and worfe would it be-
' come me to receive the Careffes of a Man,
' who, by the faintnefs of them, denotes
' he is no longer influenc'd by Inclination.
' ———For Heaven's fake then throw off
' this forc'd Complaifance! I have now
' brought myfelf to a Difpofition to en-
' dure your abfence without complaining;
' and as I am perfectly acquainted with the
' Change in your Sentiments, fhall make
' no fcruple to declare mine, and affure
' you that it is my defire we fhould meet
' no more as Lovers, and that you fhould,

but

‘ but as a Dream, remember what has paſt
‘ between You and

ZELINDA.

Her new Admirer being in the Room
while ſhe ſtep'd into her Cloſet to write this,
ſhe was in ſo much haſte to return to him,
that ſhe entirely forgot to order the Page,
by whom ſhe ſent it, to give it into no other
Hand than that of ARIDANOR himſelf;
who being at that time from home, the inadvertent Boy deliver'd it to his Gentleman,
with whom, however, it had been ſufficiently ſecure, had not BARSINA unluckily
croſs'd the Hall the moment of its being
brought. The ſight of the Page, the knowledge of his Lady's Humour, and the Obſer-
vation ſhe had made on the frequent Viſits
which her Lord had for ſome time made
there, gave her a ſort of jealous Curioſity
to know the Contents of this Letter. The
Emiſſary of ZELINDA was therefore no
ſooner out of the Houſe, than ſhe commanded the other to give it her, which he
endeavouring to evade, increaſ'd her Suſpicion, and her Reſolution to become Miſtreſs of it. ARIDANOR, *ſaid ſhe*, has no
Secrets to which I am a Stranger, nor will
he condemn you for entruſting in my hands
any Paper directed for him : but to remove
whatever Fears your Duty may ſuggeſt on
this occaſion, I give you my Honour not
to

to open it——the Seal, till broke by him,
shall remain untouch'd, and it is only with
a design of a little innocent Raillery, that I
desire to be the bearer of it myself. The
Gentleman, who knew the perfect Agreement between them, and beside cou'd not
imagine that if there were any Affair improper to be communicated to her, ZE-
LINDA would have taken so little Care in
the delivering it, made no farther hesitation
to obey her. She retir'd immediately with
it in her Hand, but being a Woman nicely
punctual to her Word, would not venture
to break it open, but laying it carefully up
in her Cabinet, resolv'd to proceed in such a
manner, as should fully inform her of the
Contents, without running the hazard of incurring the Displeasure of her Lord, or for-
feiting her Promise to his Gentleman. She
was however in the utmost uneasiness till
ARIDANOR came in; she long'd to be convinc'd of that, which she but too much
fear'd, when known, would be far from
restoring her to that Tranquillity she was
us'd to enjoy : yet so terrible to be borne are
perturbations of Suspence, that whoever
labours under them, would fly to the most
stabbing certainty for change of Torment.
    At length he came, and she no sooner
saw his Chariot enter the Court-yard, from
a Window where she sat on purpose to ob-
serve, than she sent to desire he would come

to her inftantly : which requeft being immediately comply'd with, fhe faluted him
in thefe Terms ; My Lord, *faid fhe*, a
Letter directed for you, has fallen, by accident, into my hands; but as I have been
fo honourable not to open it, I hope you
are too generous not to communicate
the Contents of it to me, the manner of
its being brought having fill'd me with a
Curiofity, which I am the lefs afham'd to
confefs, becaufe it is the firft time I ever was
guilty of it. Thefe Words, and the fight
of the Hand, cover'd the whole Face of
ARIDANOR with a fcarlet Blufh ; never,
before, had he experienc'd fuch a Dilemma,
he knew not how either to evade, or comply with her entreaty ; and having ftood for
fome moments filent, and in a Pofture
which heighten'd her Sufpicions, at laft,
Madam, *faid he, but not without fome hefitation in his Voice*, this Letter, tho directed for me, is intended for another Perfon ;
and I cannot, without the utmoft injuftice
to thofe who have intrufted me, make even
you a partner in the Secret. O Sex moft
fertile in Invention, and practis'd in Deceit!
*cry'd fhe, unable to contain the Pangs
which Jealoufy now fhot through every
aching Fibre of her Heart*, I expected fome
fuch mean Equivocation from a Guilt like
thine.——*Man*, however imperious, lord-
ly, and unforgiving when in power, is ever
fawning,

fawning, fearful, and poor in Spirit, when detection's near, and stretches out her uncorrupted Hand to draw from off his Crime the Vail which has obscured it. ——Ungrateful Lord! *pursued she*, Is it to the Lover of ZELINDA I have preserv'd myself so true a Wife!——Is it thus, that Virtue, Truth, and Tenderness must be repaid!—— O could I as easily throw off those Principles in which my Youth was bred, forget, like thee, all sense of Honour and of Shame, how might I make thee tremble at my Revenge ?——In spite of thy Indifference, I am still thy Wife, and by that Title, am impower'd, when e'er I please, to load thee with Disgrace, great as the Indignity thou hast offer'd me——But well, alas! thou knowest, I too much fear the Gods, and prize my own unspotted Purity, to retaliate in kind the wrong thou hast done me. ——Go on then, sin in security, and laugh at my Reproaches; but think not that high Heaven will always suffer thee to triumph over the sacred Laws, and abuse the Virtue of an enduring Wife.

In this manner did she continue, venting the tempestuous Passions of her Soul, for a considerable time, without his offering one word of Interruption; but at length, that Tenderness which had at first engaged him to marry her, and had never since forsook his Breast, gave way to the natural

ve-

vehemence and impatience of his Temper.
——He now ceas'd or to deny, or to excufe his Crime ; and telling her, That whatever Faults the heats of Youth might have
made him guilty of, it ought not to be a
Perfon who had fo well profited by the Folly
of his amorous Inclination that fhould upbraid him with it, flung out of the Chamber, leaving her; when Rage a little abated,
and gave room for cool Reflection, to repent that fhe fo far had urg'd him.

When ARIDANOR had enough recover'd
himfelf from that fudden diforder which his
late Rage had involv'd him in, he read the
Letter which had been the Caufe of it; he
would have thank'd ZELINDA for difcharg-
ing him from his Attendance, had fhe done
it in any other manner : but the imprudence
of her Conduct, in expofing both herfelf
and him, to that very Perfon, from whom
of all the World fhe fhould moft carefully
have conceal'd their Amour, made him now
defpife and hate, what before he had but a
fmall fhare of efteem for. He blamed his
Wife alfo for the Terms in which fhe had
exprefs'd her Refentment, much more than
for the Refentment itfelf; but as he truly
lov'd her, he eafily abfolv'd her this little
Fault, which he was fenfible was more occafion'd by the extreme Tendernefs fhe had
for him, than by any thing of that *womanifh
Pride*, which, as frequently as *Love*, renders

ders a Wife tenacious of her Prerogative, and jealous of her Right. He would not, however, feem to forgive what fhe had faid, refolving to make his own ufe of the opportunity fhe had given him, to execute a Defign which he had for fome time been forming, but could not till now bring to perfection.

ALMIRA began to fhow the Misfortune which her inadvertent Paffion had drawn on her, in too vifible a manner for him not to fear it would foon become fo to the whole World; and having of late no opportunity of fpeaking to IDOMEUS concerning the Affair, that young Lord abfenting himfelf from his Houfe, and keeping for the moft part out of town, he had for a long time been prodigioufly uneafy, that fhe did not make fome pretence to remove; which perceiving fhe made not the leaft Effort to do, he thought he had now a fit Excufe, on his Quarrel with her Sifter, to defire fhe would quit his Houfe. He therefore refolv'd to keep up his Refentment; and tho' BARSINA, fenfible of the wrong ftep fhe had taken, entreated to be admitted, he fhut himfelf up, refus'd to fee her, and fent her word, that if fhe defir'd to expiate the Fault fhe had been guilty of, her beft way would be not to remind him of it, by coming into his prefence, till he fhould let her know he had forgiven it.

But

But not being able long to counterfeit this
cruel Humour to a Woman he so sincerely
lov'd as BARSINA, as well as because he
thought it full time ALMIRA should be
gone, he order'd his Page to carry a Letter
to her Chamber, which contained these
Lines.

To ALMIRA.

'YOU are not ignorant that no other
' Motive, than the most pure Affec-
' tion to BARSINA, made me become her
' Husband, nor that the Love I bore her
' made every thing which was dear to her
' esteem'd by me. As a Sister, you have
' been treated by me with a Brother's Ten-
' derness; but as the Circumstances in which
' we once stood have changed their face,
' accuse it not as a Levity in me, that I
' desire you to remove to some place where
' you may reside with more ease, than you
' can at present in the Family of the

Discontented

ARIDANOR.

P. S. ' The sooner you provide yourself,
' the better, because here may happen Rup-
' tures will no way please you to be wit-
' ness of. Farewel; every thing is not what
' it seems, nor I so much unkind as this
' Epistle may make me appear in your Ima-
' gination.' Let

Let any one put themfelves, if Imagination can fo far tranfport them, one moment into the Condition of the unhappy
ALMIRA; and they may then, but no otherwife, be able to conceive what 'twas fhe
endur'd. She doubted not but the Secret
of her Misfortune was divulg'd, and fuppos'd that only that was the occafion of
thofe Ruptures mention'd in the Poftfcript.
ARIDANOR had indeed contriv'd it with fo
much Art, that fhe might believe it to be
fo, yet no other Perfon to whom fhe
might happen to fhow it, have fufpicion of the Truth.————What could fhe
now do? To whom could fhe have recourfe
for Advice? IDOMEUS fhe had not feen for
fome days, and fhe guefs'd the reafon of
his abfence, was on account of what had
pafs'd between them being difcover'd. Her
Sifter was in fo great a diforder, that fhe
defir'd none might come into her Chamber, and this afflicted Beauty now look'd
on that alfo as proceeding from the fame
Caufe: Believing herfelf therefore the occafion of the whole Difturbance which had
happen'd in the Family, fhe refolv'd to go
out of it immediately; and as none of thofe
to whom fhe imagin'd her Shame was known
demanded to fee her, had little Inclination
to defire it. Diftracted therefore with the
various Idea's that ran that moment thro'
her

her whirling Brain, fhe bid her Woman
pack up her Clothes, and every thing belonging to her, in order to leave a Houfe
which had been fo fatal to her.————Let
us make hafte, *faid fhe to her*, to be gone
from this detefted place, this Scene of Ruin,
Perjury, and Deceit, and where even Nature fails to take the part of one, who ought
to be moft dear by Blood and Intereft; even
BARSINA, that once dear Sifter, that engaging Friend, here forfakes ALMIRA, and
drives her out to Mifery and Shame, and all
the Woes that attend helplefs and betray'd
Innocence.———— Gods! *continued fhe*, is
the Fault I have committed of that unpardonable nature, that none will vouchfafe
a hand to help me!————If I have thrown a
Stain on my Family, and thereby forfeited
my Pretenfions to the Favour I might expect from a Sifter fo feverely virtuous, muft
ARIDANOR too abandon me ? Muft he expofe and thruft me out to the wide pitilefs
World?————He, whom had I never feen,
I had been happy, IDOMEUS had been then
a ftranger to my Eyes, nor had I ftood in
need of Friendfhip, or Affiftance! ————
O Monfter! Villain! perfidious, ungrateful
IDOMEUS! *added fhe, after a little Paufe*,
to what unfathomable Depth of Wretched-
nefs haft thou reduced me!————She utter'd
thefe Words with too much Vehemence
for them not to be obferv'd, by her Woman

man and another Servant, who were then
waiting in the Room. It was not, however, their bufinefs to take notice they obferv'd any thing farther than what fhe had
commanded ; and 'tis poffible, tho' not
exceeding probable, according to the Difpofition of the greateft part of thofe of their
Profeffion, that their Lady's Secret might
have been fafe in their poffeffion, had nothing elfe happen'd to betray it : But alas!
the Diforders of this poor Lady's Mind
wrought fo far on her Body, that the Effect was prefently difcern'd in more than
Words——each Limb began to tremble
with convulfive Strugglings, and every Nerve
confefs'd an Agony before unknown. In
fine, fhe fell into that Condition, which
thofe who are moft experienced in it dread,
but which in its firft tryal is fcarce to be
fupported.—— No longer now had fhe
the power of retaining Senfe either of Shame
or Fear ; Refentment too was banifh'd from
her Breaft, and all the Wifh was left her,
was to be eas'd by any Means, or Perfon.
Her Woman prefently conceiving what her
Condition was, and fearing the Agonies
fhe faw her in, if not immediately reliev'd,
would be her death, ran to acquaint BAR-
SINA with the News. At firft fhe was deny'd admittance by the Lady's Page, who
waited in an outer Room ; but her crying
out that ALMIRA was dying, and the Shrieks
of

of that unhappy Creature by this time reach-
ing the Ears of the whole Family, her Sifter open'd the Door, to know the meaning
of so confused a Noise; which being whifper'd to her by the Attendant of ALMIRA,
she accompany'd her, almost wild with Afto-
nishment and Grief, to her Chamber, where
she indeed found her in a Condition such
as could leave no room to imagine it any
other than really it was. Utterly impof-
sible is it to express the mingled Rage and
Concern, which at this Object invaded the
whole Soul of the virtuous BARSINA: yet
in this juncture, testifying a more than ordinary Presence of Mind, and prizing the
Reputation of her Sister above even her Life,
she order'd a Hackney-Chair to be brought
immediately to the Door, and forced her
into it, giving the Charge herself to the
Men to what place they should carry her,
which was to the House of a Midwife,
whom she knew she could oblige to keep
the Secret. She had no sooner dispatch'd
her from view, than she sent her Woman
after her with such things as were proper
for the Condition she was in, but continued in the most terrible Agonies for so
unexpected and so shameful an Accident.

In the mean time, the Author of this
Misfortune, inconstant IDOMEUS, was engaged in Adventures, which made him
wholly negligent of what might befall this
wretched

wretched Victim of his wavering Defires.
By accident, he had one day ftray'd into
the Temple of the Sun, a place he was
ufed but little to frequent; but as if the
God had determin'd to take vengeance on
him, for the little regard he paid to his
Altars, he no fooner approach'd the facred
Shrine, than he was ftruck with a fudden
Fire, more fierce than even his Rays, un-
aided by the Charms of Beauty, had the
power of kindling. The fparkling Eyes of
LUTHELINA, a young Virgin of noble Blood,
being placed oppofite to the fpot on which
he ftood, fhot into the very Soul of the
amorous Youth fuch Flames, as were not
to be extinguifh'd but by Enjoyment: Strong
as fwift he felt their mighty Force; but
that not being a place in which he could
accoft her in the manner he wifh'd to do,
the facred Ceremony over, he order'd his
Page to follow and obferve into what Houfe
fhe went, and not to return without a full
Information of her Name, and the Circumftances of her prefent Condition. IDO-
MEUS was of a Difpofition arbitrary over
thofe on whom he had power, refolute in
having his Commands fulfill'd, and fufficiently generous in rewarding Services, to
engage the utmoft from his Dependants.
The Perfon whom he employ'd on this Errand, had too much to fear from his Indignation, and alfo to hope from his Li-
berality,

berality, not to make him diligent in his Enquiries; and he so well succeeded in them, as to bring him an account that this young Beauty was the Daughter of a *Dalmatian* Lord, who, having wasted the best part of his Fortune in an unsuccessful Quarrel, had left her, with two other Sisters, wholly on the dependance of an Aunt, who was happily married to one of the most wealthy Commoners in *Caramania*; by whom having no Children, and now of an Age too much advanced to hope for any, the three Orphans had been educated as her own: and that the two elder being married with her Consent, had received from her Bounty Portions equal to what might have been expected with them, had they been really her own. But this blooming Charmer attracting the universal Admiration of the Men, the old Lady kept in a very close Restraint, never permitting her to go abroad without her, or receive any Visits but such as she was pleased to think proper. This Account was but little pleasing to IDOMEUS; he had not only the Virtue and Virgin-Fearfulness of the young one to combat with, but also the watchful Diligence of the old one to deceive: he was resolv'd, however, not to give way to Despair, without having first made a tryal of the Difficulties which he must surmount to become Master of his Wishes. Having no acquaintance

tance with any of the Family, nor with
any who could introduce him, he made it
his bufinefs to find out what publick Places
the Uncle moft frequented ; which having
learn'd, he never fail'd meeting him, and
by degrees brought himfelf fo much into
his good Opinion, that he invited him to
his Houfe. This was all at prefent our
young Adventurer requir'd ; and being one
day prefs'd by him in a very friendly manner to go home with him from the Ten-
nis-Court, where they had been at play,
he joyfully accepted the Offer ; and the
more gladly, becaufe it being before Din-
ner, he was certain of feeing the Ladies.

Thus far every thing fucceeded according
to his wifh ; but never was Man fo con-
fufed as he, when, the Table being ferv'd,
the Aunt and Niece appear'd ; the fulfome
Compliments he receiv'd from the one,
and the Beauties of the other rendring him
incapable of judging in what manner he
fhould behave. He no fooner began to
fay a gallant thing to the one, than the o-
ther would interrupt him, by telling him
how like her Niece was to her, and twenty
times over affuring him, that tho' fhe was
her Aunt, fhe was very little older ; that
her Brother was a Man when fhe was no
more than a Child, and that LUTHELINA
and fhe, by thofe who knew them not,
were taken for Sifters. Had it been at any

other

Other time, the Vanity of this Beldame would have been a fufficient matter of Diverfion to him; but the Impertinence of her Chat now hindring him from declaring his Sentiments to the young Lady, made him almoft diftracted; and fcarce cou'd he refrain from letting her fee by his Anfwers, that it was of little confequence to him of what Age fhe was: but with the Praifes fhe was inceffantly giving herfelf, fhe mingled fo many of him, that it was not in his power to be rude, and at laft put a thought into his Head which he refolv'd to cherifh as a fortunate one.

He judg'd, with Reafon, that when a Woman takes an over-care to appear amiable in the eyes of Mankind, it is not without an ambition of being told fhe is fo; and that fuch a Perfon might, with eafe, be brought to believe any thing by him fhe imagines is her Lover. To counterfeit that Character, he prefently perceiv'd was the only means to engage one of hers to his Intereft; and tho he could not, as yet, form any direct Rules in what manner he fhould proceed hereafter, he fancy'd it would be the beft beginning he could make; not doubting, but when he was once become free enough in the Family, to have an opportunity of talking to the young Lady, he fhould eafily convince her, it was not the antiquated Beauties of her Aunt, which render'd him fo affiduous.   In

In fine, he turn'd the whole Frame of his
Behaviour and Difcourfe in fuch a manner,
that fhe who had not for a long Series of
Years known what it had been to have fuch
fine things faid to her, was perfectly tranfported, and believing him really enamour'd
with her, had not the leaft jealous thought
that he was fo elfewhere, as otherwife the
natural Envy of her Difpofition would have
made her prefently obferve ; and was fo far
from denying him admittance to her Houfe,
as fhe.had done many who had profefs'd
themfelves the Lovers of LUTHELINA, that
fhe intreated him to come as frequently as
he could, affur'd him her Gates fhould be
always open to receive him ; and not only
by her Words, but alfo by her Eyes, if
Glances of a Woman turn'd of Fifty may be
allow'd to be intelligible to a young Man
of twenty five, made it her endeavour
to convince him a more welcome Gueft
cou'd not arrive.

Purfuant to the firft ftep he had taken, he
manag'd the Affair fo well in the fucceed-
ing Vifits he made her, that in a very fmall
time fhe became enamour'd of him to the
utmoft pitch of Dotage ; which is all the
Term one can afford to a Woman, who,
at her Age, confeffes a Paffion that even
Youth is put to the Blufh to acknowledge.
But being belov'd by her, was the leaft of
what he aim'd at, and as his Defign was

through

through the Aunt to make his way to the
Niece, he took the opportunity her mistaken Fondnefs gave him ; and, counterfeiting too well for one who fo much contribu-
ted to her own Deception to fee into the
Cheat, perfuaded her to pretend a Journey
to a Relation in the Country, and abfcond
for a fmall time with him. It is not to be
believ'd with how much greedinefs fhe fwal-
low'd the Bait he had prepar'd for her, and
telling her Husband that fhe had receiv'd
Letters that a Coufin of hers was extremely
ill, would needs go immediately away ; and
that, not only becaufe fhe was in hafte to be
gone to one, who fhe faid was fo dear a
Friend, but alfo pretending a Frugality,
which fhe knew was not difpleafing to him
whom fhe endeavour'd to deceive, that fhe
would fave the Charges of travelling with an
Equipage, and go privately in the Stage-
Coach. Every thing favouring her Defigns,
fhe, like the Moon, was loft in Clouds, to
have the better Opportunity of indulging
her expected Raptures with the lov'd EN-
DIMION, invifible by mortal Eyes. IDO-
MEUS contriv'd the place to which fhe went,
fhould be fo near the Town, that he could
with eafe go thither every day, and return at
night, which he was always punctual in doing, to take off all fufpicion that he had
any other defign in vifiting the great City,
than to prevent the fcandalous Obfervers of
the

the Intimacy between them, from imagining they were gone together.

Now was the beauteous LUTHELINA left
a defenceless Prey to the subtile Invader :
the watchfulness of her Aunt had, hitherto,
taken away all occasion for her setting that
guard over herself, which all Women are
instructed in, and which, when ever they
stray, most certain Ruin overtakes their
Steps; and she was as incapable of resisting
the Impulses which Love and Nature create
in a youthful Breast, as she would have been
to have subdu'd an Army by any other
Weapons than her Eyes. IDOMEUS needed
no more than to declare his Passion to inspire an equal share in her; the little she had
been suffer'd to hear of Discourses of this
kind, made her now listen to what he said
with double Pleasure; and by reading of
Romances, having been taught, that to be
ador'd was the Prerogative of her Sex, had
too often look'd on it as a hardship to be
deny'd that Triumph, not to consider the
Liberty she now enjoy'd, as the greatest Blef-
sing could have befallen her. This was indeed a Disposition which might have been
fatal instead of advantageous to his Designs,
because the same Motives which induced her
Vanity to give ear to him with pleasure,
would certainly have inclin'd her to receive
the same Declarations from others also; but
to prevent this Evil, he took care never to

Y 3   be

be abfent from her but in thofe hours which
call'd him to her Aunt, and in which fhe
could not, with decency, admit the Vifits of
Perfons of a different Sex.

What is it that continu'd Importunities,
when mix'd with Inclination, and favour'd
by Time and Place, bring to pafs! The Vanity of this young Charmer firft inclin'd her
to receive his Addreffes; his Accomplifh-
ments and agreeable Perfon, brought her afterwards to be as well pleas'd with the *Lover*
as the *Love*; and the Softnefs of her Sex at
laft, to think nothing too much to reward
an Affection, which fhe imagin'd no lefs *fincere* than it appear'd to be *violent*. In a
word, as he wanted not Courage to ask every thing of her, fo there was nothing he defired, that he did not obtain. This indeed
muft be faid of him, that in fome meafure he deferv'd her, fince never QUIXOTE
of Romance did more to obtain the DUL-
CINEA of his Hopes, than he, in conftrain-
ing himfelf to counterfeit Ardors for a
Woman, whofe Experience render'd it very
difficult to impofe on her, and who would
not have fail'd to have remark'd the leaft
deficiency in Behaviour: but this was a Merit of which he durft not boaft, but which
alfo brought with it its own Conveniencies,
to make amends for the prefent Toil; becaufe whenever he grew tired with the Poffeffions of the Charms of his young Miftrefs,

ftrefs, he had no more to do, than by growing cold to the old one, occafion her return
to Town, and by that means be releas'd
from his Obligations to that undone Beauty, without incurring the Reputation of
Ingratitude or Falfhood. He was too well
acquainted with the Inconftancy of his own
Humour, not to know that this would infallibly happen fome day or other; and felt an
infinite deal of Pleafure in his own Mind,
at thinking how well he was provided of an
Expedient to rid himfelf, whenever he
pleas'd, of Embraces in which he no longer
cou'd find a Joy.

But this fell not out immediately; it was
in the very height of his Amour with LUTHE-
LINA, that that unfortunate Accident hap-
ned to ALMIRA; and his time being wholly
fhar'd between the amorous Aunt, and lovely Niece, he had not appear'd in the Palace
of ARIDANOR for many days. His abfence
adding to the Diftraction which her prefent
Condition involv'd her in, made her fall
into Ravings, which foon difcover'd, to all
about her, who it was that was the Author
of her Shame. The News was foon communicated to BARSINA; and that Lady
thinking what fhe had to fay, a fufficient
Plea for breaking through the Injunction
her Lord had lately laid on her, told ARIDA-
NOR; who, fhe fufpected not, had before
any knowledge of the Affair, IDOMEUS

being

being unmarried, she propos'd that he should
repair the Injury he had done her Sister, by
marrying her with all convenient speed:
nor could less be expected from a Lady
of so much Virtue, and who had all the
Affection for the unfortunate ALMIRA, that
could possibly be paid by one so near by
Blood. But ARIDANOR, who knew the
Disposition of his Brother, and also that his
Circumstances could not well admit of such
a Match, endeavour'd to silence her by these
Words; It is not, Madam, *said he*, in the
power of a younger Brother to marry according to his Inclinations, and I, by following mine, have render'd him yet less
able to do so, than had I enrich'd my Family by bringing a Lady into it more eminent
for her Wealth, than for those more worthy
Qualifications I found in you. And is this
all the Reparation, *resum'd she*, that you
think is owing to the poor ALMIRA for her
Loss of Honour, and the Disgrace which
it has brought on all ally'd to her? The
Title of my Wife defends you from that
fear, *reply'd he*; and tho I truly pity your
unhappy Sister, and equally with yourself
condemn the Action IDOMEUS has been
guilty of, yet will I never advise him to
atone for it by the way you mention——
I beg therefore, *continued he*, that for the
sake of mine and your own Peace, you will
cease to urge a Suit which it is the fix'd de-

ter-

termination of my Soul for ever to refuſe.
BARSINA, whoſe only fault was having
a Spirit a little too great, could not contain
herſelf at theſe Words, and forgetting how
dear her late Raſhneſs had coſt her, relaps'd
into a worſe and more dangerous Exceſs of
it; and if ARIDANOR wanted a Stock of
Patience ſufficient to endure her Reproaches,
even when they were occaſion'd by a Fault
of which he knew himſelf guilty, how
little could he ſupport them for a Crime
tranſacted by another, and in which he had
no hand? In fine, Paſſion on both ſides
grew too high at laſt to be confin'd within
the bounds of even good manners, and that
decorum, which ought always to be preſerv'd among People of Condition, and
which, indeed, more than by their Titles,
diſtinguiſhes them from thoſe of a mean
Education : which ARIDANOR perceiving,
and fearing he might be tranſported to
ſomething unbecoming his Character, was
enough Maſter of himſelf to quit the Room.
But BARSINA thinking ſhe had now a more
juſtifiable reaſon for Reſentment than before, and beſides that rage of Temper ſhe
was poſſeſs'd of, being continually kept
warm by the daily Complainings of her
Siſter, and the Whiſpers ſhe heard concerning her, as her Misfortune grew more reveal'd, could not entertain the leaſt thought
of ſubmitting, and reſolv'd in her own
Mind,

Mind, as much as a Woman who truly loves can do, never to be reconcil'd to her Husband without he confented to ufe his utmoft endeavours for the Nuptials of Ido- meus and Almira.

In this diftracted Pofition were the Fa- mily and Mind of Aridanor, when A- drastus fought relief and mitigation of his Sorrows in his Advice and Society : how little he was able to afford it to another, the Reader will eafily judge by the knowledge how much he ftood in need of it himfelf.— Clearchus was the only Perfon who knew the Truth of this noble *Anatolian's* Misfortune, and was capable of talking freely to him concerning it; all means, therefore, as has been before obferv'd, ha- ving been try'd and found ineffectual for the removal of Ismonda, it was his Coun- fel, that his Friend fhould no more add to the Torments he endur'd, by profecuting an Endeavour which he had fo often experi- enc'd was but fruitlefs: and the Perfuafions of this known faithful Man, together with the apprehenfions of offending the King by too long an abfence, at laft prevail'd on him to leave *Caramania*; but with what Grief of Soul, none but a Husband who loves, and has like him been injur'd, can con- ceive. But whatever were his Anxieties, they could not furpafs the Tranfport which his departure afforded his tranfgreffing

Wife,

Wife, and her enamour'd Prince. The one, now become paft the care of Reputation, and the other believing himfelf fafe from all Reproach, gave a loofe to Rapture greater than ever they had durft to indulge before, and for a time, one would indeed have believ'd the Poet's Divinity had been in fuch a Love as theirs, fo much beyond the ordinary Extafies of that Paffion, were the Portion of their every meeting; but as nothing but a real Godhead can be immutable, the Fiend at laft difclos'd itfelf, and fadly transferr'd this Scene of heavenly Delights, to one all black and horrid.

There is nothing more certain in the Affairs of Love, than that Security is the Parent of Satiety; and if we in the leaft confult either Philofophy or Nature, 'tis eafy to be accounted for. What a Man fears to lofe, he is for ever endeavouring to preferve; but when Doubt is no more, and you have no farther to do than to go on in one continu'd round, the moft pleafing Circle, in time, grows dull, and the once ardent Lover flackens in his Race; the Spirits cool, and Defire begins to nod, when free from all Interruptions in the way, and unalarm'd by any purfuing Fears. Befides, of the moft lufcious Fruits we fooneft furfeit : what is given us but fparingly, would never fail to excite our keeneft Appetite; but when allow'd at large, and the rapacious

Will

Will is left without a Check, with too
much greedineſs we devour, and the rich
Sweets with too much Plenty cloy. To all
this may be added, that ISMONDA buoying
up Ambition with fancy'd Merit, and the
Plea of having now abandon'd every thing
for Love, was loſt to all but the return of
that dear ruinous Paſſion ; imprudently ex-
acted from the Prince as a Right, that which
is never with pleaſure granted when expected.————Love ſhould be free, and un-
confin'd as Air; the leaſt reſtraint deſtroys
the Bliſs, changes its very Nature, and per-
verts that to forced Complaiſance, which
was before all Extaſy and Joy.

Little did MARMILILO imagine, when
he brought VIOLETTA for the better continuance of indulging his Paſſion for CA-
RICLEA, that the Beauties of that Virgin
would occaſion him the Troubles he was
now involv'd in. ADRASTUS had ſcarcely
forſaken the *Caramanian* Confines, before
the Prince became as much eſtrang'd in his
Affections to the fair Wife of that unhappy
Nobleman, as he had cauſed her to be to
him; the untaſted Sweets of VIOLETTA's
innocent Beauties kindled in his Heart a
Fire, which nothing but their Poſſeſſion
could extinguiſh. He knew MARMILLIO
was the Perſon who introduced her to
the Service of HYANTHE, and that ſhe
de-

depended on his Advice and Care, as she would do on that of a Parent.

It was therefore chiefly in his power to seduce her, and to persuade her, that Virtue would be of little advantage to her in a Place where the contrary was so much in fashion. He had conferr'd too many Obligations on this Favourite; and, indeed, knew him too zealously devoted to his Service, to suppose he would make a scruple of any thing which might afford him satisfaction; he therefore communicated his Thoughts to him on this occasion with the utmost freedom, and talk'd to him in a manner, as if he doubted not to be in an almost immediate possession of his Wishes by his means: but he had not intirely finish'd all he had to say, before he perceiv'd MARMILLIO to change Colour, and by many Symptoms denote, that he was either unwilling, or unable to execute this Commission; which obliging him to change the form of his Discourse, What, *said he to him*, is the Happiness of a Prince, who desires nothing more than to make thee happy, of so little account with thee, that thou canst hesitate at woking to my Will a silly Girl, who would doubtless rejoice to find herself so considerable to her Sovereign. Ah, sacred Sir! *replied* MARMILLIO, the Gods of *Caramania* can witness for me, how much I bless their Bounty, when-

whenever they afford me an occasion of testifying the Regard I pay your Highness: Had VIOLETTA any thing in her of the Disposition of her Sex, I might indulge my Wishes with the hope of serving you; but she is colder than the frozen *North*, not to be warm'd by all the Artifices of melting Love; and less ambitious than the poor Cottage-maid, who never heard of Grandeur, or had a Wish beyond her Milking-pail.———— How often have I seen her fly, obscure her Charms in Solitude, or run for Protection behind the Princess's Chair, to shield herself from hearing the Courtier's Address?———— How regardless does she view the admiring Crowd? How little does she adorn her Beauties? How negligent is she in pleasing?———— Is not this, *continued he*, my Lord! a Behaviour which may make me justly fear all that I can urge will be of no effect?———— I have remarked, *resumed the Prince*, the artless Innocence which appears in all her Actions; and did I not believe there were a difficulty in gaining her, would think the Employment unworthy of thy Skill.———— Were she to be won by rich Presents, and Promises of future Greatness, my Page might, in my name, convey them to her, and bargain for her Heart.—Or did the Court-Amusements please her, in publick Balls, and private Pressures of her Hand, I might have hope

to

to catch her Senses: but so perfect a Modesty can only by Time and Argument be won; and that alas! the ARGUS Eyes, which daily are upon me, deny me to make tryal of.———But thou, MARMILLIO, art admitted even in her retir'd Moments, and under the sanction of a Guardian's Name may'st steal upon her Thoughts, and, e'er she is aware, inspire her with Desires in favour of my Passion; with amorous Chat melt down her Soul, and warm into yielding.——— Then, when thou findst her moulded to the purpose, stamp the Impression of thy Prince's Image——— Say how I languish, burn, despair, and die; say any thing, to prove it Murder, Treason, Parricide, to deny my Suit.

The Prince utter'd these Words with too much Vehemence for the other not to know all opposition would be in vain; and tho' he could not promise himself any great Success, resolv'd to try his utmost Skill for the obtaining for his Prince the Happiness he requir'd. He therefore assur'd him, in the most submissive Terms, of his Attachment to his Interest, and that he would omit nothing which might be conducive to promote it. The Prince, who doubted not his Sincerity, urg'd no more, than that he would be as speedy as possible in the execution of this Commission; and telling him, that, till he was the Master of

VIO-

VIOLETTA's Beauties, he could not hope
to know one eafy moment, left him at liberty, to ftudy on the means which might
make him fo.

The Reader will, perhaps, be furpriz'd,
that, confidering the Character of MAR-
MILLIO, and the Services he had done of
the fame nature for his Prince, he fhould
now with fo much difficulty be prevail'd
on to engage in this. The Ruin of a
young Virgin, like VIOLETTA, and the Injury he fhould do a Family, by whom he
had been treated with the utmoft refpect,
would appear but faint Obftructions to a
Man of his Humour, who, in every Action
of his Life, had teftify'd no Senfe of Pity,
Gratitude, or Honour; nor indeed would
he in the leaft have hefitated, had nothing
but what I have mention'd deterr'd him :
But, befides that he knew fhe was poffefs'd
of all that Modefty and Strictnefs of Virtue
he had reprefented to the Prince, he knew,
that happening to be in the Anti-chamber
of the Princefs's Apartment, fhe had overheard fome Conference between THEODORE
and ISMONDA, which had let her into the
fecret of their Amour. She had frequently fpoke of it to him with Wonder and
Deteftation ; and he no oftener had endeavour'd to excufe, than fhe to reproach
fuch a confequence of Love. The Senfe fhe
had of the Crime, was fufficient to make
him

him know it would not be eafy to prevail on her to become guilty of it : but
to work a change in her Sentiments, in
favour of a Perfon, whom fhe was certain
was not only married, but alfo engaged in
an Amour with another, feem'd to him an
utter Impoffibility; nor could all his Wit
furnifh him with one Pretence, which he
could think would be received.

To fave his Credit therefore with the
Prince, he had recourfe to the moft cruel
Stratagem that ever enter'd the Heart of
Man. Defpairing to corrupt her Principles,
or infpire her with any Tendernefs for a
Man, of whofe Heart fhe could not hope
to poffefs above a third fhare; after having told THEODORE that all the Arguments he could ufe had been of no effect,
he perfuaded him to force the Joy, which
he found it was impoffible for him to obtain by any other means.

Rafh, amorous, and ungovernable as
this Prince was in all his Paffions, fuch a
Propofition extremely fhock'd him : he had
an inimitable fhare of Good-nature, and as
much Honour as was confiftent with the
Inconftancy of his Temper; and told MAR-
MILLIO, that he could not confent to fuch
an Action, though the perpetrating it was
all for which he wifh'd to live, and charg'd
him to renew his Endeavours to make her
his by other means than thofe. The other

Z   pro-

promis'd him to obey, not daring to let him know the reason why he believed they would be eternally in vain.

In fine, without uttering one syllable of the Prince's Paffion to her, he continued every day to affure him, that he found her Heart impregnable as a Rock, that he had try'd her every way, and that there was now no remaining hope, but in the course he had before advis'd. What will not the fubtile Infinuations of the Perfon one loves, when concurring with one's own Inclination, in time prevail on one to be guilty of!

The Prince, impatient to poffefs, and made to believe that nothing but Force could afford the long'd-for Blifs, at laft half yielded to the Perfuafions of his Favourite; who, to remove the only now remaining Scruple, that of the thing being known, contriv'd this Stratagem, that he fhould not appear in his own fhape, and the deftin'd Victim of his wild Defires be ignorant to whom fhe ow'd her Ruin. Honour now lull'd to fleep, and all the nobler Faculties drown'd in the Excefs of an o'erflowing and tumultuous Paffion, he confented with pleafure to the Propofal, and left the management of it to him, who promifed to accomplifh it in a very fhort time.

No-

Nothing could be more eafy, than for him, who was fo intimate with her, to be-tray her in this manner: And the Method he took to do it was this; he caufed an *Egyptian* Habit to be made for the Prince, and a tawny Mask, fo artificially contriv'd, that whoever had it on, would appear to have no other Face, than that which Na-ture had beftow'd: And intreating the Prince to come into his Apartment, You muft condefcend, my Lord, *faid he*, like JUPITER, to affume a Shame unworthy of you, when you attempt an Enterprize of this kind. The things being try'd, and fit-ting exactly, never Man was more delighted than THEODORE; but yet could not con-ceive of what fervice this Difguife was to him, or how defign'd to be made ufe of, till MARMILLIO pluck'd out two Letters, the one directed for himfelf, the other to VIOLETTA: Thefe, *faid he*, are written by a hand fo exactly counterfeiting that of CARICLEA, that were herfelf to fee them, fhe would imagine them dictated in her Sleep.———They contain a Recommen-dation of an *Egyptian* Eunuch, whom this careful Sifter entreats the young VIOLETTA to entertain as the Guardian of her Virtue: So many Stratagems being daily contriv'd at Court to deftroy the Innocence of a Vir-gin, fhe cannot think her fafe without this watchful ARGUS, who, incapable of in-juring

Z 2

juring her himſelf, will be her Security from all others. He is therefore to lie in her Chamber, leſt any Attempts ſhould be made on her ſleeping Virtue. Your Highneſs, *continued he*, has nothing to do to carry on this Plot, but to perſonate this Slave for an hour or two, for it ſhall be near night when I preſent you : and to excuſe your abſence, you muſt pretend a little Indiſpoſition, and diſmiſs all but me from your Attendance. The tranſported THEODORE agreed it ſhould be done that very Evening; and having appear'd in the Drawing-room long enough to give a colour to the thing, cry'd out on a ſudden, that his Head ach'd, and retir'd haſtily to his own Apartment; where being follow'd by all the Gentlemen of his Bed-Chamber, he order'd a profound Silence to be kept, and that none but MARMILLIO ſhould ſtay in the Room.

Every body being remov'd, he began to equip himſelf in the *Egyptian* Habiliments, which the aſſiduous Favourite had before convey'd by a back way into the Chamber; by which alſo, as ſoon as dreſs'd, they went, and ſo to the Apartment, who, being not then in waiting, they found at home. MARMILLIO preſented her with the Letters of the Slave; which ſhe had no ſooner read, than ſhe bluſhed prodigiouſly, at the thoughts of permitting any thing that bore

the

the fhape of Man to lie in her Chamber;
but MARMILLIO affuring her, that it was
the Cuftom in all thofe Countries where
the Men are jealous of the Honour of their
Families, fhe at laft confented to obey the
Injunction of her Sifter. But here immediately rofe another Obftacle, which was,
that according to the Cuftom of *Caramania*,fhe having but one Bed in her Chamber,
he muft lie in another till one could be
put up : But this was not an Obftacle which
was beyond the Wit of MARMILLIO to fur-
mount; he prefently told her, that thefe
Slaves never lay but on Carpets, which
could be fpread in a moment, and as eafily
remov'd.

The good Opinion fhe had of him, the
obfervant Care with which he had ever
treated her, and her Sifter's Commands,
left her no room to hefitate, whether what
they injoin'd was for her good, or not;
and fhe order'd her Woman to fee it perform'd. The Royal Slave, who pretended not
to underftand one word of the *Caramanian*
Language, was entertain'd by the Servants, in
as civil a manner as poffible : but it was no
fmall diverfion to him, to behold the wonder with which all the Women look'd upon him, and the Mirth which his fuppos'd
Condition occafion'd among them, every
one fpeaking according to the Sentiments
of her Heart, without referve before him,

in

in confidence he knew not what they said.

But when Night came, and he saw the lovely VIOLETTA in her Bed, how difficult was it for him to restrain the Impatiencies of his burning Passion, till she was asleep, not daring to stir from his Carpets till then, lest she should alarm the Family: but a more than ordinary Drouziness, by her ill Angel cast on her Senses, made her presently fall into the Condition he wish'd; which he no sooner perceiv'd, than he quitted the uneasy Position in which he had lain, the Eagerness of Desire with which he seiz'd upon her Beauties leaving no time for the Preparatives of Kisses, and Degrees of Caresses, he in a moment became Master of too much, not to put it past her power to keep from him any part of what he wish'd. But in what words is it possible to set forth the Rage! the Horror! the Surprize with which she waked, and found this bold Intruder! She struggled, would have shriek'd for help, but Kisses stopp'd the one, and more prevailing Strength rendred the other of no effect.——— In fine, she was undone, and he as happy as the full Possession of her Charms could make him; but Tears, and Vows, not to out-live the loss of Honour, allay'd the Joy, and turn'd him all into Endeavours to mitigate the Tempest of her Soul———He

spoke

spoke to her, excuſing what he had done
by the Violence of a Paſſion, which diſdain'd all Bounds, and would fly to any Artifice to ſhun Deſpair.

Oh! by whom, *cry'd ſhe*, have I been
thus abus'd?——yet, if thou loveſt thy Life,
continued ſhe, I charge thee do not tell me,
for be aſſur'd, I will revenge this Wrong.
It was not to ſhow that he not fear'd this
Threat, but believing the knowledge of his
Quality would eaſe the preſent Horrors of
her Soul, he diſcover'd to her who he was;
at which indeed her Surprize increas'd, but
a ſmall Portion of her Griefs abated ——the
Rank of her Undoer took not away the
Shame of being undone, and tho' ſhe ceas'd
to *revile*, ſhe did not to *complain*——Oh
Cruel Prince! *ſaid ſhe*, what could provoke you to the Ruin of a harmleſs Maid,
who never injur'd you even in a Thought?
Your Heart and Vows elſewhere devoted,
how ſmall your Satisfaction, and how im-
menſe my Woe!——Wretch that I am, *purſu'd ſhe, after a little pauſe*, Death only
can put a period to my irreparable Shame.
In this manner did ſhe go on, nor could
leſs be expected from a Woman of her
ſtrict Modeſty; yet had the Prince the pleaſure to obſerve, that either the Reſpect ſhe
paid him as her Sovereign, or a ſecret Inclination to his Perſon, made her ſuffer his
continued Endearments with leſs reluctance

than

than before. As he was indeed one of the
moſt lovely and accompliſh'd Men on
earth, it was not difficult for him to make
the moſt favourable Impreſſion on a Heart
ſo entirely unprepoſſeſs'd as was her's: to
add to this, he addreſs'd her in the ſofteſt,
moſt engaging terms that Love and Wit
could dictate; and before Morning, if ſhe
was not brought to think what he had done
no Crime, ſhe was at leaſt to wiſh it were
not ſo: and though ſhe did not in words
declare ſo much, the tender Preſſures, the
Languiſhments, which, unawares even to
herſelf, her Arms, and Eyes beſtow'd on him,
confeſs'd the melting God had pleaded in
her Heart ſo powerfully in the defence of
his Votary, that ſhe now more than forgave
the Effects of his embolden'd Paſſion.——
Tranſported with this Diſcovery, he purſued his Conqueſt, and ſwore to hold her
for ever Priſoner in his Arms, if ſhe would
not ſeal his Pardon, and conſent henceforth
to give a looſe to Rapture. Faintly ſhe
ſtruggled to get free from the ſweet Confinement, but could not ſpeak: A thouſand,
and a thouſand times he repeated the ſame
Requeſt, before her Tongue could utter
what her ſwimming Eyes ſufficiently made
known and when, to prevail on him to riſe,
it being now broad day, all ſhe could bring
forth was, *Yes*. Enough confirm'd that he
was Maſter of her Soul, as well as Body,
he

he now forfook the happy Scene of Pleafure; and having clothed himfelf in his Difguife, retired to his Carpets: from which,
as foon as her Woman came into the Chamber, he rofe, and went into another Room;
whence, taking his opportunity, he pafs'd
to his own Apartment, where MARMILLIO
waited with impatience to know the End
of this Adventure.

The Prince making him a full relation
of all that had pafs'd, he was not a little
alarm'd, when he firft heard he had difcover'd who he was, not knowing how far
the Fury of a Woman, thus abus'd, might
tranfport her: but when he was told how
kindly fhe forgave the Deceit, he as much
applauded himfelf for the Contrivance. The
Prince exprefs'd his Senfe of it in terms
the moft obliging to him, and paffionate
to VIOLETTA; which let this Favourite
know, that his Defires being yet unfatiated,
he would ftill have need of his Affiftance to
procure their future Interviews.

He managed this Affair, as he had done
all others of this nature, with which he had
been entrufted, fo much to the fatisfaction
of the Prince, that he became more in his
favour than ever.———The Intimacy between him and VIOLETTA, was known by
every body, and fhe met the Prince at his
Apartment, under the pretence of vifiting
a Perfon, who was look'd upon as her
Guar-

Guardian, without the leaft fufpicion, for a
confiderable time. But what can efcape the
Eyes of jealous Love? ISMONDA finding the
Prince more than ordinarily cool in the Devoirs he was accuftomed to pay her, bent
her whole ftudy on a difcovery of the
Caufe; which fhe at laft difcover'd, and
that MARMILLIO alfo was the Perfon to
whom fhe owed her Misfortune: having
an opportunity of fpeaking to him foon
after fhe arrived at this knowledge, fhe upbraided him in the fevereft terms; wept,
threatned, rail'd, entreated, by turns did
every thing that an amorous and impatient
Woman would do on the like occafion.
Finding her too well inform'd of the Secret,
he would not heighten her Rage of Temper by any Endeavours to conceal the Truth,
but again made ufe of the fame Arguments
he had before urged on the fcore of EURI-
DICE, and advifed her indeed to the wifeft
Method fhe could now purfue: Her Reputation loft, her Intereft with the Princefs
changed to its reverfe, rendred an Alien to
her Family, and for ever abandoned by her
Husband, her whole dependance confifted
in the favour of THEODORE; which, if fhe
once forfeited, by an imprudent Attempt to
controll him in what he efteem'd a Pleafure, fhe muft expect the worft and moft un-
pity'd Fate to which a Woman can poffibly
be reduted, that of a forfaken Miftrefs:
Whereas

Whereas if she seem'd not to know, what
by resenting she could not remedy, she
would not fail of retaining his Respect,
and perhaps too retrieve his Love. To arm
her to go through this Task with less difficulty, he ventur'd to let her know this had
not been the first false step the Prince had
made; and by reminding her, that in spite
of all the new Attractions which had hitherto fallen in his way, she had still preserv'd her Empire o'er his Soul, flatter'd her
with the opinion she should always do so;
and by degrees moderated the first Emotions
of her jealous Rage so well, that she consented to seem blind to what she but too
well saw: But alas! she had now reduced
herself to a Condition, which made it the
only Expedient to preserve her from Misery,
Contempt, and all those Ills a Woman in
her Circumstances must be obliged to bear,
when abandon'd by him for whom she incurr'd them.

As for VIOLETTA, her Character as yet
remain'd untouch'd; the *Egyptian* Slave, who
lay in her Chamber, and was never heard
of after, was by MARMILLIO's Artifices
suppos'd to have taken that opportunity of
robbing her of some Jewels which she had
worn that Day; and confiding in his Ho-
nesty, had not order'd to be secur'd: and by
the Diligence of the same Person, the enamour'd Prince has frequent Opportunities
of

of revelling with her to the height of that
Defire, which fhe now feels in equal proportion with himfelf. How long a Space of
Time their prefent Ardours will continue, or
what muft become of unhappy ISMONDA,
hereafter muft reveal: but 'tis highly probable,
that in a Paffion liable to fuch Viciffitudes,
as have been obferv'd in the courfe of thefe
Memoirs, there will happen Occurrences
worthy of Obfervation ; which fhall then,
as they fall out, be communicated to the
Publick.

F I N I S.